Rachael Stewart adores conjuring up stories, from heartwarmingly romantic to wildly erotic. She's been writing since she could put pen to paper—as the stacks of scrawled-on pages in her loft will attest to. A Welsh lass at heart, she now lives in Yorkshire, with her very own hero and three awesome kids—and if she's not tapping out a story she's wrapped up in one or enjoying the great outdoors. Reach her on Facebook, Twitter @rach_b52, or at rachaelstewartauthor.com.

Nina Singh lives just outside Boston, USA, with her husband, children, and a very rumbustious Yorkie. After several years in the corporate world she finally followed the advice of family and friends to 'give the writing a go, already'. She's oh-so-happy she did. When not at her keyboard she likes to spend time on the tennis court or golf course. Or immersed in a good read.

OFF-LIMITS FLING WITH THE HEIRESS

RACHAEL STEWART

THE PRINCE'S SAFARI TEMPTATION

NINA SINGH

MILLS & BOON

First published in Great Britain 2023
by Mills & Boon, an imprint of HarperCollins*Publishers* Ltd,
1 London Bridge Street, London, SE1 9GF

www.harpercollins.co.uk

HarperCollins*Publishers*, Macken House, 39/40 Mayor Street Upper, Dublin 1, D01 C9W8, Ireland

Off-Limits Fling with the Heiress © 2023 Rachael Stewart

The Prince's Safari Temptation © 2023 Nilay Nina Singh

ISBN: 978-0-263-30652-1

09/23

MIX
Paper | Supporting
responsible forestry
FSC™ C007454

This book is produced from independently certified FSC™ paper to ensure responsible forest management.
For more information visit: www.harpercollins.co.uk/green.

Printed and Bound in the UK using 100% Renewable Electricity at CPI Group (UK) Ltd, Croydon, CR0 4YY

OFF-LIMITS FLING WITH THE HEIRESS

RACHAEL STEWART

MILLS & BOON

For all the Survivors xx

CHAPTER ONE

Gabe

I HAVE A few rules in life.

One, don't get distracted from the job.

Two, don't get attached to anyone.

And three, don't, for the love of all things holy, get anyone pregnant.

That's it. Short and sweet and to the point. You see, when you have a father like mine, you learn quickly that money makes the world go your way and sex is for fun. Procreation is for other people. Because heaven forbid I'd bring a child up like my father did me.

And my life is near perfect. Take now, for example. I'm in an exclusive New York club, enjoying the finest whisky money can buy and—

'Now, *that* is some fine piece of...'

Okay, so my company could be a little more refined.

I turn to my companion who adds a low whistle to his unsavoury observation. I'm being schmoozed by a tech start-up with ample promise, if only their frontman weren't such a Grade A jerk. Trouble is my dad owes his dad and I've been roped in to clear the debt.

I wouldn't do it if it didn't work for me too. I want this

company. I know what I can do with it. What I don't want is this particular breed of man working for me.

'Oh, my God, is that…' Grade A frowns '…is that Avery Monroe? Aiden's little sister?'

My head snaps around, my body going into overdrive before I even see her.

It can't be…it shouldn't be…but it's her all right.

Did I mention I broke my own rule?

Kind of…

I've known Aiden since we were kids. He's my best friend. There isn't anything I wouldn't do for him, or anyone associated with him. But his little sister…she's trouble.

And right now, she's rocking that and then some. Her long auburn hair falls around her face and bare shoulders, as free and easy as the vibe she's giving off. Bold red lips, heavily lined eyes, an abundance of smooth creamy skin on show with an inch-thick choker sitting tight around her neck. The black velvet housing a crucifix at its centre that's taunting the man above and a barely there figure-hugging dress that's taunting every man on the ground. Every woman too, judging by the looks she's getting.

I bite back a curse. At twenty, she's underage. In this state anyhow. She must know the press will be here, somewhere? That at any moment someone will work out who she is and have her shown to the door. A display worthy of tomorrow's headlines and another bashing of the Monroe name, which in the last few years has suffered plenty thanks to her and her wild ways.

'Hey, where are you going?' Grade A stares up at me as I stand, wondering where the fire is, I'm sure.

'I'm done for the night. I'll see you at the office for eight. We can draw the papers up then.'

Grade A sinks back into the dark leather, a glint of excitement taking out the surprise now. He thinks he's got what he wants, and I don't have the time to correct him.

Avery's weaving her way to the bar, the crowd parting like royalty is in attendance, and I clench my fists. Either they're setting her up for a fall or she does this often enough, it's a thing. I should have known she'd be around, New York becoming her playground since she dropped out of Oxford last year, but this club should be more selective with who they let in.

I pull my phone from my pocket, issue a message to my driver so that he's primed and push my way through the crowd. She has barely a second to register my presence as I hook my arm through hers and take the quickest route to the back exit.

'Gabe?' She stumbles along with me, her green eyes wide as she blinks up at me.

Even in her skyscraper boots I have inches on her and my jaw is gritted so tight I can't respond. Her perfume is more intoxicating than the whisky, her arm through mine, a heated magnetic field. It takes everything I have to fight the burning connection, to remind myself that she's Aiden's sister—too young, too forbidden, and too much…even for me.

Too clever and wasted on the path she has chosen too.

We break out into the fresh air, the drizzle an icy wash against my skin, and I suck in a breath, release her with a flourish. I need the space, the air to breathe without her in it. 'Get in.'

My driver already has the door to my gunmetal-grey Aston open and she gawps back at me, hand propped on one hip, chin at a defiant slant.

'Who do you—?'

'I said, get in!'

I'm already scanning the dark alleyway for unwitting passers-by ready to snap a pic of our standoff. It'll be all over social media in seconds and I don't want to face that kind of the scrutiny. Neither should she. But Avery's been courting bad press for years now. Loves it, by all accounts.

And grief will only get you so far. Sympathy for the daddy's girl suffering the sudden loss of her father has long been replaced by hostility for the rich, spoilt heiress with no care for anyone but herself.

Not that I believe the half of it…though faced with the defiant woman before me it's hard to keep sight of that.

'No "Hello, Avery. How the hell are you?"' Her eyes flash gold under the solitary amber lamp hung over the door we broke out of. 'It's been months, if not years…'

Rain drips off the railing to the fire escape above us, trickles down my neck, but I don't even flinch. It's been three months at most, something she'd remember if she hadn't been so drunk or drugged up. I'm not sure which. Maybe both.

'Hi, Avery. How the hell are you? It's been months, if not years. Now get in.'

She folds her arms, doesn't budge and my driver's mouth quirks but he doesn't dare smile. No one defies me. No one save for Avery, it would seem.

'Or do you want me to call your brother and tell him where we are, where you were?'

She blows out a breath, says something I can't decipher and moves. Clambering onto the back seat without a care for the plush upholstery or the shortness of her skirt that rides far too high.

I curse the heavens and follow her in, readying myself for the backlash. I should have instructed Jenkins to take her home alone but I wouldn't put it past her to get him to stop the car once out of sight and do an about-turn.

'Where are you staying?'

'Why?'

'Unless you want to come back to my place, I suggest you disclose it now.'

'"*Suggest you disclose it?*"' she mimics with a curse. 'You're as bad as Aiden.'

'I'll take that as a compliment.'

'You would! Ten years my elder and you're both ancient and boring with it. Or is this what happens when you pass thirty?'

'It's twelve.'

'*Twelve?*'

'There are twelve years between us. And wanting to keep one's personal life out of the public eye isn't ancient or boring, it's the right thing to do. Especially when one seems to have a predilection for doing wrong.'

She gives a harsh laugh. 'And what happened to fun, Gabe? What happened to living your life and enjoying every second? You know you only get one, right?'

I suppress a sudden smile. Sparring with her is too much fun and beats the company I was enduring not ten minutes ago. If it weren't a by-product of her poor judgement call, I'd allow myself to enjoy this little interlude. 'Address?'

She gives it through gritted teeth, her sullen expression deepening and tugging my gaze south, to her mouth—far too full and far too taunting cloaked in red. Reminding me that, for all she is Aiden's sister, she is indeed a woman, a woman who sparks thoughts that I have no place entertaining.

I clear my throat, look away and catch Jenkins' raised brow through the rear-view mirror. He's questioning the destination and frankly I am too. I don't recognise it. And I know this city. The parts you want to know at any rate.

I give him a silent nod to proceed.

'You realise my friends will wonder what's happened to me?'

I flick her a look. 'Are they underage too?'

'I'm perfectly legal back home.'

I want to ask where she considers that to be. Her family have homes across North America and Europe but, as far as I'm aware, since dropping out of uni she's barely been back to any. For a girl that used to be such a homebody, the last six years have seen her grow more and more distant. From the people that matter, *should* matter...can she not see that?

'And you think that makes it okay? Do you really want to be splashed across the tabloids come morning? Do you really want to bring that disgrace on your family?'

'What difference does it make? They'll print what they like anyway.'

'Not if you don't give them fodder to pore over.'

'Whatever.' She slumps back in her seat, arms tightly crossed around her middle and emphasising her feminine curves. Curves I don't want to acknowledge. I don't want to appreciate. Not when they belong to Aiden's sister and she's as forbidden as she is messed up. I want to help her but I know my help is unwelcome.

I force my eyes away, stare out of the window. Take in the shiny towers and bustling sidewalks that shift into the dark and dingy...boarded-up windows, litter filling the streets, abandoned sleeping bags and rolled out boxes lining the ground—just where in the hell are we?

She can't be staying here. 'Who were you meeting?'

'None of your business.'

'Are they staying with you?'

She flicks me a look that says the same—*none of your business.*

'You should message them at least, let them know you're safe.'

She scoffs. '*Now* you're worried about that?' She spies

something outside that has her leaning forward in her seat, bringing her closer to my driver. 'You can pull over, thanks. I can walk from here.'

'Are you serious?' I choke out in surprise, panic even.

'What?'

'I'm not letting you out here.'

'This street not up to your standard?'

'This isn't up to…' I grit my teeth, try again. 'I'm not leaving you here.'

'This is where I'm staying.'

'Over my dead body.'

'That can be arranged.' She stares back at me, hard, her jaw pulsing, her throat a livewire.

'Sir?' Jenkins breaks through the tension, asking for instruction and there's only one I can give.

'Home, and step on it.'

She starts beside me. 'Oh, no, we're not.'

'At the risk of sounding like some pantomime audience, oh, yes, we are.' My car is already attracting too much attention crawling the sidewalk—any moment now one of the semi-naked women pacing out there is going to tap the glass and ask if I want company. I give a silent curse. What is Avery doing here? She can afford New York's finest, she can afford… Hell, anything is better than this.

And who is it that lives here? A guy she's seeing? Some, heaven forbid, drug dealer?

My skin crawls and a fire burns in my gut. 'I am *not* leaving you here. Your brother would never forgive me.'

And I'd never forgive myself… She's his sister, which makes her near enough blood to me.

'And I'll never forgive you for humiliating me back there.'

'Better to be humiliated in front of me than the entire world come morning.'

'Like I care.'

'You *should* care!'

'Who do you think you are, Gabe? You're not my father, my brother, my mother even, you don't get to tell me what I can and cannot do!'

'Wanna bet?'

She makes a sound akin to a grunt and I'm done arguing with her. The sooner we're back at my place, the sooner I can get to the bottom of where she's staying, why she's staying there and where she'll be staying until her departure from the city.

'You must have better things to be doing with your evening than babysitting me?'

'You'd think that, wouldn't you...?'

Truth is, I don't. Even in light of the takeover bid I want to make come morning, the millions I'll make the Curran empire have nothing on her. Because everything else pales alongside Avery Monroe, right now, and the press debacle I want to save her from.

But now we're stuck together. Confined quarters. No escape and I'm no longer sure what's worse, the way my body's responding to her against my will, or the press and their insatiable hunger as far as this rebel heiress is concerned.

A hunger that I don't want her to feed.

As for my own... I can control that. She's Aiden's sister, totally off limits, and, in her eyes, I'm ancient. She outright told me as much.

But ancient? I shift in my seat, swallow back another curse. *Well, I'll be...*

Avery

I sit very still, my lips pressed together, my thighs too.

Because this is Gabe Curran. Gabe *freaking* Curran. The

man that has fuelled my fantasies since I came of age and the one man that will never see me as more than his best friend's little sister. An annoyance. A child. Someone to be disciplined and quieted and kept out of sight.

And I want to scream.

I'm sick of being pigeonholed. Pigeonholed and pitied. Poor little rich girl. Lost her father and hasn't known what to do with herself since. Or worse, spoilt and selfish with it, she's an embarrassment to the Monroe name.

I'm not sure which I resent more, the public opinion of me, for which I only have myself to blame, or my family's ignorance, which I've done my best to counteract. But newsflash, people—money doesn't make you happy. And life sucks.

Seriously, what is the point in any of it when death comes a-knocking whenever it likes? All that hard work, all that time spent studying, working, investing in *stuff* and none of it really matters. We all end up six feet under or burnt to ashes. And you can't take it with you.

Not that I have anything to take with me any more...

I wonder if Gabe knows my brother has cut me off. And I don't just mean capping my allowance, I mean nothing, *nada*, you're on your own, chuck. I sneak a look his way and instantly regret it as my pulse leaps, my body contracting over the rush of heat. Though the sensation beats that of the depression, the loneliness, the chill...

I angle my face to the window so Gabe can't see the tears that spike. Depression doesn't discriminate. It doesn't care how wealthy, how blessed, how lucky on the surface you are. And I'm trying to get better. I *am*.

But when your friends are the people who showed an interest, who cared when your own family didn't, you don't get to be picky and selective about who you let in. Though the drugs, the drink, I know I need to break free of them and I'm getting there. I *am*.

'What's happened to you, Avery?'

I ignore the gruff timbre to his voice, the way it ripples along my spine, excites, provokes. The way it rings with concern too. Grip my middle tighter.

I pretend I'm more interested in the world outside than I am in the man beside me. The man who emanates power, stability, reassurance and warmth. A man who has the scent of the taboo wrapped up in the rain. A hint of whisky and woody cologne and the wet outdoors. It's doing strange things to my insides, things I have no control over, and I need it to stop.

Which will only happen when I get free of him...

'Just drop me at the nearest hotel and I'll—'

'You'll what? Check yourself in? Do you think I was born yesterday?'

The slightest smile plays about my lips. 'As we've already established, I've classified you as ancient so...'

'Funny, Avery. Very funny.'

'I know. I'm a full-blown riot.' It drips with sarcasm but I can't help it. He brings out the worst...and the best in me, depending on how you want to look at it. 'But if you think I'm staying at your place, you can think again.'

'What's wrong with my place?'

'You're in it, for a start.'

And now he's laughing at me, his mouth—that thick bottom lip and sharp cupid's bow to the top—twitches at the corners, his eyes glitter in the low light... I should look away, do anything to douse the heat he's kicked up down low, the kind of heat that can only land me in further trouble. Or deeper humiliation. And neither scenario bears much merit.

'Does that really appeal so little?'

It appeals far too much and that's the issue.

'If I'd wanted company akin to that of my brother, I would have joined him in the Rockies for our annual Christmas ski trip...'

'Why didn't you?'

I purse my lips, unwilling to say, though many answers come to mind. Because Dad died at Christmas and I'm sick of pretending that it didn't ruin that time for ever. Because I'm the last person my brother wants around. Because I can't bear to be around my mother and not have her see me...like really see me.

'In his bad books again?' he guesses.

'When am I out of them?'

He studies me quietly and I fight the urge to take it back. I know how sullen I sound. I know I'm playing up to the image I've curated over the years, intentionally or otherwise, but I'm angry. Angry at the world for taking my father away. Angry with my family for not being there when grief consumed us all. Angry at my brother for not seeing me now. My dreams, my desire for a career outside the Monroe firm. For dismissing those dreams as a foolish whim and stripping me of our wealth in the hope I'd come to my senses and toe the family line.

But it's no whim and I'll show him. I'll show them all... once I work out how.

'You have the power to change that, you know that, right?'

'If you truly believe that, then you don't know my brother as well as you think you do.'

'I take it things have gone downhill since you quit your degree.'

A degree my brother chose for me...

I huff, getting the sense that he's in my head reading my thoughts. 'Wasn't like the hill was that high to come down from.'

'Come on, Avery, he just wants what's best for you.'

'You have no idea what you're talking about.'

'Then give me an idea.'

The last thing I need is this man dishing out sympathy or, worse, more of the condemnation my brother did when I told him of my dreams to study jewellery design. To launch my own brand one day. A line of ecological and unique statement pieces, something that's all me but in the name of Monroe and as far from wealth management, the focus of our billion-dollar firm, as you can get.

'Your brother loves you.'

I scoff, shake my head with a sneer of a smile. He really does have no idea and I'm not about to argue it out with him.

We sit in silence until the car pulls up outside the sky-scraper that houses his penthouse and as he turns to me I'm already shoving open the door and getting out. I need the space, the air, a moment without him and his disorientating presence.

'Thanks, Jenkins.' He climbs out behind me before I can take a full breath. 'We're done if you want to call it a night.'

'Will do, sir.'

I nod my thanks to his driver but I'm too distracted to see if he notices. I'm singing the lyrics to a Christmas song in my head, using it to distract from where I'm about to go. It's a technique I've used to cope when the voices in my head get too much, the voices that do me down, that tell me I'm no good, that remind me of my loss too. Of Dad.

'This way.'

He beckons me along the sidewalk and I follow a safe step behind. Doesn't mean his scent doesn't carry on the air, his warmth too as his large frame protects me from the swirling wind. That's when I remember I left my jacket at the club. I curse. I'm not one for waste. I'm accustomed to my friends leaving possessions behind and not giving a damn, but life is wasteful enough, I don't want to add to it.

It also doesn't escape my notice that I've not once felt the cold until now…despite my skimpy outfit and the winter air.

The reason for that turns to me, his dark brows drawing together and sharpening his blue gaze to the point of distraction. 'What's wrong?'

'My—my jacket's at the club.'

'I'll have it collected.'

Of course he will. This is Gabriel Curran, contacts across the globe let alone New York. He says jump and people immediately ask, 'how high?'… He likely has a woman in every continent, every state, too.

Will he have one here? Waiting to greet him home?

It'll be like Mum and Dad's ruby wedding anniversary all over again. Aiden had arranged it as a surprise and Gabe had turned up with some glamorous opera singer on his arm—all air and grace and so much more than I could ever be. I'd been thirteen, young and easily swept up in him. A simple smile and my cheeks had flamed, something his date had been quick to notice. And when she'd pulled me aside, taking pity on my crush, and offered out advice, I'd wished for the ground to open up and swallow me.

Some things don't change…

'Is that a problem?' He's looking at me strangely and I realise I'm frowning, stalling on the sidewalk like some lost soul…which I am, I guess.

'What?'

'Getting the jacket collected?'

'No. No, of course not.'

'I should take the rolling of the eyes as a positive gesture, then?'

Oh, God, had I? My shoulders hunch about my ears, my

folded arms screaming defensive, but if he knew the true reason for the eye roll I'd be even redder than I am now.

'Sorry, I was distracted.' I stride inside the building and he follows close behind. 'Thank you. For getting the jacket collected, I mean.'

'You're welcome.'

He gestures to the doorman who goes to call the elevator, but his gaze doesn't leave me.

'How are you doing, Avery? Truly?'

My eyes drift his way of their own accord, something about the earnest way he says it, the rough edge to his voice, making me want to talk. To let it all out. And then I remember who his best friend is and what this isn't. A loyal, friendly ear. No judgement, no reporting back.

And let's be honest, the last thing I want to turn tonight into is a pity party on top of everything else. I just want to forget life exists, that Dad's gone, and I've never felt more alone. As for Christmas, it can do one.

Smiling wide, with my most photogenic smile, I say, 'How do you think?'

'I don't know, Avery.' His voice is a low murmur that I don't want to react to, but my body warms all the same. 'That's why I'm asking.'

'I'm fine.'

'I don't think you are.'

'Oh, really.'

'I think you've been on a downward spiral ever since you lost your father and you don't know how to get out of it.'

His bluntness winds me, my lips parting on a sharp inhalation. Tears sting at my eyes as I travel back to that day almost seven years ago. A day that I spend my life trying to forget, trying to pretend it never happened…only it did.

'And what would you know of it?'

'I know what the gossip columns say. I know what your brother thinks. And your mother. The drugs, the drink, the partying…your presence in that club tonight only reaffirms it.'

My blood fires, my hackles rise. 'Tell me something, do you have to work hard at being a pompous know-it-all or does it just come naturally?'

The lift arrives and I step inside, craving the distance, but his stride far outreaches mine and he's beside me in a heartbeat.

The doors slide closed and we're alone for the first time. Truly alone. There's a whirr in my ears and I can't catch my breath. The voices in my head escalate. Judging, condemning, full of scorn.

'I'm being honest. More honest than you are right now.'

I don't look at him as I snap, 'And as I've already told you, you have *no idea* what you're talking about.'

The lift ascends in a silent rush that has my knees weakening or is that the effect of his body at my side, the gentle pressure of his palm as he cups my elbow? Is he scared I'll run? Because I can hardly make a break for it in his lift. Try as I might.

Crazed laughter rises up as I ponder a ninja-style move through the elevator hatch that involves monkey-climbing him first. Not happening.

But this is.

One second, I'm heading for the bar, looking to lose myself in a few hours of reckless fun and the next, I'm being manhandled to the door, my body on fire with the heat of his. Burning up with instant recognition. Physically attuned and visually enraptured. By him. Gabriel Curran. My biggest fantasy and my heart's deepest desire.

And now he's asking how I am, wanting to dig beneath

the bold exterior to the real me, the broken me, and I want to give it to him. Against all my better judgement, my well-rehearsed lines, I want to spill all.

But I'm not here because he cares about me, he only cares about my brother and making sure I fall into the Monroe line. The reminder is timely and as the elevator slips into position and the doors open onto a vast space filled with high-gloss marble, black walls and glass, I shiver.

'You're cold?'

'I wasn't.'

But I am now.

Gabe doesn't have a heart, you see. It's a known fact. He cares about making money and he cares about my brother, but outside that... I'm not sure anything else breaks through the cool and ruthless surface.

'I'll get you something to change into.'

'You'll get me...' My voice drifts away as I watch him leave, my head shaking as my feet remain rooted to the cold floor. I say cold but it won't be. It'll be heated. I'm the one who's cold, cold and on edge, and as I wrap my arms around my middle, I accept I'm just a smidgen over naked—one hundred per cent exposed, vulnerable, and entirely susceptible to him.

I'd call myself a cab out of here if I didn't think he'd do exactly as he threatened and contact my brother. And it's not that I'm scared of my brother. Tired of him, more like. Tired of being judged and put down and made to feel inferior. My voice ignored.

I broke free of his hold and look where it's got me. Practically naked and ready to bare all to his best friend. Stupid, stupid move. Not that I had much say in it. The story of my life.

I take a breath. Tell myself to calm down. To ignore the

inner voices, ignore the rising panic…at least I can breathe without taking in his scent now, except I'm surrounded by him. His mark is everywhere. The masculine colour scheme, the dark furnishings, the hard angles and cut glass…how does anyone concentrate with this man in their orbit?

He's back too quickly for my liking but I'm relieved to see it's menswear he offers out to me. No obvious feminine wardrobe to hand, thank heaven.

'The guest room is down the hall, second door on your left. Why don't you get changed and then we can talk?'

'Talk?' I raise my brows at him. Does he really think it's that easy?

'Or not.' The deep concerned rumble is back, his blue eyes softening as he holds my gaze. 'The choice is yours.'

Does he have to act like he cares, cares and be all hot and sexy with it?

I move before I say something—*do* something—I'll later regret. I lock myself in the guest room and toss the clothing on the bed, wishing I could dive beneath the duvet too and hide. From him. My life. The world.

I mean, I love my brother, I really do, but when was the last time he paused to ask me how I was? Truly was. Took the time to sit down with me and just be together. No outside world looking in, no pressure, just a brother and sister enjoying one another's company.

Mum gave up on family time the day we lost Dad. As for Aiden, he took on his responsibilities as head of the Monroe family and firm and forgot I even existed. Until it was shoved under his nose by the school, the press, anyone with a bad word to say about me. He came running then and only then.

And now it's Christmas. A time we Monroes used to cherish, sacred family time, as Dad called it. Well, not any more.

It's all about hitting the slopes with friends, socialising, keeping busy, busy, busy. No time to just be.

It's exhausting. Physically and mentally. And they wonder why I run.

Run and end up just as bad. Living life at a hundred and ten miles an hour.

A rap on the door makes me jump, his voice quick to follow. 'Are you hungry?'

Am I? I don't remember when I last ate properly but I can't say I'm hungry. 'Not particularly.'

I can just make out his footsteps retreating, and I scan the room for a way to close the blinds. The glass window that takes up one wall may look like it's not overlooked but it also feels like a fish bowl and I'm always on the other end of some lens or other whether I choose to be or not.

I find a control beside the bed and set them to close. They slide smoothly into position and I take in the rest of the room. Cool white walls, white bed, white furnishings…does the man not do colour in any shape or form? I shudder as I strip out of my dress, tossing it onto the bed and taking up the items he gave me.

A grey T-shirt and dark grey sweatpants with a drawstring waist.

Mmm, sexy…

Except as I slip them on, his scent engulfs me and the buttery soft fabric rasps against my now sensitised skin…okay, so he makes even the simple sexy. I shove the top into place more abruptly than necessary and tug on the bottoms, tying them in a double knot to be extra secure.

I catch sight of myself in the wall of mirrors and suddenly a showdown with my brother feels far more appealing than walking back out there dressed like this. I grab my bag and pull out a hair tie, scrape my hair up into a messy knot, but I still look ridiculous. My make-up is garish and incongruous against the monochrome and I want it gone.

I head towards the only other door in the room. It leads to a private bathroom stocked with every luxury known to man. I grab a towel and some face wash and scrub my skin clean.

Fresh faced, I feel better but no less out of place and, sucking in a breath, I make for the door.

Everything will be okay. A night under Gabe's roof and then tomorrow life will resume as normal…

Though the thought leaves me colder than his choice of décor.

CHAPTER TWO

Gabe

I PICK UP my phone for the umpteenth time and navigate to Aiden's number, my fingers hovering…

I should tell him.

But then, what good would it do?

I got to Avery before anything bad happened so there's nothing to tell. Not really.

But what's to say something bad won't happen tomorrow or the day after, when I'm already out of here and she's been left to do as she will?

What's to say she won't try and hook up with her friends that can't be a great influence if they're encouraging her into a club underage?

And what's so bad about that? You're saying you didn't do that at her age…you and Aiden? Don't you owe her some flex…some benefit of the doubt…some freedom?

But that street, the place she was staying at…

'Telling tales?'

I almost drop my phone as I spin towards her and gawp. I never gawp. But at her…right now.

This is why you never give a woman your clothing. It marks them, brands them, makes them yours. I feel the visceral force of it even as I discount the reaction as ridiculous.

But she looks…she looks hot. Hair twisted up high, her face clear of make-up, cheeks all pink…

She cocks a brow. 'Well?'

I clench my jaw, realise I'm still staring and turn away. 'Not at all.'

I place my phone on the side and go back to making the hot chocolate I started earlier.

'Here.' I offer the mug out to her. 'I figured you could do with warming up.'

She pads bare foot across the floor towards me and I school my features, prepare myself for her nearness. I want tonight to be about her. Her and whatever hell she's going through. There were times when I thought she might tell me, glimpses of trust and a desire to let it all out before she shut down again.

'You made me a hot chocolate?' Her voice is laced with bemusement. Her eyes shine with it as I dare to meet them again.

'I guess I did.'

She purses her lips, like she's holding back a laugh. 'Are you trying to make me feel more like a child?'

If she could read my mind she'd know better. 'It's not my fault the law makes you a year off drinking age, but if you don't want it…'

I turn away and she reaches out, eases it from my grasp. 'I didn't say that…but if you have a splash of brandy you could add…'

'If I was your legal guardian then I would, but as I'm not, I won't.'

'I won't tell, if you won't.'

And why does it feel like she's talking about so much more than alcohol…?

Because there's a fire behind her eyes, a fire you know well and should be doing your utmost to put out.

I step away, take up my own drink. A fresh whisky to make up for the one I bailed on. 'You ready to talk?'

'You sure you want to listen?'

'Is everything a fight with you?'

'Is everything black and white with you?'

I frown, unsure of her meaning, and she waves a hand around the room, her lips curving up. 'Don't you think a splash of colour might be nice?'

She's all the colour this room needs, her flame-red hair and vibrant green eyes a striking contrast. I almost say it out loud too, it's on the tip of my tongue as I throw back a swig and treat her to silence instead. Because I have no place thinking it, let alone saying it. She's Aiden's sister and I know, beneath the tough exterior, she's hurting.

'I haven't noticed.'

The upward twitch to her brows tells me she doesn't believe me, but I'm not interested in talking about me and my interior design choices. 'You going to tell me what's going on, why you're so determined to act out all the time?'

She sips her hot chocolate, a delighted hum resonating through her that I try to tune out.

'Who says I'm acting out?'

'Everyone.'

She cocks her head as her eyes hold mine, quiet, contemplative. 'Define everyone.'

'Your brother, your mother, the press…'

'And you? Do you think I'm acting out?'

'I think you're giving the performance of a lifetime and I want to understand why.'

'So, you think being my brother's best friend gives you the right to probe into the whys and wherefores of how I behave?'

'As your brother's best friend since we could walk, I care about what happens to you, yes.'

'You care?'

'I do.'

And I can't explain it better than that. It must come from her connection to Aiden because why else would I have intervened tonight when I should've been focused on work and what comes first? My father's demands. And not this. Not her.

'I behave like I do because I want to.'

'You choose to behave like some out-of-control party animal with no care for anyone but herself?'

Her lashes flutter over eyes that flicker, the only sign that my words have found their mark. 'Gee, don't hold back on my account, Gabe. Why don't you tell me what you really think and be done with it?'

I don't react, my voice as even as my gaze. 'You see, I wouldn't care if it wasn't an obvious front to hide what's really going on with you.'

'And why are you so convinced it's a front?'

'Take it from a man who's spent his life perfecting his own. I can tell when someone isn't being true to themselves, and, in your case, I *know* this isn't you.'

'Really?'

'Yes. Because the girl I knew, the girl who couldn't go on a walk without bringing flowers back for her mother, or a special-looking rock for her father, or a stray animal given half a chance, wouldn't lose that good heart. You care.'

Her face scrunches up. 'I was a child, Gabe.'

I shake my head, dismissing her reasoning. 'Even in your early teens, you couldn't go a week away without phoning home, at boarding school you always checked in… Aiden would joke about it but—'

'Would he now…?'

'But he loved it. He loved that you were sweet and innocent and loving and everything us men aren't permitted to be.'

'Whatever.' She rolls her eyes, but I know I'm getting to her.

'You always sought your father's approval in everything you did.'

'Yeah, well, Dad isn't here any more, is he?' She stalks away from me, heads towards the fire where the flames dance beneath a suspended wall that doubles up as a room divider. Not that I think she's seeing any of it.

'No. He's not. And is that what this is, some extended act of rebellion now you don't have him to look up to, behave for...?'

She laughs but it cracks, her 'As if!' a broken scoff.

'Come on, Avery.' I resist the urge to reach for her. 'How do you think it feels for your brother and your mother to witness the way you're choosing to live your life?'

'I'm not doing it to hurt them.'

'I know.'

'Do you?' she throws back at me. 'Because the disapproval in your tone says otherwise.'

'I think you're scared, Avery. Scared and sad and—'

'Scared? I'm not scared.' But there's no power behind her voice, no conviction.

I walk towards her, careful to keep my stride slow. She's too easy to spook and I don't want her running from here at this late hour. I've already overstepped as far as detaining her goes—to keep her here against her will is a step I'd rather not take. Even if it is for her own good.

'Why would I be scared?'

Her chin is up but her lips quiver around the words.

'You tell me.'

'You're the one that said I was scared.'

'And you're the one acting like it.'

She stares back at me, trying to be tough, and I reach out unable to stop myself now, tuck a stray auburn curl behind her ear. 'It's okay to admit you're scared, Avery.'

'Oh, really? When was the last time you admitted to any kind of fear?'

'I'm a man, it's different.'

'And now you're being sexist.'

'Perhaps. I also have over a decade on you, so...'

'Ageist too. You really are rocking it tonight.'

A smile teases at my lips. I love her fire. Even at her weakest, the spark is there, pushing back.

'Why is it a problem how I behave? I'm not hurting anyone.'

'You hurt your family every time a bad word is printed in your name.'

'And you really think that will stop if I clean up my image tomorrow?'

'No, it'll take time and effort but eventually they'll leave you alone.'

'How can you be so sure?'

'Because it's the nature of the game. Don't add any fuel to the fire and eventually it will go out.'

'The smoke will remain.'

'For a time, but you will know better, your family will know better because what's the alternative, you carry on down this path of self-destruction and end up where, Avery? For what purpose?'

She can't answer me. She looks so lost, so vulnerable and I pray I'm getting through to her.

'When will you know you've had enough? When will you know to stop? When you get yourself arrested or, worse, hospitalised with your stomach being pumped? Pregnant by some loser boyfriend who couldn't care squat about you or a child?'

Her pallor deepens until she looks more grey than white. Maybe I've gone too far, said too much, but my imagination is running away with itself, triggered by the latest press reports of the wealthy heiress courting trouble.

'You don't know what you're talking about.'

'So you say.'

'I mean it.'

'Then tell me, give me the honest truth. From you. I could talk to your brother, get him to ease up if—'

Her laughter cuts me off. 'You're deluded if you think he'll listen to you.'

My frown is sharp. 'Your brother and I often give one another counsel, value each other's opinions, share advice.'

'Not where I'm concerned. Trust me. The only counsel he's keeping is his own and I'm done with it. Done with being controlled and forced onto a path I don't want.'

'Millions would give anything to have your wealth, your independence, a family like—'

'He's cut me off, Gabe. Okay? I am a Monroe heiress no more.'

I laugh at the absurdity of it. 'Don't be ridiculous, he can't—'

'Oh, he can and he has.'

'But...' I think of where she was staying, the squalor, I think of all the reasons Aiden can't have done this, his love for her, his desire to keep her safe, to save her from herself. 'I'm sure you've misunderstood.'

'Bank cards don't lie.'

'But—'

'Look! I quit my degree, told him I wanted to do something else, that his dream to work for the family firm was just that—his. Not mine.'

'And he cut you off?'

She drops back into the sofa and looks immediately swamped by the deep-set seat, her hair a bright splash of colour against the charcoal cushions. 'I think he hoped I'd come crawling back, contrite and ready to return to university. But he's wrong. I don't want to go back to how things were. I don't want to study a degree that puts me on track for a position within the Monroe firm, a position I never wanted but had pegged for me anyway.'

'Then tell him it's not what you want.'

Her eyes are wide as she blinks up at me. 'I did. But he doesn't listen. He doesn't care what I want. So now I'm free. Free and penniless and no more a part of the family than I was before.'

'You're still a Monroe. You're still his sister, his family.'

Tears fill her eyes. 'And you really think that, don't you?'

'You should think it. You should *know* it.'

'I haven't felt a part of the family in years. The day Dad died I became an outcast. Aiden was always too busy and Mum was too wrapped up in her own grief to see mine. The day Dad died I might as well have died too.'

Her words slam into me. 'You can't mean that.'

'Can't I? And you wonder why I have the friends I do. They were the ones who cared. They were the ones who listened when no one else would.'

'You sure about that, Avery, or were they just the ones that flocked around you because you had the money and the means and the notoriety to feed the toxic world you've lived in?'

She pales again but I won't take it back. I need her to see this isn't where she belongs. That, for all her family failed her, the future, the path she's on can change. And for the better.

'Take that down-on-his-luck rap singer you've been snapped hanging out with, he—'

'Emcee.'

I frown. 'What?'

'He's an emcee not a singer.'

My laugh is dark. 'Well, right now he isn't anything but trouble and seeing you fall out of clubs with him when you're underage and—'

'He's the same age.'

'It doesn't matter and you know it. Rumour has it, it wasn't just the parties you were funding but all that studio time for him, too.'

'He has talent.'

'He's a freeloader, Avery.' I'm so angry my voice shakes with it. 'A leech who'll bleed you dry.'

'Not any more.'

'What's that supposed to mean?'

She gives me a twisted smile. 'I'm penniless, remember, there's nothing left to bleed, as you so delightfully put it.'

'So, he's left you?'

'We were never together in the first place.'

I don't want to ponder what that means. They certainly *looked* together enough in the paparazzi snaps. Was she just using him for fun, for sex…? My stomach rolls and I ignore the reason why.

'This isn't you, Avery.'

'And maybe you're wrong, maybe the Avery you think you know no longer exists.'

'No!' The very idea does something to me that I'm unwilling to acknowledge. 'I don't believe it. I refuse to.'

Avery

'You *refuse* to?' Something about the way he says it has me back on my feet and closing the gap between us. 'You're wrong, Gabe.'

I'm goading him, I know it. But there's an undercurrent

in his voice, in the air, something I want to probe, provoke, bring to the surface…

'Am I?'

'I'm not the little girl seeking out stray animals to bring home, or the teen forever seeking her father's approval, I'm a woman who does what she wants, when she wants…'

And what I want right now is him. I've done a lot in my twenty years, experienced much the world has to offer, but a man… I've kissed plenty, done a little more too, but I've never had the true desire, the burning need to go all the way, to want more.

I fear it. The connection. The attachment. The inevitable loss and abandonment too.

But something about Gabe calls to the very heart of me and the whirling, swirling heat that's been building ever since he hooked his arm in mine tells me I want this. I want him and the pleasure I know he can deliver.

'And that includes this singer, this emcee? You wanted him? Want him, even?'

His voice is rough, his jaw pulses, a tension emanates from his rigid stature and it's building with every step I take.

'If I so choose…'

'And do you?'

'Do I what?'

'Do you choose him?'

His voice gets lower with every syllable, vibrates with something that I'm desperate to understand. Because this is Gabe. My brother's best friend. A man who's never looked at me like I swear he is right now.

'Does it bother you if I do?'

'You could do better.'

I pause, barely a foot away, breathe in his scent, feel the warmth radiating off his body, the open collar to his shirt drawing my eye to the hint of hair there. I wet my lips. He's all man, so much more than the boys I have dated, I have kissed…

'Better? How so?'

His throat bobs. 'Any man has to be better than a failing musician with a reputation for drugs and alcohol.'

'Got an issue with musicians?'

'More the drugs and the alcohol.'

I dare to press my palm against his chest. Wow, he is hot, in every way. 'Do you *mean* any man, or…' I lift my eyes to his '…you?'

'No.' His throat bobs, his chest pulses beneath my touch. 'Not me. Never me.'

'Why?'

His eyes are dark, dangerous, they burn into my lips as he wrestles with whatever he's thinking. 'You're playing with fire, Avery.'

'When that fire is you…' I smooth my palm over his shoulder and savour his strength flexing beneath '… I like it a lot.'

And then I kiss him, the briefest sweep of my lips against his, and my body is torched alive. Every nerve ending craving, reaching… He tenses and I fear he's going to pull away and when he doesn't, I'm emboldened, passion licking fire through my veins. I reach into his dark hair, feel the carefully groomed strands give way beneath my fingers, feel the hardness of his chest against my front and a whimper rises up unbidden, overridden by the growl he gives.

'Avery, don't do this.'

My lashes lift, my eyes colliding with his. 'Stop me, then.'

Lightning bolts through his blues, a curse tearing from his lips as he claims mine. And then he's kissing me, hard and fast, walking me back until the sofa hits the back of my calves and we're tumbling onto it. I've never felt anything like it, the need so deep within me it's painfully acute and I'm tugging his shirt from his trousers, raking my hands underneath to get to his skin.

I wrap my legs around him, urge him closer. Desperate as his tongue invades my mouth, plunges as his body shifts over me in tune. 'This is madness.'

'The best kind of madness.'

'We shouldn't do this.'

'We should.'

'I'm supposed to be looking out for you!' He scrambles back, fighting with himself, his head shaking but I move with him, straddle him.

'You're not my brother, Gabe.' I pull the T-shirt over my head and his eyes drop to my naked skin, my lack of bra an accidental benefit as the desire in his depths deepens. 'I'm not your responsibility.'

'Your brother...' More head shaking and I dip to kiss him, try to distract him.

'I don't want to talk about Aiden.'

'Avery.' He squeezes his eyes shut, lifts me away, launches himself off the sofa as he tosses the T-shirt I discarded back at me. 'Put it on. I won't be a part of this.'

My skin prickles, goosebumps rife as his rejection washes over me, cold and brutal with it. And then I register his words. 'What do you mean? A part of this? A part of what?'

'This!' He thrusts a hand at me before raking both through his hair, grips the back of his head. 'I'm such a fool. I don't know why I didn't see it before.'

'See what?'

'I'm just a part of this act, this performance, the ultimate act of rebellion.'

My head is shaking, my voice quiet with confusion. 'I don't know what you're talking about...'

'*No?* Seducing your brother's best friend?' His laugh is pitched, his face full of distaste. 'Was this your plan all along? To get back at him, to spoil what friendship we have, to get between us…if you can't have your brother in your life, neither can I, is that it?'

'*You* were the one who brought me here.' I launch to my feet, grip his shirt to my chest as I feel every exposed inch. 'How could I possibly have planned it?'

But he's not listening, a wall has gone up that I can't surmount. As for the hate in his eye…

'I don't know, Avery, but I won't be a part of it. This life you portray, the whole rebel heiress with a chip on her shoulder, angry at the world and everyone in it. I was wrong to try and see any more in you.'

My gut turns over, tears sting the backs of my eyes, but I refuse to break down any further—he's seen enough. I've given him enough. 'How can you say that?'

'Because it's true.'

I raise my chin further. 'You were the first person to see me properly in a long time. The first person to ask me how I was and genuinely want the answer. It felt good. Too good. And I was a fool to trust you with it.' He pales as though I've slapped him but I'm not done. 'A fool to give into whatever this is between us, but I tell you now that kiss, that kiss was no act.'

I pull his shirt over my head, grab my handbag from the table and stride for the exit.

'Where are you going?'

'Anywhere you're not.'

'Avery, get back here. It's late. You can't go out there dressed like that.'

I pluck my shoes from the floor and spin to face him. 'And that's where you're wrong, Gabe. I'm Avery Monroe and I can go anywhere the hell I like, dressed however I like, and no one will bat an eyelid. It will just go down as yet another way in which I can embarrass my entire family.'

'Avery—'

'No!' I'm done listening to him. 'If you want me to keep this dirty little rendezvous to myself, I suggest you leave me to it.'

'Please—' There's a flash of regret in his eyes, or is it panic? Either way, I don't care. I'm done.

'Goodbye, Gabe.' I strike off once more. 'If I ever see you again it'll be too soon.'

CHAPTER THREE

Three years later...

Gabe

I HEAR THE car approach on the winding cobbled driveway and head to the upstairs window.

Hands deep in my pockets, I watch the rear door open and all I see is the top of her flame-red head, the sight enough to pulse right through me.

Well, she's here in Dubrovnik, that must count for something.

Three years and I haven't seen her. Three years since that kiss that blew my world apart. And now it's time to put it back together and fix what I broke.

A reset of sorts.

She's avoided me and I can't blame her. The things I said, saw, did…

And if Aiden knew, had even an inkling of any of it, she wouldn't be here now…she wouldn't be here and our friendship would be over.

But she is here and at her brother's request.

Her consent is another matter.

Is it under duress? A desperation that her brother forced upon her when he stripped her of her wealth? Or has she come by choice? That's what I've yet to discover.

She talks to my driver, who beams back at her, clearly smitten, and I turn away. Take a breath. Well, here goes…

Time to meet and greet.

Avery Monroe. Housekeeper to my Croatian Castle for the summer. A well-paid job to fund her studies and a home away from home.

For Aiden, it gives her a place to stay that he trusts, thanks to his ignorance of what went down.

For me, I get a chance to fix our relationship, put that kiss to bed and move forward. In a healthy, platonic, future-proof manner.

For her, she gets the money and the space she needs to work on her degree. I'd say she gets protection from the outside world, too, with acres of private land to wander and a press-shielding security line in place, but she's kept a low profile in the last three years. And her brother wants to keep it that way, his need to have her out of the family home and in safe confines questionable but understandable. I'll do what I can to support him and her in the process.

It's a win-win… I hope.

Car doors slam, heels clip against the cobblestone drive-way, suitcase wheels a constant burr and my veins thrum. Nerves. Apprehension. A whole heap of what the hell am I doing raging through my bloodstream. I take the winding stairs down to the treble-height entrance hall just as the front door swings open and in she strides.

She hasn't knocked. Of course, she hasn't. And I'm all out of staff to greet her thanks to a virus that's sweeping through the city. It's just me and her and my driver standing cautiously back.

She freezes when she sees me, a second's hesitation and a, 'Don't even say it!'

I pause on the bottom step, raise my hands. 'Say what?'

'That you missed the news.'

I frown, my next step as cautious as I feel. 'The news?'

'About hell freezing over...?'

'Hell freezing...?' I scratch the back of my head and then it clicks. 'I don't think you said anything about hell freezing over, more that if you ever saw me again it would be too soon.'

Because those words have been ingrained in me ever since that night. Those words and the papped photo of her leaving my apartment building. The oversized sweatpants—mine. The oversized T-shirt—mine. The kiss-swollen lips—my doing. The flushed cheeks, too.

She'd hidden her eyes behind designer shades and given the cameras a smile so wide you'd think she was accepting an award. Not doing the walk of shame out of *my* apartment building.

God knows how Aiden hadn't put two and two together and hit a very accurate four. Come beating down my door in a rage. Not that he'd needed to. I'd had enough anger and disgust to cover the both of us.

'My mistake.' She cocks a hip, eyes hidden behind a very similar pair of shades as she pins me to the ancient floor. She's a vision of confidence. From the flowing trousers in flamboyant burnt umber and barely there fabric, to the loose vest top that hangs just above her midriff and shows off her slender frame, to the haughty air...

How much of it is an act? I wonder. Is she really as confident, as unaffected as the vibe she's giving off?

I say unaffected but she's angry—the fire in her gaze unmistakable.

'Where would you like me to put Miss Monroe's luggage, sir?' My eyes leave her to take in my driver, Emerik, standing on the sidelines. His hands are gripped before him, eyes wide as he takes in our little exchange and I smile to hide my edginess, promptly smother it when the gesture startles him. Do I really smile so little?

'Just there is fine.' My tone is clipped and I grimace, it's hardly his fault. 'I'll take them up shortly.'

'Of course.' He props up the two cases he has in hand. 'I'll go and get the rest.'

'The rest?'

I look at the bags, frown from him to Avery, who blushes. 'I'm here for the whole summer, and I have my work too...'

'The summer, yes, I didn't expect you to move yourself in.' Again with the edge. The loss of cool. What is wrong with me?

You really need to ask...?

'Regretting your agreement to this madness already, Gabe?' But her tone is soft, sensitive, worried, her sudden shift drawing me up sharp.

'No.' I say, truthfully. We need this opportunity to break the ice. She can't avoid me for ever, and I can't avoid the elephant in the room. Every date, every woman since, Avery's there, burning up my mind, unintentionally intervening. I haven't been able to kiss another without recalling that night. I tell myself it's the guilt, the broken trust, the bad way I handled it. I play it over and over. But by having her here, as a favour to Aiden and a job for her, I hope we can put it behind us. Find a platonic footing, a friendship once more. But first, I need to convince her that she's welcome. 'Not at all.'

She studies me a moment longer, looks like she's about to say something but stops herself.

I step forward and she turns away, hurries into the room. 'This place isn't what I was expecting.'

It comes out rushed but her head is held high. She has the grace of a swan and the confidence of a queen, and for a second, I just leave her be. Leave her be and appreciate the woman she has grown into. The colour in her cheeks, the healthy curves, a sign that the ex-party girl maintaining a low profile isn't just a front.

'How so?'

She pauses and looks up, takes in the high ceiling with its cast-iron chandelier and twirls on the spot. 'This place is more quaint castle than contemporary home. I guess I shouldn't be surprised though.' She looks at me now, a smile on her lips and I anticipate the tease before she even gives it. 'I always fancied you to have been a king in a previous life.'

'A king, you say?'

'Yes.' She waves a hand at me. 'All that superiority you've got going on.'

Is she still teasing? Or is she recalling that night, my treatment of her? She wets her lips and I'm helpless to track the move...remembering how it felt to kiss those lips, to have her...

A scuffle to the left announces a returning Emerik and she moves first. 'So, is there someone who can give me a tour? I'm sure you have work you'd like to be getting back to and I don't want to keep you. If someone can just show me the ropes, I can take care of the rest.'

'You don't have to get stuck in straight away.'

'You're paying me good money, Gabe. I'm going to earn it.'

'I don't doubt that.' Because I don't. Something about this new woman means business in an entirely different way. 'I just mean, you've had a long journey. You should freshen up first, take some time to settle in.'

'I'll take some time once I have my bearings.'

I nod. 'Okay, this way.' I cross the hall and realise she hasn't moved. 'Something wrong?'

'You don't need to do this, Gabe.'

Does she mean the job? Does she see it as some kind of pity offering? I open my mouth to object but she gets there first. 'I'm fine with someone else showing me around.'

My shoulders ease. 'There's no one else, Avery. Save for Emerik and he's busy bringing in your luggage.'

'No one else?' Her eyes widen a fraction.

'You heard me.'

She hurries after me as I set off down the corridor that leads to the rear of the house. 'You don't have any staff here? But this place is...this place is huge.'

'They're all off sick.'

'*All?*' She shoves her shades up into her hair, her green eyes bright as she stares at me. I've never met anyone with eyes like hers. Emerald cut with amber and fascinating with it. Especially as they dart up and down the hall now. 'Are you kidding?'

'No. It's just you and me.' I blow out a breath. This tour is going to take for ever if she keeps stopping me. And then I take in the panic in her face and wonder if I called it wrong— maybe she *is* worried about the amount of work she's taken on. 'At least for a little while. Don't look so worried. I'm sure you'll cope.'

'Cope?' She swallows, the tiniest line appearing between her brows.

'With all the housework...?' I explain. 'I'll do my fair share.'

'No, no that won't be necessary. I can take care of it, I just...'

I frown. Her response as disorientating as her fluster. 'Just?'

'Nothing. Nothing at all. Let's get back to the tour...'

'What is it?'

She flicks me a look. 'I just hadn't expected it to, you know, be just you and me.'

'You, me, and the security team at the gates. Emerik when he's needed, too.'

She blinks back at me. And that's when I realise this isn't about work at all, it's about us. Being alone.

I clear my throat. 'Is that going to be a problem?'

'No,' she blurts, then proceeds to worry over her bottom lip and I know it is. I also know that the glossy pink flesh I'm now staring at will be the death of me if I don't set her straight and get this tour over with.

'You really don't need to worry. You'll have plenty of space in the east wing, we'll hardly need to cross paths.'

Her eyes flicker up at me. 'Is that what you'd prefer?'

'I thought that's what...' I stop myself and start again. There's no point beating around the bush with this. As soon as it's dealt with, the sooner we can move on. I hope. 'Look, about what happened, the things I said to you—'

'Don't, Gabe. Please.' Her hand is on my chest, quick as a flash. 'Let's not relive it. Just know that I'm sorry.'

'*You're* sorry?' I stare at her dumbfounded. Meanwhile her palm is burning a hole through my shirt but I can't think to step away, not when her apology is so sincere and so unnecessary. She was scared, lost, alone and I pushed her, goaded her, and then crushed her. Consumed by my own disgust, my own guilt. Hating myself.

'Yes.' The sudden tears in her eyes slay me. 'I never should have behaved like that. You were trying to help me and—and it was wrong. I was wrong. I'm—I'm so ashamed.'

Her cheeks burn and my brain races, words tumbling over themselves, reassurances I want to give, but the one thing I have been desperate to say for three years overrides. 'I'm the one who's sorry, Avery.' I cover her palm on my chest, desperate for her to see I mean it. 'What I said to you, what I accused you of...'

She shakes her head. 'You were right though. Not about the—the kiss, but everything else. I wasn't trying to jeopardise your friendship with my brother. I wasn't trying to come between you.' Her eyes are awash with her honesty, her sincerity and the hurt I put there. 'I wasn't thinking of him at all.'

No, she was thinking only of the kiss, the chemistry, the burn that persists even now.

'I know.'

Her scent, more subtle than that of before but no less intoxicating, feeds my veins and I see the reciprocal fire come alive behind her eyes, feel the dangerous lure of her and say the words that need to be said before we end up back where we shouldn't.

'But you have to know it was a mistake.' My desperate need to ignore the force that's drawing us together adds strength to my words. 'It should never have happened, and it can never happen again. Understood?'

I grimace. Fearing she'll see it as an order from above, not a request to get us both on the same page.

'And there goes that superiority complex I was telling you about.' She teases but her smile lands flat, the fire in her emerald depths going out. 'I understand, Gabe.'

She slips her hand out from under mine. 'You don't need to worry. There won't be a repeat performance. I promise.'

The mood is meek, the air heavy.

'Shall we get back to the tour?'

I nod, but I can't shake the sadness. Surely she has to understand that once can be dismissed as a mistake, a moment of madness when caught unawares. But twice?

Twice would make me the worst kind of friend imaginable.

Loyalty means more to me than family. Aiden means more to me than blood. I don't do relationships and that puts Avery firmly out of reach. A fling with your best friend's sister is never a good idea, no matter what rule book you live by...

Avery

I plaster on a smile. I've done one of the things I came to do. The hardest and most important, too. I've apologised. The shame almost killed me, but I had to say it. The second he brought it up, I knew it was my chance. Especially after I erupted on his doorstep.

I'd wanted to bite off my tongue. But seeing him again, feeling that intense rush of attraction, that fire that I'd hoped would have at least dimmed in the intervening years, had thrown me for a loop and I'd said the first thing to come to mind. Fighting talk.

Not the gratitude I wanted to lay at his feet. Gratitude for the job. Gratitude for not telling Aiden what I did. And, of course, the apology.

An apology I never in a million years thought he would return.

And to have him respond like he did, to hear him say *he* was sorry.

I should be happy, ecstatic even. We've agreed a reset, a fresh start of sorts. It's more than I could have hoped for and makes the next few weeks brighter by far. So why do I feel so cold?

You know why...

Not only has he made clear that the kiss was a mistake—which it was.

He's also stated in no uncertain terms that it can never happen again—which it can't.

But that connection I've been pondering for three years. Pondering and comparing every connection to since...well, it was no exaggeration, no figment of my overactive, highly tumultuous, emotional state. It hasn't been intensified by my shame, my imagination, my wrongdoing. It's still there. And it's stronger than ever.

Which puts another important reason for my visit here in jeopardy. To get over it. To get over him.

I want to laugh at my own stupidity, my naivety even. Faced with him now. His piercing blue eyes, the carefully styled hair and chiselled jaw, those broad shoulders and tapered waist, a behind that looks incredibly fine in the shorts he wears and don't even get me started on how well his pale blue T-shirt stretches across his pecs... How could I have been so foolish as to think I'd have it under control?

I've come a long way in three years and I intend to prove that to him. I want him to forget the incident three years ago, not because we've agreed to move on, but because he sees me as the woman I am now. Unrecognisable as the 'rebel heiress with a chip on her shoulder' as he so aptly put it. And letting this desire get the better of me can only scupper that and take his mind right back to her.

'On this level you have access to the library...the lounge... the dining room...the kitchen...the laundry...'

He vaguely points in either direction as he speaks. To grand double doorways and stone archways, corridors filled with warm stone and carved wood and relics of many a yesteryear. It's an interior untouched by the modern age and charming with it.

Is this really his home? I hadn't been lying when I'd said I was surprised by it. Trying to cover up for my nerves, my attraction that I desperately wanted to hide, yes. But not lying.

I'd expected something cold and contemporary, much like his place in New York. Instead, I feel like I've stepped back in time, into an ancient fairy tale full of whimsical magic and dreams come true.

I want to understand its owner, too. The compassion I've glimpsed, the concern and the loyalty, they all strike me as characteristics of a man with a heart. A real heart and not the cold, callous tech mogul he is renowned as being.

Has he spent three years reliving that kiss? Dwelling on it?

He's been beating himself up about it, if his heartfelt apology is any indication.

But has it tortured him like it has me? Ruining every attempt at a relationship, a fling even? Has he been stuck in some strange kind of limbo, hounded by this futile, impossible want?

Twenty-three and still a virgin, not through intent but by inescapable choice. One that he made for me when he kissed me back and lit me up from within. Made me want only him, through no plan of his own. Made me his in some weird, twisted way.

And what makes it so much worse is that he has no idea.

He turns to look at me. 'You okay?'

'Yeah, why?'

'You sighed.'

'I did?'

He nods, his head tilted to the side as though he thinks I'm losing it. Ha, maybe I am!

'This place is just—well, it's incredible.'

A second's hesitation and then he looks away, carries on, and my body sags with relief.

'I'm glad you think so.' I think that's all he's going to give when he surprises me with, 'It was built over three centuries so it has an eclectic mix of architectural styles that you won't find anywhere else.'

'Each telling its own story through the ages,' I murmur and his eyes flit my way for the briefest spell.

'Something like that...' His mouth tugs off to one side. 'You never know what you'll find around the next corner.'

'I can believe it.' I let my gaze drift over it all, my smile one of genuine wonder, and I realise he's still looking at me. 'What?'

'Nothing.' He's moving off again and I have to hurry to catch him up.

'No, you're looking at me funny. Did you think I wouldn't appreciate it?'

'No, it's—that's not—okay, yes, I guess.' He flicks me a look. 'It doesn't strike me as your cup of tea.'

'Cup of tea? Can you get any more British?'

'You know you're British, too, right? That just because you live all over you haven't lost your place of birth.'

I ignore him as I press, 'Is that why you bought it?'

His blues eyes dance back at me. 'Because I didn't think you'd appreciate it?'

'No!' I shove him, failing to resist the impulse and loving the spark of camaraderie but as soon as the sparks fly through my fingers too, I snatch my hand back, fist it against my chest. 'Because it's unique, an eclectic mix!'

'In part.' He's off again and I hurry to catch him up.

'So why Croatia? Why Dubrovnik?' I shake my fingers off, unaware that my questions have made him stall until I almost collide with him. I step back. 'I get that it's beautiful but...'

'But what?' He rakes a hand through his hair, seems to ground himself before his pace picks up again.

'It seems an unusual choice, that's all.' I step in line with him, try to catch a look at his face, which feels permanently averted now.

'How so?'

'For someone like you, I mean.'

'Someone like me?'

'When you could live anywhere in the world, buy anything.'

'Not up to your standard, hey? I thought you liked it.'

'I do like it.'

'I don't remember you being so fussy in New York.'

My cheeks warm. 'I told you I like it.'

But I get the impression he isn't listening. 'What happened with your friend that night? Did you go back there?'

No, I didn't, but I'm not about to get into a conversation about it. 'Can we just forget about that night?'

He scans my face and whatever he sees there has him acquiescing. 'Of course.'

'But if you must know…' I fold my arms against the spreading chill within '…that friend is a distant memory.'

'Glad to hear it.'

'And it has nothing to do with the neighbourhood he lived in, Gabe, and everything to do with him, okay?'

'If you say so.'

'Will you stop?' I bluster.

'Stop what?'

'Stop being such a—such a—'

I wave a hand up and down, gesture at the whole of him like it somehow completes the sentence and, finally, he gives me his full attention, only I don't want it now.

'Such a…?'

'Pompous buffoon!' I blurt, pressing my lips together as soon as it's out. Name-calling is hardly the brightest, most mature of moves, but, man, he drives me crazy!

'A pompous buffoon?' His brows disappear into his hairline and the impressive sweeping quiff he has going on. I mean, who even has hair as perfect as that? How long does it take him to achieve that look every morning? Or does he just get out of bed that way? I bet it's the latter. Someone as flawless and enigmatic as Gabe probably came out of the womb looking pristine!

'Is that really how you see me?'

I fist my hip, eye him with all the fight I can muster. No going back now…

'When you look down on someone based on where they live, yes.'

'Even if my opinion was clouded by my concern for you.'

Concern? Gulp. Ignore. Be still my beating heart because it means nothing!

I raise my chin. 'Where someone lives has no correlation to who they are so get out of your entitled behind and accept that.'

'I do accept that.'

I snort, I can't help it. Dignified or not, it's the sound that best fits my reaction.

'It was your safety and the company keeping those streets that time of night that had me concerned. Not the certain someone you were choosing to stay with.'

And why am I disappointed at that? I shouldn't care that he doesn't care about my potential love interests.

He cared that night, though. Remember. It's how you got yourself into this mess…

He stares back at me and I suddenly feel teeny tiny and never keener to change the subject. 'So, Croatia? Why choose here for a holiday home?'

He hesitates, a look chasing over his face that I can't identify but I feel the sudden shift in power my way and grab hold. 'Gabe?'

'It's in my blood.'

Not what I expected… 'But I thought your father was—'

'On my mother's side.'

'Oh…'

And he's moving off again, running from the conversation as much as me. He never talks of his mother, ever, and I realise I know next to nothing about her.

'Your mother was Croatian?'

He doesn't answer me right away and I wonder whether he will at all when he admits, 'Yes.'

I touch the gold fringe to a tapestry that hangs on one wall, feel the delicacy of it as well as the conversation. 'I've never heard you talk of her…' I try and make it sound like it's not a big deal 'Your mother, I mean.'

'Because I don't.'

There's an edge to his voice, an edge that I want to probe… even though I know it's not my place. 'Why?'

'Why does anyone not talk about something, Avery?'

He does an about-turn, the look on his face telling me that this conversation is over.

'You can get to the pool and gardens through here. There's a pool house you can change in with towels, refreshments, and suncream. I'll show you to your rooms upstairs.'

I follow his rigid stride back to the front of the house where my luggage has formed a mini mountain. His step falters as he takes it all in and I curse my inability to travel light. But in truth, my work takes up a lot of it. My precious designs, my portfolio two years in the making…something that may not have happened if it hadn't been for him.

His rejection had cut deep, of course it had. But his encouragement, his understanding, and his belief that I was doing what was right for me, that my family would come around, had spurred me on. Given me the confidence to sign up for my course…

True, he didn't know about my dream in detail. I never got so far as to tell him. But it was enough that he'd believed in me.

He shakes his head and hits the stairs two at a time, his burred words a command. 'Watch your heels on the stairs, it's uneven in parts.'

'You worried about the ancient rock or me taking a fall?'

'I'm not going to dignify that with a response.'

He doesn't look at me as he says it, doesn't see the growing smile on my face, but I do take a second to assess the higgledy-piggledy stone and slip off my heels. As much as I'd love him to come to my rescue—just to show he truly cares and *not* because I want his arms around me—I'm not sure his extended stride could get to me before I suffer a nasty bruise or two.

Hooking the backs of my sandals in one finger, I take them with me as I follow him up. He heads east across the galleried landing with its peculiar statues, intricate tapestries and weapons that look as old as the castle itself. Does he like all this stuff? Is there a secret love of all things old and mystical underneath the tough, businesslike exterior?

Or does this have more to do with his mother and her family? His heritage?

'This is your domain.'

'Huh.' I'm so lost in the memory of his face, his voice, his entire posture when he spoke of her that I don't realise we've come to a stop and he's looking at me expectantly.

'Your private area. You have your own reading room, dressing room, bathroom… If you want to make yourself at home, I'll go get your bags. If there's anything you're missing let me know and I'll have it sourced.'

'I'm sure that won't be necessary.'

He gives me a nod and hurries away, so fast it's as though

he has a small dog yapping at his heels. And what's he running from? Truly?

Me, or the past that I accidentally touched upon.

The past I now want to understand, just as much as I want to understand the man it belongs to. Because one thing's for sure. Gabe is not the heartless man the media depict and he himself projects.

Not by a long shot.

CHAPTER FOUR

Gabe

I RETURN TO the hall and stare at the mountain that is Avery's luggage and pull out my phone.

My text is brief:

She's arrived.

Aiden replies instantly and I know he's been waiting for my message.

Thank you for letting me know, and for agreeing to this.

Guilt gnaws at my insides. He wouldn't be saying that if he knew what had happened three years ago. How I crossed the line when I should've been looking out for her, protecting her...

But you're making up for that now.

How is everything at home?

So-so. I'll keep you posted. Mum's procedure is scheduled for next week. I know you disagree, but please don't tell Avery.

I pause. I don't like that I'm keeping something from her. Something she should know. But at the same time, I owe Aiden. More than he can ever know. And though he's right, I do disagree, I'm not her brother. He is. And he's doing what he believes is right.

I won't, but you should seriously reconsider...

So you've said, but now isn't the time.

I could press further but it would only add more stress to his already full plate.

Okay. Keeping you in my thoughts. Take care.

You too. And of her.

I will.

And then I go back to the luggage and scratch my head. How can one woman need so much stuff? And how on earth did Emerik fit it all in the car?

'That's everything, sir.' The man himself appears in the doorway, mopping his brow. 'Would you like some assistance taking it upstairs?'

'No, no, it's okay.' I slip the phone back into my pocket. 'I've got it.'

'Are you sure, sir?'

'Absolutely.'

And I can treat it as something of a penance...just as this whole trip will be. Living under the same roof, sleeping under the same roof...a torture I deserve. Because it doesn't matter that my head knows she's off limits, my body still wants her.

But lucky for me, willpower is one thing I possess in spades.

My father trained it into me from a very young age. Made me stubborn. Deny all that is bad for you and work hard for the good. What makes you sweat and pushes you to your limits reaps the greatest reward. Love makes you soft. What you crave will be your undoing. It's far too easy to devour the cake, hit the lighter weights, take out the smallest company...fall into bed with the wrong woman.

'You get yourself home, Emerik.' My fingers are back in my hair, my aching jaw protesting all the clenching. 'I'm sure your family will appreciate having you back.'

'That they will, sir, this virus is a nasty one.'

'Just keep yourself safe.'

'Will do, sir. I'll see you tomorrow.'

'Take the rest of the month, Emerik. If we need to go anywhere, I can take us.'

'But I'm—'

'Fully paid.'

His eyes widen. 'But, sir, Marija can manage.'

'I'd be happier knowing that she's managing with your help, Emerik.'

'That's very kind of you.' He stands to attention. 'Thank you, sir.'

'Not a problem.'

With one last look at me and the array of cases, Emerik leaves, and I start hoisting as many bags as I can manage onto my back, and head upstairs. Focusing on the job in hand and not the mutterings in my mind questioning my ability to handle this situation. Handle it in an agreeable, acceptable, and wholly platonic way. Just as I had planned. But planning it when Avery was on the other side of the world had been so much easier than handling it with her under the same roof.

And if I hadn't been working so hard to get my head and body on the same page, maybe I wouldn't have stepped into the bedroom. Maybe the sound of the shower running would have been a sign to leave the bags outside the door and go back for more. Instead, I'm rooted to the rug beside her bed, listening to the water fall and the unmistakable sound of Avery singing over it.

Singing in the shower is one thing. Singing the way Avery does it is something else…free and easy and utterly hypnotic. An alien warmth spreads through me, discombobulating and immobilising with it. I guess I don't need to worry about her making herself at home…at this rate she'll be the one settled and I'll be the one eager to move out.

Then I remember why she's here, the many reasons she's here, and the one that she doesn't know about yet, and the thought is as sobering as it is concerning.

I drop the bags, go to turn and realise too late that the shower has shut off, the singing fast approaching and—

'Gabe!'

I blink. Blink again like it will somehow magic her out of view. But no. She's still there. Very wet. Mostly naked. Gripping the smallest towel imaginable to her breasts.

'I'm sorry.' The apology sticks in my throat but seriously… I'm sure there are bigger towels in her bathroom. Towels that would at least reach her knees and not end so high on her thigh that they leave little to the Imagination. 'I was dropping off your bags, I didn't mean—I wouldn't have come in if—I wasn't expecting you to be…'

I gesture at her like it explains everything my mouth seems unable to.

'Thank you,' she says, her cheeks a fetching shade of pink as she stares back at me.

'I'll just…' I point in the direction of the door but my feet don't budge.

'You'll just…?' Her mouth twitches, her eyes sparkle, her amusement the kick I need.

'I'll go get the rest.' And turn and flee, fingers raking through my hair.

I head downstairs and load up again. This time I don't stride right in, I leave the mountain outside her door and tell myself she's more than capable of doing the rest.

Then I hit the gym. Hard.

Avery

Gabe wasn't lying when he told me we could go about our lives without crossing paths. I've not seen him since he appeared in my room and promptly scarpered.

Maybe I should have donned the bigger towel. Maybe I should have been a bit more coy about coming out when I knew he was there. But the devil in me, the one that has spent the last three years pining for him against my will, wanted me to toy with him just a little. Toy with him and test the waters, the attraction—is it just one-sided or is Gabe suffering too?

Regardless of his loyalty to Aiden and his assurance that the kiss would never happen again, is he in the same boat? Because at least that would be better. Fairer, even.

But now he's nowhere to be seen and I can't hear another soul within the house. The walls are so thick, the outside world doesn't intrude either so all I have are the voices in my head and it's starting to grate.

I make it a priority to surround myself with noise. Noise and a healthy dose of chaos. To be busy, busy, busy and not let the little voices in. Which is kind of hard when I'm in new territory with no one to talk to, not even a member of staff to harangue. I say harangue because that's what my brother would call it. I prefer to see it as taking an interest.

And I really can't bear this—this nothing.

I explore the house but leave the upper west wing be. I assume it's his domain and, though I'm keen to seek out a distraction, some company, I'm not about to invade his space to achieve it.

I sweep down the stairs, humming to myself, take a turn about the kitchen where I spy a well-stocked wine fridge and pluck out a bottle. 'While the host's away the guest will play…'

'Play?'

I spin on the spot, grip the bottle to my chest as my heart gives a thrilling little jig.

'Is that what you call helping yourself to my wine?'

He's lounging in the doorway, his eyes dark and brooding, and I'm drowning in that look, struggling to catch my breath.

'Well, I assumed anything was available for the taking…'

If only that extended to the host himself...

And why did that thought have to race through my mind? And why do my cheeks have to colour and my eyes give it all away? Because they have. I'm sure of it.

He shoves away from the door frame and strides towards me, reaches out. My eyes widen, my body arches back—is he reaching for me? But then his grip closes around the bottle and my heart trips out. 'I'll take care of that if you want to get two glasses.'

'You're j-joining me?'

'I can hardly let you drink alone your first night here.'

Close your mouth, Avery, it's just a drink...

'I would have thought dinner would be the more appropriate thing to join me in,' I say as casually as I can, 'but I'll take a drink.'

He checks his watch. 'Forgive me, I didn't realise how late it was.'

'Too busy with work?'

'Something like that…'

'Is there a plan?'

'A plan?' He's busy extracting the cork from the bottle but he takes a brief moment to frown at me.

'For dinner?'

'Oh, right. Uh…'

He scans the kitchen like it will produce an answer and I laugh. 'I'll take that as a no.'

'Normally Ms Novak would have it covered but she was struck down by the virus…'

'Ms Novak?'

'My cook.'

'Of course. Did she leave instructions? A list of what she intended to serve up? Cooks are nothing if not organised. Do you have food in the cupboards at least?'

My eyes narrow on the streak of colour that sweeps across his well-defined cheekbones and deepens with every question I pose… Sheepish Gabe is even more handsome than carefully composed Gabe. If that were even possible.

'You didn't listen, did you?'

He doesn't answer and I fold my arms, rest my hip against the stone countertop. 'Ms Novak told you what was what, and you didn't listen.'

'I was busy. For one, I had your arrival to prepare for…'

Prepare for mentally or physically? I want to ask, but I don't dare.

I shake my head and mutter, 'Typical man,' instead.

'I was also more concerned with getting her home so that she could rest.'

That earns him a genuine smile, plus brownie points that I'll keep to myself as I start opening drawers, checking cupboards…

'What are you doing?' he asks as the cork pops free.

'I'm looking for a note of some sort. Failing that I'm looking for ingredients to cook with.'

He pours two glasses and offers one out to me, the near brush of his fingers enough to make my own warm. I take a sip, praying the burn won't reach my cheeks, and busy myself with the task at hand, anything to avoid the way he's making me feel.

I find lots of ingredients I recognise and some I haven't a clue about. 'Are you planning on getting some temporary staff in?'

'I have.' Then he grins. 'You.'

I raise a brow at him. 'Just me?'

'Just you. And as we've already discussed, you said you were fine with it.'

'I am.'

You're not.

But not for the reasons he's thinking. Then I find a binder containing handwritten recipes and give a big, 'Aha!'

'What's that?'

'I believe it's Ms Novak's recipe collection and a list of staples that she keeps stocked up.' I brandish said list with a triumphant smile. 'What would you do without me, hey?'

It's meant as a tease, instead it feels loaded with so much more and now my cheeks are definitely burning and I look away from him sharply, focus on the sheet. 'On second thoughts, *don't* answer that.'

'Does it help?'

'It looks like she was up to date on the shopping. There's plenty we can rustle up.'

'In that case, give it to me and I'll sort dinner.'

'Isn't that part of my job description?'

'It's your first night. You can start tomorrow.'

I should be pleased that he's going to cook for me. Instead it makes me uncomfortable. Uncomfortable because it's a thoughtful thing to do. A caring thing. And it's too easy to confuse such gestures for more.

Especially when I'm so unaccustomed to it.

The last three years I've been on my own. Paying my way through university in London by taking every job I can get and studying around them. Trying to prove to my brother that I'm serious, that I'm making a go of my life on my own terms. But it's not come easy. My so-called friends gradually upped and left just as Gabe had predicted and my life at uni is split between work and study. I haven't had the time to make new friends, people I can lean on, depend on and vice versa. I haven't been taken care of like this in… I don't know how long.

'Why don't you take your wine outside?'

'Huh?'

He's looking at me strangely and I wonder what it is he's seen in me, or thinks he's seen.

Or maybe he just wants rid of me? Just like my brother, who when I suggested coming home for the summer, getting a job locally, a chance to show him my studies and prove to him how hard I *can* work, offered me this opportunity instead.

I'd like to think it's because he's coming around to the new me. The one that's serious about life, my career and making a go of it. But I doubt it.

'The sun is setting.' Gabe tugs me back to the present, gestures to the impressive vista beyond the glass. 'You should go outside and enjoy it.'

'You sure you don't want help?'

'I've got it all in hand.'

Is his tone dismissive or have I put that there, my brother's dismissal of me overshadowing what is another thoughtful gesture on Gabe's part? I smile to hide my uncertainty and do exactly as he suggests: head outside with my wine in hand and breathe in what is the most breathtaking view I've ever had the pleasure to witness.

As picture perfect as a postcard, especially with the sun setting over the blue sea and the walled city of Dubrovnik. The undulating terracotta roofs, forts and ancient castle are a distant beauty, while up here the air is fragranced with flowers that are potted around the veranda, a splash of vibrant colour against the yellow stone. A large mosaic table fills the middle while steps lead off in either direction, down to a stunning manicured lawn that is carved into sections, a recreational area complete with pool and sun loungers positioned to make the most of the view.

It really is beautiful.

'The house may be unique but even that has nothing on this.'

I clutch a hand to my chest as my heart threatens to vacate it. 'You scared the life out of me.' I turn to face him. 'I thought you were cooking.'

'I am, or at least the oven is. Seems Ms Novak left some dishes prepared in the freezer.'

'See, I told you she'd have a plan.' I smile. 'I'm surprised you didn't try to pass them off as your own doing.'

'I am many things, but a liar isn't one of them, Avery. And I never take the credit for someone else's hard work.'

I shake my head at him, bite back a smile. 'Don't you ever get tired of being so serious all of the time?'

'Serious? I was just being honest.'

'And I was joking, Gabe. You know, having a laugh.' I shake my head and turn back to the horizon, bask in the warmth of the setting sun. Well, if he's in the mood for being serious and honest… 'Why did my brother ask this of you? And before you give me the same reasoning he did, save your breath. I know there's more to it.'

'Like what?'

'You tell me…'

I sense him tense. 'And what makes you think I know any different?'

I turn to face him head-on, search those eyes that can hide from me as readily as his words, but I trust him when he says he doesn't lie, and I know he won't lie to me now. 'Because you know him better than anyone.

'My brother hasn't intervened once in the last three years. I've worked jobs you wouldn't believe, hours that have seen me run into the ground and not once has he intervened. Until now.'

'Sounds like it's time he did something.'

'I don't need his charity. Or yours.'

'This isn't charity. You're earning your keep.'

I stare back at him. He's right. I'm here to work. Work and study. But in surroundings such as these when what I'm used to these past few years are poky student digs and food I can rustle up cheaply and easily, it's hard not to see it as such.

Not that he'll truly understand because he's not the one who's lived through it.

'I know. But considering his lack of any involvement these last three years, it's a marked change and something is driving it.'

'Maybe he feels bad and wants to make amends, show you some support?'

I scoff into my glass, take a sip.

'He knows how hard you've been working, Avery. Your mother does too.'

'Then why not welcome me home for the summer? Why ask you to give me this opportunity instead? No, it doesn't make sense.'

The more I think about it, the more it really doesn't. And as I sneak another look his way, I see the truth in his face too. 'What's going on, Gabe? What isn't my brother telling me?'

'You should take it up with him.'

I'm on high alert now. 'So, there is something else going on?'

'It's not my place, Avery. You need to talk to him.'

'Don't you think I've tried?'

'It isn't my place,' he repeats.

'But it's about me, my family...?'

He opens his mouth, closes it again and moves away. I watch him go, unwilling to break the silence, not when I sense I'm so close to learning the truth...

He reaches the terrace edge, places his glass on the stone balustrade and leans into it.

I come up behind him and he offers me the briefest of glances—sympathy and regret a storm in the glittering blue.

'I can't tell you Aiden's reasons without betraying his trust. I've done that once already where you're concerned, and I won't do it again.'

'You hardly betrayed his trust. What happened was between you and me, my brother had nothing to do with it.'

'Not how I see it. But trust me when I tell you he has your best interests at heart. He's looking out for you.'

I sip my wine. 'I don't need him looking out for me. The past three years should have proven that.'

'And the past three years do not rewrite history, Avery. It's going to take him a while to accept you've changed.'

'You were the one who once told me I had the power to change how he saw me.'

'And you do. You have.'

'It doesn't feel that way.'

'Give him time. He'll come around.'

'And you? Will you come around, Gabe? Or do you believe I'm the same troubled young woman running scared?'

I don't know why I ask it, but I wish I hadn't. Because now he's looking at me, really looking at me, and I can't breathe.

'I think you've come a long way, Avery.' The compassion in his gaze shifts with appreciation, admiration. 'But it's more important that you know it in yourself, that you're proud of yourself, just as you should be.'

'Thank you.' It's breathless, the power of my voice lost in the intensity of his gaze. Does he know I have him to thank for it in part? I might have done it on my own, my brother having forced my independence upon me, but it was Gabe's encouragement and rejection that saw me go after it all.

'Don't thank me.' The smallest of smiles touches his lips. 'This is all your doing.'

I blink up at him. 'You had a hand in it too.'

'I did?'

'I listened to you, Gabe. I meant it when I said you were right, and when you turned me away assuming the worst...' I swallow the pain of it '...you crushed me.'

'I'm s—'

'Don't apologise, Gabe. I needed that. I needed that wake-up call. My brother cutting me off, you rejecting me, it gave me the fire and determination I needed to sort myself out.'

'There are so many ways I could have given you that nudge...better ways.'

I press my lips together, a subtle fire in my blood. 'I don't know. I think it was the most effective.'

The most fun for a time too...

He stares back at me and I'd give anything to read his thoughts. Is he reliving that kiss like I am now? Is he wondering how it would feel three years on? My gaze falls to his lips, the memory clouded by the present and the line he's once again drawn.

A line that feels so very unfair when every urge wants me to step closer and I do, the smallest of steps. 'Gabe?'

He straightens, looks away. 'I should check on dinner.'

'But you've only just put it in.'

He's already moving off. 'I don't want to risk ruining Ms Novak's creation.'

Ruining Ms Novak's creation or ruining his friendship with my brother?

Most definitely the latter.

I watch him go, my thoughts and pulse still racing. But as the lustful haze clears, I'm left with one question above all else: what is my brother hiding from me? And how bad can it be for Gabe to keep it a secret too?

CHAPTER FIVE

Gabe

AN HOUR LATER, dinner is served but I have no guest. I find her on her bed, poring over her sketchbook, and for a moment I watch her. Earbuds in, she hums as she works, pencil scratching over paper, an intense look about her face. I almost don't want to disturb her but...

'Gabe?'

Too late. She plucks her earphones out of her ears.

'I'm sorry. I knocked but you didn't answer... Are you working?'

She sweeps up the pages, tucks them into a binder. 'I was.'

I eye the binder, wanting to see what's inside, but I sense she's not in the mood to share. I know from her brother that she's studying jewellery design. I likely know more than she thinks I do, but I also know my abrupt departure outside is hanging over us, as is the secret I won't share...

I drag my eyes back to hers. 'Dinner is ready if you'd like to come and join me.'

She swaps the binder for her empty wine glass and follows me downstairs.

'I thought we could eat outside,' I say, pulling open the door to the veranda and waiting for her to go on ahead but she freezes on the threshold, her gasp putting me on edge.

'What's wrong?'

'What—what is this?'

I frown at the arrangement. 'Dinner?'

'But, Gabe...' she looks from me to the table and back again '...you did all this for me?'

'I'm a man not a Neanderthal, Avery.' I walk ahead, pull out her chair. 'Quite capable of laying a table for dinner.'

She gives the tiniest sniff, moves forward once more, but her steps are slower, more cautious. 'I just wasn't expecting something quite so...romantic.'

Inside I cringe. Maybe the lanterns and the candles are a bit OTT, but then, they're always lit when I dine outside and tonight should be no different.

'Ms Novak is the kind who believes we eat with our eyes and that your surroundings have as much to do with your pleasure as the food itself.'

'You eat like this every night?'

'Not every night but when the weather and mood suits.'

She shakes her head, lowers herself into the seat. 'You really are full of surprises, Gabe.'

'How so this time?'

I move to take the seat opposite, feel her curious gaze on me the whole way. 'The cold, hard exterior you give off...it contradicts this entire place.'

'I don't know, the structure's pretty hard and cold.' I flick out my napkin, lay it across my lap, act indifferent but I'm not. For some unfathomable reason, her words sting. She's right. I am cold. Hard. Calculated. It doesn't pay to be soft in my line of work or life in general. Another of my father's life lessons. 'You ought to see this place in the winter.'

'Whatever you say, Gabe.' But her eyes dance as they shift from me to her plate, freeing me to breathe again. 'So, what do we have here?'

'One of my favourites: *pašticada*. It's a sweet and sour stewed beef. Ms Novak's family recipe.'

'It smells amazing.'

'And tastes even better.' I take up my cutlery and she follows my cue. We eat in silence, the mood oddly easy, the sounds of nature and the distant city providing a soothing soundtrack.

'I was wrong, Gabe.' Her sudden voice in the quiet makes me start, as does the soft, contemplative tone, the hint of tease. 'This place is perfect for you.'

She leans back in her seat, sips at her wine as I meet her sparkling gaze across the table. 'I'm not sure I want to ask this after you just told me, quite brutally I might add, why it's the opposite.'

She gestures around us with her glass. 'You're king of the world up here.'

'Back to the castle and the king references?'

'It's also very isolated.' Her eyes sharpen with her words. 'You can choose to never see another soul, save for your staff when they're here, of course.'

She's not wrong. It was part of the appeal. And I rarely bring anyone here. Dubrovnik is too personal, too steeped in my own history…a history I barely understand myself.

'It has a certain appeal.' I take up my wine, wash down the emotion she has successfully stirred up once more.

'Does it make you feel close to your mother too?'

The drink catches in my throat. 'You don't give up, do you?'

'You know me, always the tenacious one.'

I stare back at her. No one challenges me. No one dares probe. If I say I don't want to talk about something it doesn't get talked about, full stop. But Avery's not like everyone else and damn if I don't have the sudden compulsion to share.

Whether it's where we are, the past she's provoked to the surface, guilt that I'm keeping a secret in the name of her brother, a secret she has more right to than me...

'Something that affects you as deeply as your mother shouldn't be buried, Gabe. I have years of therapy under my belt, trust me when I say you're only giving it the power to hurt you more.'

Avery and her therapy. Something else I know a lot about thanks to her brother. I wonder if she knows how much he talks of her, how much he truly does care...

'And does it work?' I say. 'The therapy?'

'In what sense?'

'Does it hurt less?'

She shrugs, her eyes drifting to the sea, her expression turning distant. It doesn't *look* like it hurts any less and I feel her pain reach across the table, take my heart in its icy grip.

'I'm saying I've learnt ways to cope with it...' Her eyes come back to me—sad, reflective, open. She isn't shying away from me, or how she feels...how would it feel to do the same? To let it in? Be honest with oneself and let oneself be vulnerable.

Admiration swells, even as I acknowledge how different we both are.

'I've learnt to accept its presence and not lose myself in it.'

By it, I assume she means grief. The loss of her father.

'To steal the words of a great lady, grief is the price we pay for love, Avery.'

'And the risk of love is loss, and the price of loss is grief. I've heard it all.'

'But at least your father was a man worthy of that love. He was a good man, Avery. If only we could all be so lucky as to have had a father like yours.'

Her eyes glisten gold in the lanternlight. 'I know and I

wouldn't change him for the world. I know how lucky I am…
just as I know how lucky you're not.'

She says it softly. It isn't a dig or a tease or anything but
the truth.

'I came to terms with who my father is a long time ago.'

'But your mother?'

'My mother walked out when I was eight and didn't look
back. She's hardly someone I want to think on now.'

'You state that like it's fact.'

'I was there, I know what she did.'

'And as you admit, you were eight, you were a child, how
can you know what truly happened?'

'I watched her leave, Avery. She hugged me, told me she
loved me and I never saw her again. She died. Five years ago.
A motorcycle accident not far from here. She moved back
home when she left my father, my grandparents took her in
when she refused my father's money, and she cut us out like
we didn't exist.'

'And yet you choose to have a home here now?'

'I've owned this place for a long time.' I take in the architectural delight, the imposing stone that is somehow softened
by its age and buttery hue, and is now as close to my home
as any that I own across the globe 'Granted, it didn't look
quite so habitable when I first took it on.'

She sips at her wine, her eyes still on me, her brain working overtime. 'You really are a dark horse, Gabe.'

'Because I've owned a place in Croatia all these years?'

'No, because you bought a place to feel close to your
mother, to your heritage. The sentiment is—'

'There is no sentiment.' My stomach twists as I'm quick
to correct her. 'I bought it to rub their faces in it. To make
my mother realise what she walked away from. I bought it to

show that I survived without her and her family. More than survived, I succeeded.'

'Do you truly believe that?'

'Are you questioning my motives?'

'I think you have more heart than you give yourself credit for. Did you ever seek her out? Speak to her? Get her side of the story.'

I swallow the sudden tightness in my chest, the hollow ache I don't want to acknowledge. 'I thought that one day, maybe...but then, the accident happened and the opportunity was taken away.'

'The opportunity...?' she repeats quietly, and I ignore the condemnation in her tone. 'But her family are still here? You could—'

'*They* could have come to me. Word spreads here, the people are everything, they know where I am and they've made no attempt to reach out. Not them and not my mother when she was alive. That tells me enough.'

'It doesn't give you closure though.'

'I don't need closure.'

'Don't you?' Her eyes pin me to my chair, cloudy with doubt. 'Until you take matters into your own hands and reach out to them, you can never truly know how they feel or trust the eyes of an eight-year-old boy and a father with a view of his own.'

'My father may not be a kind man, a loving man, but he isn't a liar, Avery.'

'I'm not saying he is, but she left him, Gabe, and for a man as powerful and as proud as yours, it had to have cut deep. You can't trust everything he told you...or didn't tell you.'

There's nothing I can say to that because she's right. And having it stated so plainly, so reasonably, and hit that age-old nerve, that ancient niggle of doubt... As a child, I hadn't wanted to believe it. My bond with my mother had felt unbreakable. The idea that she would walk away, unthinkable. But she had. That was an undeniable fact.

She'd left and I'd heard nothing. I moved here and still, heard nothing.

Forcing me to accept that both my mother and her family cut me out when they cut my father out. But what if there *was* more to it? What if it wasn't as black and white as I'd been led to believe?

'It doesn't hurt to reach out to them, Gabe. What have you got to lose? You knock on their door and they close it in your face. You're no worse off than you are now. But if they open it and open their arms to you, you gain. If not love and family, you gain their side of the story and your mother's version of events. You gain her truth. And that must be worth the risk, surely?'

Avery

What am I doing?

I should be uncovering my own family's secrets, not pushing him to discover his. But in this moment, I can't imagine caring about anything or anyone else more.

Gabe wanted for nothing financially growing up, but a life without love, without his mother… I'm sure there's more to that tale and, though I know it's too late for them now, it's not too late for his grandparents and any cousins, aunts, uncles… His family could be huge for all he knows. In fact, he likely does know. He likely has a report on them all, but he's written them out just as his dad would wish.

I can count on one hand the number of times I've met his father and once was enough. I've never met anyone who, with a simple look, can leave you quite so chilled to the bone.

'Can I get you any dessert?'

He gestures to my empty plate and I smile. 'No. I'm fine, thank you.'

Because compared to Gabe I am fine. I've had years to get to grips with my anger at the world, my loss, my depression. I've pushed myself to my limits with the hours I keep, trying to earn enough to make ends meet while pursuing the career I want. And it's exhausting, but it's also fulfilling. And it means something…to me at least.

One day, I hope it'll mean something to my family too.

Can he honestly say the same?

'That really was delicious.'

'Well, hopefully you'll get to meet Ms Novak in person and tell her yourself.'

I smile. I like hearing him talk of Ms Novak. There's an affection in his voice that I don't often see in him.

'More wine? A *rakija*?'

'A what now?'

His smile still bears the strain of our conversation, and it claws at my insides, nags at my heart.

'I'll be right back.' He heads inside, leaves me to the sounds of the city and the wildlife and then he's back, two small shot glasses in hand. 'It's another of Ms Novak's specialities.'

I get to my feet, take the one he offers out to me and I'm not so careful this time. Our fingers brush, my breath catches, our eyes connect and I swear he feels it too.

'And what exactly is it?' I say, focusing on the drink and not the thousand butterflies taking flight within me.

'*Rakija*. It's a traditional drink of the Balkans and, here in Croatia, many households like Ms Novak's distil their own.'

I eye the amber liquid. 'But *what* is it?'

'It's essentially a fruit brandy...' I go to take a swig and he raises his hand. 'It's strong so go steady.'

I give it a cautious sniff. Wowzer, he's not joking. 'Are you trying to lead me astray, Gabe?'

Oh, man, why did I have to say that? Not in this moment when I'm all about the conversation that I feel isn't yet done.

You're not all *about it, clearly.*

I dare to reach his eye, take in the strange look there as he says, 'I'd like to say I'm trying to lead you back.'

'I thought you believed in me and the changes I've made.'

'I do... I also think you still have a bit of the wild in you.'

That burr is back in his voice, the low rumble that works its way through me, excites and ignites, and I realise just how close we are, just how close his lips are and his scent—he smells of the sea and sex. Not that I can truly know, but he makes me think of it. He makes me think of being naked and wrapped up in his sheets, mouths and bodies entwined.

'*Živjeli,*' he says, tugging me from my thoughts, my desire to ask him why, what makes him think that about me, but it's as risky as my thoughts.

'*Živjeli?*' I hesitate over the word that I don't recognise.

'It means cheers,' he explains. 'Life is beautiful; let's live.'

I want to laugh, as strange as it is hearing those words come out of his mouth. 'Life is beautiful, let's live...'

'It's what Croatians mean when they say it.'

I nod, still unconvinced by the tiny shot of amber liquid. I can be a lightweight at times, something I'm sure Gabe doesn't know or suspect. Not with the party-girl reputation I once possessed...and still do, depending on who you talk to.

'You know, for a guy who claims not to be sentimental, you know an awful lot about the customs here.'

He doesn't comment, doesn't smile, just raises his glass and drinks, his gaze holding mine as I do the same and I swear the connection arches between us stronger than ever. But then I made the mistake of believing in its two-sided existence before and look where that got me. Humiliated and rejected and never again.

But you're not the same person you once were.

I'm still his best friend's sister though. Off limits and out of reach…in his eyes at least. And, oh, my, that drink *is* strong. I splutter as it catches the back of my throat.

'Are you okay?' He touches a hand to my back and my entire body pulses, my eyes striking with his. 'Sorry.' He snaps his hand back to his side. 'I did tell you to go steady.'

He did, and I was too distracted by him, by this…this persistent want. Is it my innocence that makes me so susceptible to him? The memory of how he made me feel, the very real need to feel that way again. Passion, arousal, a heated pleasure that wraps around me, coils right through me…after years of feeling numb, lost, so empty, he'd filled me with it all.

Until that moment of rejection and humiliation. Both deserved, lamented and never to be forgotten. But what had come before, what I can feel building here now… I want more of that. And I've had three years to feel it again, to meet someone capable of triggering it and not even a spark. Until now, until him. Again.

And how do I change that? How do I break free of it?

I press my fingertips to my lips that seem to thrum, my pulse still racing, my body too warm with the proximity of his. I need to move. Occupy myself with something. Anything.

'I'll help you clean this away.' I back up, sloshing my drink as I place the glass down far too quickly and he steps forward.

'I can take care of it, Avery.' Why does he have to step closer? Can't he tell I'm trying to create some distance, some space…trying to abide by his wishes? 'You must be tired after your journey.'

He's right, I am tired. Maybe I can blame my extreme response on that.

'Avery?'

'Yes,' I say, still piling up the plates, my focus very much off him.

'I said I can do it.'

'Contrary to popular belief, I like to make myself useful.' It comes out filled with frustration. Frustration that I still want him and cannot have him. Frustration that, although I have freed myself of the negative press, my brother and my mother are still prone to think the worst. So much so they're keeping something from me and making him do the same.

He touches his hand to my arm, forcing me to pause and though I want to snatch it back, break the tantalising contact, I don't want to appear like a resentful child.

'What?'

'If I said something to upset you, I'm sorry.'

I swallow impulsively. Tears clamber up my throat. 'I'm fine.'

'You're not.'

'Then tell me whatever it is my brother is keeping from me!' I go on the attack, because attack is far safer than what I really want to do right now. Safer for him. Safer for me. Safer for whatever this tentative footing is that we are on.

'I can't.'

'Why?'

'You know why.'

'Because my brother asked it of you.'

'Yes. After everything we've discussed tonight, you of all people should understand how important your brother is to me, why I'm so loyal to him. To all intents and purposes, he's all I have.'

You have me too, I want to scream.

But I know that exposes me and confirms my deepest fear. That Gabe is the only man for me. Always has been, always will be.

And though I have my career now, there's a part of me that I'm desperate to ignore. A part of me that wants the impossible. Love. A husband. A family to call my own.

Because if my mother and my brother can't love me for who I am, how can I ever hope that someone else will?

'Oh, to be my brother and to know how that feels, Gabe.'

He frowns, his fingers on my arm pulse. 'Avery...'

'You're right, I'm tired.' I free myself of his touch, I only wish I could free myself of the way he makes me feel as easily. 'I'll see you in the morning. Thank you for tonight.'

And with that I walk away, teeth gritted against the tears and head held high because I won't let him see me crack. I'm done with this frustrating unrequited lust that is just that— lust. Because I can't love Gabe. I. Just. Can't.

CHAPTER SIX

Gabe

I WAKE WITH a start. A siren piercing my eardrums.

The fire alarm—*what on earth?*

I throw back the covers and run from the room, then the scent hits me. The unmistakable smell of burnt toast...

Avery!

I check my watch as I head for the kitchen. Three in the morning.

What in the blazes?

I find her brandishing a flapping tea towel at the sensor just inside the door, body outstretched, a crop top that barely conceals her breasts, and shorts that can only just be considered a millimetre off underwear, and curse.

'Avery!'

She starts, freezing mid-flap, the tea towel flopping onto her face as she gives a muffled, 'Gabe.'

I tug the towel from her grasp, resume the vigorous flapping as I scowl down at her, anything to keep my body from reacting to the sensual sight she makes. 'What are you doing?'

She blushes deep, her eyes like a startled rabbit. 'Making a snack.'

'It's three in morning, Avery.'

The noise finally quits and I toss the towel on the side, rake a hand through my hair as my heart starts to beat to a more normal rhythm. 'Are you trying to give me a heart attack?'

'I'm sorry, it was an accident. I lost track of time.'

And that's when I see it. The telltale powder on her face. I'm across the room in seconds, the dregs of sleep lifting as I grip her wrist and tug her to me. Up close I can see her eyes are dilated, covered in a glassy sheen. I curse.

'How could you?'

'How could I what?' She blinks up at me, gives the tiniest shake of her head. 'I just wanted something—'

'Let me be very clear, Avery. I won't have drugs in my home.'

'Drugs?' Her brows knit together. 'What are you—?'

She tries to tug her wrist from my grip, but I hold her firm, swipe my thumb across her upper lip, her cheek, clearing away the remnants that make me so mad the sensation's burning a hole through my middle. How could she be so stupid, so foolish, and under my roof, my watch, my protection? She was supposed to have changed, be different, better!

'Let me go, Gabe.' She struggles against my hold. 'I don't know what you're talking about but—'

'You've got it on your face,' I say through gritted teeth, not wanting to believe but seeing it all the same.

'Got what?'

'I don't know, you tell me! What is it that floats your boat these days?'

'Gabe, what are you...?' Her eyes widen, her brows arch. 'It's flour, Gabe! *Flour!*'

'What?' My grip slackens and she takes advantage, tugging herself free.

'Flour!' She strides across the kitchen and grabs up a white bag, thrusts it in my direction. 'You know, this *stuff* you bake with.'

'But…' I drag a hand down my face, relief weakening my posture. Flour. She's baking. She's not… 'But it's the middle of the night.'

'Is that your excuse for thinking the worst of me?'

'I'm sorry.' I take a breath. 'I just didn't expect…what are you doing baking?'

She thrusts the flour back on the side and pulls out the cremated toast, lobbing it in the bin beneath the sink. 'I was hungry, okay, and I couldn't sleep, and I had all these voices going around and around in my head and I was getting angsty and I was craving Mum's muffins. You had the ingredients, so I thought, why not?'

'The voices?'

'Noise, just noise. And when I get like that, I need to distract myself. Focus on something else.'

'And the toast?'

'I put it on while I was waiting for them to bake and lost track of time. I didn't expect the toaster to set fire to it.'

That's when I see the strip of pills on the side. I step forward, finger them as I try to read the name. 'And these?'

'Huh?' She turns to see what I'm pointing at and snatches them from my reach. 'Antidepressants.' Her cheeks heat as mine drain further. 'Legally obtained on prescription, before you ask.'

'I—' I feel like a cad. A cruel, thoughtless cad. She hadn't just been talking of her grief that evening, she'd been talking of her mental health. Her ongoing mental health. I should have realised. Why hadn't Aiden said something? He was free and easy in telling me everything else. Or maybe he only knows about the therapy and not the meds? Her depression. 'How long have you been on them for?'

She slips them into the band of her shorts. 'Not that it's any of your business, but a few years. And no, I'm not replacing recreational drugs with a legal high if that's what you're thinking.' Her green eyes shoot fire at me, daring me to say as much.

'That's not what I was thinking.' I rub my face with both hands now, wishing myself to wake up, to think clearly because what I'm actually thinking she doesn't need to know either.

Not that she believes my denial.

'I'm not, Avery. Far from it.'

She chews the corner of her mouth, her hesitation killing me. 'Well, I'm coming off them but it's a gradual thing. I'll get there. I will. It just takes time.'

'I'm not judging you, Avery.'

'But you were.' She turns away. 'And my brother would too, so please don't tell him.'

'I won't. Of course, I won't. But you…you shouldn't be ashamed of it.'

'I'm not ashamed,' she throws back at me and I know she means it. 'I just don't want to have that showdown on top of everything else. It's bad enough he can't support my studies…if he knew about this…'

She starts putting things away and the heavy weight of guilt swells in my gut. The fact that I thought the worst, suspected her of taking drugs in my home when in reality she was doing something so normal, something designed to soothe and calm. I can feel the disappointment in her, see it in the slump to her form, the quietness in her voice, the way her eyes evade me.

'I'm sorry.' Her head lifts a fraction but she doesn't turn. She sniffs though. So quiet I only just hear it. 'Avery?'

'What?'

I walk up behind her, pause a step away. 'I really am sorry.'

She shrugs. 'Don't beat yourself up about it. You wouldn't be the first to suspect the worst and you won't be the last.'

'You mean your brother?'

'My brother, my mother, take your pick.' She forces me to back up as she reaches for a cloth at the sink, sweeps up the crumbs from the toast.

'I shouldn't have jumped to conclusions.'

Another shrug. 'People do all the time.'

'But I shouldn't have and I'm sorry.'

'So you say.'

She tries to walk past me but I reach out, gently touch her arm. 'Look at me, please.'

Slowly she does as I ask, and the pain in her gaze, the tears she hasn't let fall steal my breath. 'I'm sorry. I panicked. I was still half asleep and when I saw you… I don't know, I'm not the best when devoid of sleep but that's no excuse. I shouldn't have said what I did. I shouldn't have thought it.'

She takes a breath, long and slow and barely steady. 'Just to be clear, Gabe, I haven't touched recreational drugs in almost four years. I'm clean and I have no interest in going back to those days. It's just a shame you and my family can't see that.'

A timer sounds and she blinks up at me, something unreadable in her face, and then she breaks away, heads to the oven at the other end of the kitchen. Through the acrid scent of burnt toast, I smell something pleasant, something appetising now. Her mother's muffins.

If only I'd caught that scent earlier, maybe I wouldn't have jumped to conclusions, been so quick to accuse, so unintentionally brutal.

'I'm sorry I woke you.' She pulls the tray out of the oven, slips it onto the awaiting heat mat. 'You should go back to bed.'

'When there are fresh baked goods to enjoy?' I try for a

smile. There's no way I can leave her like this. Walk away from the pain I've created. 'I don't have that kind of will-power.'

She looks at me, her eyes and smile hesitant. 'You want one?'

'I do...that's if you can forgive the idiot in me enough to share?'

Her lips quirk, a subtle light behind her eyes, taking out the dark, the sad, the disappointed. 'My waistline will thank you.'

'Your waistline has nothing to worry about.'

She gives a soft huff. 'You can ease off with the flattery, I've forgiven you already.'

I close the distance between us. 'I truly am sorry.'

'You've said that already.'

She looks up at me, her eyes awash with tears again and I reach up, cup her cheek, refusing to shy away from the pain I caused and wanting desperately to take it away. Even if it means exposing some of myself.

'I care about you, Avery. I know it's no excuse but I wasn't thinking clearly. The past and the present collided and I acted on impulse. I wasn't thinking with my head, and it was wrong.'

'It was,' she agrees, no dismissal now, no letting me off and I'm grateful for it.

'How can I make it up to you?'

Her eyes flit to my lips, her cheeks warm. So many answers burn in her gaze and sear my brain, so many ways in which we could bury this right here, right now. Lose sight of everything but this incessant chemistry...

'You can get two glasses and the milk from the fridge,' she murmurs.

'Milk, you say?' My voice is as gruff as I feel. Not what I was expecting her to say but safer, definitely safer than what I had in mind, and I curse my overactive imagination that refuses to stay in check where she's concerned. 'Easiest penance I've ever done.'

'Oh, the milk is just the beginning...'

And there it is, the fire, the spark, the Avery I know and—

'I'm not sure I like the sound of that.'

Liar.

Avery

'Tough.' I smile to hide the hurt. The way my bruised heart feels ever more broken.

You see, I'm used to my brother doing it, my mother even, but Gabe...

It only confirms what I've known all along. I'll never out-run my past. It'll always rear its ugly head and tear me down when I least expect it. Just as it had three years ago when he rejected me, dismissing our kiss as some twisted attempt at revenge on my brother. And I know we've had it out already, dealt with it, attempted to move on but he hasn't. Clearly.

Living with my brother's constant suspicion and doubt is bad enough, living under Gabe's roof and having him feel the same...

But his words come back to me: *'I wasn't thinking with my head...'*

And what does that mean? That he was thinking with his heart and, if so, just how much of it was for me? Not the loyalty and the bond he shares with my brother, but me.

I watch as he takes two glasses out of the cupboard above the sink, his naked chest flexing as he stretches up, and my body warms over the sight... It doesn't care that he's hurt me, crushed me with his suspicion. It only cares about the chemical reaction and the hormones he stirs up...and now

I'm wondering if there's any part of him that isn't tanned. Perhaps there's a striking band of white beneath those snug-fitting black briefs…the visual far more entertaining than dwelling on the rest.

Far more entertaining but no less frustrating…

I occupy myself extracting the muffins from the tin and placing them on the cool rack as he fills two glasses with milk and brings them to the centre island. He slides onto the stool and eyes the fresh-baked goods. 'May I?'

'Sure. They're hot, mind.'

'I can take it hot.'

'I bet you can.' It's out before I can stop it, my party spirit still in there somewhere, and I'm relieved when he laughs. Loud and easy. The sound provoking the warmth that's never far from spreading in my lower belly when he's around.

'I'm not going to ask what that's supposed to mean.'

'I wouldn't waste my breath on giving an answer.'

I give him a jaunty smile, fight the chaos inside as his blue eyes, dark and glittering, spark back at me. I should have turned the overhead lights on. The subtle accent lighting that runs along the wall creates a far too cosy atmosphere. But when my original goal had been to encourage my body into sleep mode, it had been sensible. Now it's plain provocative.

I grab a muffin for myself, throw my focus into its yumminess and not his.

'These are delicious,' he says around a mouthful, his pleasure undeniable, and it coaxes out a laugh that I don't need to feign. Lightening the mood as readily as I wish I could.

'So says your lack of manners.'

He grimaces as he swallows. 'Sorry, I forgot myself. Ms Novak can cook, but these are something else.'

I shake my head, laugh some more as I dare to slip onto the bar stool beside him and peel away the paper from my own. 'I forgive you. These things are good enough to get the best of most of us.'

'The epitome of naughty but nice.'

I smile in the face of his genuine appreciation and don't shy away from holding his eye as I lick my lips and take a bite. A deliberately slow, flirtatiously big bite—if I'm to suffer, he can too. I clean away the remnants from my lips with the pad of my thumb, suck it clean and all the while he tracks the move, his eyes darkening, his pecs flexing... Am I getting to him?

'It's funny you say that...' I cross my legs and tuck them under me, anything to ease the dull ache that's pulsating out, spreading the warmth, the heat, the coiling tension. 'Naughty but nice is me all over.'

'Avery...' His voice is a low warning.

'Oh, hush, Gabe, I'm not about to jump you. Though...' I'm treading a dangerous line, maybe it's the lateness of the hour, the low lighting, the earlier misery I want to forget but '...you could jump me if you wanted.'

'Avery, seriously...' He chokes on a stray crumb, or my words, probably both as his eyes blaze back at me. There's barely a foot between us, barely any clothing on us too— if ever there was a moment to take advantage of, it's now. 'We've been—'

He's interrupted by his phone making itself known, the device vibrating on the centre island where he must have tossed it on his arrival, and he reaches for it. A brief look at the screen and his scowl deepens. 'I need to take this.'

I nod, expecting him to leave. He doesn't, he walks up to the glass doors that lead outside, his eyes on the distant city. 'Father?'

Well, that explains the scowl... I double-check the time: a little after three. Is this normal for him? Taking calls at such an hour. Regardless of where in the world his father currently is, the man must know where his son is, what time zone he is in…

'Look, I'm sure—no, no…why would…? Right. No, that's fine. I'll take care of it.'

From where I'm sitting, he's not getting a word in edge-ways and it makes me think of my relationship with my brother, the number of times Aiden would interrupt me. Not listen. To see Gabe treated like that though… Gabe, a well-regarded tech tycoon in his own right, bowing down, taking instruction.

It continues on until eventually he cuts the call, but he doesn't move from the glass. I wonder what's stalled him—me or his father?

'Is he always like that?'

His head shoots up, his eyes pin me. 'Like what?'

'Short, abrupt, not letting you speak?'

His mouth lifts to one side. 'You got all that from one side of the conversation?'

'I did. It felt all too familiar.'

'Your brother?'

I nod.

'So, is he?'

'My father has one focus in life, to make money.'

'One can never have enough…'

'In his world, no. So, in answer to your question, yes. Yes, he's always like that.'

'Does he always keep unsocial hours too?'

'It's not so late where he is.'

'I assume he knows it's the middle of the night for you.'

'Money never sleeps.'

I stare at his rigid back, take in the stress that radiates like an aura around him. Maybe his father doesn't know where he is. With the history of the place, his mother… 'Does he know you're here, in Croatia?'

'We never speak of it, but he knows. My father makes it his business to know everything.'

'Don't you ever get tired of living under that kind of microscope?'

He shrugs. 'I've learned how to do it in such a way as not to provoke him.'

I give a tight laugh. 'Twenty-three years and I still haven't perfected that skill.'

He gives me a twisted smile. 'I guess it is quite similar.'

'Don't you ever just want to tell him where to go?'

'Because that's served you so well?'

I shrug. 'At least I've tried.'

He goes quiet, his eyes back on the glass and I wonder if he's pondering it. Whether he truly does draw a parallel between our lives and the men that try to control them. I've never seen Gabe in that light before, but I do now. Having witnessed it first-hand. Having heard the tale his father spun with regards to his mother too. The more I think about it, the more I think there's more to that story.

'Ever think about branching off on your own?'

He doesn't turn, doesn't answer but I wait and eventually he nods. 'Sometimes.'

And even just that tiny acknowledgement gives me hope, hope that one day he'll do just that. Branch off financially and visit his mother's family too.

'Well, I highly recommend it.'

His laugh is gruff. 'Noted.'

'Don't get me wrong, I'm not about to say I'm the perfect role model, but cutting those puppet strings has been the best thing to ever happen to me. We can all make money, granted not quite as much perhaps, but to be free of its trappings and the hopes and dreams of others, it really is quite liberating.'

He smiles back at me, a hint of admiration in his depths, but there's the sadness too, and I push myself to standing, determined to shake off his father's shackles for tonight at least. 'Right, you need to relax before you go back to bed and I have the perfect suggestion.'

'You do?'

'Strip poker, works every time.'

He chokes out a laugh, the lightness in his demeanour worth every racing thought I'm now entertaining thanks to my impulsive, save-the-mood suggestion.

'I don't think that's a good idea.'

'No.' I pout and give a playful sigh. 'Such a pity.'

He surprises me by coming back to the table though, surprises me all the more when he sits back down and eyes the muffins. 'May I?'

'Another?'

'Please.'

'I never took you for a comfort eater.'

'There are probably a lot of things you don't know about me.'

'True. But I'm learning.'

He takes up a muffin. 'And what have you learnt so far?'

'I think most of what I've learnt can be summed up in one.'

He cocks a brow, takes a hearty bite.

'You, my dear Gabe, present an alpha front but beneath all that muscle and hard-set mouth, chiselled jaw and steely gaze, which I will admit is a very fine package indeed, you are as beta as they come.'

He struggles to swallow, his eyes watering. 'I'm *what*?'

I slip off my stool and close the distance between us, rest a hand on his shoulder and savour the way his muscles twitch, the way the heat from his bare skin warms my palm.

'You're beta, Gabe,' I lean into his ear to say, 'and very sexy with it.'

I'm already walking to the door now, desperate to leave him hanging...

It was too racy, too flirtatious, too daring...but it felt oh so good.

CHAPTER SEVEN

Gabe

DO YOU EVER pause and wonder how you got to a certain point?

Take a breath and stare at the life in your hands and wonder what on earth happened?

That's me. Right now.

Standing in my laundry room, a place I've never really ventured, clutching a pair of red panties in one hand and what was once a crisp white shirt that's now a garish shade of pink.

I know *how* it happened, or rather *who* happened to it, I just can't fathom how I ended up like this. My orderly life in ruins. My body permanently wired and my every sense attuned. To Avery. And I'm exhausted.

Throwing myself into my work to try and distract myself from her presence. From the guilt too, because I know she's missed my company. That each time she's ventured into the city to see the sights, she's wanted me to accompany her, and I've always had an excuse at the ready.

Fearing the easy connection, the risk that I'll cross the line like I very nearly did that first night. Pouring my heart out to her, all the stuff about my family, my mother, the desire to reach down and taste those lips that had offered up such wisdom, such truth and flirtatious fun too.

And then where would we be?

Back where we were three years ago, making a huge mistake and breaking the trust of my closest friend while at it. All for a fling. A fleeting bit of fun in exchange for the only solid relationship in my life? I don't think so.

Because that's all it could ever be. I know I have a warped view of love and marriage. But knowing it's warped doesn't make it wrong or any less real. I've met plenty of women over the years to reinforce my belief that love isn't for me.

But there's something about Avery. The way she gets beneath my skin, the way she's pursuing her dream and works hard at it too. With her visits to the city tapering off, she now spends her time split between chores and her studies. I rarely see her relax. When I'm working, she's working, and if I'm tired, she must be too.

She chooses that moment to appear in the doorway—denim shorts, a simple vest, her hair a messy knot atop her head and her mouth in a provocative 'O'.

'Oh, hey, everything okay?' Then she spies the shirt, her gaze flitting to the panties in my other hand and widening with a gasp. 'Oh, I didn't!'

'Oh, you did.'

She snatches the offending number from my grasp, clutches them to her chest. 'I'm so sorry!'

She's mortified and I'm weak. Weak in the face of her shame, weak with this longing I can't throw off. 'It's okay,' I say. 'Accidents happen.'

She shakes her head. 'They seem to be happening far too often of late.'

She's not wrong. The past fortnight has seen a sofa ruined by bleach, a curtain pole tugged out of the wall by an overzealous vacuum cleaner, a precious vase broken and a case of wine hitting the deck. All because she was doing her job… and I happened to walk in.

But is it any surprise when she's burning the candle at both ends?

'I'll have to start charging your brother danger money on top of paying your salary.'

It's a joke, my keenness to lighten the mood backfiring as the colour leaves her cheeks and I'm quick to add, 'I'm only teasing.'

'It's not funny.'

'It's okay, Avery. Honest. Perhaps you ought to take a break for a bit. When was the last time you had a holiday? Some real time off?'

'Just the other day when I took the bus to Trsteno Arboretum and did the whole *Game of Thrones* thing.' She frowns at me. 'I told you this.'

'No, I mean a real holiday, several days of nothing but relaxation, not a few hours snatched here and there.'

She doesn't answer and I have the distinct impression she can't remember. Something else we have in common.

'I'm here to work, Gabe. You're paying me, remember?'

'And as your employer, I can insist you take a few days off.'

I sense the cogs turning behind her eyes, her continued refusal and then an idea comes to me, an idea I know she won't be able to resist.

'We'll both take a holiday.'

She frowns up at me. '*You're* going to take a holiday?'

I nod. 'And you're going to join me.'

'Where?'

'You'll see…'

Avery

My cheeks are still burning an hour later. Just the thought of Gabe holding my knickers in his hand…my skimpiest, sexiest... I'd love to say I did it on purpose to provoke him, only the idea of ruining his clothing is so abhorrent and wasteful.

And what makes it worse is that it isn't the first time I've messed up and he knows it. What he doesn't know is that it's all down to him. I hadn't been able to sleep the night I set the fire alarm off because my body had been too alive with thoughts of him. Being around him again bringing forth a rush of heat no one could sleep through.

I sucked the curtains up the vacuum cleaner because I was more busy paying attention to him walking by than I was the location of said curtain hem. I knocked the box of wine over because I backed into it when he startled me coming out of the gym, all sweaty and chiselled and... I swallow. The vase had been the same. The only thing I can truly blame myself for is the bleach and even then, I had been trying to get a wine stain out of it. Wine I had spilled because I'd been thinking of...yes, him!

And now we're going away together. I flop face down on the bed with a groan, savour the cool sheets against my burning skin.

What is wrong with me?

I twist my head to the side, blow the hair out of my face with a frustrated huff and stare at the closed door like I can see him on the other side, striding through the house, putting things in motion for whatever this little trip entails.

I flip onto my back, stare at the ceiling and still my body feels alive. A buzzing hive of activity that no amount of singing, breathing, rolling around is going to cure...well, there's one kind of rolling around I *know* will work but he isn't about to offer that up.

Because whatever this trip means, it doesn't mean that.

I scramble across the bed and tug my binder out, empty its contents onto the bed. Time to plough this energy into something productive, at least until I know what we're doing and can pack for it.

I stick my earbuds in, blast out my playlist of favourites and pick up my pencil. Tongue in teeth, I sketch and lose myself to the page. My latest design.

A necklace that I can envisage on my mother. A stacked trio of pear-shaped emeralds, brilliant cut and graduating in size, accented by diamonds set in a tapered design to either side and crafted in solid platinum. My signature is in the dragonfly that falls from the lowest teardrop…a touch of nature and something I include in all my designs.

It's important to me and the message I want to convey—that nature has to be at the heart of what we do, that the planet has to take priority. And those that have the most have the responsibility to give the most. All my pieces are recycled in some shape or form, and unique to my brand. One day I hope my brother will get it and support me in this venture but, right now, he's still too bitter that I've carved out my own path. Or at least that's how it feels.

I'm so engrossed in what I'm doing I finally start to calm, so much so that I'm humming along in my own world when a shadow suddenly blocks the light over my page.

My eyes snap up. 'Gabe!'

I tug my earbuds out and gather up my sketches, a sense of déjà vu kicking in.

'Sorry, I didn't mean to startle you, I knocked…'

'You said that last time.'

'You really don't hear much when you're working, do you?' He looks at the binder I'm clamping closed, and I feel my cheeks start to warm…for an entirely different reason now.

'I like to get in the zone.'

'Can I see?' He gestures to my work.

I hesitate. He's been supportive of me pursuing my own

career thus far, but to show him what that career is, to show him my designs and open myself up to his critical eye…his potential condemnation too. It's one thing to take it from my brother, but from Gabe…

'Please?'

I nip my lip and he holds out his hand but my grip is iron clad. I know he's not my brother but still…

'Fine.' I thrust the binder at him and look away as he opens it up. He's quiet. Quiet for far too long. I can hear him rustling through the pages and eventually I crack. 'Can I have them back now?'

'These are amazing. You did these? All of them?'

I peek at the top page, up at him, feel my cheeks burn with his praise. 'You don't need to be all gushy.'

'I'm not, I'm speaking the truth.'

I eye him, the contrast between my brother and him so very marked. 'If only Aiden agreed with you.'

'Have you shown him?'

'What? My work?' I look at him like he's crazy. 'He won't even entertain a discussion on it, let alone take an interest.' I clamber off the bed, toss the binder on the dressing table. 'You know, I think he'd rather I continued burning through the family coffers than study something so airy-fairy and fanciful.'

'His words?'

'A polite variation of.'

'He'll come round.'

'So you keep saying.'

'Look, Avery, I know nothing about jewellery design, but I know art and you have a talent that should be lauded, not hidden away.'

My cheeks continue to heat and my heart swells. I wish he wouldn't speak to me like this. Tease me like this. Make me feel special when I know I'm nothing to him, nothing other than his best friend's sister at any rate. I fold my arms, shield myself as I turn back to him.

'Yeah, well, my brother isn't one to agree.'

'Then make him agree, make him see you for the strong, independent woman you are. Talented and going places.'

I smile, I can't help it. 'The only place he wants me is back in the company fold and until then, I'm invisible to him.'

'That's not true.

'It isn't, Avery,' he says when I say nothing. 'Have you thought that maybe, just maybe, your brother is struggling with his own life? That he envies you in a way for being able to break off as you have done, to make something of yourself, something of your own, something he never had the opportunity to do?'

I frown. 'What are you talking about?'

'Your brother was twenty-six when you lost your father, his idol. He became CEO and head of the family overnight but long before then he was earmarked for that position. The subjects he studied, his summer jobs, the social functions he attended, all grooming for the day he would take over. His entire life revolved around it. There was no choice, no opportunity for something else.'

'But it's what he wanted…'

'Was it?'

I think back, think on all those years of witnessing my brother at my father's side, envying him almost for having that attention over me but now…to see it in a different light, to twist it…

'Are you saying…?'

'I'm saying maybe you should ask him.'

'Has he said something to you?'

'We're men, we don't often talk about the things that

bother us, not when it runs as deep as that. You know more about my life, my history in a fortnight from my lips than I've ever told your brother, but I imagine he knows most of it because he's lived through it with me.'

'But I…' My words trail off, my thoughts too.

'I'm just saying there are two sides to every story and maybe you should hear his.'

'Does this have something to do with the reason he asked you to have me for the summer?'

'What?' he starts.

'The reason he asked you to give me this job. Is he about to quit, too?'

'No. No, of course not.' He suddenly looks gaunt, panicked even. 'That has nothing to do with it.'

'But something does, something you still won't tell me?'

'I can't.'

'Right, it's not your place.' And now I'm angry. Angry that my brother couldn't be honest with me. Angry that Gabe managed to see what I couldn't. It makes so much sense now. The shackles, the pressure, the need to keep me on the Monroe path. Dad's dream.

'I wish I could.'

'Of course, you do.'

'I promise you, I do.' He reaches out and I sidestep him. I can't have him touching me, can't have him looking at me with all that compassion and sincerity in his gaze. And on the back of all his encouragement, his admiration for my work…it only makes me want him more, care for him more. And I can't care for Gabe. I can't.

'So, are we going away or not?' I'm trying to change the focus but now I've asked, I'm wondering if he's going to retract the offer. Especially when he doesn't answer straight away. 'Gabe?'

'Yes.' He turns away, starts for the door. 'Can you pack a suitcase?'

'Sure.' I let go of a breath I hadn't known I'd been holding. 'How long are we going for?'

'I'm not sure. A few days. A week.'

'Where are we going?'

'It's a surprise.'

'What will we be doing?'

'Why does that matter?'

'I need to know what to pack, how much to pack...'

'I don't know. Swimming. Eating. Drinking. Don't worry about it, there will be no one to impress but me.'

No one but him...

Doesn't he know that, aside from my brother and, long ago, my father, he is one of the very few men I've always wanted to impress?

'We'll set off when you're ready, and, Avery...' He pauses on the threshold, looks back at me.

'Yes?'

'*One* case. No more.'

I smile and nod. I should be wary. I should be cautious, afraid of the way he makes me feel, but the promise of some time with him, some real bona fide downtime...

I'm too excited and relieved it's still on offer to care.

CHAPTER EIGHT

Gabe

AND FINALLY I can breathe.

We're on my yacht. We have staff. Every need catered for. No need to vacuum the walls down. No need to ruin clothing. No need to cook up a fire hazard. Avery's taking a well-earned break and already enjoying every second of it, by the looks of her.

Hair all windswept, head tilted to the setting sun, cheeks aglow as she grips the rails of the bow...

'This is stunning, Gabe.' She breathes in the fresh sea air, her eyes closing on a sigh before opening again on me. 'Truly stunning.'

And she means it. For a woman who's grown up with money I can't help but be surprised. 'Surely you've been on your fair share of yachts?'

I know the last few years have been different, tough even, but you don't forget the wealth you grew up with.

No? Isn't that part of the reason you've brought her on this idyllic trip, to remind her, to spoil her, to give her back a little of what her brother has taken away for reasons you disagree with...?

'A few, but I was always in the thick of a party. I never got to appreciate the vessel or the actual joy of sailing. In fact, I think this is the first *sailing* yacht I've been on.'

I look away from her beauty to be blinded by the sun instead, hoping it does something to ease the irrational urge to do what I shouldn't and pull her to me, to hell with her brother and our friendship. A moment's insanity for a lifetime of regret.

'In that case, I hope you'll sit back and enjoy it.'

'If you will…' She nudges me with her hip. The briefest sweep of contact and my body burns with it.

I give a tight smile. 'What's that supposed to mean?'

'I've hardly seen you in the time I've been here. Two weeks and you're always cooped up working.'

Working, otherwise known as avoiding her, and I wonder if she knows it.

'And I've promised you a holiday. A holiday for the two of us.'

Us. How easy it slips from the tongue. Wrong and yet so right.

'And so long as you promise not to interfere with the staff, the cleaning and, under no circumstances whatsoever, the laundry, we're good.'

She laughs softly. 'Deal.'

Was the laundry incident really only this morning?

It feels like a lifetime in my Avery-injected world.

I'm already contemplating burning the rest of the ruined laundry in the hope it'll exorcise those red panties from my memory, but something tells me that pink will remind me of her for ever…pink or red for that matter.

'So, where are we heading?' she asks.

'Tonight, the Elaphiti Islands. We'll drop anchor and dine on the yacht.'

'When there's so much to see on land?'

'When you see what Tom serves up for dinner you won't question it.'

'Tom?'

'The onboard chef.'

'Okay, I'm sold. But I wouldn't mind a swim beforehand. Just a little one… It's been an age since I've taken a dip in the sea.'

So long as she's not suggesting skinny-dipping, I have no reason to refuse her. I almost say as much but common sense prevails. I don't want to give her any ideas, not when she's full of her own. Strip poker being right up there as one.

'You'll have time, we'll be dropping anchor soon. Until then, champagne?'

'Huh?' She turns just as Nadia, the chief steward, arrives, two glasses already poured and a smile for us both.

'Oh, thank you,' Avery says, taking a glass and a caviar-topped blini. 'You read my mind, or my grumbling tummy. I hope it was the former.'

Nadia laughs, instantly entertained and smitten. Is there anyone Avery can't coax under her spell? Besides her brother, that is…and just the reminder is enough to put me on edge. Why can't the guy see that she's changed? Why can he not see her talent for what it is too? Encourage her passion, support her…put his bitterness aside?

'Is something wrong?' I refocus to find both women staring at me, waiting for me.

'Nothing at all.'

'Glad to hear it.' Nadia's smile makes a return, Avery's eyes remain watchful, curious. 'Is there anything else I can get you?'

Nadia asks me and I look to Avery. 'Anything else you would like?'

'So long as you're leaving the rest of those blinis here, I'm good.' Avery's smile is friendly and warm as she gives Nadia her full attention. It strikes me how different she is from the other women I have dated. Other women I have brought on this very yacht, who come from the same world as her yet distance themselves from the staff. A haughty tilt to their nose, a polite smile that barely lands, their attention all for me or the view. Polite but removed.

I doubt any of them would know how to turn a vacuum cleaner on, let alone suck a curtain up it. The memory teases a smile to my face as I take a glass and a blini, thank Nadia myself before she walks discreetly away. 'You are quite the anomaly. You know that, don't you?'

She flicks me a look as she chews over her food, the subtle upturned edge to her luscious pink lips and her effervescent eyes telling me I've amused her. She swallows and I follow the move, take in the delicate bob to her throat that looks all the more delicate for the sheer shirt she wears. Sleeves rolled back, the white fabric bright against her fresh tan and un-veiling what I tell myself is a bikini beneath because heaven forbid I get any more glimpses of her underwear.

'How so?'

I look away before I lose myself in her, tell myself the sun is just as captivating as it dips into the ocean. 'You know how many women I have brought here?'

She chokes on her champagne, wrinkles up her nose. 'Not the conversation I want to be having, Gabe.'

'No?' I grin.

'But I'll let you elaborate though.'

'You just told me you didn't want to talk about it.'

'I don't want to talk about the many notches on your bed-post, no.' Her eyes trail over my face, land on my lips as she wets her own and I don't want to notice how they glisten now.

'But I do want to know what that has to do with me being different, so enlighten me.'

Her green eyes collide with mine, their rolling depths so deep I can almost sense the herd of cattle on the hills coming at me, daring me to remain on this path. To accept the risk of giving too much away. But doesn't she deserve the truth? Her brother talks her down enough. Who does she have to bolster her?

'Why do you assume I was talking about women I have slept with?'

'Why did you specifically say women if you didn't mean that?'

'Because in case you hadn't noticed, you're all woman, Avery.'

'Oh, I'd noticed.' Her eyes flash. 'I just wasn't so sure you had.'

My teeth bite together. 'I've noticed.'

And the blood rushing south proves it—this woman will be the death of me. Death by denial, I wonder if that's even a thing.

'Good.'

And she's loving it, her eyes positively sparkle, her lips barely contain her smile.

'No, not good. You're my best friend's sister, Avery, of all the women in the world, you are the one I cannot touch… You're also the one who intrigues me the most.'

'And I'm supposed to feel sorry for you now?' She smiles around the edge of her champagne glass, takes an agonisingly slow sip that I can't tear my gaze from.

'No. But I expect you to understand and help me out a little.'

She laughs. 'Help? I'd ask how but I have a fair idea. We're talking dressing in overalls, a bit of—'

'Hell, no!' Because Avery in overalls conjures up images of her sprawled over the bonnet of one of my sports cars and I *really* don't need that image to add to my fantasy repertoire.

She cocks a brow at me. 'Dowdy, then. Like a grandma.'

'Better. Yes, much better.'

'Or I can rock a nun's habit if you'd prefer?'

'No!'

And now I'm laughing, turned on but laughing and the release is heavenly. This is Avery all over. Fun, playful, teasing, but she can be ever so loving, ever so caring too. Why can't Aiden cut her some—?

I stop. My brain quits. There's a look in her eye, a look that has ants dancing over my skin. 'What is it?'

'I've never heard you laugh like that.'

Because I don't laugh like that. The realisation floors me. As does the fact that I can physically feel her burrowing deeper. Forget ants on the surface, they're under my skin, my ribs, my shield.

I purposefully evade admitting she's right. 'So, are you going to help me out?'

It's as much a distraction tactic as it is a serious request.

'Help you out?'

'Yes, no more flirtation or parading about, scantily clad or otherwise, and I'll—'

'Parading, you say?'

'Would you prefer serenading? Because I hate to tell you, Avery, you are many things, a talented artist being right up there when it comes to those hands of yours, but those vocal cords...' I gesture with my champagne before taking a sip, fearing I've insulted her when she turns to face me head-on, one fist on her hip as she does that loaded pose of hers.

'Are you saying you don't care for my singing voice, Gabe?'

'I'm saying I care for much of you, but I would gladly leave that bit out.'

She laughs, shakes her head as the colour in her cheeks deepens.

'I will admit, though, there is something quite…' I struggle for the right word '…captivating when you are in full swing.'

She purses her lips off to one side, smooths her sea-swept hair out of her face. 'That'll be the scantily cladness when you caught me post-shower.'

'No, Avery. That'll be you, in your many shapes or forms, clothed or otherwise.'

It's serious, too serious, and her eyes soften, her blush deepens, but I'm not about to take it back. She needs to hear it. The truth, the positivity. None of the negativity she's received from all sides over the years. It isn't my place, her brother should be giving her it and I should be steering well clear because every second I'm around her, the risk increases exponentially that I'll do the wrong thing. Losing not only her but her brother in the process.

'Here's to our holiday?' I raise my glass once more.

'A holiday where we're free to spend time together, no stress from the outside world, no pressure from our respective families. Time to just be.'

'Just be… I like the sound of that.' And I do, more than I ever thought possible. My life revolves around my work. Take that away and I'm left with not a lot else. But 'just being' around Avery, there's nothing I want more.

She smiles, long and slow. 'Though you do realise that swimming will involve a bikini or two?'

I laugh softly. 'I'll allow you that.'

'And what, pray tell, will you be wearing?' Her gaze drags along my body and I hold my ground though every nerve ending urges me to run…to run or tug her to me. And I know which one it wants most of all. 'Because if I'm to be on best behaviour, the same applies to you too.'

The very idea that she would find me attractive when she could have her pick of far less problematic men aggravates me and I can't say why. Is it frustration? The fact that this would be so much easier if she would play by the same rules, be restrained by those rules. Rules that centre on her brother, her blood, not mine.

It's not like you're dealing with the attraction much better...

I cling to humour, the best and only defence in this moment. 'I don't think I'll get away with a nun's habit.'

She laughs, the sound high and free and as glorious as the birds that fly overhead—and since when have I paid attention to birdsong?

'No, but I'd definitely pay to see it.'

'Not going to happen, Monroe.' I use my name for Aiden on purpose, remind myself why I'm behaving, why it's essential that I keep this side of the line.

'Well, on that note, I'm going to take that swim. Are you going to join me?'

My instinct screams 'no!', the last thing I need is her in a bikini up close and personal, but the careful arch to her brow reminds me of my promise—to just be. 'Of course. I'll meet you on the swim deck in ten.'

'Excellent.'

She skips away, happy in her ignorance of my inner fight, and I groan into my champagne, throw the rest back and let it dance on my tongue.

Bubbly perfection.

Much like someone else I know.

Another groan and I'm striking off in the direction of my cabin, a safe distance from hers but still not far enough away.

Though let's be real, she could be on another planet and it wouldn't be far enough to see off the way she makes me feel.

Avery

I can't kill the smile that's busting my cheeks. Whether it's because I've yet to come down off the high of being here on this yacht, *his* yacht, or his agreement to spend time with me, I don't know.

Liar—you know. Just as you should also know that he has absolutely no intention of repeating the kiss you once shared, let alone the imaginings you have going on inside your head.

I ignore the voice of reason and tug my sexiest red bikini from the glossy white chest of drawers. It's more bondage style than bikini and designed with seduction in mind. Hardly dowdy-esque.

With a sigh, I shove it back and pull out a black one-piece. Its style isn't exactly sedate but it's certainly not as risqué. The cross-over front cinches in my waist, enhances my curves, but it feels relatively tame.

I change my mind the moment Gabe spies me—spies me and looks away, the sudden tension that ripples through his body and the sharpness of his evasion telling me he thinks otherwise. I smother the smile that threatens to give me away—I can't help it if he finds me attractive. I can't help *liking* the fact that he finds me attractive either. It's too new a realisation and gives me a real buzz.

So, head held high, I walk right past him and execute a perfect dive into the water. I don't, to use his words, parade about in front of him and tease him like my heart desires. I *do* cop an eyeful on my way though. Of a perfect male physique—tanned, toned, and only partially covered by black swimming trunks that I would happily do away with.

Water rushes against my sensitised skin, cool and stimulating with it, and I stay under until I hear him enter behind me before breaking the surface and turning in one. He emerges just in front of me, flicks his hair out of his eyes and grins.

'Happy?'

'Perfectly.' I could be happier though…the urge to close the gap between us and wrap my arms around his bare shoulders, hook our bodies together, is so great I kick away before I do exactly that. I'm a competent swimmer and the need to burn off the adrenaline his presence has triggered has me striking off at a decent pace.

'Hey! Where are you heading?'

'Anywhere and nowhere,' I call back, loving that he follows. It's like we're playing an unspoken game of chase and I'm more than happy to be his target.

I hear an engine start up in the distance, turn to see one of the crew heading out on the rib. 'What are they doing?'

'Keeping us safe. It's getting dark and, though it's relatively quiet on the water now, it pays to have an escort.'

'Right.' I nod though it feels strange being paced by a small boat, not quite the private bit of fun my mind was imagining…

Not that you should be thinking any of it.

I switch from front crawl to breaststroke and we swim side by side for a spell. He leaves me to my thoughts as I take in the islands in the distance, the lights on land twinkling as dusk settles and the moon lights up the ocean. The ripples in its surface are dark and soothing and oddly alluring. It's late but I have no desire to go back, not yet.

I wonder if he will stop me. Suggest we return.

I keep going, waiting for him to do just that but he swims beside me, his thoughts his own.

I wonder how long we can go on like this, how far he'll

let me go before he's forced to say something. It's my own private game, see who can last the longest.

'What are you thinking?' He doesn't look at me as he asks the question but I feel like he's sensed my thoughts.

'I'm just wondering how far you'll let me swim before suggesting we head back. What about you?'

'I was wondering whether you were trying to swim to land so you can make a break for it.'

I laugh, hear the laughter in his own voice too. 'Never. I like being around you, Gabe. I happen to like your company.'

He's quiet and I sneak a look his way but it's impossible to make out his features. It's very dark now, the light from the rib turning him into a silhouette. 'What is it?'

'Nothing.'

'I sense it's not nothing.'

'I like your company too, Avery.' He says it quietly, something about his tone making my chest warm and my heart skip a beat.

I swallow the rush of emotion and kick out. 'Race you back?'

I don't wait for him to respond. Keen for a head start and desperate to get away—from him and my thoughts—I do an about-turn and strike off for the boat. He's alongside me in a heartbeat and I know I'm beat but I don't give up. The adrenaline coursing through my veins as heady as the chaos he's stirred up. Not that I can outswim it. Try as I might.

We reach the boat and he's pushing up out of the water as I touch the deck, my breath coming in short pants. 'You're a strong swimmer.'

'A skill my father insisted I learn from a very young age.' He leans down, offers a hand to help me out. I don't need it. I could just use the steps. I *should* use the steps. It's what they're for, and I hesitate for the briefest second, knowing what his touch will do to me and craving it all the same.

'So, he did care…' I wrap my hand around his, press my lips together as the contact fizzes through me.

'He cared about the potential shame of having a son who couldn't take care of himself on the water, yes.'

My eyes snap to his, my frown as severe as the pang in my chest. He can't be serious. Yet, he is. And I'm so floored by the realisation, so sad for the boy he was, that I struggle to gain my footing as he tugs me up in one swift move and I find myself pressed up against him. I gasp, at least I think I do, there's a whirring in my ears, my blood rushing forth, flooding my breasts, my lower belly…chest to chest, wet skin to wet skin, his face is so close, his mouth parted in surprise and so ready for the taking.

'Gabe?' I'm all for acting on it, all for—

The rib whizzes up behind us, its engine drowning out my voice. 'Tom's on the radio, Mr Curran,' Carlos, the deckhand, calls across the water. 'Dinner is served.'

Gabe holds my gaze, holds me still too. Has he not heard him?

'Gabe?' I whisper.

'Tell him we'll be right in.'

His voice is a low rumble, almost a warning—for me, for Carlos, who knows? I swallow as his eyes glitter down on me, the pulse working in his jaw as rapid as my own.

'Sure thing,' Carlos calls back. If he's aware of the tension between us, he makes no show of it. He's probably used to it. After all, Gabe himself all but admitted I'm not the first woman he's brought here. But I bet I'm the only one he's refused to bed…

It's that chilling realisation that has me stepping back sharply, severing the connection. 'I best hurry, I don't want to be late for Tom's first dinner…you know how chefs are.'

I duck to grab one of the towels that have magically appeared for us to use and run. Feel his eyes on me until I'm out of sight but he says nothing. Not even *I'll see you soon*.

And maybe he won't. Maybe getting *that* up close and personal is enough to see him bring an end to this flight of fancy, or, rather, platonic sailing…

But I seriously hope not because being around Gabe, this new Gabe, makes me feel alive. More alive than I've felt in years and I'm not ready for it to end.

No matter the risk to my heart, I want this time with him for as long as he will gift it to me.

CHAPTER NINE

Gabe

I CURSE AND curse again. I'd come so close. So very close.

If it hadn't been for Carlos I would have…

My teeth grind, my body fires and my fingers drum against the dining table. Anything to distract from the direction of my thoughts, the memory of Avery's wet curves pressed against my body. Her hair slicked back, cheeks all flushed, lips mere inches from my own…and those eyes—big and green and full of want.

'I hope this is okay?'

I narrowly miss biting off my tongue as I shoot forward, my head snapping to the left, to where she's now standing. One hand resting on the door frame, one foot over the threshold and making no further progression, as though she's truly unsure.

'Of course, it is.'

She could arrive dressed in a potato sack and she'd still make it look elegant and dinner-worthy. But wearing a blue dress that shimmers with her eyes, its straps barely there and her tanned skin aglow, she's simply exquisite. And she's stolen my breath along with my ability to think straight.

And you're forgetting your manners again…

I push up out of my seat and pull back her chair. She joins

me, her lashes lowered, her stride slow. She touches a hand to her hair that's still damp at the edges and pinned into a twisted knot at her nape. 'Men only have to slap on a shirt and, hey presto, they're dinner-ready.'

'Don't forget the all-important trousers too,' I joke, seeing off the gushing compliment I'm eager to give and daren't. 'Or the comb through the hair.'

That coaxes out a smile that fires my blood more than it should. It's just a friendly smile, a polite smile… nothing suggestive, or coquettish, or provocative… but it's Avery.

She looks up and her eyes assault me, their depths so green and vibrant against the ambient lighting from the deck. She wets her lips that already shine with some neutral-looking gloss, her cheeks flush a deeper shade of pink highlighting the dusting of freckles along the bridge of her nose. 'I happen to like it when it's a little askew.'

I smile and wonder whether it looks as perplexed as I feel. I've been conditioned to see anything less than perfection as a flaw, something to be picked out, dissected, removed or corrected.

But not Avery…

She lowers herself into the chair as I ease it forward, her scent lifting on the sea breeze—fresh, tantalising, disturbing my senses and messing with my head…until she shivers and goosebumps prickle over her exposed skin.

'Are you cold?' I rush out. 'We can dine inside if you would prefer?'

'And miss out on this view?' She gestures to the islands in the distance, the moonlight dancing on the water, and I have to agree what a waste it would be. 'No, thank you. And I'm not cold.'

Her skin tells me otherwise and I want to protest but there's something in her eyes that stops me. Something that tells me she's not lying. She's not cold. Instead, she's too aware. Her skin alive because of this, this dogged chemistry, firing the very air that we breathe. Is it destined to always be this way between us?

Or is it possible to put the fire out? To indulge it and move on.

Like anything in life.

Enjoy it and walk away satisfied.

Gorge on it and make yourself sick, unwilling to go there again.

I need the latter, but the damage such a fling would cause, the irrecoverable damage, potential heartache and pain. The trust it would destroy. These are the things I cling to, remind myself of, arm myself with. If only I could make myself numb to her too.

'Good evening, Mr Curran, Ms Monroe.' Nadia appears, stepping up to the table, two plates in hand. 'To start this evening, Tom has prepared a traditional Dalmatian octopus salad.' She places our food down and takes up the bottle of wine that's been waiting on ice. 'He's selected an oak-aged *pošip* to accompany it.'

'*Pošip?*' Avery says.

'It's a white wine from the Dalmatian region of Croatia,' Nadia explains. 'It's very similar to a Chardonnay and utterly divine.'

Avery takes up her freshly poured glass for a sip and gives an appreciative hum.

She looks less keen on the food though and as Nadia discreetly hurries away, I lean in. 'Something wrong?'

'I have a weird aversion to tentacles.'

I grin. 'Are you kidding?'

She shakes her head, her eyes still on the dish. 'I blame

Aiden for chasing me around our villa with what I thought was a live octopus once.'

I chuckle, enjoying the visual and the rare easy reference to her brother. 'The joy of siblings.'

'Or lack thereof.'

'You love him really.'

She meets my eye, her sudden sobriety cutting deep. 'If only the feeling were mutual.'

'Avery…' I lean back in my seat. 'You know he loves you.'

'He has a funny way of showing it—anyway…' she takes up her fork '… I don't want to talk about him. Though in truth…' she looks at her plate '… I'm not sure I want to tuck into this either.'

I study her a moment longer, wanting to push it and knowing I've likely said enough on the matter already. No one, other than Aiden himself, can convince her otherwise and I'd be better off telling him my concerns. Which I will do, just as soon as the opportunity arises.

'Do the suckers ever get stuck?' Her nose wrinkles as she asks, the move too cute to bear and I chuckle, the sound tight and as uncomfortable as I feel.

'Live ones can, yes.'

'Live ones?'

'Your face is a picture.'

'Who would eat one while it's alive?'

'It's considered a delicacy in some parts of the world, like Japan, Korea…'

She shudders. 'Well, they can keep it.'

'This really isn't encouraging you to try it, is it?'

'I'm sorry, Gabe, but when you asked if I had any dietary concerns, I didn't think I needed to specify a fear of—'

'Close your eyes,' I interject.

Said eyes widen instead. *'What?'*

'Close your eyes,' I repeat, taking her fork from her un-resisting fingers.

'Are you—why?'

'Are you always so mistrusting?'

'I'm not mistrusting. I'm—I'm—'

'Understandably wary after what your brother did but trust me.'

Her brows arch, her lips purse together. Then, 'Trust you?'

'Is that so hard to do?'

'When you're best friends with said brother?'

'But I'm not him.'

'No. You're not.' There's a glint in her eyes now, a glint I should ignore but it's already set something alight within me. She takes a breath, sits up straighter and closes her eyes. For a second I don't move. Being able to take her in, unobserved...

The delicate angle to her collarbone, her pulse flickering at its heart. The graceful arch to her neck and tilt to her chin. Her lightly pressed lips, full and pink. Her closed lashes falling like soft auburn crescents upon her cheeks and the faint dusting of freckles beneath the subtle veil of make-up.

'What now?' she murmurs, her voice snapping me out of my trance-like state, and I clear my throat, fork up both tentacle and salad from her plate.

'Open your mouth.' Her lashes flutter, her cheeks warm and I realise this is hardly my smartest move when trying to strip the evening of its intimacy.

Her lips part and I take the smallest of breaths.

You started this...

I lean closer, carefully slip the fork inside her mouth. She takes it willingly, trustingly, her lips closing around the food as I slide the fork away and I've never been more captivated or more attuned to another in my life. My own tastebuds salivate as she moves the food around, the blissful hum she makes provoking one of my own. 'Good?'

She covers her lips with her hand, her eyes opening into mine. 'Heavenly.'

I smile. 'Glad you listened to me?'

Her eyes dance. 'Don't let it go to your head.'

'I wouldn't dare.' I offer back her fork, which she takes, her fingers brushing against mine as she does so and the urge is there, to take her hand in mine, to pull her closer, to taste the wine and food on her lips... I snatch up my glass before I can be so stupid and focus on eating and drinking and anything to keep my hands and attention where they belong.

'Can I ask you something?' she pipes up after several strained minutes—strained in my world at least, in hers I'm not so sure.

'Of course.' Though I'm already regretting my agreement as her eyes narrow. The way she's now studying me has the hairs prickling at my nape and I run a finger through my collar.

'Why are you so determined to go through life alone?'

'Who said I was determined?'

And why do you sound so defensive?

'You did. Not in so many words, but the way you act, the way you talk about your father, the family you don't know... plus there's the articles that have been written about you. I assume some of what they say is true.'

'And what is it they say?'

'That you're a declared bachelor. That you live for your work and feel no need to share your life with another.'

I shift in my seat, force myself to relax back and fend off the tension. 'Your brother isn't so different.'

'I don't approve of the way he lives his life either, but he isn't here right now, you are.'

'Lucky me.'

Her lips quirk off to one side. 'Drop the sarcasm.'

I raise my hands. 'Apologies, but I wasn't expecting to defend my way of life over dinner.'

'Well, I wasn't expecting to face my fear of tentacles either but hey-ho…here we are.'

I laugh—surprise, disbelief, a very definite case of being put on the spot cutting it short.

'I just think it's sad.'

'You think I'm sad?' I choke out, waving a hand at our surroundings. 'Have you seen where we are? What we're doing? We have an award-winning chef at our beck and call, a fully crewed yacht that will take you anywhere on water you want to go, I have—'

'Yes, you have a lot, Gabe. More than most men can ever dream of, but has it brought you happiness, contentment, true pleasure?'

The way she says pleasure ripples through me. The devil on my shoulder demands I show her exactly that, the pleasure we'd be capable of having before the inevitable storm would hit. But I'm agitated too. I don't like where this conversation is going.

'Happiness is a never-ending goal, Avery. One we're never destined to achieve, only seek.'

'That sounds like some weird guru nonsense…do you truly believe that?'

'It's what puts fire in our blood, pushes us to get out there and achieve what we set out to. And then we move on to our next goal and the next.'

'And what's your next goal, Gabe? Is it your next big win for the Curran Empire, for your father?'

Her words chill me. 'Not for my father, no. I do it for me.'

She studies me quietly. 'So you don't crave his love, his

affection, his pride?' She says it softly, like she knows she's overstepped but can't stop herself.

'I told you; I came to terms with who my father is a long time ago, what he is and isn't capable of giving.'

'I know you did. But it doesn't stop you from wanting it. From wanting more for you and your life. You're thirty-five, Gabe, aren't you tired of doing it all alone? Wouldn't you like someone to share all of this with? Someone other than your father, who actually appreciates you, cares for you…loves you.'

My jaw aches with the effort of staving off her words. 'I'm sharing it right now and frankly,' I quip, 'it's not all it's cracked up to be.'

'You don't like being cracked open and poked at, that's all.'

'Who does?'

'It's why some of us who need it go to therapy and get our heads screwed on straight.'

'While the rest of us simply flounder?' I suggest, the tease in my voice evident. Because I'm not floundering. Far from it. And she needs to know it.

'Not how I would have put it, but yes, that seems fairly accurate to me.'

I laugh, stunned, bemused, in awe of the firecracker that she is. She has me on the hunt for an escape, which comes in the form of our next course. I just hope Nadia hasn't been standing there for too long. It's enough to have Avery think all she does, to have others think it too, my staff at that… I raise a hand to beckon her forward, give Avery a tight smile. 'And on that note, it looks like our main course is ready.'

Nadia steps forward and clears away our plates. I only wish she could clear away the remnants of our conversation too.

Is there a part of me that still craves my father's approval? Is that why I never broke away, set up on my own, even when I could have done it numerous times over by now?

Look at Avery, comes the inner voice, *look what she's managed to achieve all under her own steam*.

She's done what I've never had the courage to do and the realisation does something to me...even as I try to deny it all.

Avery

I know I've backed him into a corner. That the look on his face when he spied Nadia waiting in the wings was that of a drowning man being handed a life jacket. But I couldn't stop myself.

Especially when each and every conversation we have unveils another piece in the Great Gabe Jigsaw—a puzzle I am desperate to solve, to fix.

But why? What is it I hope to achieve by understanding him better, by helping him? It's not like he's about to change his mind where I'm concerned. I know there's no world in which Gabe will see me as a woman, someone other than Aiden's sister. No matter what my heart desires. But if I can make him see how much better his life could be, how much more fulfilled...then at least I will have helped him as he has me.

'So what about you?' he says.

'What about me?'

He smiles, that dazzling, slow, *I've got you* kind of a smile. 'You're twenty-three with dreams of owning your own jewellery empire, but what do you want outside that?'

'Don't make fun.'

'I'm not. You have a gift, Avery, and I wholeheartedly support you with it.'

'Thank you.' Though it comes out weak with where this conversation is heading. Picking holes in the way Gabe lives his life is far easier than letting him pick holes in mine. Hypocritical I know. But when the reason for my single status is sitting across from me asking the very questions that will expose me, the very questions he doesn't really want to know the answers to, I'm allowed to be a hypocrite.

Though there's more to it than him, and you know it.

'So?'

'So what?' I take up my cutlery, keen to tuck into the chicken that looks far more appetising than the octopus and definitely carries more appeal than this conversation.

'Come on, Avery, you're so quick to judge my single status, to question it. What about you? Don't I get to do the same?'

'Are you asking if I'm in a relationship?'

'I would hope not.'

My heart gives the tiniest leap, a ridiculous reaction to a statement that doesn't mean what I want it to. 'Why?'

'Because I'd pity the fool that let their girlfriend stay with another man.' His eyes carry an unreadable force, a strength that I don't understand. 'Especially alone.'

I wet my lips, my mouth ridiculously dry. 'Don't you think that's a bit outdated?'

'No. No man wants their girlfriend staying under the same roof as another unchaperoned, no matter what they may say otherwise.'

I give an awkward laugh. 'Unchaperoned? What century are you in? People do it all the time, Gabe.'

His focus doesn't shift, his intensity doesn't ease. 'I wouldn't like it.'

My lips quirk. His stubbornness, jealousy even, over something that is hypothetical, that isn't even about me... Yet I feel the possessive heat of his statement and wish with all my heart that it were. Even if the feminist in me would strive to change his stance while revelling in the caveman attention.

'Anyway, the point is moot...' I slice up my chicken, determined to eat it this time. 'I don't have a boyfriend.'

I thrust the fork in my mouth and my tastebuds sing. Fresh tomato, basil, olive oil, mozzarella. Delicious.

'Good.'

My eyes lock with his, all taste forgotten as I struggle to swallow. 'Good?'

I swear my heart is lodged with the food in my throat. Good. Did he really just say *good*?

He blinks across the table at me, his expression easing, his eyes losing some of their intensity. 'What I mean is, I'm glad I don't have a jealous boyfriend to add to my already pressing conscience.'

I shake my head, the fog lifting as the flood of disappointment descends, cold and unrelenting. 'And by that, you mean a three-year-old kiss and the trust of my brother, which you believe you broke.'

And I'm angry now. The heat of passion, the way I feel about him, twisting up with the humiliating reminder of that night.

'I don't remember you being all that concerned about a potential boyfriend back then, Gabe...unless it was to pass judgement on them not being good enough. Do you want to revisit that conversation now?'

'No.'

'Perfect. Because I have no interest in discussing my love life either. Now can we eat before this gets cold?'

'I'm sorry I hurt you.'

'And I think we've already covered that off, too. So, moving on.' I overfill my fork this time and chew with gusto, making clear I'm done with this conversation. Done with feeling uncomfortable. Done with feeling anything but pleasure for this delicious meal.

'You're angry.'

'You don't say.'

You were the one who started it...

I chew over the inner gibe.

'And yet, you were happy to probe into my situation.'

He's got you there.

I swallow. Breathe. 'Well, I don't have a situation to probe, okay? In fact, I can't imagine ever having a situation to probe—satisfied?'

He frowns across the table, his food untouched. 'What does that mean?'

I drop my knife and fork with a clatter, clean my lips with my napkin. 'I don't want a relationship, okay?'

Liar.

And he knows it, looking at me as he does, a glimmer of scepticism in his eye.

'Why?'

His question spears right through me. One too many therapy sessions coming to the fore.

'You want the truth?'

'Always.'

'Of course you do. Perfection. Discretion. Honesty. Discipline. They're all things you value.'

'What's wrong with that?'

'Nothing, Gabe.' I shake my head, blow out an unsteady breath. I might as well have listed all the things my brother believes I lack thanks to my unshakeable past. 'Nothing at all.'

'I would expect for someone like you, brought up as you were in a happy family, a happy home, to want that.'

'And I did, you're right. Growing up I wanted what my parents had. I wanted the marriage, the kids, the white picket fence and the nuclear family. I wanted it all.'

'And then you lost your father?'

The pang is fresh, severe. 'I did. It broke me. It broke us. I just never realised how deep the damage went. If what you say about Aiden is true...'

'I don't know for certain, but I do know your brother and I know how hard it was for him living a life that had already been mapped out at birth.'

And then it hits me. 'Because it was mapped out for you too.'

It's not a question, it's a statement, his nod so very small.

'We each deal with it in our own way.'

'Or not, in my case.'

His mouth quirks up. 'I'd say you dealt with it pretty well... in the end.'

'In the end,' I repeat, mimicking his smile.

'But now you avoid getting close to another to avoid experiencing that crushing loss again?'

'To some extent,' I admit. 'I can dream of a career because it's in my power to achieve it. But a family, true love...' I shake my head, feel the cold set in '...it feels too much like a pipe dream.'

'And yet, you think it's attainable for me.'

'Because it is, Gabe. You are lovable, dependable, adorable in your own grumpy ass way. You can have it all.'

He doesn't even flinch at my teasing descriptor. 'And you can't?'

I laugh—cold, harsh, bitter. 'Let's look at the evidence, shall we? I'm surrounded by family who should love me unconditionally and yet struggle.' He opens his mouth to object but I hurry on, unwilling to listen and adamant in my hypothesis. 'The idea that I would find a man, or anyone else for that matter, who *chooses* to love me, feels like a fantasy and, frankly, I'd rather dream big for my work and plough my energy into that. Keep the fantasies as that, pure fantasy. Then there can be no heartache, no devastation.'

'No true happiness?'

And what can I say to that? Nothing. So I don't.

'You're wrong, Ave.'

I huff, throw back some wine to douse the warmth his shortening of my name triggers. It's too familiar, too sweet, too…too heart-provoking.

'I've had years of therapy, Gabe, and not a second of that has been able to convince me otherwise. Come to terms with my father's death, get over my addiction, handed me tools to manage my depression and get on in life, yes. I'm used to the voices in my head, used to being able to manage them and quiet them as I need to. I don't deal well with silence so being alone can suck, but I can now cope with that too. And I'm doing fine, Gabe, really, truly, so don't be getting all sentimental on me. You can save your breath and your worries for someone else who needs it.'

'You seriously cannot think—'

'Gabe, please.' I look at my plate, unable to hold his eye any longer, when he's looking at me like he is right now. 'I want to eat. I want to enjoy this time. I didn't come here for more therapy but keep pressing me and I'll turn this back on you and then some.' Now I look up, needing to add fire to my words. 'Because, believe me, I'm quite happy to explore what happened three years ago and this time, I won't take your panicked attack as a reason to walk away.'

'But what if I—?'

I raise my brows at him, cock my head in challenge.

'All right. All right. I'll quit. But know this, Ave, you deserve a man that will make you feel like the woman you are—worthy, lovable, frustrating beyond measure but with a heart that's always in the right place. Please don't doubt that.'

I still, my heart stills, my ears ring. I feel the response on the tip of my tongue, so very similar to the one I gave three years ago when I pressed him into telling me whether he was that man. But I'm no masochist. I'm not about to pressure him into rejecting me all over again.

But how can I keep my distance, protect myself when he says such things? Such things that suggest he feels more, more than he's willing to admit to because of my brother, because of his loyalty to him.

I want to scream at the unfairness of it.

'But then…' he picks up his cutlery and I realise he's the one switching focus now '…what do I know about any of it?'

'It?' It's a rhetorical question but I find myself asking anyway. 'You mean love?'

'Yes, Avery, I mean the L word. I didn't grow up with it. I only ever experienced it first hand in your household and the truth is, as a teen I craved what Aiden had, what you had. But when you live without something long enough, you realise that maybe you're not quite wired right yourself.'

His meaning hits home with chilling precision. 'You think you're *incapable* of falling in love?'

He chews over his food, his eyes dark in the low light. 'I think I've been on the dating scene long enough to come to that conclusion, yes.'

'And what if you just haven't met the right woman?'

He studies me, long and hard. 'Who says I ever will…?'

CHAPTER TEN

Gabe

'THIS PLACE IS just beautiful!'

Ave looks like a child on Christmas morning as she says it, her face alight with her pleasure as she takes in the island of Korčula and its medieval town.

'And I *love* that they call it Little Dubrovnik…it really is like a miniature version. Quietly pretty and utterly serene.'

She truly is gushing and I'm captivated. By her. Not the island, which I've seen several times before. It's the same everywhere we go. Day five of our trip and each new location, each new sight brings such unprecedented delight, and the more energy I put into provoking that response and making her happy, the more I lose myself in her.

'It's a masterpiece,' I say, forcing myself to look away and focus on the town's history.

'A masterpiece?' Her arm is looped through mine, her body ever more at ease with me and it feels good, it feels natural, it feels right. I don't pause to question it as I nod and expand on the tiny detail.

'The Venetians built the town in the form of a fishbone. It acts as a medieval air-conditioning system controlling which winds are permitted to flow through the streets.'

'Ah, now that's clever.'

'Isn't it? They say the winds are to Korčula as the canals are to Venice, shaping its geography, its character and its fortune.'

She twists into me, gives me a look that makes my body warm and the ants come alive beneath the surface of my skin again. 'What?'

'You.'

'Me, what?'

She shakes her head, her grin as wide as her eyes that return to our surroundings, the narrow streets and its bustling cafes, tables spilling from the inside out. Flowers trailing from balconies overhead. People chatting, kids playing, bicycle bells ringing…

'I think you're a closet romantic, Gabe.'

'A what?' I choke out.

'You can laugh, but I reckon you're a romantic at heart, the way you describe things…the places you've taken me. If I were a woman in the mood to be wooed, you would have had me on day one of this yachting adventure. And don't look so worried.' She tugs on my arm. 'I'm not about to misconstrue anything. I know the score.'

Did she? Because right now, with the glow reaching all the way from her eyes to her toes, I'm not so sure.

I pause and extract my arm from hers. 'Stay here, one second.'

She frowns at me. 'I wasn't trying to scare you off.'

'Not at all.' I smile to reassure her. 'I just need to call in here.'

She eyes the old bakery with its traditional front and hanging display of treats. 'Oh, how sweet.'

'Quite literally.'

I step inside and converse with the owner, who boxes up a selection. I don't hold back either—these are really good and I know Ave will love them. When I return outside, I find her chatting with a group of locals who are all sitting around a gingham-topped table. As I approach, they quieten down and she straightens with a blush. 'You all good?'

'Yup.'

She loops her arm back in mine.

'Making yourself at home?'

She looks back at the group, gives a wave and starts off in the direction we'd been heading before I broke away. 'They were asking if you were treating me to some Croatian delights.'

'Did they?'

She hums.

'And?'

'And I said I thought you were.'

'And?' Because the look in her eye tells me there's more to this tale.

'And they said you were a good man who clearly knew how to treat his lady.'

'Aah…'

Well, you did ask.

'Do you ever go anywhere without drawing people into conversation?'

'Can I help it if I have one of those faces?'

I chuckle and shake my head. 'I suppose not.'

'So, come on, what did you get? Those crescent-shaped buns floating about in the window looked mighty odd. Like crabs…though I'm relieved there wasn't a tentacle in sight.'

'You mean the *cukarins*?'

'I thought that was the name of the bakery?'

'It is. It's also the name of their staple cookie.'

'Did you get one?'

'Of course, along with a selection of others.' I open the

box and offer it to her. She licks her lips—a sight I try in vain not to react to—and selects the chocolate-covered one. 'I should have known.'

She looks up at me, all wide-eyed innocence. 'What?'

'You're all about the chocolate…'

'I'll share.'

I grin. 'You'll want to, it's seriously rich.'

'Even better.' She takes a bite, her eyes close and the look of heaven on her face is enough to make my mouth salivate, my stomach rumble and my entire body warm. 'Wow, that is *good*! Cream. Walnuts. Chocolate. So much chocolate. What more could a girl ask for?'

'It's a Marco Polo *bombica*.'

Her eyes open as she thumbs her lips and I tear my gaze from the gesture—you'd think I'd be used to watching her eat by now. Used to it and desensitised to it, yet it feels the total opposite. Is this what denial does to you?

'After the Venetian explorer?' she asks.

'Huh?' What were we talking about?

'Marco Polo, the *bombica*?'

'Oh, yeah…you know your history,' I say.

She nudges me with her elbow. 'Don't look so surprised!'

'No insult intended. You're a woman with many hidden talents.'

'Is this you bigging me up again because seriously, Gabe, you can give it a rest.'

'I wouldn't dare.'

'No? Yesterday it was my jewellery designs. I thought you were trying to sell my services to the great coral master himself on Zlarin.'

'And why not? You were in your element as he took you through his jewellery design process and it was obvious you knew what you were talking about in return.'

'I loved it.' She beams, unable to hide the truth from me. 'There was something so special about the way he spoke of his work, how the coral spoke to him and shaped itself in effect—don't look like that!'

'Like what?'

'Like you're about to laugh.'

'Hey, far be it from me to judge a master at work. Especially when that devotion produced the earrings you have on right now. They suit you.'

She blushes, touches a hand to the loop of glossy red branches that hang from each ear, the colour vibrant and perfect for her. 'And there you go again with the compliments.'

'I hardly think twice is a crime...'

'Then there were the comments you made about my athletic ability on the beach the day before...'

'You *were* impressive. You beat many of the locals to that ball and prior to our arrival on Uvala Šunj you didn't even know the game of *picigin* existed.'

'I'm a quick learner and it was fun.'

'Having you join them certainly upped the appeal of the game for the locals too,' I tease—*and me*.

She shakes her head, eyes me funny but the look is gone as quick as it came and she tucks into the chocolate ball. 'So why Marco Polo?'

'Well, for a start the locals believe he was born here, not that there's any actual evidence to support the theory and the Italians certainly don't agree, but he was captured in a sea battle not far from here and it's the reason the *bombica* is shaped like a cannon ball.'

'What about the rest?' She eyes the box. 'Any more fascinating stories behind those?'

'No, but don't let that put you off. They're just as delicious. I prefer the *cukarin*. The one that was hanging in the window… It's a dry cookie that tastes of lemon and orange and it tastes even better when dipped in *prošek*.'

'*Prošek?*'

'A local dessert wine.' I lift the paper bag hooked under my arm. 'I picked one up for later.'

'Perfect. And the rest?'

'This one is *klašun*, also known as a little ball of joy. It's made from the same dough as the *cukarin* but inside they have a nutty filling flavoured with rose brandy and vanilla. Sometimes a touch of marmalade too.'

'And this one?'

'Another of my favourites, an *amareta*. Crispy on the outside, soft on the inside.'

'Sounds like someone else I know.'

I chuckle and shake my head anew. 'No prizes for guessing…'

'How did you know I was talking about you? I might have been referring to Aiden.'

'Were you?'

'No. But come to think of it, the same does apply…that's if a heart still beats within that steel shell of his.'

I catch her eye, feel her sudden shift in mood and it takes me with her. 'Go easy on him, Ave. He lost his father too and took on the firm when he was still young. He gave up more than you realise.'

'So you say…'

I fight the urge to cup her cheek, to offer up more sympathy and empathy that can only soften me to her more. And it won't help maintain the distance I've been trying to keep, the wall that I can feel crumbling with every hour she's in my orbit.

'So…what's in it?'

'Hmm?'

'The *amareta*?'

She's changing topic and I'm grateful. I am. Only...

'It's a ball made from ground almonds, citrus zest, dried figs and something sweet. I think it's honey. It's another one that goes well with the wine.'

'And this one?'

'*Harubica*. It's a muffin made from ground carob fruit and topped with marmalade and sugared orange peel.'

'Yum!' she says, nibbling on more chocolate. 'You want some?'

She offers it to me and I wave it away, 'No, you look like you're enjoying that one too much to share.'

And I'm enjoying her enjoying it, not that I'll say it out loud.

She covers her mouth as she chews. 'I really hope Tom wasn't planning a huge dinner tonight because I'm going to be ruined for anything proper.'

'It's okay, I gave him the night off. Figured we could visit a street vendor on the way back if you were still wanting something.'

'Sounds like a plan.'

'But first, come on...' I lead her through a stone archway, down some steps. 'There's something I want you to see.'

'There is? But didn't we exhaust this part of the town on arrival...?'

'Not quite.'

She doesn't press any further and after a few twists and turns she says, 'You come here a lot, don't you?'

'What makes you say that?'

'The way you know your way around these streets, know the traditions, the food...' She gestures to the box. 'If you ever need to pack in the billionaire day job, you could always become a tour guide.'

I smile. 'Now there's a thought.'

'You really do love it here, this country, this island…'

'My father would think it ridiculous but there's something about Korčula that resets you. It's unlike any other place I've visited. The tourism isn't as oppressive as Dubrovnik and the history runs just as deep. Each time I visit, I find something else to appreciate.'

'And what have you found to appreciate today, other than your fabulous company in the shape of *moi,* of course?' Again, she teases, but she doesn't realise how close to the mark she is. Just how much I do appreciate her. How much I've enjoyed wandering the same city walls with her, the same streets…

'Oh, wow!' She slows as we round a corner and above us the sky is adorned with colourful umbrellas floating mid-air. She hands me the small piece of remaining *bombica* and pulls out her mobile to snap a pic. 'That's so pretty.'

It's not the only thing.

I stuff the chocolate in my mouth to stop myself from saying as much.

'Hey!' She pokes me in the ribs. 'Thought it was all for me.'

'I thought you were done with it.'

She presses her lips together on a lively grin that I desperately want to kiss from her lips.

'Come on…' I take her hand in mine and move before I act on the foolish impulse. 'We're almost there.'

'Where?'

'You'll see.'

It's getting late, the setting sun breaking through the alleyways bathing the ancient walls and us in gold. It's narrow here and with the tables, stalls and potted plants taking up half the passageway it forces us to walk in single file. Hand in hand.

I don't think about the symbolic intimacy, the ease with which it keeps happening, the physical link and the budding invisible bond…it just is.

We reach the fifteenth-century tower of Revelin with its plaque depicting the winged lion of Venice. Something she'd pointed out on our arrival.

'We've definitely been here.'

'We have.' Not that I stop.

'What did we miss?'

'You'll see,' I repeat. I don't take the stairs to the top of the tower, though I know the view over the port at this time of day will be enhanced by the setting sun. The glow from the terracotta roof tops and the fort wall as spectacular as that of Dubrovnik. Instead, I lead her into the courtyard where a small crowd is gathering, filling up the seats set out in rows. A group of women dressed in traditional costume—black dresses, white blouses, red sashes around their waist—sing in a circle, entertaining the arriving guests.

I purposefully tuck us into the back row and she leans into me. 'Why do I feel like a naughty schoolgirl trying to hide out in the back?'

I laugh. 'It's far safer up here, trust me.'

'Okay…' She leans back to eye me. 'And what's that supposed to mean…? Don't tell me—*you'll see.*'

'Got it in one. You fancy another while we wait for it to start?' I open up the box and she peeps inside.

'What did you say this one was?' She points to the cup-cake-looking one with a blob of marmalade for icing.

'Harubica.'

'Yum!' She scoops it out, takes a nibble as she watches the preparations under way on the makeshift stage. The men arriving in divisive costumes—one group in red and gold, one in black and silver—both elaborately embroidered. She eyes the swords hooked over their shoulders and leans into me again. 'I wouldn't mess with them.'

'Wait until the dance gets going.'

'A dance with swords? That's a new one on me.'

'I thought you might enjoy it. It's a tradition that dates back hundreds of years and takes place here twice a week in the summer. It's known as the Moreska dance.'

She nods but doesn't tear her gaze from the stage and I struggle to tear my gaze from her. Watching Avery enraptured is like watching the most interesting story unfold... even if I have paid for us to watch the tale on stage.

The singing ends and the shows starts up. The leader of the blacks entering the ring dragging a veiled woman in his wake and the leader of the reds steps forward. An argument rings out between the opposing men, the woman caught in the middle.

'What's happening?' she whispers, eyes on the action.

'What do you think is happening?'

'I think they're fighting over the girl.'

'On the surface, yes. The armies of the Red King and the Black King battle it out over the honour of the veiled princess, a Korčulan maiden who is in love with the Red King. But at its heart, it's a tale of morality that pits the East against the West.'

'But she gets the man she loves—right?'

I laugh softly. 'Back to the important bit...'

She looks at me all hopeful and the sight of her so caught up in it is enough to make me want to wrap my arm around her and assure her a thousand times over.

'You'll have to wait and see.'

'Spoilsport.'

I chuckle softly as she hooks her arm in mine, her focus returning to the stage as the dancing armies face each other off. The battle ensues, shouted taunts over escalating music, the kings fight, the armies clash, swords clang. Bits of metal flying into the crowd as seven different dances unfold and the noise builds to an almighty crescendo.

Through it all she watches, the sweet treat in her hand forgotten, her eyes sparkling in the lights ensconced in the walls. When, finally, the black army is defeated, their king is captured, and the veiled maiden is returned to the arms of her one true love...

She sighs against my shoulder. 'Well, I didn't expect that.'

'Which bit? The flying metal or...?'

She laughs. 'You were right about the back seats being safer. I'm surprised they let people sit so close.'

'They get warned by the ushers, the risk is their own and I guess some people like to be in the thick of the action.'

She looks up at me and before I know what she's about, she presses a kiss to my cheek. The rush of sensation has my lips parting of their own volition, heat feeding my veins and warming the area she touched.

'What was that for?'

'Thank you for bringing me here. Thank you for all of this.'

'It's nothing.' Though it comes out tight, strained. She's still so very close, I only have to dip my head and...

'It's everything, Gabe...' her voice is a soft whisper '... but it has to stop.'

'Stop?'

She nods, disturbing the air between us, caressing my cheek. 'Because I won't want to go back.'

I don't want her to go back.

The words come from nowhere as instinctual and impulsive as the warmth spreading through me. 'You've worked hard the last three years, Ave, it's time you caught a break.'

Her green eyes glisten as they search mine and she inches closer or am I moving…?

And what does it matter? You kiss her and you're done for!

'Come on.' I launch to my feet, almost losing both bottle and box in the process. 'It's late. We should head back to the yacht.'

She rises a second later and I know I've startled her.

But I have no business thinking such things, let alone acting on them.

Avery

'Do you want anything else to eat?'

For a moment I don't hear him, I'm too busy analysing the connection between us. Working out whether it's all in my head, my heart, or whether Gabe feels it too. The last few days I've been floating on air, buoyed up by his attention, his thoughtfulness, his care. Keeping a clear head and clear heart has been all but impossible.

'Ave?'

'No.' I shake my head, give him the smallest of smiles. 'I'm fine.'

He raises the box and the bag holding the wine. 'Cookies and wine it is, then.'

My smile grows. 'Cookies and wine, sounds so bizarre.'

'Not to be knocked until you've tried it.'

We walk in silence the rest of the way and I get the impression he's deep in thought.

Whether he's wrapped up in the same conundrum as me, I'm not sure, but I swear his eyes are on me when he thinks I'm unaware. And though we walk close together, I avoid wrapping my arm through his or taking his hand. Testing him. Waiting to see if he initiates the contact…

He doesn't.

And though the beauty of Korčula by night, the moonlight dancing on the water, the glow of the lights on the ancient harbour wall is enough to warm the coldest of souls, I'm not sure he's seeing any of it.

Nadia greets us as we climb back on board and Gabe quickly dismisses her for the evening.

'Shall we take this up to the flybridge?' he says to me when she's gone. 'The breeze is quite mild tonight.'

'Are you trying to get me in that hot tub, Gabe?'

I shouldn't have said it. I shouldn't have and yet the way his eyes flash, the way the muscle works in his jaw... I can't help but feel the thrill of it.

Have I given him the same idea? Injected him with the same thrill?

'If that's what you want to do.'

'So long as you're joining me this time. Hot tubs are nowhere near as much fun alone.'

He doesn't say anything, only leads the way and I'm intrigued by the change in him...or maybe there's no change other than what's going on inside me. Maybe I'm going to land us right back where we were three years ago and I definitely don't want to relive that.

He swipes two glasses from the bar and leads me to the top deck. Tiny flutters start up low in my abdomen. I'm nervous. Why am I nervous? We've been around each other all day, every day since our arrival on this yacht and we've been at ease. Comfortable.

Or at least, I have.

Maybe it's because we're alone, truly alone for the first time. The staff all dismissed. The deck to ourselves. The wine, the cookies, the thoughtful gestures that could so easily be deemed romantic...

He wanted me to experience the delights of the island. Just as he's wanted me to have the most amazing week. How can he believe he is incapable of love when everything he's done comes from that same place? The warmth, the care, the thoughtfulness.

'You've been sporting that pensive look ever since we left the dance.' He sets the box and glasses down on the table, pulls the wine from the bag. 'What's wrong?'

'I'm not pensive.' He cocks a brow. 'Okay, I am, but I'm taking it all in, the day, the week, the things you've done for me...'

I slide onto the cushioned seating that hugs the intimate round table, keep my eyes on the spectacular view that is just as amazing at night. If not more so. It's certainly got the romantic edge.

'I've enjoyed myself too. It's not entirely altruistic.'

'I'm glad.'

He's not enjoyed it in the same way though, because if he had, he would have kissed me back at the dance, he would be kissing me now too.

And I shouldn't want him to. It isn't fair on him. On us. On what this is. A friendly trip together, a break from it all.

But I can't help how I feel, I can't help how my heart feels...

He pours us both a glass and joins me on the sofa. 'Cheers.'

I take up my glass, clink it against his, my cheers as quiet and reflective as I feel but my smile is all for him. I lift the drink to my lips, watch him do the same. He doesn't look away, doesn't blink and under the power of that look my body warms, my limbs soften and I know the warning signs enough to know that I'm as caught up in him as I've ever been.

I'm more than caught up in him. I'm in love with him.

Head over heels, utterly besotted and in love.

In love with a man who claims he can't love anyone.

And yet, he's made me feel that. He's made me feel special and worthy.

A few weeks ago, I would have said I was unlovable. Hell, I told him as much. But in this bubble he's created I've lost sight of that and felt loved. For the first time, in a long, long while. Loved.

No matter his intention, his true feelings beneath the surface...

'Don't you like it?'

I register the grimace on my face. 'No, it's lovely.' I aim to distract. 'How's about that *cukarin*?'

He opens the box, slides it towards me but his concerned expression doesn't lift.

I take out the funny crab-shaped dough and break off a piece, offering him the rest. 'I will if you will.'

I'm flirting because it's what I do when I'm at ease around him and I don't want him to think there's something wrong. I don't want to ruin what's been a perfect day, a perfect week even.

His mouth quirks as he takes it, and together we dip and bite. So in tune with one another, I almost feel like it's him I'm tasting... It's definitely him I'm enjoying. The warmth of his body mere inches away, the intensity of his gaze, the fullness of his mouth, the subtle hint of stubble along his jaw.

'What do you think?' he asks as I swallow and I realise I have no idea.

I hold up a finger. 'Let me try that again.'

He chuckles. 'Any excuse for more sugar.'

It really is rather delicious, the sweet wine softening the biscuit, the flavours merging into a citrus explosion that has the density and satisfaction only a baked good can provide. 'Oh, yes, that's heaven in a bite.'

'I told you.'

'You did.'

I beam at him, alive on the joy and pleasure reflected back at me. 'This really has been one amazing week, Gabe.'

'You sound like it's over already.'

'All good things have to come to an end at some point, I'm just preparing myself.'

He shakes his head, takes another sip of wine. 'How about just living in the moment?'

I laugh. 'Hearing you of all people say that sounds wrong.'

'What can I say, being around you this week, taking a long-overdue break, it's been good for me too.'

'You do have a more relaxed edge to you—less perfection, more rugged male.'

He laughs heartily now. 'I'm not sure how to take that.'

'As a compliment. Definitely a compliment.'

Silence falls, easy yet charged.

Whatever this is between us, it's leaving me tongue-tied, unsure, and neither suits my disposition. It's what has me leaning forward and saying. 'Gabe, if—'

'Avery, I—'

We both stop and I laugh, my cheeks warming with a confession I hadn't even thought through. 'You first.'

'No, you go, I'm nothing if not a gentleman.'

My mouth twists at the corner. 'That you are.'

'So you were saying…'

What was I saying? Something stupid, something foolish, something which would only cross the line and run the risk of ruining this evening, if not this entire stay. 'It was nothing, really, probably just more gratitude.'

I wave a hand, dismissing it away like it's nothing when it's really not.

'I don't need you to be grateful, Ave.'

Ave. I love the way he says it. I love the bond that's led to it. The bond that makes me feel like I do. Cared for. Loved. It makes my heart turn over just that little bit more.

'If I've done as I intended and shown you a good time—not *that* kind of good time but…hell, you know what I mean. Then I'll consider it a job well done.'

'A job?' His words register with a heavy thud. 'I thought I was the one with the "job", not you.'

'It's just a figure of speech.'

'A figure of speech that turns me into a problem in need of fixing, just like my brother, a burden—'

'No, that's not…'

I'm on the defensive attack because isn't that how I saw him, as a project in need of fixing, someone to help? And look where it landed me. In love.

And now what? This trip will come to an end and we'll go our separate ways, only my heart will go with him and I'll be left with…

'Ave!' He moves so fast I have no time to adjust, his thigh pressed up alongside mine, his arm around my back. 'No! That's not what I meant. Ave, I—'

He stops. His face so close, I can smell his cologne mixed up in the wine and biscuit. I can see the ring of gold around his pupils, the flecks of fire in the blue. I don't move for fear he'll break away, don't speak for fear I'll give my heart away.

'I could never see you like that.' His gaze is intense, his desperation for me to believe his words blazing in his depths. 'I will admit I feared your arrival, the risk…the temptation…'

'The temptation,' I repeat, helpless, enthralled, wanting. His eyes dip to my lips as I wet them.

'*Yes.* You *have* to know that.'

'I know I want you, Gabe. I know I've wanted you for a long time and that hasn't changed.'

'But you *can't* want me.'

'I don't have a choice.' I find the courage to lift my hand to his cheek, savour the hard line of his jaw, his stubble, the fact that he doesn't flinch or move away. I rest my thumb beneath his lip and hold him steady as I confess, 'It's as instinctual and innate as my need to breathe.'

'But your brother…he's my best friend, Ave.'

'So? There's no law against it.'

'There is in our world. You know that.'

'Why? Why can't—?'

'I can't lose him.'

'You won't lose him.'

'We do this, I will.'

'He doesn't need to know. We can keep it between us.'

His hand flexes at my back, his eyes hesitate as they search mine, but I can feel the tension, the fight within him and I move closer, raise my nose to nudge his, bring our lips a hair's breadth away. 'Kiss me.'

'I can't, Ave.' He presses me back but doesn't release me. 'I can't risk our friendship for what can only ever be a fling.'

'There's no risk if he doesn't know.'

'He'll find out, somehow.'

'And so what if he does? I'm a grown woman, capable of choosing who I sleep with. It has nothing to do with him. Nothing at all.'

'It does if I hurt you.'

'Who said anything about getting hurt?'

He stares back at me, quiet.

'I won't beg you, Gabe. I won't be the vulnerable woman I was three years ago. If you don't want me, tell me now and we can end this and move on, no hurt feelings, no resentment, no anything.'

'You don't know what you're asking.'

'That's where you're wrong. You've spent this past week convincing me of my own worth, convincing me to continue on the path of my choosing, to ignore the naysayers and the doubters and go after what I want. Don't ruin it all now by becoming one of them.'

'You're twisting my words.'

'Bending them, perhaps, but their essence remains. I want you. Right here. Right now. And I'm owning that.'

'And what about after? What about us, Ave?' He strokes a hand through my hair. 'Are you saying we could just move on like it never happened?'

I swallow the lie I can't give. Because I know things will never be the same, but the truth is this trip has changed me for ever. I'm in love with him and that's what makes it right. That's what makes it okay. Because I can't imagine giving my virginity to anyone else, and though he may not return that love, the making of it could never be deemed a mistake. Or a regret.

Even if I can't spell it out to him, I know it in my heart and I'll make sure we're okay.

'I'm not asking you for for ever, Gabe. I'm not asking you for what you cannot give...' *love* '... I'm asking you for now. I'm asking you to live in the moment just as you have me and tomorrow, we'll be just the same.'

Because I'll still love him just as I do now.

'Will we? Because I won't turn this into a relationship, Ave. I don't—'

I press a finger to his lips, smile into his eyes. 'I know.'

Because I do know. I know him better than he likely knows himself.

CHAPTER ELEVEN

Gabe

IT'S ONE NIGHT. No broken promises. No change to the future.

A chance to sate this need that's been driving me crazy, her too…

And then what?

Can we truly go about life as normal? Forget about it and move on?

No, not forget about it. Never forget about it. But to know her, to know how it feels to be…

'Gabe.' She strokes her hand through my hair, her green eyes blazing and pleading. 'Stop thinking.'

I make a sound that I don't recognise—a tortured groan, a desperate growl—and then I'm kissing her like my life, my sanity depends on it. Because it does. I swear. Kissing her with all the desperation that has been three years in the making. Three years of being haunted by that night, the want in her eyes, the depths of passion only she has ever truly stirred.

We can have this. She's right. She's old enough to make her own decisions, to deal with the consequences. To deal with Aiden or not. He doesn't need to know. And if he does, we'll deal, we have to. Because I can't stop this now. I can't.

I squeeze my eyes shut against the vision in my mind's eye. The look of thunder on my friend's face. Like it can somehow rid me of the guilt, my conscience. I hate my own weakness. But I desire her more.

I kiss her deeper. Drown him out with the taste of her, the feel of her, the sounds she's making…tiny whimpers as she opens up to me. Her lips parting to the pressure of my mouth. Her tongue, dainty and tentative, twisting with my own.

'Gabe.' She claws at my hair, tugs me closer. 'I want you'

Another crazed growl as her whispered words send fire through my veins, tightening up my core. She shifts over me, pressing me back into the sofa as she straddles my hips, caresses my groin through the fabric of our clothing and pushes me to the brink. Losing my cool like some inexperienced teen, but right now, I feel just like that. The intensity is unlike anything I've ever known.

But then, this is Avery, the one woman with the power to break me. Haven't I always known that deep down, run from it even?

Was I really so afraid of losing Aiden or losing my control?

Both I'd wager, and the thought streaks through my brain, bringing enough lucidity to know that this isn't the place.

I tear my mouth from hers, rasp out, 'Not here.'

The flybridge is hardly private when we're sitting in port, the fort wall towering over us with its many visitors taking a late-night stroll.

'Come.' I'm on my feet, my hand in hers and I can't look at her with the continuing fight under way inside. I lead her to my cabin, praying we don't meet a soul and wishing for it all the same. Someone to save me from this madness.

She sweeps in front of me, kisses me as she continues backwards dragging me with her. It's like she can sense my hesitation, my doubt and she's forcing it out, her hunger driving out the cold and feeding my own.

We reach my cabin and I spin into her, kiss unbreaking as

I force her back against the door to close it. Her fingers are in my shirt, fumbling over the buttons and I take over, tear it from my body and toss it aside.

'I'm sure you broke a button or two,' she murmurs against my lips.

'I'll buy another.'

I tug her top up and she raises her arms to let me strip it from her. I trap her hands above her head, hold her wrists in one palm as I take her in, stretched out before me. Temptation of the highest order.

I trail my free hand down her arm, her neck... Her skin is like silk. Soft and warm and prickling under my caress.

'Gabe?' She wriggles.

Her breasts heave, the red lace of her bra delightfully sinful, the flush to her skin, her cheeks, her chest all the more so.

'You are too hot for words, Ave.'

'Says you.'

I shake my head. She's on another level to me. How can she not see it? How can she not see she deserves better than me? I don't know, but I swear she doesn't. Just as she doubted her own worth, the love of her own family, she doubts my words now. And I won't stand for it. She needs to see how perfect she is, how wonderful and exquisite.

I cup her breast, feel the heat of her skin through the lace, watch her eyes as I stroke my thumb over the hardened peak and her responsive whimper pulses right through me.

'So hot...'

She nips her lip and I keep up the caress, dip to tug her earlobe between my teeth, feel her body writhe as she struggles to take a breath.

'Please, Gabe, don't tease me.'

'I'm not teasing you,' I say against her ear.

'I want you,' she breathes.

'And I want you... I want you ready for me.'

'I am.'

I lean back, look down at her. 'You will be.'

It's a promise and she knows it, her eyes flaring up at me.

'Good sex shouldn't be rushed, Ave.' I reach around her back, unhook her bra and grit my teeth as her breasts spill free. Their taut peaks, peach against cream, pointing up as she arches back, pleading for my touch.

'What other kind is there?'

Fire licks through my veins. So all sex is good sex. Has she been that lucky before?

I clench my jaw against the thought. I've hardly been a monk. How can I condemn the men that have come before me? But the idea of anyone else having her, of anyone else touching her... I want to obliterate every other man from her mind and her body. Make her mine.

And I know how dangerous that sounds, but I can't stop the force that's driving me...even if I don't understand it.

Avery

I wince at my naivety. What a foolish thing to say.

But it hasn't stopped him. If anything, it's pushed him on, goaded him. Like a man possessed, he growls and kisses me deeply, releasing my wrists to grip my thighs and draw them up around his hips. His hot, hard body crushing me to the door.

'Yes,' I cry out as he rocks against the aching heart of me. The lace of my thong and strip of my skirt no hindrance to the delicious friction he delivers.

And then it hits me, this is jealousy. He's jealous of the others he believes I've had.

Somewhere my head is telling me to be honest with him, to tell him of my innocence, but the fear that he will put a stop to this—no, the knowledge that he'll put a stop to it—keeps the confession trapped inside and I cling to him as he traces kisses down my throat, my front, the curve of my breast...

'Don't stop, Gabe, please don't stop.' My words express my deepest fear as he hooks his fingers into my skirt, shimmies it down my thighs, his kisses travelling with him, and then his tongue is caressing me through the lace of my thong and a telling shiver ripples through me. I curl my toes into the floor, tighten up my limbs. He's taking me to the brink and he hasn't so much as touched me fully.

No one has ever coaxed me to this point, no one but myself and to feel it at the hands of another, their mouth even, my eyes roll back, my head too.

'You feel incredible, taste incredible,' he groans over me, the movement of his mouth a caress upon my heated flesh. 'The idea of any other man...'

I don't know whether he knows what he's saying. Whether he's so caught up in sensation that the words are falling from his lips unbidden, but I find myself confessing, 'I don't want any other man, only you.' This is why I know this is meant to be, why I've been destined to reach this point with him. 'It's always been you.'

It's the raw honest truth and he's on his feet, claiming my lips before I can take another breath. I wonder at his force, his desperation. Was it my confession? My truth? Or his jealousy? Is he trying to bury his own fears? His own regrets?

'Heaven help me.' He breaks away, presses his forehead to mine, our ragged breaths in tune as he palms my cheeks. 'I want you too.'

'Then take me.' I hold his gaze with all the confidence I possess that this is right, that this is what's meant to be, that he should be my first. That no one else could ever compare.

He carries me to the bed and moves away. I shoot up on

my palms, suddenly alone, vulnerable, panicked by his quick departure. 'Where are you going?'

'To get protection.'

I flop back with relief, stare up at the ceiling in wonder. This is really happening. Me and Gabe. Gabe and me. I circle my belly button, feel the chaos just beneath, the heat, the dull ache and coiling tension that I trust him to coax and placate, my inexperience that I trust him to take.

Doesn't mean you can keep him, though...

My fingers still. 'No,' I whisper, that's not what this is but... I look to the door that he disappeared through, prop myself up on one elbow.

What if things are different now?

Three years ago, he broke our kiss and I walked away broken.

But he didn't know me like he does now. We didn't know each other like we do now. And he isn't stopping. This doesn't have to end the same way... It doesn't.

Things are different. Aren't they?

If you truly believe that then tell him the truth...see what he does.

I bite my cheek, the confession catching in my throat as he appears in the doorway, a foil packet in hand.

'Any second thoughts, now is the time, Ave?'

Gabe

She shakes her head, her 'Never...' a quiet whisper and a rush of something rises up within me. I tell myself it's desire. I know desire. I understand it. And I want her. It pumps thick and fast through my veins as I stalk towards her, her body outstretched and waiting for me, nothing but red lace to protect her modesty. So why do I feel like I'm walking into the gates of hell? Succumbing to my greatest desire? About to make a huge mistake and wanting it anyway?

'Are you just going to stand there and ogle…?'

Her eyes are laughing but her chest and cheeks are full of colour, her nipples forming tight little peaks as she presses her thighs together and twists into the sheets.

'You always were so impatient.'

'And you were always so careful and considered.'

'And look at me now…'

Breaking my own rules, doing the unthinkable. I should have put a stop to this before we'd gone too far. But it's too late now. I'm a man not a saint. And right now, she's not Aiden's sister, she's an independent woman and she's mine—for tonight at least. My heart swells, my body heats and I drop to the bed beside her.

I pull her to me and kiss her until the thoughts empty out and all I can hear are her panted moans, my own rasping breaths. I can't get enough of kissing her, of feeling her every curve, her warm inviting body moulded to my own. Her hands are on my belt buckle, looping it free, my fly descends next and I kick my trousers free… There is no stopping this.

I stroke her over her thong, feel her need through the fabric. She's ready, so ready and I want to be there, surrounded by her heat, her wetness…to know how perfectly we fit together.

'Please, Gabe, please.' Her nails dig into my back, the rocking of her lower body as she seeks to deepen my caress telling me she's almost there. Almost.

'Please. Please,' she pants, and I slip beneath the fabric, tease her, stroke her under the pad of my thumb as my fingers sink in deeper. She jerks against me, her breaths shorten, her nails break the skin and then she shatters, her body wracking beneath mine, her pleasure everything.

She sags beneath me, her eyes wide, her surprise taking

me by surprise. I want to question it. I want to understand the depth of her reaction, but I can't find my voice.

'I want you,' she whispers.

'I know,' I manage, shoving away my briefs and realising that this is different. Different for her as much as it is for me. The bond we share. The bond that ultimately makes it right, even if it comes with such risk.

The thought undoes me, exposes me, leaves me vulnerable.

But we've called it. One night. No more.

And her brother will never learn of it.

She'll never tell and neither will I.

And if he learns of it…it's a bridge we'll have to cross.

'I want only you, Gabe.'

Hearing her say it, the husky plea, the big green eyes that blink up at me… I curse. I could get addicted to that look, crave that look…

One night only, Gabe. Stick to your rules.

But my rules and the Monroes don't mix well. They never have. They're also all I have.

I shake my head, feel my fingers tremble as I tear open the condom packet, take a steadying breath.

'Are you sure, Ave?'

She combs her fingers into my hair, hooks her legs around my hips, telling me without words what she wants, what she needs…and she's driving me to the edge as she does it. My control slipping through my fingers as I sheath myself. I know the line we're crossing can't be uncrossed, I know what we're doing, who I'm betraying, but there's no holding back the tide.

I lean forward, kiss her as I smooth my hand down her front, caress her until she's crying out my name again and then I shift my hips, close my eyes as the pleasure threatens to consume me and sink within her, sink within her and freeze. She's so still, her cry more pain than pleasure. And through the haze I register the resistance, the tightness…

No!

My eyes flare open with a curse. Her face is pale, her eyes and mouth are clamped shut. Sweat like a sheen across her skin.

'Ave?' I say through gritted teeth, panic setting my blood cold. 'Please don't…don't tell me…don't…'

But the evidence is there, I can feel the truth of it, the lining, the innocence…

No! God, no!

'Ave! Look at me.'

Slowly she does as I ask and the tears I witness crush my soul. She can't be. I can't have…

'Ave, tell me you're not. Please, tell me you're not.'

She shakes her head, one tear spilling free.

'Ave!'

'I can't.'

Goosebumps spread like an icy wash across my skin and I try to pull back but she's locked around me tight. Her green eyes flash with pain, with panic. 'Don't, Gabe, please don't. It's okay, please, it's okay.'

'It's not okay, Ave. It's *not*.' I pulse within her, the reminder that we're still locked together, so close and yet a gulf has opened up between us. A gaping great abyss that makes my gut roll. 'You *should* have told me.'

'You didn't ask.'

'Why would I ask? Why would I *think* to question it?'

She clings to me, pale cheeks wet with tears. 'Because you told me you didn't believe the gossip, everything you'd read, everything you'd heard.'

'But all those men, all those rumours…'

'Rumours, Gabe, all rumours.'

I curse. How could I be such a fool? Such a hypocritical, prejudiced fool?

I stare down into her wide green eyes—vulnerable and trusting and tainted with fear. Fear that I will walk away, abandon her, like this. There is no way. The pain I would inflict, the pain and the regret. Three years ago, I almost lost her entirely, her and her brother. But this...this is so much worse.

'Please, Gabe. I want it to be you. Don't leave me. You can't. Not like this.'

My lower body is disconnected from my brain, shifting with her as she urges me back but my head is screaming at me. My heart too.

This wasn't the deal, this wasn't...

'Gabe,' she whispers, her mouth brushing softly against mine. 'Please, I want it to be you.'

'There really is no going back from this, Ave.'

'I don't want to go back.' There's a spark behind her eyes now, a flash of courage. The Avery I have come to know, come to know and... I swallow to dislodge the lump in my throat. 'I want to move forward knowing what it's like, what this is like, with you. Gift me that memory, Gabe. Please. Three years ago, you told me I could do better when it came to the men I dated. Show me what better feels like, show me what I've been missing out on, be the one...'

That night comes back to me in full technicolour. How experienced I thought she was. How jealous I had been. How wrong could I be?

Untouched. A virgin!

Not any more, thanks to you.

'Gabe, I'm not asking you for more, but I am asking for this. I trust you with this.'

I ease my body over her, my words desperate and soft. 'You should have told me.'

'I know and I'm sorry.'

She strokes my hair back from my face, her apology written in the fresh tears that glisten in her gaze. But this is my fault too—my own prejudice, the assumption that *I* made.

'Please.' Her legs pulse around me. 'Don't leave me like this.'

I swallow the curse that wants to leave my lips, drown out the angel on my shoulder telling me I've ruined her, and listen to the devil, the one that says give her this night, this one and only night and make sure she measures everyone against you in the future.

Be the man who sets the bar so high, it can only take a good man in return, the right man to take her there again.

Make sure her first time is something she never regrets.

'Please, Gabe.'

I shift slowly, my body straining for release as I seek to ease her discomfort, all the while I can feel something inside me creaking open, something deep that was once contained. A part of me I've always ignored but not any more.

She pulls my head to her, tries to kiss me but I can't. It's taking everything I have to give her this without giving away that part of myself. I lower my hand between us, caress her as I sink deeper within her, her body tense as it takes my length, adjusts to my size.

'That's it, Ave, relax, let me in.'

She nods, moves with me and I cherish the colour returning to her cheeks, her panted breaths and escalating moans… my body riding higher with her every response.

'That's it, sweetheart, let go, let go with me.'

Her eyes are locked in mine, her lips a parted haven that I dare not dip to taste, and when she cries out my name, her head thrown back, her legs crushing me to her, I'm gone. My release robbing me of all control as I shudder and let go. My mind, my soul, my…no, not my heart. Never my heart. But I can feel it…beating warm in my chest. The thud deep and visceral and getting louder at the sight of her, the feel of her around me…

I drop to my back and pull her into my side. Stare at the ceiling though I know her eyes are on me, questioning me, but I'm too busy questioning myself. Hating myself.

Avery

I feel the mood change, the chill that seeps between us. He's unmoving beside me but I know it's only a matter of minutes before he ups and leaves. Sanity has already crept in and now he'll be hating me for my secrecy.

You should leave before he does. Be the strong one. Show him it's okay. You're not broken this time.

I go to look at him, but his hand is there, encouraging me back down. He presses his lips to my hair. 'You should sleep. It's late.'

There's a strange edge to his voice, an edge that I don't recognise and instantly hate.

Just as much as I hate myself.

Is that the power of sex? To go from such an amazing, almighty high. To this. Regret. Ice-cold regret. And we promised we wouldn't. There was to be none of that.

But then, we don't get a say in how we feel, just as we don't get a say in who we fall in love with. And I love him just as much as I regret this. Not the sex. Not the loss of my virginity. But this, the aftermath. And now I have to make it right. Somehow.

I press away from him, plant my feet into the rug, feel some semblance of normality in the reassuring solidity of the ground.

'Where are you going?'

'I should shower.'

Shower. Clean away the remnants so he doesn't have to face the reminder.

'Did I—did I hurt you?' He's up on his side, his hand on my back and I flinch away, because I crave that touch, I want to fall into that touch and know I can't. 'Of course, I did.'

'You didn't hurt me. Not intentionally. You could never—'

I can't even finish that sentence because my heart is breaking in two and my voice cracks with it. He didn't intend for this to happen. And neither did I.

I get to my feet, smothering the wince my body urges me to give. Hell, I'm sore, but not as sore as my heart. I feel his eyes follow me to the door, fight the urge to turn and beg him for more. To break the deal we made. I need to show him that I meant what I said. I need to show him that I'm capable of walking away without a backward glance. That nothing has changed. Even if it's killing me to do so.

I take a shower, find what I need in the well-stocked cupboards and dress in the robe hanging on the back of the door. For the briefest moment, I breathe in his familiar scent on the fabric, cherish its softness against my skin and then step out.

He's gone.

Not only that but all trace of 'us' has gone with him. The bed has been freshly made, the old linen stripped, the new untouched. Where is he?

And what do I do? Am I supposed to stay here, or go back to my room? Which proves to him that I'm okay more?

My legs decide for me. They feel like jelly and I don't have the strength to wander the yacht looking for him, especially when I have no idea what I'll find, which Gabe I will find.

Instead, I sink into the sheets, close my eyes and hope that sleep will claim me.

Sleep and a returning Gabe. And then everything will be okay.

No matter how fanciful I know that is…

CHAPTER TWELVE

Gabe

THE SUN IS on the rise and I wish it away. Wish the night away like I somehow have the power. Wish myself away like she had the night before. She couldn't even bear to look at me as she walked away.

And I'd done what I could to make sure that when she returned, the evidence would be gone. Cleared away the mess. Left the room immaculate for her.

Hoping it would somehow help her sleep while I came up top and poured myself a whisky. I barely touched it though, my head already fit to crack with the headache of it all.

I'm a monster. A complete and utter monster. Taking her innocence when I know I can't give her a future. Oh, she hadn't asked for one, of course she hadn't. She knew better. But hell... I growl, rake my fingers through my hair, grip my skull as I stare at the glossy white deck. What do I do now?

'Morning, Mr Curran, I wasn't expecting to see you so early.' Nadia's bare feet appear beside me from nowhere, her morning voice enough to make my head pound. 'Can I get you a coffee?'

'Please,' I say to the floor, my voice unrecognisably gruff.

She disappears and I pick up my phone. Almost six. I think of Aiden. I think of Aiden entrusting me with Avery. I think of Aiden and the painful secret he's keeping from her, that I'm keeping too. It makes everything so much worse and the guilt is eating me up inside. It's bad enough that she couldn't get away from me fast enough last night. That in all likelihood she'll want off this yacht and to return home immediately. But going home means learning the truth and for that I need Aiden on board.

On board and treating her like she deserves to be treated. Like the adult that she is and not some vulnerable child incapable of dealing with the harsh reality of life.

A reality you just made a whole lot worse.

I curse and dial his number. The phone barely rings before it connects. 'Curran, is everything okay?'

'In a sense.'

And what sense would that be?

'It must be the crack of dawn over there, what's going on?'

'You need to tell Avery the truth. I can't keep it from her any longer.'

'We've already been through this.'

'And it's wrong, she needs to know. I don't care how you do it, whether you come here, or she comes home, so long as you do it face to face, but it's not fair to keep it from her.'

'It's not about keeping it from her, it's about protecting her.'

'She doesn't need protecting, not like this.'

'How can you say that, knowing her past?'

'Because it's the past. She was a kid, Aiden. She's not any more.'

'She's still in therapy.'

I think of the pills too, her depression, and what Aiden does or doesn't know but I'm not about to enlighten him. 'She's in therapy because it helps her. She hasn't quit and run away from how she feels. She's dealing with it. You should be proud of her, not using it as a reason to wrap her up in cotton wool and infantilise her.'

'I *am* proud of her.'

And he is, I can hear it in his voice. If only Ave could see that too. Believe it, even.

'We just worry. Mum worries and she hasn't the strength for it.'

'But she's not a child any more, Aiden, and you need to stop treating her like one.'

'And since when have you cared so much?'

Since she cracked me open and messed with my head.

Your heart, you mean.

'I've always cared,' I say over the frustrating inner voice. 'She's your sister.'

'That's right, she's *my* sister and I know what's best for her.'

'In this case, you're wrong and if you won't tell her, I will.'

'You can't. Seriously, man.' He curses. 'Gabe, I don't have time for this right now.'

'Make time.'

'That sounds like a threat…' I can hear the strained laughter in his voice. 'Are you threatening me?'

'She deserves to know, Aiden. Hell, what if the worst happens and she finds out too late?'

'That isn't going to happen.'

'You can't know that for sure. Your mother's chances of surviving the next year are slim enough as it is…'

'Thanks for your optimism, mate.'

'I'm trying to point out what she stands to lose. You think knowing now is bad, think—'

'The treatment is experimental but encouraging. They're making progress all the time, changing the odds.'

'It doesn't change the favour of those odds!' I wince, hating that I have to say it. 'Look, I love you like my brother. My mother is gone, I don't get to fix my relationship with her, I never had one. Don't run the risk of her doing the same.'

'Avery doesn't need to fix their relationship.'

'That's not what she thinks.'

'What are you talking about? Mum loves her, I love her, we're family.'

'Then treat her like she's a part of that family, because she doesn't feel like it right now.'

'Look, when she walked away from the family business, I admit, I said some things, did some things I regret. But we're still a family. I may not like the career she's chosen—'

'Don't get me started on that.'

'What? The jewellery?'

'Have you seen her work? What she's capable of?'

'But it's jewellery, Gabe. You know how many designers there are in the world?'

'You know how many fund managers there are in the world?'

'But it's not a serious career.'

'Who says it isn't?'

'She's clever, Gabe, she'll go far in finance, make a mint.'

'She'll go far with her jewellery and make money there.'

He scoffs. 'It's not the same.'

'No, it's not Monroe Wealth Management and that's where your problem lies, Aiden. Because if you saw what she's capable of, actually took time to look at what she's created with her own bare hands, we wouldn't be having this argument now.'

He doesn't answer.

'Look, we took on the roles destined for us from birth, and they've served us well, but don't force that choice on her just

'I've hardly forced her.'

'You took away her financial support.'

'And look where that got us.'

'I don't know. I think she's done all right with it, more than all right and you know it.'

He's quiet again and I'm hoping it's because I'm getting through to him. 'Take a look at her work, Aiden, a real look. She has a talent that you should be encouraging, not dismissing. Especially when it makes her happy.'

A heavy breath, then, 'That's all we want at the end of the day, for her to be happy.'

'Then give her the respect she deserves and bring her back into the family fold, trust her with the truth and trust her with her dreams too.'

Movement behind me makes me turn, a polite smile in place to thank Nadia for my coffee but it freezes midway. It isn't Nadia. 'Ave...'

'The truth?' Avery stares back at me, face pale beneath her tan, her arms hugging my robe around her middle. 'And what exactly is the truth, Gabe?'

Avery

I shiver. I'm sore in places I don't recognise and it's all his fault. No, not his fault. Not entirely. I was as much a part of what happened last night as he was.

But I'm angry. I'm angry that he didn't come back to bed. I'm angry that he's complicit in this secret of my brother's. I'm angry that I've fallen in love with him knowing full well he can't love me back. Just angry.

'I have to go.' Gabe's already lowering the phone. His expression would be comical if it weren't for the fact that my presence is the cause.

My brother says something down the phone, his muffled voice reaching across the way, but Gabe cuts him off, his eyes fixed on me. 'How are you feeling?'

Like you care.

'Fine.' I'm not and he knows it. 'Care to tell me what's going on?'

'How much did you hear?'

'Enough.'

'How much is—?'

'I know you were talking about me and whatever it is that my family are keeping from me.'

He gets to his feet and Nadia appears, a fresh coffee in hand. 'Ms Monroe, I didn't realise you were awake. You're both early risers this morning.'

Her smile dies in the strained atmosphere and I press my lips together, take a steadying breath through my nose. 'Could I get one of those, please?'

'Of course.'

She places Gabe's drink down on the table before him, the same table we enjoyed wine and *cukarin* at the night before. I stare at where they would have been, unable to believe that was only a few hours ago and how different things feel now.

So much for everything staying just the same...

'Do you want to sit down?' he says, once Nadia has left.

'No. I want you to tell me what's going on.'

'I told you it's not my place.'

'But you think I should be told.'

'Yes. I don't think it's right that something so—something so important should be kept from you.'

'How noble of you.'

'Please, Ave. Don't—don't be like that.'

'How else should I behave, Gabe? You abandoned me last night as though what we shared meant nothing and I wake up this morning to find you already on the phone to my brother. What was it, your guilty conscience? Or did he ring you?'

He visibly pales under my assault but I'm done playing nice. Done playing tolerant. I want answers and I want them now.

'I phoned him. I—I figured you'd want to return home as soon as possible.'

'Did you now…?' I shake my head, stare off into the middle distance. So now he wants rid of me. I shouldn't be surprised. I certainly shouldn't let it sting like it does.

'About last night, Ave…'

My head snaps around, my eyes spear his. 'You really want to go there?'

'I think we should at least talk about it.'

'Last night was a mistake,' I say, giving him what he wants to hear. 'You know it and I know it. There's nothing more to say on the matter.'

He stares back at me, his eyes unreadable, the pulse in his jaw working overtime. 'Why didn't you tell me before things went too far?'

'We've already gone over that.'

'You *should* have told me.'

'*You* didn't ask.'

'Because it didn't even occur to me that you would be—be—'

'A virgin. You can't even say it, can you? Is the thought so repulsive to you?'

His throat bobs. 'That's not—I've never, not ever, not when—' He rakes a hand through his already tousled hair, his eyes wild. 'I make it my business not to sleep with inexperienced women, Avery.'

My cheeks burn, shame a heat I cannot douse. And I'm Avery now, not Ave. Could he stick the knife in any deeper?

'Wow, the female population thanks you for your humble consideration.'

'This is coming out all wrong.'

'You're telling me.'

'If I'd known I'd never have—I could have taken my time, been more gentle, looked after your needs, your—'

My laugh is harsh in the face of his sudden compassion. 'Oh, really? Or would you just have come to your senses sooner and brought an end to it?'

The lines around his eyes deepen, the shadows just beneath appearing like bruises under the glow from the rising sun. It's a glorious morning, set to be another glorious day on the surface but its warmth fails to reach me.

'Yeah, I thought as much. You would have rejected me just as you did three years ago, my innocence condemning me. Too young. Too naive. Too innocent. Aiden's little sister through and through.'

'That was different. You know that was different. After the week we've had and last night, you and me, what we shared...' He shakes his head. 'I knew who you were and I made love to you anyway.'

Something about the way he says it, *what* he says, tugs at my brow. 'What are you saying?'

'Damned if I know!' He throws his hands in the air, starts to pace the deck, exasperation a frenetic energy around him. 'You just should have told me!'

'I know!'

He spins to face me and I clamp my mouth shut. His stance is foreboding, his gaze too. 'A man has a right to know that kind of detail before he gets into bed with a woman.'

My gut twists. 'I know,' I say, softer now. Because I know he's right on that score and I swallow, lift my chin to say, 'And I'm sorry.'

He stares back at me, the distance between us a couple of metres at most and yet it feels like miles. He looks sick, harrowed, the agony of what he believes he's done to me eating him alive and I can't bear it.

'It's too late for sorry when the damage has already been done.'

'The *damage*? Gabe, it's a hymen, okay! A tiny little membrane that is no more so get over yourself.'

His head jerks as though I've slapped him but I'm not taking it back. I'm hurt, angry, humiliated. I don't want to regret what happened between us but if he carries on like this…

'Women give their virginity away all the time, it doesn't make it special, it doesn't mean they're in love. It doesn't have to mean anything more than a bit of fun. It was sex, Gabe, between two consenting adults. *Just* sex.'

My stomach rolls with every word, my heart sinking deeper in my chest. I don't even know where the words are coming from. I just need him to know that it doesn't matter. None of it does. I don't have any expectations of him, any hope, I just want off this yacht, out of this country and his condescending radar.

Condescending—are you confusing him with Aiden now?

I shake off the thought. What does it matter? The longer I stay here for, the longer this goes on and I can't bear it.

'If you can make the arrangements, I'll be out of your hair just as soon as transport permits.'

I turn to leave but he's upon me, his hand on my arm forcing me to pause. 'Ave.'

Ave. I close my eyes and breathe, press his hand and the emotion away. 'What?'

'I'm sorry, too.' I open my eyes to take in his above me, so wide and confused, tormented and ablaze. 'I'm sorry you wasted something so precious on me. I had no right to take it.'

I blink up at him. Wasted it? *Wasted* it? No *right*?

How wrong can he be? My thoughts choke up my throat. I could never see it as a waste giving it to the man I love but I can't tell him that. And oh, how it hurts, my heart shattering into a thousand tiny pieces.

I shake my head, words failing me, and run, run so fast, so blinded by tears that I don't see a returning Nadia. I collide with her, hot coffee sloshing over us both but I don't even feel the sting of it. 'I'm so sorry, Nadia. I'm so sorry.'

And I race before the tears can fall. It's one thing for me to know my own heartbreak but for others to witness it, for Gabe to witness it…no, just no.

CHAPTER THIRTEEN

Gabe

SHE'S BEEN GONE three weeks. Three weeks and it feels like another three years.

Only this time it's worse. Much worse. Because not only do I miss her, I feel like a part of me left with her. It's the only way I can explain it.

The castle feels too vast without her presence, too empty. The staff have all returned and yet it feels quieter than ever. I've been driving myself crazy in the same four walls. Chasing Aiden for updates, wanting to call her and knowing I'm not welcome. Reliving every moment we spent together and wishing I could go back. Recalling her insightful words with regards to my family, my history, and knowing that she's right.

It's the reason I'm here now, staring at the door before me. A door that's aged with time and steeped in history. My history.

I swallow. I've come this far, I can't back away now. But the uncertainty of what will greet me, who will greet me, renders me immobile.

A young lad runs past shouting in Croatian at me, a small dog yapping at his heels, and I realise how ridiculous I look. Ridiculous and dodgy.

Be a man, for goodness' sake. Be the man Avery thought you were.

I step forward and knock.

No running now. No changing your mind. You're here and you're doing this.

It's as though she's beside me, egging me on. I can almost feel her hand in mine, my palm tingling with the imagined contact as the ancient door creaks open and a weathered face peers around it. Wise blue eyes squint up at me, paper-like skin crinkling at the corners and then she gasps, hands flying to her cheeks.

'Gabriel?'

Grandmother?

'Baka?'

'Da... Da!' Her eyes well up as she swings the door open wide and steps forward, reaches up to grasp my arms. 'It is you.'

'Yes.'

She shakes her head, her wispy grey hair escaping her bun as she ushers me inside. 'Come. Come.'

She leads me to the back of the house, constantly checking over her shoulder as though she can't believe it, her little frame travelling faster than I would have thought possible. Furniture fills the hallway, dark wood that looks like it's been here for ever, clean but well-loved. The walls are filled with photos—black and white through to colour, portraits and reportage snaps and then I see one that makes me pause. Pause and forget to breathe. It's my mother. My mother and a little boy, a toddler...*me.*

I lean closer, take in her smile that's full of love for the boy I was, the arms that are wrapped around me, the smile I give in turn.

A hand touches my arm, my heart pulses in my chest.

'Come,' my grandmother says softly, her smile both sad and warm.

There's a scent in the air that's growing stronger. A scent I vaguely recognise from my childhood. Something my mother used to cook. It has the strangest power over me, a sense of calm, of comfort, of...home.

The sound of voices grows until we are upon them, fourteen—no, sixteen people from a baby through to a man who must be my grandfather, all sitting around the kitchen table. They all go quiet when they see me. Mouths hanging open, food forgotten.

'Vidi, vidi!' My grandmother claps her hands together, her smile wide as she beams up at me. 'Gabriel, *vratio se kući*!'

Gabriel, he's come home...

Avery

'How are you feeling, Mum?'

'I'd feel a lot better if you and Aiden would stop fussing.'

'Tough.' I smile. 'The doctor said you needed to rest up so quit complaining and accept it.'

She shakes her head. 'I knew telling you was a bad idea.'

'Say that again and I'll make sure you get nothing but gruel for dinner.'

'I don't think gruel is in Chef Leo's repertoire.'

'Still not funny, Mum.'

'I know. I'm sorry.' She reaches for my hand, pulls me in to sit on the edge of her bed. The curtains are drawn, the light from the bedside lamp highlighting her hollow cheekbones, the thinness to her skin, but her green eyes shine with such vibrancy.

'You do know that, don't you, darling? We never should have kept it from you. But after your father... I didn't want you reliving it. The idea that my diagnosis…' She swallows, her lashes fluttering over eyes that show her pain, her worry but not over herself, over me. 'That it would set you back to those days. Living in fear that one day a police officer would come knocking on our door. I couldn't bear it.'

'I know, Mum, I know, and I'm sorry I put you and Aiden through all that, but I've been getting the help I need for a long time now. Those days are behind me, I promise.'

She searches my gaze and I see the love there, the love and the admiration. 'I know, love. I only wish I'd seen it sooner.'

'I guess I wasn't really home enough for you to see it for yourself.'

'And that's our fault too.'

'No, Mum. It isn't. I'm glad Aiden did what he did. It forced me to grow up and work hard for what I wanted.'

'But you will be home more often now, won't you?'

'While you're going through this, I'll be here. I can study remotely and go back for my exams. You'll have a hard time getting rid of me.'

She chuckles softly. 'Music to my ears.'

I look at our fingers entwined and the rings she still wears from Dad, feel his absence with a sense of sorrow but also pride. Pride at the man he was, gratitude that he was a good man, a loving man, one who set an example worth following.

'You've grown up to be a beautiful, talented young woman, Avery. Your father would be so proud. *I'm* so proud.'

Her words are a salve to an ancient wound and tears catch in my voice. 'Thank you, Mum.'

She gives me a watery smile. 'And to be honest, knowing you're here to keep tabs on that brother of yours is a weight off my mind too. He's taken on too much. What with me and the business and he's showing no sign of settling down. It isn't right at his age.'

I laugh softly. 'You'd be surprised, bachelorism is all the rage these days.'

She wrinkles her nose. 'It's not right. Both him and Gabriel. They're good men. Kind. They need a woman to soften up those tough exteriors, give them something more to live for than their work.'

Gabriel. I bite my cheek as my entire body contracts over the mere mention of him.

'You okay, darling?' Mum's astute gaze narrows. 'You do this little thing every time his name crops up.'

'Whose?'

'Don't act all coy, you know very well who I'm talking about.'

'I'm absolutely fine.'

She nods but I can sense the cogs still turning in her brain. 'Do me a favour, darling?'

'Anything.' So long as she isn't about to bring up the state of *my* love life.

'Go and fetch your portfolio again. I'd like to take another look through it.'

'Mum, you've seen it a thousand times over.'

'And I can enjoy it a thousand more. There's a reason diamonds are a girl's best friend. And when they're designed by your daughter, they're even more exquisite, especially with all those little creatures.'

I laugh. 'Okay, Mum, flattery will get you everywhere.'

'Oh, and can you pass me my phone on your way out? I promised I would message Great-Aunt Joan back.'

'I still can't believe you and Great-Aunt Joan are texting.'

'Yes, darling, she's ninety but she's not inept.'

I shake my head, pass her the phone and head across the hall to my room and the portfolio she's requested. I may not have Gabe but I do have my family. I do have their love and their support and I have him to thank for that, in part. From his rejection to his encouragement, his pressure on my brother to see me for who I am, his insight into my brother's own demons, which between us we have put to bed, and his ability to see me, truly see me.

All isn't lost, even if, right now without him, I feel like a part of me is missing. A whopping great big Gabe-shaped chunk.

I take up my portfolio and head back onto the landing, and that's when I hear it...or rather *him*!

His voice travelling up from the entrance hall of our Toronto home. Not that it can be him. He's still in Croatia, Aiden told me as much.

It's just my mind playing tricks on me. It's not enough that I have to dream about him every night, I have to conjure him up by day too. It'll be Mum's fault for mentioning his name.

Like you weren't thinking of him anyway...

I pick up my stride. The sooner I get this to Mum, the sooner I can stick my earbuds in and drown out his voice with—

'What do you mean you're here to see Avery?'

I freeze. That's my brother.

'I'll explain as soon as—'

I lean over the banister just as he looks up. 'Gabe!'

The portfolio slips in my grasp and I clutch it tighter. 'What are you...?'

I'm barely aware of my brother eyeing us both, I'm too caught up in my first sight of Gabe in weeks. His hair is longer, his stubble too and my mouth is drier than the Sahara. How dare the man let himself go and look all the hotter for it?

And why, oh, why does he have to come here now when I'm still coming to terms with my feelings for him? I need time. Time to deal and time to heal and then I can face him without turning to hot jelly…if such a thing were possible.

'Can I speak to you, please?'

'Is this about the damage she did to your house?' Aiden's saying. 'Because I thought we'd been through all that and—'

'No, no, of course not. We just—we have unfinished business to take care of.'

'What kind of—?'

'It's okay, Aiden.' I hurry down the stairs and shove my portfolio at him. 'Can you take this to Mum? She was asking for it.'

'But—'

'Shall we talk in the study?' I say to Gabe, ignoring Aiden's dumbfounded look and hooking my arm through Gabe's like I have all the confidence in the world and I'm not a quivering, questioning wreck inside.

'Please.' His voice is gruff, gruffer than it was seconds before. Is he burning from the contact too? Or is this guilt? More guilt at what happened and how we left things?

The second we're through the door, I break away from him. 'If you're here to apologise again for what happened between us, you've had a wasted trip.'

I turn and rest my behind against the edge of my father's antique desk, channel his strength as I stare Gabe down and ignore the crazy dance to my pulse.

'I've come for many reasons, that being one.'

He looks oddly hesitant, his eyes travelling over me hungry but unsure. So he wants me still, wants me but doesn't know how to deal with it. Well, good.

That makes two of us.

If only the heart could be connected to the head—love, libido and logic. The three 'L's. Life would be so much simpler.

He still hasn't spoken and my patience is wearing thin.

There's only so much of his presence I can take before I lose it so completely. 'And the rest?'

He steps towards me and I raise a panicked hand. 'Close enough.'

'I'm not going to hurt you, Ave.'

The alarm is written in his face and I soften a fraction.

'Not intentionally no, but I would prefer it if we kept a decent amount of air between us.'

He nods, swallows. 'I visited my family in Croatia.'

'You did?' It comes out in a rush, forced out by my heart that leaps just a little.

'I did, and it was—it was enlightening.' His eyes brighten with his words, his smile reminiscent. 'I wish you could have been there to see them all.'

'All?'

'They were sat around having dinner. The entire family.'

'Timing.'

'Yes, timing.'

'My *baka*—grandmother,' he adds at my tilted head and confused expression. 'My grandfather, aunt, uncle, my cousins and their children.'

'You walked into all of that?'

He nods. 'I walked into what felt like home. The scent, the photos on the wall, their faces, the familiarity, similarity to my mother.'

I'm so happy for him, I can feel it welling up inside, out of my control. But being happy for him is so close to my love for him that I feel like I'm choking on it, unable to speak.

'They explained so much. They told me that my father made it very difficult for my mother, for any of them to have any access to me. There were threats, financial constraints, even political steps taken. He gave her no choice but to walk away. There was a letter too, a letter she wrote in the hope that one day I would read it...'

His voice breaks and I am powerless to stop myself from crossing the room, my arms wrapping around him as I choke out, 'Oh, Gabe, I'm so sorry.'

How could a man take that love from his child? Steal that time. That precious, sweet time.

His arms come around me slowly and I know he's surprised, shocked by my sudden embrace when not two minutes ago I was telling him to stay away, but...

I look up, see the pain in his gaze and something else, something I haven't witnessed before.

'It was a beautiful letter, Ave, so full of love and regret. But most of all love. She told me all the things we used to do together, the hobbies I enjoyed, my favourite toy, my favourite book, all things my father wouldn't know or care. She left me this too...'

He reaches into his pocket and pulls out a locket that he opens up. Inside is a picture of him and his mother. 'She wore this every day. She never forgot me.'

'Oh, Gabe.' I launch myself up, press an impulsive kiss to his lips and instantly drop back. 'I'm sorry, I shouldn't have...'

He pulls me back in, reignites the kiss and for second, the world falls away and it's just me and him and this.

My love overflowing. My love that he doesn't want. And it's that which has me breaking away, shaking my head. 'And what about your father?'

I focus on the villain in all of this, use it to douse the heat coursing through my veins, the love that I want to declare and he doesn't want to hear.

'I've had it out with him and I've cut my ties. You know,

he didn't deny it, didn't even try. Said she would have made me soft. That I should be grateful.'

I curse, I can't help it.

'He said I was his mirror image and that I'd realise it soon enough.'

'You're nothing like him, Gabe. *Nothing.*'

'I told him that too.'

The relief that he knows it is huge but then all the questions come racing. 'But what about the business, your livelihood? What will you do?'

'I have ideas, ways to raise the capital I need. I'll get there again but under my own steam. Much like someone else I know.'

And there's the admiration, the appreciation all for me. But it's not love, I tell myself. Don't confuse that look with love.

'And your father?'

'Some blood isn't worth keeping.'

'Oh, Gabe.' I reach up, stroke the line from his brow, unable to keep my hands away now I've broken the seal. 'You have us, you have the Monroes.'

'And I have my mother's family, which is a whole lot more than I had before.'

I nod, press my lips together, bite them as I fight the continuing roll of emotion, the tears that want to fall.

'But I'm being greedy.'

I frown. 'Greedy?'

'I want even more, Ave.'

'M-more?'

'Yes.' His hands smooth down my back as he holds me closer. 'I want *you*, Ave.'

I shake my head, blink away the tears. 'I don't think us continuing to have sex is such a—'

'That's not what I mean. Though, yes, I want the sex! But I mean I want you. I want us. I want a relationship.'

My heart is beating so hard I fear I'm going to break a rib. 'A *relationship*? But why? Just a month ago you told me you'd never, not ever…'

'Just a month ago, I thought I couldn't love anyone.' He strokes a hand through my hair, his eyes deepening in their intensity and locked with mine. 'I was wrong. I'm not my father. I'm more my mother than I ever realised. And I love you, Avery Monroe. I was in love with you before I knew what love was, and now that I know, I can't imagine going another day without you by my side.'

I laugh, the sound husky and tight and disbelieving. 'Is this some weird, twisted joke? Is Aiden switching you up from employer to full-time escort? Does he still not think I can cope with mum's illness? Because I'm telling you—'

He presses his thumb to my mouth and I try to break away but he has me held fast and I'm barely putting up a fight. He feels so good, so warm and inviting and that look in his eye…is it? Can it be?

I don't want to let that kind of hope in…to hope and then have it dashed.

'Ave, this is no joke.' He smooths his thumb away, his hands cupping my face. 'And your brother doesn't have a clue. In fact, he's the last person I want to tell but I'll face his wrath every day for the rest of my life if you will accept my love for you.'

'You *really* love me?'

'With all my inexperienced heart.'

I search his gaze and realise that's exactly what I can see blazing back at me. The look I didn't recognise, the warmth and conviction. Love. It truly is love.

'I don't expect you to say it back, I don't even expect you to *take* me back, not that we had anything before, but—'

I kiss him to shut him up. I kiss him because I feel like I'm about to explode with my own confession and when I break away, I let it all out. 'Gabriel Curran, you are the most infuriating, dizzying, confusing hunk of a man, but I love you.'

I enjoy the way my words dance across his face, light up his eyes.

'I've loved you for far longer than my sanity would like but I'll carry on loving you regardless because that's the annoying thing about love, you don't get to choose when it suits, who it suits, it kind of chooses you.'

He wraps his arms around me, squeezes me closer. 'I couldn't have said it any better.'

I laugh, feel the tears I've been holding back start to roll down my cheeks.

'Oh, I don't know.' I link my fingers behind his neck. 'You did a pretty good job of it yourself.'

'So why are you crying?'

'Because I'm happy, so happy.'

'You and me both.'

And then he kisses me and everything feels right with the world.

I know there's a painful road ahead, Mum's health is by no means certain, and I also know I could get through it on my own, but doing it with Gabe...

'I feel like the luckiest girl alive.'

'Now you just need to hold onto that thought because there's one more thing we need to do.'

'What's that?'

'Someone needs to tell Aiden.'

'And Mum.'

'Oh, your mum knows.'

'What?' I tuck in my chin. 'How can she possibly…?'

'Who do you think gave me kick up the ass I needed to come and get you? I was already going to hunt you down, of course, but she gave me the extra nudge to do it now. I think her message said something along the lines of "grow a pair and come get my daughter".'

'She never!'

'She did.'

'When?'

'She's been on at me for the last fortnight, but that text came through all of ten minutes ago. Lucky for me, I was already outside.'

'*You're* Great-Aunt Joan!'

'I'm who, now?'

'She told me she was texting Great-Aunt Joan. I didn't believe her and she made out I was being ageist. Of all the sneaky little…she kept fishing and I kept dismissing.'

He chuckles low in his throat. 'She's a wise woman.'

I beam up at him. 'It runs in the family.'

'As does the fire…and speaking of fire, are you going to tell him, or am I?'

'Wanna draw straws?'

'I'd rather take you up on that game of strip poker you once offered…'

EPILOGUE

One year later

Gabe

'I STILL CAN'T get used to this.' Aiden adjusts his tie for the umpteenth time and stares through the floral wedding arch to the view of Dubrovnik beyond.

'Which bit?'

'Any of it.'

I laugh and squeeze his shoulder. 'Do I need to remind you that you agreed? To me proposing *and* you walking her down the aisle.'

'Did I? I must have been drunk.'

'Well, there was a fair amount of whisky involved on both occasions. Ave felt it would soften the blow a little.'

Aiden chokes out a laugh. 'I still can't get used to you calling her that either.'

'Pretend it's another woman. Whatever helps, my friend.'

'I prefer the whisky...'

'She's ready.' The officiant approaches through the make-shift aisle behind us, so many faces looking to us expectantly, and we both straighten and sober in one.

'I best go and...' Aiden gestures to the glass doors that

lead back inside the castle, and knowing Ave is in there some-where, my bride-to-be, makes my heart skitter.

'Give my love to your mother, remind her that I'll take good care of her daughter, I promise.'

'You'd better, Curran, else it'll be me you answer to.'

'And don't I know it.'

We share a knowing smile and then I watch him leave. I feel his absence and for the briefest spell my gut sinks, feel-ing his absence roll into that of my father's. I don't miss him though. I've trained that out of me. The need for his respect, his love, it's never going to happen and I don't want it. Not now I know the truth of what happened with Mum all those years ago. But it's my wedding day, a day I never thought would happen...

A sniff behind me has me turning further and there's my grandmother, handkerchief to her nose, eyes welling. I smile at her, smile at them all. My beaming family.

I have them because of her, because of Avery, and as the doors open and she steps out, Aiden on one side, her mother on the other, all the worry, all the doubt evaporates. I only have eyes for her. She is my world, my everything and I know, in my heart, my mother would have loved her too.

'Volim te, Mama,' I whisper.

And meeting Ave's eyes through the delicate lace of her veil, I mouth, *I love you.*

* * * * *

THE PRINCE'S
SAFARI
TEMPTATION

NINA SINGH

MILLS & BOON

For my mother,
who brilliantly adapted to a world
in which she at first did not belong.

CHAPTER ONE

PRINCE DANTE ANGILERA made his way down the cavernous hallway in the north wing of the main castle, his shadow casting a long dark path behind him. He'd been summoned. Maman had messaged him before dawn this morning to meet her bright and early as she took her breakfast on the north garden patio facing the majestic mountains of Nocera, the island kingdom Dante was heir to. Located in the Mediterranean, several miles from Cyprus, Nocera marketed itself as a prime vacation spot throughout the year, but particularly during the summer season.

He knew the reason she needed to speak to him. And the tightness of anxiety gripped his chest as it came to mind. His father, the king, had been experiencing heart palpitations for the past week. The doctors were concerned but not alarmed. Yet.

Arriving at the patio, Dante found Maman sipping tea from a steaming delicate porcelain cup. No doubt it was at least her third or fourth given the hour. She was scrolling hastily through her tablet and taking notes in a leather-bound notebook with her gold-casted pen. A devoted supporter of many causes, Maman always had one project or another on her plate.

Hence the reason for this visit. The king's heart issues had thrown a major glitch in one of her most important endeavors. The prince and she needed to figure out what to do about it.

A wide, friendly smile spread across her face when she looked up to find him approaching. She gestured with her cup to the chair next to her and motioned for Vito, their trusted butler, to bring Dante's cup of espresso.

"How is Papa this morning?" Dante asked, unnecessarily as he'd been adamant that the rotating group of royal doctors keep him updated at all times on his father's condition.

Her lips tightened and she frowned. "The same. But now, on top of his health concerns, he's started to become restless and bored."

Dante shrugged. "Well, he will have to deal with his boredom. He is not to strain himself in any way until the physicians get his condition under control."

"You and I know that. Which brings me to why I called you down here."

Dante didn't have to guess.

"The dignitary tour for your and Papa's conservation foundation. I suppose it will have to be canceled now."

She blinked at him. "But I don't want to cancel it, my dear son."

Dante didn't bother to ask if she intended to go alone. If he knew his *maman*, there was no way she would leave his father's side at a time like this, when his health was in question. Dante's parents were the rare exception when it came to arranged marriages. They genuinely cared for and loved each other. Somehow, they'd found the wherewithal to combine duty and love. So different from his own lot in life. His marriage had been a failure from the start. A failure that had ended in tragedy.

"Then what…?" he began, but didn't finish the sentence as realization dawned. Of course, how could he not have seen this coming? "You'd like me to go on the safari in your stead."

She nodded slowly. "It's the only way that makes sense. We already had to postpone this trip once."

His mother was referring to the accident, the tragedy, two years ago that had claimed the life of his wife, the princess who would have been the future queen.

The kingdom's papers still found his marriage, as well as the accident, an endless source of content. At some point, they'd deemed him the ever grieving widower prince, speculating whether there would be a princess again at some future point. Dante hadn't so much as had a date since Rula's passing. He felt a twinge of guilt. The people of the kingdom and the worldwide tabloids attributed his lack of a romantic life on speculation that he was still heartbroken over the loss of his spouse. Everyone assumed Dante had married for love as well as duty.

If they only knew.

The truth was a bit less fairy tale worthy, the reality being that Dante had failed as a husband. His wife had been unhappy. Maybe she'd guessed that his heart wasn't in the union, and she'd paid for the mistake of their failed marriage with her life.

An image of a smiling face with bright hazel eyes and golden tanned skin formed in his mind's eye. Dante mentally pushed the image and the wayward thoughts away. No use dwelling on any of it now. Never mind that the guilt of his failings would haunt him the rest of his life.

The trip was certainly going to put a major dent in his schedule. He had meetings lined up all next week with various ministers and his most trusted economists about the kingdom's current political and financial status. He supposed that some of that could be done remotely, even from a far corner of Africa, but it wasn't going to be easy. Dante sighed with resignation. If he knew his *maman*, there was no point in arguing.

"All right. I'll go start making the arrangements. Please have Vito bring my espresso to my office."

Before he could rise from his chair, Dante noted the expression on Maman's face. His mother's eyes scanned his face expectedly. Clearly, there was more she wanted to say. "Why do I get the feeling there's something else?" Something he distinctly got the impression he wasn't going to like.

"Your father and I have discussed it, and we've decided that a true representation of Nocera will have to include more than just the crown prince on such a trip."

Dante didn't like the direction this conversation was headed. Her words could only mean one thing. "I won't be going alone?"

She shook her head. "Think about it, dear. Many of these visits involve ceremonies, meetings and formal events. Both men and women will be present. You will need a prominent female presence to complete the delegation, just as your father and I would have been."

Only one person made sense as a possibility. Perna, their trusted royal aide and decades-long employee of the royal family. "Has anyone told Perna that she'll be traveling to Africa in a few short weeks?"

To his surprise, Maman shook her head once again. "No, not Perna. Someone a bit more representative as an extended member of the royal family. Besides, Perna is needed here. You know how much your father depends on our most trusted aide."

"Then who?"

Maman lifted an elegant shoulder. "Someone who's worked at the palace in the past, someone who will represent the Angilera name with dignity. Someone who knows us well and has her entire life."

Alarm bells began to ring in Dante's head as his mother's words echoed through his mind…

An extended member of the royal family… Someone who's worked at the palace in the past…

Maman meant her goddaughter, a woman he'd known since childhood.

No, that had to be wrong. She couldn't possibly mean to suggest—

But she did. The name his mother uttered was the last one he wanted to hear as a possibility. The same vision of the smiling face once again intruded behind his eyes.

This time, there was no pushing it away.

"You've outdone yourself with this one." The voice came from above her head as Sierra adjusted the hem of the cocktail dress she'd just completed that morning, mere moments before the model had arrived for the fitting.

Camille, the model in question, was one of Sierra's favorite to work with. The two women had grown somewhat close during the period of time Sierra had been hired as a sketch artist for the House of Perth and her recent promotion to assistant designer.

"Thanks," she responded, rising to stand then stretching her aching back. She'd been huddled over her desk then the sewing machine for most of the night. Now, her muscles were screaming in protest.

"One down," she added. With several more to go. Darned if she knew how or when the rest would come to her. She'd been creatively blocked for longer than she wanted to admit, with no designs coming to mind that she would deem worthy of putting down on paper, let alone cutting fabric for.

On top of the creative block, there was also a distraction to deal with. How to respond to her godmother, Her Majesty Naila Angilera, Queen of Nocera.

Sierra stifled a giggle. Calling the honorable queen of an island kingdom a mere distraction seemed beyond silly of her. If she were smart, she would drop everything she was doing and respond to the queen right away. But Sierra couldn't seem to bring herself to do so. The queen wanted a personal face-to-face visit. For what, Sierra couldn't begin to guess. But she had a season to prepare for with no ideas to show for it. She had to show the mega designer house in New York's fashion district she was lucky enough to work for that she had the chops to deliver.

Besides, Nocera seemed worlds away, a different lifetime. Aside from sporadic calls from her busy parents, she hardly thought about her old life in the tiny island kingdom.

Right, a nagging voice teased. As if her hesitation about traveling to her old home nation didn't have everything to do with the risk of seeing *him* again. "Him" being Crown Prince Dante Angilera, her once best friend's widowed husband.

"What's the matter?" Camille asked, drawing her back to the here and now. "You've got a faraway look in your eyes and your forehead is drawn tight."

Sierra made a concentrated effort to smooth out her facial features.

Camille gave her a critical look. "That's not much better. You're going to get several wrinkles if you insist on scrunching your face that way."

Sierra sighed and rubbed at her hairline, as if she could smooth away the dreaded wrinkles the other woman warned about.

"I just have a lot on my mind."

"Please tell me it involves a tall, dark and handsome someone you have yet to tell me about."

Sierra chuckled. "Not quite."

Though perhaps Camille's statement was more accurate than she wanted to admit. But the truth was, despite her colleagues and a few of the models' repeated attempts to set her up on dates, Sierra didn't have much of a dating life. Or one at all, for that matter.

There was too much to do; her job was too demanding, taking all of her energy and time to come up with new ideas and designs. She refused to speculate as to any other possible reason.

"You know," Camille began, "my cousin's friend from the Upper East Side just broke up with his girlfriend—"

Sierra cut her off before she could say any more. Another blind date was the last thing she wanted to attempt right now. "Thanks, but no."

Camille hopped off the block and began carefully removing the dress, starting with the delicate straps. In moments, she was down to wearing nothing but a delicate lace thong, despite the myriad of staff and others roaming about the room. No one so much as stared.

The modeling life didn't lend to shyness or modesty. These women had to get dressed and undressed in mere seconds during runway shows. The lot of them were professionals who'd been modeling since their teen years.

"Well, if you change your mind, yada yada."

"Sure," Sierra answered with smile, not meaning it in

the least. The chances she was going to let Camille or anyone else for that matter set her up were slim to none.

Camille threw on the tiny tank top and fitted jean leggings she'd walked in with earlier that afternoon, then strode away after throwing an air kiss in Sierra's general direction.

She simply wasn't interested in pursuing anything romantic. What was the point anyway? Her dear friend had fallen in love and married a literal prince. What had it gotten her in the end?

Her eyes began to sting with the memory of her loss, and Sierra had to suppress a sniffle. Guilt combined with loss was a potent combination. But she had nothing to feel guilty for, damn it. One couldn't be faulted for thoughts and emotions they'd never acted on.

So why did her heart feel so heavy?

Sierra drew in a deep breath and tried to wrangle her emotions. She couldn't be seen crying here, for heaven's sake. It wasn't very professional.

Someone cleared their throat behind her. Not quite ready to turn around and reveal the potential evidence of tears in her eyes, she sucked in a breath and summoned her voice.

"You're back. Did you want to try on the dress again? I was just about to hang it on the completed rack."

She didn't receive an answer for several beats. Then, "I don't think it's quite my color. A bit too much of a pastel." A deep, masculine voice had spoken behind her. Definitely not Camille.

Sierra's blood froze in her veins and her breath locked in her chest. It couldn't be; she had to be imagining things.

But then the scent of mint and sandalwood reached her

nostrils, and Sierra knew her mind wasn't playing tricks on her. This was all too real.

She would know that voice and that scent anywhere, heaven help her.

"Hey, Sisi."

Any remnants of doubt fled her mind at the two simple words. Only one person had ever called her that.

Dante almost felt guilty for the way Sierra's eyes grew wide with shock when she finally turned around and saw him standing three feet away.

"Dante. What are you doing here?"

He began to answer, but she waved it away with her hand. Apparently, it was rhetorical.

"Never mind. I guess that's what I get for not responding to the queen right away." She answered her own question. "She sends her son in person."

Dante tried to remain unaffected at seeing Sierra Compari again. She appeared the same, yet so very different. Her face had matured yet remained as beautiful as he remembered. She wore her hair straight now, the silky auburn strands flowing past her shoulders. Her catlike hazel eyes remained as bright as he remembered. And right now, they were boring right through him.

"On the contrary," he told her. "No one sent me. I'm here of my own will. Completely."

She crossed her arms in front of her chest. "You could have given me a heads-up."

Dante took a step toward her. The scent of her familiar rose and vanilla perfume tickled his nose. "Would you have agreed to see me if I'd announced my visit beforehand?"

Her answer was simple and direct. "No."

"I thought so."

"I was going to reply to Her Grace's emails soon enough. You hardly needed to fly halfway across the world."

Dante shrugged. "Maybe so. I thought it would be considerate of me to do so. The least I could do was to sit down with you in person. Given that we're the ones requesting a favor of you."

She visibly swallowed. "Favor? What kind of favor?"

Dante glanced about the room. Various women were in the stages of undress. Racks of clothing were being rolled from one end of the room to the other. A high-tempo techno song played loudly in the background, heavy bass thudding through the room.

"Perhaps we could go somewhere a bit more private to discuss it."

Her chin lifted defiantly. "Whatever you have to say, you can say it right here."

Dante should have expected a refusal. Sierra was...well, she was Sierra. Try as he might, he couldn't help but compare her to his former wife. Whereas Rula had always been gentle and soft-spoken, Sierra was always straight and to the point. She didn't mince words when she wanted to get her point across. And she was often stubborn. So very stubborn.

He made a show of glancing at his watch. "It's just past noon. Surely you can get away for lunch."

"What makes you think I haven't eaten already?"

"Have you?"

She didn't deign to give him a response. "I have a lot to do, Dante."

He could be stubborn as well. Especially given the stakes. "This won't take long, Sisi. Believe me, we need to have this discussion. The sooner the better."

Her lips tightened. "Fine."

His shoulders sagged with relief. The sooner he got this over with, the sooner he could begin to try to convince her to go along with his mother's idea.

"Great. I have a suite rented at the Grand Ritz. We can eat there. There's a car waiting outside."

"Fine," she repeated, turning on her heel. "But just know that I'm only agreeing to hear you out because it's really the queen who's asking." She threw the words over her shoulder.

He had absolutely no doubt. The queen always had a lot of sway with Sierra Compari. Dante could only hope that hadn't changed.

Within minutes, they'd arrived at the hotel and were riding the private elevator to the suite of rooms on the top floor.

Dante couldn't recall the last time he and Sierra had been alone together, let alone in such tight quarters. That familiar scent of hers was wreaking havoc on his senses.

He'd taken great comfort in that scent once. Before circumstances and fate had cost him the friendship of the only woman who had ever truly known him for who he was, and not the crown prince of Nocera.

He led her out of the elevator when they reached the top floor and past the foyer into the dining area. A table had already been set up with polished, glinting silverware and bone china plates. A server appeared immediately, wheeling a cart of platters full of steaming food.

Dante pulled a chair out for Sierra and sat down next to her as the man served their meal.

"What's this all about?" Sierra demanded to know as soon as the other man had left. She hadn't so much as glanced at the stuffed lobster shell placed on the plate before her.

So much for actually eating lunch.

Dante took a deep breath before beginning. "The king and queen have been scheduled for quite some time to visit a few different locations as part of a tour to call attention to my mother's foundation."

Sierra nodded then took a bit of her French roll, chewing slowly. "Environmental and wildlife conservation."

He nodded. "That's right. The tour was to highlight all the ways people can be environmentally conscious despite where they live throughout the world. Even in places such as the African savanna. And that animals are an integral part of the environment they're native to."

"I know all this, Dante," she said, her voice holding no small amount of impatience.

Better to just spit it out, Dante figured. "It turns out they won't be able to go, after all." He wasn't ready to tell her exactly why just yet. Guilting Sierra into making this decision because of concern for his father didn't sit right with him.

Concern washed over his features so he went on before she could ask. "I'll be going in their stead."

"I see." She took another bite of her baguette roll. "What does any of this have to do with me, then?"

"The queen would much prefer if I didn't go alone. She thinks I need someone to accompany me. Preferably female. Someone who can represent Nocera as a true daughter of the kingdom."

Once again, Sierra's eyes grew wide at his words. She looked as if she couldn't decide whether to swallow the morsel of bread in her mouth or spit it out instead. Luckily, she decided on the former.

"You can't possibly be suggesting what I think you are."

There was no other way than to just say what he'd come all the way to New York to say. "The queen thinks you should be that person, Sisi. We are asking you to accompany me."

Sierra's mouth went dry and she dropped her half-eaten roll on the table. She'd suddenly lost all her appetite, which was quite a shame. It really had been quite a delicious baguette, crusty on the outside and flaky soft on the inside. Not to mention how gourmet the seafood entrée looked. But she had more important things to contend with right now than an empty stomach.

She couldn't have heard Dante correctly. "I'm sorry, I could have sworn you just said that you wanted me to accompany you on some kind of dignitary trip on behalf of the royal couple."

His response to that was nothing whatsoever. He just thinned his lips and continued to stare at her. It took all of Sierra's will to remain calm and unaffected. Of all the gall.

Slowly with one smooth motion, she pushed her chair back from the table and rose to her feet. "It appears you've wasted your time, Prince Dante. As well as a pointless trip halfway across the world. Maybe you can see some sights to make up for it. The Statue of Liberty, perhaps."

Dante sighed deeply before speaking. "I take it your initial reaction is to say no."

"Initial and final, I'm afraid. Now, if you'll excuse me." But she hadn't made it more than a couple feet away from the table before he'd reached her side. Long, tan fingers gripped her elbow gently.

"Just hear me out, Sierra. That's all I ask."

"Why?"

He tilted his head, took a step closer. That familiar cologne of his taking her mind to a past she had no business thinking of. So much had happened since then that she couldn't allow herself to forget.

Dante answered as if he'd just read her mind. "For old times' sake?"

Sierra felt herself bristle from head to toe. "What's that supposed to mean?"

"Would traveling with me be so bad?"

"You do not want me to answer that question." Neither did she. Because she didn't even want to think about it—flying halfway across the world with him, seeing him every day. The whole problem was that it probably wouldn't be bad at all. Not in the least. And she so couldn't go there.

He let go of her, pinched the bridge of his nose. "We were friends once, Sierra. The best of friends."

She chuckled. "Right. That's why I'm hearing from you now after all these months. When you need me to do something for you." Rula's funeral service was the last time they'd so much as spoken. And that had hardly been any kind of true conversation given the cloud of grief hanging over them both.

His eyebrows lifted. "Did you want to hear from me?"

Damn it. The answer to that question was beside the point. The point was he hadn't made any kind of attempt.

He blew out a long breath. "Don't leave. At least finish your lunch."

"No, thank you. I seem to have lost my appetite."

"Look, this was the queen's idea. Did you expect me to flat-out refuse to try to honor her wish?"

"I expected you to try to have her see reason."

He lifted an eyebrow. "Her reasoning is quite sound.

You are a daughter of Nocera. You've done work for the queen before you left the kingdom and relocated. Some of that work involved the very foundation we'll be supporting with this trip."

Sierra hated that he was making sense. NEWEF, the Nocera Environmental and Wildlife Ecological Foundation, was one of the royal family's most esteemed organizations worldwide. "Nevertheless, you should have tried to persuade her this was a bad idea, Dante."

He laughed briefly. "You really have been gone too long if you think that would have worked on Maman."

Sierra pointed a finger at him, nearly jabbing his chest. "It's too bad my dear friend isn't around anymore to join you on such travels."

His obvious and sharp flinch sent a rush of guilt through her. That was a low blow. Dante's stricken expression had her wishing she could somehow take the words back. They were harsh words, admittedly unfair. Dante might not have been what Rula had needed in a husband—he always seemed distant with her the few times Sierra had seen them together—but no one person could be faulted for the car crash that had claimed Rula's life. Rula had been the one driving late at night in a foreign country without any support staff or bodyguards. No one could guess why she'd gone off on her own. Sierra had figured she had needed to get away, needed some time to herself away from the demands placed on her as the future queen. But the truth was anyone's guess. In any case, it was needlessly reckless of her friend, and the impulsive trip had cost Rula her life.

Dante stepped away from her, his eyes shuttered now in shadow. "Just think about it, Sisi. That's all I ask. I'll be here until tomorrow afternoon." He motioned to the elevator. "Stewart will see you out."

The same car was waiting for her when she made it down to the street. The driver stood next to the vehicle with the passenger door open.

She shook her head in his direction. "No, thanks. I think I'll just walk and get some air."

The driver merely shut the door in response, gave her a friendly tip-of-the-hat wave.

Sierra rushed down the sidewalk, thinking of no particular destination. Her mind was a jumbled mess of thoughts, her heart a jumbled mess of emotions.

The nerve of that man. To shock her by simply showing up at the studio and then to throw such a request at her. What was he thinking? He had to know in advance that her answer would be a resounding and flat "no."

So why had he come here unannounced? Dante wasn't spontaneous or impulsive by any means. There had to be a piece of the puzzle she was missing, something he hadn't told her.

She was still pondering that question when she found herself entering Central Park. Being here always helped to clear her head. Something about the open air and all the strangers going about their business served as a balm for frazzled nerves. Right now, she needed clarity more than anything else. It worked. The fresh air and greenery surrounding her shifted her focus away from the turmoil of her emotions.

A question nagged at the back of her mind. Dante had never stated exactly why it was that the royal couple couldn't attend the trip. Something had to have come up.

She could call the queen herself to find out. But then she'd be subjected to Her Majesty's persuasive efforts. Sierra didn't think she had the patience or nerve for that right now. There was one other person who came to mind.

Someone who happened to be a woman Sierra consid-ered a friend.

Pulling out her cell phone, she clicked on the icon for one of her contacts. Perna answered on the first ring.

After a few pleasantries and general catching up, Si-erra had the answer to her question about why the king and queen wouldn't be traveling anytime soon. Her heart sank when she found out.

Perna was still speaking in her ear. "At his age, they say he'd be foolish to attempt such a taxing itinerary given the irregularity of his heartbeat."

Sierra absorbed the news as she made her way to the nearest bench. Her shoes may as well have been made of bricks. "I see."

"We've been trying to keep it quiet until the doctors had some definitive answers about his condition."

"Thanks, Perna. You've been as helpful as I knew you would be."

With that, Sierra hung up and tucked the phone in her jeans pocket. Then she pulled out the card Dante's aide had handed her in the elevator. Releasing a resigned sigh, she began to dial.

CHAPTER TWO

Three weeks later

SIERRA SHUT HER suitcase and tucked it away in the vast
closet in the corner of her even vaster room. The last time
she was here at Castle Angilera had seemed like another
lifetime. It felt odd to be here again. Which made no sense.
She'd spent countless days here as a child. She and Dante
running through the miles of hallways, playing hide-and-
seek for hours in any of the numerous royal gardens. This
castle had been like a second home to her while growing
up. So why did she feel like a stranger here now? How
had things changed so much in her life that the familiar
now felt odd?

Three knocks on the door jostled her out of her reverie.

She didn't need more than one guess to know that it was
Dante. He always knocked three times, a slight hesitation
just before the third. Funny how little details such as that
one could remain lodged in one's memory. But then, she
had several memories of Dante, some prone to rising to
the surface at the most inopportune times. Sierra sighed.
Looked like she would be adding more to her collection
given the trip they were about to take together.

"Come in."

He strode into the room to stand before her. Sierra

thought her knees might buckle at the sight of him. He must have been returning from some sort of ceremonial event. He wore a formal, fitted suit jacket with the crest of the house of Angilera on one side of his chest while the coat of arms adorned the other. A slew of honor ribbons sat below the crest.

"Glad to see you've made it. Sorry I wasn't there to greet you. I had a swearing-in ceremony for a new minister."

"How is your father?" she asked, pulling her focus away from the way he looked in his formal attire.

"There has been no change. Which is both good news and bad."

"You should have told me that first day you flew to New York. About his condition."

He stepped farther into the room, leveled a steady gaze on her with those steel gray eyes that were all too easy for a woman to lose herself in. "I didn't want the knowledge to sway your decision about coming. Didn't want any kind of guilt to play a part. I was hoping I could convince you in other ways."

Was it her imagination, or had his voice grown deeper as he finished his words? If he meant any kind of double entendre with the way he ended that sentence, she wasn't about to follow that path.

"My change of heart had more to do with concern for my godfather than any kind of guilt." Enough concern that she'd pleaded with the head designer at House of Perth to give her leave for several days, then wrangled Camille into sitting for her pet hamster while she was away.

He nodded once. "Be that as it may, I should have guessed you would find a way to discover the whole truth, whether I told you or not."

She wasn't sure how to respond to that, so she ignored it. "So, we leave in two days?"

"Correct. We should reach Valhali by Thursday afternoon."

This was all happening so quickly, so unexpectedly, Sierra was having trouble processing all the details. "Remind me exactly where that is again."

Dante said, "It's a small independent nation in the south of Africa, bordering Botswana. The prime minister and his wife will be there to greet us and take us to the Melekhanna lodge, where we'll be staying."

"Followed by a safari starting the next day," she said.

"Correct again."

Sierra had to admit that a feeling of excitement hummed through her veins. An African safari trip sounded so adventurous and exotic. She'd never thought of herself as the safari type. In fact, she hadn't thought about visiting that part of the world at all. Now that she was about to, she couldn't deny the excitement of it all. Despite the potential for disaster, given the company she'd be traveling with.

Her best option was to do her best to keep a safe distance between her and Dante. Surely they'd be surrounded by others most of the time. It wasn't as if they'd be traipsing the African grasslands by themselves.

"There will be two journalists who work there locally who will be with us from the beginning to chronicle our journey through the game reserve and hopefully lend some more visibility to the cause," Dante told her. "A gaggle of reporters from all over the world will join us a few days later to cover the scheduled news conference and meeting with the local conservationists."

Her excitement turned to trepidation. She wasn't used to being the center of attention. Being in front of a group of journalists with cameras flashing in her face—the thought of it made her stomach queasy. Sure, Dante would be the primary attraction, but she was bound to have at least a few questions thrown her way. What if she made a fool of herself with a stupid answer that made no sense? If only she had some of Rula's savvy. Even when Rula said the wrong thing, she could find a way to charm her way out of any sort of embarrassment. A rush of sadness washed over her. These halls held so many happy memories from her youth. Memories that were all at the forefront now that she was back. How she wished she might be able to turn back time and return to the carefree days spent in this castle with Dante and Rula.

"Penny for your thoughts?" Dante's question pierced through her musings.

She blinked at him, trying to come up with a way to answer. "I was just thinking how much I'm looking forward to seeing your mom and dad again," she said, fibbing. "The last time I was in Nocera…"

She didn't need to finish the sentence. The last time Sierra had been here had been for Rula's funeral service.

"They're looking forward to seeing you as well. Your visit is all Maman has talked about for the past several days. Though it's unfortunate that your own parents are out of the country."

Grateful that he'd changed the subject, Sierra offered a small smile. "I'll see them when they come to New York for my birthday."

"Next month. The seventh," Dante said.

"You remember?"

He playfully tapped her nose. "I remember everything, Sierra." The amusement faded from his eyes and his lips thinned. "All of it, before everything changed."

Changed it had. When Dante had gone from being a dear childhood friend to someone akin to a brother-in-law. But Sierra couldn't deny that there'd been a slight shift in their relationship even before his courtship of Rula. Unguarded moments as they'd both grown older and matured. The way Dante's eyes had lingered on her the first time he'd seen her in a ball gown at the king's jubilee soiree. How he'd held her just a moment longer than he might have the first time they'd danced together.

"I'll let you get settled," Dante said after several heavy moments of silence. Sierra had to wonder if his thoughts had traveled down a path of memories as well.

"See you in a couple hours at dinner."

She watched silently as he turned and walked out of the room, shutting the door softly behind him.

The flight to Botswana three days later took a little over nine hours from Istanbul International Airport, where they'd departed after leaving Nocera. The moment they'd landed, Sierra and Dante had hit both the proverbial and literal road running. Now, they were in a Landcruiser their way out of Botswana, headed toward the Valhali border.

A second SUV trailed behind them carrying two bodyguards and a palace aide.

Sierra glanced over at Dante's profile as he sat in the passenger seat next to her. The man was perpetually tanned, his skin a natural golden hue despite the season. Now, sheeted in a thin layer of dust from the bumpy dirt road, he still somehow looked every bit the royal crown prince and heir to a kingdom. Yet, somehow in a rugged, edgy way.

Wow. She really needed to stop focusing on Dante's looks. Or focusing on the man in general. What was wrong with her anyway? She was in Africa! Plenty to see here, no need to fixate on the handsome, alluring prince she was traveling with.

There she went again. Sierra sighed and turned her gaze to the road. Their driver was a jovial young man who frequently turned to give them friendly smiles as he drove. He'd introduced himself as Banti when he'd picked them up from the airport.

"We'll be there in no time," he said over his shoulder in a charming accent. It never ceased to amaze her, throughout her travels, how so much of the world was fluently bilingual, English flowing smoothly from the lips of many people no matter where she was.

Rula had been fluent in three different languages. Her best friend had always said any queen worth her salt should be bilingual at the least. She'd been determined since barely past her toddler years to marry into the royal family, with no small amount of influence from her ambitious parents, and had worked steadily toward that end.

It had all gone so horribly wrong.

Sierra had wondered more than once over the years if Rula might have chosen a different path had it not been for the urging of her mother and father to aspire to become queen. How different might her life have been?

"What's the matter?" Dante's voice asked above the loud rumbling of tires over rugged road. He'd always been very in tune to her moods.

"Is the ride too rough? I can ask him to pull over for a bit."

She shook her head. "No. I'm fine. Really."

He didn't look convinced.

"Seriously," she began. "Don't worry about—" But she couldn't get the words out as particularly drastic jolt threw her first against the door than hurtled her in Dante's direction. The next thing she knew, she was practically sprawled in his lap. His arms immediately wrapped around her shoulders to hold her steady.

Stunned, she could only stare up at his face. His eyes were shielded behind a pair of aviator sunglasses, but there was no doubt about the tension in his features. It took several moments for Sierra to find her breath.

"I'm so sorry." But when she made an effort to pull away, his arms remained locked around her.

He was silent for several beats before speaking. "Don't be."

Despite the rumbling of the vehicle, despite the dust kicking up around them, Earth might as well have stopped turning. Sierra continued to stare at Dante, knowing full well that she should have moved off his lap already. But she felt dazed and disoriented. Every cell in her body screamed at her to stay where she was and enjoy the scenery with his arms wrapped tightly around her, safe and secure in his embrace despite the treacherous, bouncy ride. Being this close to Dante, having him hold her, feeling his warmth against her skin felt right in a way that she had yet to experience with any other man.

Sierra squeezed her eyes shut and shook her head against the wayward thoughts. Finally, common sense somehow intervened. Forcing her muscles to work, she gave him a tight smile and removed herself from his lap.

"Border checkpoint," the driver announced from the front seat. "This shouldn't take long. No need to be nervous," he added.

Well, it hadn't occurred to her to be nervous until he'd just told her not to. Her anxiety kicked up a notch as their vehicle slowed and several armed soldiers approached.

Dante reached for her hand, gave it a reassuring squeeze in his own. The warmth of his palm on hers lowered her anxiety several notches. Their driver exchanged several words with the man who appeared to be in charge of the group. Clearly these men had no idea a foreign crown prince was in the back seat. The lack of fanfare and the bluster finally made sense. Dante was much better off pretending to be an ordinary tourist on an outing with his girlfriend or wife at this stage of their journey. The time for fanfare and publicity would come later.

Sierra gave herself a mental whack at the dangerous word. *Wife*. Lord, she had to find a way to control her thoughts and keep from wandering into such perilous territory.

Their driver was right, with a cursory glance at the paperwork, followed by a pointed look at her and Dante holding hands, the soldier gave them a nod and motioned them to move forward.

They'd driven about a half mile when Banti slowed the vehicle and pulled off to the side.

"Why are we stopping?" Dante asked.

At the exact same moment Sierra said, "Is something wrong?"

"We are in my country now," Banti answered, shooting them a wide grin over his shoulder. "Beautiful Valhali. We can do as we want. Would either of you like to drive?"

Was he serious?

"Absolutely not," she answered automatically. She'd learned how to drive a vehicle on her fifteenth birthday, but had never really had need to drive herself anywhere. And since moving to New York, the subway had been her main mode of transportation.

Dante however was already hopping out of the vehicle, a look of clear excitement on his face. "You bet I do." He glanced behind him over his shoulder. "But we have to hurry before Otto and the others catch up to play the bodyguard card to try to stop me."

He was in the driver's seat in the next moment. Banti extended his hand to her, opening her door. "Would you like to go sit in the front by your—"

Sierra didn't let him finish the sentence.

"Sure. Why not?" Though her heart was hammering in her rib cage at the prospect.

Dante seemed to be enjoying himself when he took the wheel. The expression on his face could only be described as one of pure glee. She pressed her back against the seat and braced herself as he pressed the accelerator. The Landcruiser surged forward, and soon Dante was driving over the rough terrain like he'd been driving in this country his whole life.

The second car finally caught up and pulled along beside them. The two men in the passenger seats shook their heads at the prince as if chastising a child. Dante merely shrugged and grinned back at them. A wave of nostalgia washed over Sierra at the sight. The moment reminded her so much of Dante as a preteen when he'd sneak off to meet her and Rula at the beach or to simply get away from the castle.

"Thanks, Sierra," he said with a grin as he assisted her out of the front passenger seat.

Sierra blinked at him in confusion. What was he thanking her for? "Banti's the one who let you drive."

"I just mean thanks for being a good sport and not arguing how dangerous and reckless I was being by driving."

His statement took her aback. She had the distinct impression arguing with him about driving would have been exactly what Rula would have done. Her emotions were in enough turmoil without the knowledge that Dante might be comparing her to her lost friend.

Heaven knew she did enough of that herself. And she always came up short.

The sense of exhilaration Dante had felt while driving hadn't abated even a fraction as they approached their lodge two hours later. Banti had no idea how much of a favor he'd done for him with such a seemingly innocuous offer. No way would Dante have been allowed such an indulgence if his parents or anyone else from the royal court were here. Too risky. He was the sole heir. He couldn't be so reckless with his health and safety. He had no doubt he was going to get an earful from Otto and the aide at some point. But he'd worry about that later when the time came.

He'd expected Sierra to protest as well. But she'd taken it in stride, hadn't said a word against it once he'd accepted Banti's offer to let him drive.

Rula would have no doubt done the exact opposite. He could hear his former wife's voice in his head. *Don't even consider it, Dante. You're in a foreign country, in a completely remote area. Help could be hours away if something were to happen.*

By contrast, Sierra had clearly been nervous, but she'd still jumped into the passenger seat next to him. He could still hear her excited laughter as he took a particularly sharp turn in the road a little too fast. She may not have liked it, but she'd let Dante make the decision. And she'd trusted him once he had. To this day, even after all this time having known them both, it still struck him how different the two women had been despite being so close.

Dante gave his head a brisk shake. Try as he might, he

couldn't seem to keep mentally comparing Sierra to his deceased wife, right or wrong.

He released a deep sigh. *Wrong.* Of course, it was completely wrong.

Dante stole a glance at her as they pulled up in front of the lodge. Her cheeks were glowing a rosy red, from both the sun and exertion of their ride, he would guess. She'd been chewing on her bottom lip, rendering it swollen and crimson. She'd kept applying some kind of balm to them during the drive. Every time she'd uncapped it, the scent of berries had wafted through the air. What might that taste like if he were to taste it on her lips?

Whoa.

Dante pulled up short. Now his thoughts were leading him into perilously dangerous territory. Sierra was a family friend, here with him only as a dignitary. Dante absolutely couldn't lose sight of either of those facts.

So instead of opening her door and helping her out of the vehicle when they'd come to a stop, he let Banti do it instead. Then he forced himself not to so much as look in her direction.

"The prime minister with his wife and their group will be here in a few hours," Banti informed them. "They wanted to give you both a chance to settle in and freshen up before their arrival."

Sierra's shoulders dropped, a look of relief washed over her features. She was clearly relieved at the news. Dante wanted to kick himself. He hadn't even considered how new this all must be for her. She was no seasoned royal on her latest state sponsored trip. She hadn't even been rehearsed on exactly how to behave or what to expect, aside from a brief consultation with his *maman* after her arrival in Nocera. He was going to have to do his best to guide her, and to reassure her along the way. He had no doubt she was going to be an amazingly impressive representative of his kingdom. She just had to believe it too.

He knew how much he and his parents were asking of her. It spoke to her character that she was even here in the first place to help them out. Not to mention the heavy shadow of the past that would follow them. He would have to find a way to truly thank her for all that she was doing for the sake of the Crown and this trip. Not that he had any idea what he might do for her. Sierra had always been an independent soul. She'd gone after her dream of pursuing a career in fashion and was unsurprisingly successful in one of the most competitive markets in the world. She hardly needed anything from him.

"Come, follow me." Banti broke into his thoughts, motioning them toward the lodge. The Melekhanna lodge could have made a perfect picture for an article about Valhali in a travel magazine.

The structure appeared more luxurious than Dante might have guessed. Lanterns adorned the perimeter of a wide porch that wrapped around the entire structure. Individual egg-shaped hammocks hung from either side of the wide entryway. Comfortable looking wicker furniture with thick colorful cushions adorned the patio just outside the wooden porch steps. The thatched roof was the color of dark reed, blending in well with the surroundings, as if the lodge was part of the natural environment and not a man-made structure with all the comforts of a grand resort inside.

Sierra appeared to be studying the building with awe as Banti led them up the wooden steps. "Wow," she uttered on a breathless whisper.

"It's pretty impressive."

She nodded. "It certainly is." She continued to take in her surroundings before adding, "I have to admit. I had no idea what to expect when I agreed to come here. So far, I've been impressed at every turn."

Her words sent a surge of pleasure rushing through him. "There's so much more left to see."

She chuckled with what might have been delight. "I can't wait."

Dante checked his gold and onyx watch for the umpteenth time and wondered if somehow it was actually malfunctioning. Or else it meant time was moving unbearably slowly. After a lengthy email to his parents assuring them their arrival had gone smoothly, followed by a long shower, he was more than anxious to proceed with the evening. Today was the first day he could remember in a long time that he'd actually felt…something, anything. Now, he was itching to get back out there. After Rula's death, he'd spent several weeks in a state of numbness. The people of his kingdom referred to him as the Ever Grieving Prince. But no one knew the whole truth. Not even his parents. It was hard to grieve a marriage that had never really felt genuine. He had loved Rula. And he knew she'd loved him, in her own way.

But he wasn't naive enough to believe either of them had ever been *in* love with each other. Rula had wanted to be a queen. And Dante had been her means to that end. Rula had wanted the title. It just so happened that she needed a husband who was a crown prince to achieve it. It had cost her everything, her very life. He knew he bore some of the responsibility for his wife's untimely death. Perhaps if he had tried harder, attempted to be more affectionate, things might have turned out differently.

He'd thought from the beginning that Rula understood theirs was to be a marriage of convenience, not one based on love or affection. How tragically mistaken he'd been. Rula clearly had needed more from him. Ultimately, he'd been unable to give her what she might have wanted most—a spouse who could have indeed loved her.

As the heir, Dante would have to remarry eventually. This time, he'd be better prepared. He'd make sure his next wife knew exactly what to expect from their marriage. He'd make sure that she understood the union would be barely more than a business arrangement. A marriage of convenience to ensure the stability of the kingdom and produce the next heirs.

The lady would have to understand and agree that she couldn't expect anything more from him, least of all any kind of true affection or love.

He scoffed at the very notion. People like him couldn't afford such emotion.

Dante swore, rubbed his forehead. This was useless. Why was he standing here in his room, thinking thoughts about what might have been? None of it made any difference whatsoever. Nothing would change the past now. He'd failed his wife. He would have to go to his own grave with the guilt of that knowledge.

Sierra had never actually come out and said so. But he knew she blamed him for her dear friend's fate as well. At least partially. The two women were as close as sisters. Of course she would hold him partly responsible. It only made sense. If there was any way to atone himself in her eyes, he had to be able to find a way to do so. And that was why he hadn't fought harder to dissuade his mother from asking her on this trip. To give him some time with her, to try to convince her to forgive him somehow. Maybe it was selfish of him, but he couldn't spend the rest of his life knowing Sierra Compari might never forgive him for his greatest mistake. Though he could hardly blame her.

For now, he needed some air. Enough of the melancholy thoughts tormenting his mind. Yanking open the door, he strode out onto the shared porch and toward the front of the lodge. Two things struck him at once. The color of the sky as the sun was beginning to set. And that Sierra was outside as well, just a few feet away on the patio. She sat in one of the eggshell hammocks, scribbling furiously in a sketchbook spread open on her lap.

Dante nearly turned around so as not to disturb whatever she was in the middle of. She had her bottom lip between her teeth, her bare feet dangling. Her hair was still damp from her shower, haphazardly tied up in a knot at her neck. Soft, delicate curls framed her face. She'd changed into a calf-length skirt and a white collared top that barely reached the waistband of the skirt. She fit into the picture before him perfectly, as if she belonged here, under the darkening African sky.

She must have sensed his presence. She didn't bother to look away from her page when she spoke to him.

"I'm afraid my colored pencils don't do the scene any justice," she said softly, still sketching. "And there's no way to capture this on a cell phone camera."

He moved closer, pulled up the nearby cushioned wicker chair and sat down. "It is rather striking." The sky was a deep crimson over the grasslands, waves of clouds reaching the horizon. Dante felt as if he'd stepped into a life-size painting.

"Breathtaking," Sierra answered, looking up briefly before putting pencil to paper once more.

"Are you sketching the sunset?"

She shook her head. "I'm sketching a jumpsuit. Something a woman might wear to a casual cocktail party. Or to Sunday brunch. I've decided the pant legs will be loose and flowing. Slightly pleated, like the pattern of those clouds. I can only hope to find a fabric that comes even close to that shade of red back in New York."

Dante couldn't find the words with which to respond. He'd never seen this Sierra before, not even when they were kids. Sierra at work was a novel sight. Totally focused, her right hand moving furiously over the page, eyebrows drawn in concentration. He knew she was passionate about her work. She'd left her home and moved halfway across the world in its pursuit, after all. But he'd never actually seen her create before. It was a sight to behold. Once again, he felt as if he might be intruding on a private moment and almost rose to leave.

It was as if she'd read his mind, something she'd always been rather good at. "You don't have to go," she told him. "I'm almost done."

Moments later, she tucked the last pencil into a thin silver case and dropped it into a canvas bag near her feet. Before she could close the cover on her sketch, he rose and reached her side. "May I?" he asked, gesturing to the book in her hand, genuinely curious.

A tightening of her lips, a slight hesitation, but she turned the sketchbook around and pushed it toward him. Dante would be hard-pressed to describe what he was looking at. Somehow, she'd captured the visual magnificence of the scene before them and transferred it into the design of an article of clothing. And she'd done so with nothing but blank paper and colored pencils. Plus her imagination.

"Wow," was all he could think of to say.

She tilted her head. "Is that a good 'wow' or a bad 'wow'?"

She had to ask? "Definitely the former. I don't know much about women's clothing, but what you've captured here is beyond impressive."

Her shoulders dropped, and she cast him a small smile. "Thanks. I'm really happy to hear that. To be honest, I surprised myself. I've had a bit of a rough patch coming up with new ideas lately. And then I came out here and saw this." She gestured in the general direction of the horizon. "I had to sit down and try to see where it led."

Dante glanced down at the image once more. He'd have to say it had led her well.

CHAPTER THREE

SIERRA COULDN'T HELP the rush of giddiness that flashed through her at Dante's compliment. How silly of her. After all, it was true what he said. He didn't really know anything about women's clothing. His opinion on her design shouldn't mean anything to her.

But it did. It meant more than she would have liked it to.

Now, he pointed to her drawing. "Do ideas such as this one just come to you?" he asked. "Out of nowhere?"

Sierra scoffed. If only that were the case. "Hardly. This trip might be just what I needed."

"A creative jolt," he said,

She held her right hand up, crossed her fingers. "Let's hope."

"Well, if this is any indication, I'd say you're off to a good start."

Sierra hadn't wanted to show him what she'd drawn. Given his reaction, she was glad she had. She'd sensed his presence the moment he'd stepped out of his doorway, had had a fleeting urge to flee before he could reach her side. But that was childish. She could hardly go running every time he appeared. They'd be spending several days in each other's company. Which left only one other option—she would have to try to clamp down on the inconvenient awareness of Dante Angilera she couldn't seem to shake despite all the time that had passed. Despite the fact that he was once her best friend's husband. For instance, she should not be noticing how muscular his chest appeared under the soft cotton shirt he wore, nor the way his shirtsleeves were rolled up just above his elbows and how his forearms looked like they may have been sculpted by a master artist.

"It's louder here than I would have thought," she said, by way of conversation, just to have some kind of dialogue and to redirect her focus.

Dante lifted his head, as if listening, then nodded. "I noticed that too. Cicadas humming. Punctuated by the shriek of a monkey in a nearby tree. And birds. Lots of birdsong."

Yet another sound rang from his pocket, this one much more modern. Dante pulled out his phone and glanced at the screen. "From Banti. He's texted both of us."

"I left my phone in the room," she told him. So that she could focus on what she'd wanted to draw uninterrupted. "What does it say?"

"He wants to let us know that the prime minister and his wife should be here within minutes. They're bringing along a couple of journalists. We'll be meeting them outside the lobby. Followed by dinner then an evening full of activities and entertainment."

Sierra jumped off her seat with a resigned sigh. It all sounded so exhausting. It was during moments like this that she wished she could have been more like Rula. A stab of guilt seared through her center. Rula should have been the one here in her stead.

Rula was the consummate dignitary who always knew how to present herself and exactly what to say and how to behave. Just as a future queen should. Sierra would much rather stay here enjoying the ever-changing scenery and the solitude. If she had her way, she might spread a blanket in the field, grab a sandwich and a bottle of wine, and simply sit out here to enjoy the view, watching the changing sky. But the vision her mind concocted at those thoughts didn't have her sitting on that blanket alone. Dante was next to her, pouring that wine and they were sharing that sandwich.

Stop.

"Guess we better make our way down there then."

To her surprise, he reached out and gently grasped her elbow. "Just another minute."

Huh. Maybe she wasn't the only one trying to overcome an introverted nature. It must be so much harder for Dante if that were the case. A prince didn't have much choice about socializing, did he? His whole life centered around meetings with other prominent people and public appearances. A life she couldn't imagine. Unlike Rula, who had wanted nothing more out of her own life.

"I just want to enjoy this a bit longer." He gestured generally around him. "Once the prime minister and his entourage get here, moments like this will be hard to come by."

That sounded fine by her, to enjoy the peace until the very last second. So they simply stood side by side in silence, with nature providing plenty of background noise. The sun continued its slow descent. The rushing water of a nearby river competed with the hum of the cicadas. Her fingers itched to reach for her sketchbook again, more ideas rushing through her mind. But it would have to wait, of course.

Sure enough, the moment didn't last long. A commotion of noise could be heard in the distance, clouds of dust rising in the air a few meters to the right of the lodge. The other guests were arriving.

Dante tilted his head, gave her a defeated look, then motioned for her toward the steps.

Time zero. Help me out here, Rula. So that I don't somehow say the wrong thing or act the wrong way, Sierra pleaded to her lost friend.

Though she knew she had no right to ask.

Dressed in traditional attire complete with headdresses and beaded neck chains, the prime minister and his wife looked regal and ceremonious when they exited their vehicles.

To her relief, they both set Sierra immediately at ease with their friendly introductions and smiling faces. For his part, Dante appeared equally cordial. He may have been hesitant and less than enthusiastic earlier about the festivities starting, but Sierra saw now that he was in his element. He introduced her as Lady Sierra, a family friend who would be accompanying him.

They all insisted on the use of their first names.

Nantu, the prime minister, threw a hand over Dante's shoulder, his mouth tightening in a solemn line. "Again, I want to convey in person our deepest condolences on the loss of the princess," he said to Dante, gesturing to his wife. "We were both so saddened when we heard," he added.

"Thank you, Your Honor."

"Call me Nantu, remember?" he reminded Dante.

"And thank you for the flowers you had sent all the way from Valhali. It was a beautiful arrangement that brightened up the palace during its darkest days. The lilies were particularly vibrant."

Of course, Dante would remember such a detail, Sierra thought. Or he'd made sure to look it up before embarking on the trip. Such a thing would not have even occurred to her.

"You're welcome, my friend," Nantu said.

It was then Sierra noticed the two individuals hovering on the outskirts of the circle. A strawberry-red-haired woman and a balding, older gentleman. They were both clad in western clothing. The man was furiously snapping photos with a complicated looking camera. The woman was tapping furiously away at her phone screen.

Two of the journalists who were here to ensure this trip got the publicity the queen was after for her foundation. Sierra wondered when the rest of the crew would arrive. Probably not long now.

The prime minister's wife, Kaliha, approached her. "You'll get used to them being around," she told Sierra, her singsong voice laced with a charming accent. "After a while, they just blend into the background."

Sierra wanted to believe her. But just at that moment, she noticed the camera was pointed in her direction. The reporter clicked several snaps in rapid succession. Sierra did her best to summon a smile, but it wasn't easy. She was used to being surrounded by lenses, but she was never the one in the frame. The models she worked with were the usual targets.

"I'm going to vehemently hope you're right," she said, not believing the statement for one moment. How could one get used to constantly having their photo taken as they went about their activities? A glance at Dante gave her a clue. He seemed completely at ease as the camera turned on him and the reporter snapped away.

"Come, let's get acquainted," Kaliha said, leading her away a few feet away from the action. Why did Sierra get the feeling the distance was for her own benefit and not for Kaliha? Heavens, she must look as out of place as she felt.

"And we can give those two a chance to catch up," Kaliha stated once they'd moved out of earshot, glancing in the direction where the men stood chatting. They gave every appearance of being longtime friends.

"Has your husband known Dante long?" Sierra asked, genuinely curious despite herself.

"They met a few years back at a UN summit and hit it off. Nantu has spoken fondly of him ever since."

No surprise there, Sierra thought. Most people found Dante charming and good-natured, both men and women. Particularly women.

"It's nice to see the prince finally traveling, even if it's in an official capacity," the other woman added after a beat, her gaze still locked on where Dante stood with her husband. "I know the loss of his wife hit him hard. And it's nice that he has someone like you to keep him company."

Sierra immediately shook her head. It was important to make sure no one got any false impressions of what she was doing here. Especially given the presence of all sorts of journalists and photographers. This could turn into a situation ripe for the spread of false rumors. She didn't need that complication in her life right now. And neither did Dante. "Oh, it's not— I'm his former— He used to be marr—" She stopped her sputtering to suck in a deep breath. Why in the world had she lost the ability to speak all of a sudden? "I'm only here as a representative of Nocera and the royal family," she explained, doing her best to keep her voice steady.

Kaliha tilted her head to the side. "I know that, dear," the other woman answered with a small but rather mischievous smile. "My point still stands."

Before Sierra could find a way to respond, Kaliha patted her hand. "Tell me about yourself, dear. Is this your first time in Africa?"

The tension in her midsection loosened a fraction at the change of topic. "Yes, it is. I'm terribly excited to be here. It's already given me a creative nudge, so to speak."

Even as she sat here, her creative juices were flowing. The darkening sky dotted with twinkling lights, the exotic caw of a bird in the distance, a soft breeze that carried with it the scent of the colorful flowers planted by the patio. Her senses were in heaven.

Kaliha's eyebrows lifted half an inch. "Oh? How so?"

Sierra explained what she did back in New York, the difficulties she'd been having coming up with new ideas, and how inspiring she'd found the sunset earlier. To her surprise, her words flowed freely and comfortably. She'd just met the woman, but something about her warm personality had Sierra completely at ease. As if she were speaking with an old friend and not the spouse of the leader of a sovereign nation. On the surface, she had nothing in common with this woman. But she felt as if she might have made a new friend.

Their conversation was cut short with the arrival of Banti, who announced that their meal was ready to be served. Within seconds, the prime minister was at Kalihi's side offering her his arm.

Dante followed suit, holding his hand out to Sierra.

She took it, a tingle of electricity spreading along her skin at the contact. Dante's fingers wrapped around her wrist gently, his eyes lingered on hers for a loaded second. The sound of a camera snapping a photo echoed in the distance.

Dante guided Sierra to where Banti was leading them, a long wooden table by the front patio of the lodge. In the center sat a cornucopia of fruits, sandwiches, sliced vegetables. Each plate looked exotic and different, arranged aesthetically. The vivid colors reminded him of paintings he'd seen in some of the world's most renowned museums.

"I don't even recognize some of these fruits," Sierra said as he pulled out her chair and she sat down. He planted himself in the one next to her once the prime minister and his wife found their own chairs. Tall, lit candles atop the table accented the various dishes. Lanterns hung from poles staked in the ground at each corner.

"Looks like we'll be dining under the stars." He was about to add how romantic the scene was but thought better of it. He couldn't remember the last time he'd eaten dinner outside in the company of a beautiful and charming woman.

Whoa.

It was exactly those kinds of thoughts that he had to avoid. Never mind that the whole setting he found himself in was quite romantic indeed. The soft candlelight cast a soft glow on Sierra's rosy cheeks. The sparkling silver bright stars in the velvet dark sky above. The hum of the cicadas echoing in the air around them. A myriad of unfamiliar scents mingled with the nostalgia of the vanilla rose combination he associated with Sierra. He would have to ignore all that.

Exactly when had he become so poetic anyway? This was essentially a state sponsored dinner. With journalists dining along with them for heaven's sake. There shouldn't be anything remotely intimate about it. Determined to consistently remind himself of those facts, Dante reached for the bowl closest to him, thinly sliced cucumbers dotted with marinated olives, then offered it to Sierra. Nantu and his wife had already spooned an assortment of items onto their own plates.

A server wearing a bright headscarf that matched her dress appeared between their chairs to pour them a ruby red wine. Dante recognized the label as one of the finest vintages from a well-known South African vineyard. Another immediately followed in her wake with a tray of gooey vegetable lasagna and spooned generous portion for each of them.

"This looks and smells divine," Sierra stated, taking a small bit of the steaming pasta. She practically purred with pleasure and Dante found himself having to look away.

Across the table, Nantu lifted his glass in a toast. Grateful for the distraction, Dante followed suit. Sierra lifted her glass then took a hesitant, small sip of wine. Her eyes grew wide with pleasure as she swallowed.

She held the glass out at eye level, seemingly studying it.

"I take it you like it?" he asked.

"It's like nectar from heaven. And the color is so strikingly robust. It kind of reminds me of the sky earlier as the sun was setting."

Dante couldn't help but feel a twinge of envy. Sierra's world seemed to be so vibrant, full of color. She truly took note of everything around her and appreciated the world's beauty unlike anyone he'd ever met. By contrast, most days he felt as if he were sleepwalking through his day. Saying all the right things, meeting with all the right people, providing a royal spokesman with all the right quotes. Even the events he did for charity seemed hollow at times. He wasn't the one usually doing all the work. Just a symbol of the Crown. Nothing more.

Get a grip.

He was perilously close to "the poor prince" territory here, with such self-pitying thoughts. As a distraction, he picked up the wine bottle and topped off both their glasses.

Sierra held a hand up before he'd reached close to the top of the rim. "Whoa. As good as that is, I should probably slow it down a bit."

"Fair point. It has been a rather long day." He should probably take it easy on the wine as well. "But what's done is done." He couldn't very well pour it back in the bottle.

She nodded slowly, a sly smile over her lips. "I supposed it would be a shame to waste such delicious wine."

"It certainly would," he agreed, tapping his glass to hers as gently as possible. It was rather full.

"The reporters look awfully busy," Sierra commented as they polished off the salads and the main course. "Even as they eat, they're scribbling away on their little notepads."

"At least they're here to do a job."

She lifted an eyebrow. "Meaning?"

He hadn't intended for his inner thoughts from earlier to rise so close to the surface. "Never mind. It's not important."

She set her fork down. "Tell me," she prodded.

Dante did his best to explain his meaning. It was hard to put into words but if there was anyone he'd try to do it for, it was Sierra. "What value am I providing here exactly?" he asked. "I'm not one of the conservationists. I don't take care of the animals. I'm just here as a mouthpiece. A figurehead."

Sierra's mouth fell open. "You can't believe that, Dante."

"It's the truth, isn't it?"

She turned in her seat to face him directly. "On the contrary, Dante. What you're doing here is very important. Drawing attention to animal and environmental conservation is more crucial now than ever before. So many species are close to extinction. And the way some of these animals are hunted for profit is an absolute crime."

She was right about that. "An international crime," he agreed. "Yet it keeps happening." But what was he doing about any of it? Aside from speaking about it and spending time at a safari lodge? "It's not the cause I'm questioning," he told her, once again surprising himself with the revelation.

"I don't know what that means," Sierra answered after a pause. "But it's people like you that others pay attention to."

Leave it to Sierra to find a way to make him feel better about his mostly ceremonial role. Not that he was surprised. She'd always been one of the few people in his orbit who knew exactly understood his insecurities about becoming the leader his people needed. And she always knew what to say to smooth those insecurities over. Saints above, how he'd missed that. Dante hadn't even realized just how badly until this moment.

He didn't have a chance to respond as the server who had earlier brought the wine rolled a tray cart full of pastries and cakes up to the table beside them.

"Something sweet, madam? Sir?"

Sierra began to shake her head then leaned closer to the cart. "As full as I am, I don't think I can pass up on that banana cake."

The woman sliced a thick slice and drizzled a bronze glaze over the piece with a flourish before placing it in front of Sierra.

Some of the drizzle dropped onto her lips as she took a bite, and it took every ounce of his will not to reach over and wipe it away with his thumb.

He clenched his fist around his wineglass instead. It was a wonder the stem didn't snap.

CHAPTER FOUR

SIERRA'S SENSES WERE on overload. It had to be the exhaustion. Dante was right, it had been a rather long day. And this meal was much richer than her usual nightly fare—a quick bite from a food truck on her way home or a boxed meal heated in the microwave. But she couldn't blame either of those things for the way her heart was thudding in her chest. Or for the heady feeling fluttering in the pit of her stomach. No. That had everything to do with the man sitting next to her. Despite the slew of people around them, Sierra and Dante may as well have been alone. Her focus was zeroed in on him so completely. She couldn't seem to help herself.

Everything about this night was downright magical—dinner under a clear African sky dotted with bright stars, the humming nature sounds all around them, the sound of the flowing river in the distance. The mouthwatering food. Not to mention the delicious wine.

No wonder she was forgetting herself. She barely had any kind of social life with her busy schedule, couldn't even recall the last time she'd had a date. Now all this activity was throwing her off. She'd probably have the same reaction to any red-blooded male under the same circumstances.

Right. A voice inside her head mocked her. She wasn't fooling herself.

As if she could ignore the history she and Dante had together. As if she'd forget all the times she'd felt a pang of longing when he was near, even after his engagement to her best friend had been announced.

It was all so wrong.

"Sierra? Did you hear me?" Dante's voice broke into her thoughts. He was rising out of his chair with his hand extended to her.

"I'm sorry?"

He gave her an indulgent smile. "I said the entertainment is about to start. The lodge staffers have arranged for a customary dance ceremony to welcome us here."

Sierra stood and they followed Banti and the others to a makeshift stage on the patio at the back of the lodge. A small bonfire burned several feet away. Just as they took their seats, the beat of rhythmic drums began to flow through the air. A group of people appeared from the side of the building, four women and four men. The ladies wore long woven skirts with lacey, brightly colored tops. The men had on leather ankle-length pants and white tops. All wore crowns of beads atop their heads.

Sierra watched, mesmerized, as they began stomping their feet and dancing around the fire, perfectly in sync and perfectly in tune to the music. Her eyes moved from the dancers to the bonfire. It was as if the flames had become a part of the dance, flickering and moving along with the humans performing around it. She'd never seen anything like it, and would remember the vision for the rest of her days.

After a few minutes, a different beat began to play. Slower this time, the movements of the dancers shifted in response. The men bowed before the women, their hands clasped behind their backs. The women continued to dance, circling the men then circling the fire.

After several moments the drumbeat stopped and the dancers faced them, then bowed to the audience.

Sierra felt as if she'd experienced a masterpiece performance. Belatedly, she realized everyone else had started clapping. While she'd been sitting there stunned by the beauty and wonder of what she'd just witnessed.

One of the dancers approached her, as another went over to where Kaliha and Nantu sat.

"Come, my lady," she said, reaching for her hand. "I will show you how." She turned her focus on Dante. "You too, sir."

Sierra immediately started to protest. She'd always had two left feet. Rula had been the graceful, coordinated one of the two of them. Rula had been the one who'd attended all the ballet classes and who'd taken voice lessons, while Sierra could often be found swinging from trees outside their family cottage when she wasn't down by the river sketching in the dirt with a stick.

She was likely to fall on her face if she attempted any of the moves she'd just witnessed. But the woman was not taking no for an answer, her smile encouraging. She gave Sierra an enthusiastic nod. And Dante had already stood and was looking at her expectantly. He couldn't be serious. He knew her better than to think she should really attempt this.

Apparently not. "Come on, Sierra. Nantu and Kaliha are already on the dance floor." He tilted his head in their direction. "It will be fun," he added with a smile. The light from the fire cast a halolike glow on his dark hair.

The merriment behind his eyes lent a golden light to their depths.

How in the world was she supposed to turn him down when he was smiling at her that way?

With more than a little trepidation, Sierra stood and the two of them followed the dancer to the bonfire, where Nantu and Kaliha were mimicking the movements she'd just witnessed. They clearly didn't need any kind of lesson and appeared to be pros who done this more than once before. Sierra felt like the uncoordinated nerd at the high school dance, the one so desperately trying to fit in and praying that no one was paying any attention to her. But that was fallacy, of course. Dante's eyes were focused squarely in her direction.

His unwavering attention was only making this harder for her.

The dancer took Sierra's hand in hers and Dante's in the other. "Like this," she said, first stomping her right foot twice, then the left one once. Then she repeated the action. Okay. That seemed simple enough. Sierra copied her movements. Then she did it again. Dante didn't even appear to be trying. He was just stomping the dirt indiscriminately. Somehow, he still appeared to be in tune with the beat and the other dancers.

"That's great, my lady!" the dancer exclaimed. "Now just make it faster."

Sierra tried...she really did. But as soon as she attempted the faster pace, her one foot got caught in the hem of her skirt. Her other foot only caught air as she tried to balance herself. There was nothing for it, she was about to go down. A shriek of alarm tore from her lips as her mind registered how close she was to the bonfire.

But a pair of steady hands grabbed her about the waist before she could topple.

And Dante was there, to stop her from falling into the flames.

Yet Sierra still got the feeling she'd been saved from one fire only to land in another.

The relief that she hadn't fallen flat on her face was immediately replaced by something else. Dante was holding her, his arms tight around her middle, his breath hot against her cheek. Sierra lost all sense of the here and now. She could only zero in on the sensations coursing through her core. The feel of his arms around her, the heat of his body against her body, his warm breath against her cheek.

"Steady there, I have you."

Heaven help her, the images and thoughts those words invoked had her pulse skyrocketing, already high from the adrenaline resulting from her near fall.

She looked up to glance at his face. Reassuring, protective…handsome, so devastatingly handsome. Her gaze dropped to his lips. Like so many times in the past, she wondered what it would feel like to kiss him, to brush his lips with hers. What would he taste like? Would he still have traces of the ruby rich wine they'd shared earlier? Some of the dessert he'd indulged in?

If only they were just two ordinary people. If only he hadn't been married to her closest friend who'd so tragically been lost. If only he wasn't the crown prince of her homeland.

But the reality was that Dante was heir to a kingdom. Someone like her would simply be a distraction who provided little to no value to someone like him. Unlike Rula, she hadn't been prepared or trained to be a royal in any sense. Dante deserved someone by his side who had done just that. But it was hard to remember all that in this moment, with Dante's eyes dark and focused on her face.

Sierra wasn't sure how much time passed, with her simply standing in his embrace, before Kaliha appeared at her side. "Are you all right, dear?"

Sierra nodded, straightening and stepping out of Dante's grasp. Was it her imagination or did his hands just tighten around her midsection ever so slightly when she'd begun to remove herself?

"Yes, yes, I'm fine. Just a bit of a klutz."

Kaliha's gaze darted from her face to Dante's and back again. "Well, how fortunate that the prince moved so quickly. You were in good hands."

"Quite literally," Sierra said with a small chuckle, trying to make light of things, as lame an attempt as it was. To her horror, she looked around to find every eye trained solely on her. "I'm sorry to have alarmed everyone. I'm fine, really. Just not as dexterous as you clearly are."

Kaliha patted her arm. "I grew up doing these dances. You'll get the hang of it."

Ha! As if she'd ever try again. "Thank you," was all she could come up to say.

Sierra resisted the urge to groan out loud and watched Kaliha return to her husband's side. Just as she'd predicted, she'd just made a complete fool of herself. In front of the prime minister and his wife, no less. Not to mention the lodge staff and the two reporters. Great. There would probably be color photos of her in the papers and online tomorrow tripping over her own feet.

"I'm so sorr—" the dancer began.

Sierra held up a hand to stop her. "Please, don't apologize. The fault lies solely with me and my two left feet."

The woman gave her a grateful nod before turning away to find a more promising candidate to teach.

Sierra turned to find Dante watching her. "Uh… I should be thanking you too, of course. My first night here and it could have been a disastrous one. I imagine a game drive would be tough to do with a broken leg."

He shrugged. "Don't mention it. And for the record, you were doing fine until…well, until you weren't."

She cringed. It was an obvious attempt at trying to make her feel better. Which she appreciated but wasn't falling for.

"I think I'm done on the dance floor," she told him. "I'm sure you'd be able to find another partner, one who's a bit more dexterous, hopefully." For one, the female journalist was eyeing him from across the bonfire with clear interest.

Dante chuckled. "You can't get rid of me that easily." He led her back to the table. "Can I get you some more wine?"

That was the last thing she needed. "Absolutely not," she answered without hesitation. "Actually, I think I'm ready to retire for the night." More than ready. Between all the excitement and the tiredness, she just wanted to crawl under the netted canopy of the four-poster in her room and get some rest. Maybe sleep would help her to sort out the completely inconvenient emotions that had been churning through her gut back there. To imagine kissing Dante, of all things. What had gotten into her?

"I feel bad for leaving without saying good night to Kaliha and the prime minister," she told him.

"I'll explain to them later that you were exhausted and dead on your feet."

"Thanks. And tell them I should have known better than to attempt that dance on the best of days, let alone after a day of travel and all that delicious food. Oh, also there was the cabernet."

"They will understand," he reassured her. "Here, I'll walk you to your room."

Sierra wanted to decline his offer, but there was no tactful way to explain that she needed distance right now, particularly from him. *Especially* from him.

She gritted her teeth to keep from protesting. "Thank you," she said instead, following him up the steps of the lodge then around the corner toward the suite of rooms.

When they reached her door, Dante paused, searching her face for several moments. A heavy silence hung in the air between them. For the life of her, Sierra couldn't think of a thing to say in order to fill it. Even after she'd opened her door and turned back to face him, he hesitated, continuing to linger at the threshold. For a moment, Sierra felt exposed, unguarded. Could he somehow see what had been her thoughts earlier? The way she'd reacted at the feel of his arms around her? Did he somehow guess where her imagination had led about placing her lips on his?

For one insane moment, she was tempted to invite him inside. They were friends after all, weren't they? Nothing wrong with a bit of conversation with an old friend. But she wasn't fooling herself. She wouldn't be inviting him in for a chat. They would both know it. And then what?

Not to mention, everyone still at the bonfire would no doubt notice the prince's absence. The speculation that would follow would run rampant. The journalists in particular would have a field day with the knowledge that the prince had left with his companion and hadn't bothered to return.

No, asking Dante to come inside her room was out of the question.

"Guess we have a big day tomorrow," she said instead, by way of an attempt at conversation.

"Good night, Sierra," was all he said. Then he turned on his heel and walked away.

"Good night, dear prince," she answered, but not until he was well out of earshot.

Dante lingered outside his room, waiting until he heard the click of Sierra's door shutting behind her. For one insane moment, he thought about going back and knocking on her door. And then what? What exactly would he say? That he didn't want the night to end? That he wanted to spend some more time with her because these last few hours in her company had been some of the most enjoyable time he'd spent in much too long? Since even before Rula had passed?

Of course he couldn't tell her any of that. At best he would sound like some character out of a romantic comedy movie delivering a few cheesy lines. At worst he would sound desperate and lonely.

If the shoe fits...

Enough! He needed a distraction. He also needed a shower. Not just to wash away the dust and dirt of the evening but also to clear his mind and try to regain some focus.

He should probably use cold water.

Plus he'd reached the point of tiredness where it would actually be difficult to fall asleep. All these crazy thoughts. His attraction to someone he considered an old friend had to be the result of his exhaustion. There was no other rational explanation.

Sure, he'd had a minor crush on Sierra when they were younger, kids really. But he was an adult now, heir to the throne. He'd been a married man once. Would have to marry again. Papa already regularly nagged him about meeting eligible ladies. Or, to use Papa's term, *suitable young women who may qualify*. Just last week he'd tried to set Dante up with a member of the Swedish royal family. As if his next marriage were some kind of reality game show.

In a way, Dante supposed Papa was right. Weren't there constant bets in the gaming halls of Nocera about when and who he might marry?

Dante's lack of any kind of romantic entanglements only fed fuel to the gossip fire. As well as the people of Nocera, the newspapers also called him the Ever Grieving Prince. He couldn't seem to get over losing his wife, they speculated. He couldn't seem to move on and find another woman to wed. The truth was, Dante had no intention of moving on, knew he didn't deserve any kind of happiness. When the time came, he would marry once again. But this time there'd be no false pretenses. He'd lay everything out on the table. His next wife would have no pretenses that he might actually grow to love her.

No, he wouldn't make the same mistake twice.

Dante headed immediately to the shower. But the water did little to smooth the rough edges of his rambling thoughts. Toweling off several minutes later, he accepted defeat. He wasn't going to be able to fall asleep anytime soon.

Though more than full, he grabbed a banana out of the fruit bowl on the small wooden table by the entryway. Just give his hands something to do.

Tossing it in the air and catching it again, Dante stepped outside and walked toward the patio, which was still lit up with lanterns. A movement to his right startled him as he sat down. Then he was staring into a small face with a pair of beady eyes, and short whiskers.

A monkey. And he was eyeing Dante's fruit.

"A bit clichéd, isn't it?" Dante asked the animal, who simply blinked at him and moved a dark paw in his direction. Dante could have sworn the little guy was actually pointing at the banana. A chuckle rumbled in his chest. Wait till he told Sierra about this tomorrow.

And there it was. He couldn't seem to get the woman out of his mind.

With a sigh, Dante leaned over and extended the fruit in the monkey's direction. He snatched it with amazing speed. Was it actually grinning at him now?

"Tsamaya kwa!" a deep voice ordered from the steps, and Banti appeared, shooing the monkey away with dramatic hand gestures. It responded with a series of low-pitched grunts before bounding away off the railing and into the dark, biting into the banana along the way.

Dante had to chuckle at the scene. His first real native fauna sighting and he hadn't even been on the game drive yet.

"I'm very sorry, Prince Dante. That vervet is a nuisance around here. This is much later than he's usually out. All the noise and commotion must have roused him."

Dante could relate. "I might have the same problem," he told the other man. "Speaking of which, you must be tired too."

Banti rubbed a palm over his face. "Yes, it has been a rather long day."

Dante gestured to the cushioned wicker chair next to him. "Have a seat."

Banti obliged with a weary sigh. "Thank you."

"Do you live here at the lodge?" Dante asked.

The other man shook his head. "No, I live in a village about six kilometers from here. I am usually home much earlier. But today was a special day. I was needed here at the lodge."

Dante felt a twinge of guilt. "Sorry to have been part of the reason that kept you from home. And from your family."

A wide smile spread over Banti's face at the last word. True affection flooded his features.

"Tell me about them," Dante prodded.

His grin grew wider. "I married the girl I fancied since I was a child. The smartest, prettiest girl in the village. So talented too. She weaves blankets that are true works of art. I'm so lucky she chose me."

Banti's love as he spoke of his spouse was so clear, it was nearly palpable. He was a lucky man, indeed. "Any children?"

He nodded. "A girl almost seven. Bosses me around like she's the parent." Laughter laced his voice as he spoke. "And a little boy. Just turned three." He reached in his back pocket. "Here, let me show you."

Pulling out his phone, Banti tapped the screen and scrolled a few times before extending the device toward Dante to show him a photo of a smiling woman holding a colorful blanket with a look of clear accomplishment across her face.

Banti scrolled once more to call up another photo. This one showed Banti with a small boy cradled in his arms and the same woman next to him, her hand resting on the shoulder of a little girl who stood between them both. The children had Banti's smile.

A picture-perfect family.

"You really are lucky as you said, my friend." Dante said the thought aloud this time.

The other man's grin suddenly faded. "I'm sorry. I should not go on like this. I know you lost your wife not long ago."

Dante nodded. "About two years now."

"I'm sorry," Banti repeated.

"No need to apologize," Dante reassured him, sorry that the conversation had turned to such a depressing one.

He never quite knew what to say when it came to his talking about his marriage, disastrous as it was. In more ways than one.

The lightheartedness of just a moment ago had vanished completely. Banti sat staring at him, his eyes warm with compassion. Mixed with a good portion of pity, no doubt. Dante was pitied the world over for having lost his spouse so soon after the marriage ceremony of the decade. A true debacle most of the world had watched. Rula had wrangled the publicity personally at great effort. Effort that had paid off. For a small island kingdom people barely thought about, their nuptials had been broadcast far and wide across the world. Exactly as Rula had wanted. He had indulged her, simply because he didn't care enough not to. Let her have the attention and limelight she wanted so badly. Dante had no doubt worldwide interest would fade quickly enough. And it had. Until the announcement that Rula was gone, having died tragically in a car accident in the Italian Alps.

"I recall it was an automobile accident, right?" Banti asked before Dante could come up with a way to change the subject. Apparently, he wanted to know more. Or maybe he thought he was doing Dante a favor by giving him a chance to talk about his lost wife. Given the other man's warm personality, Dante was guessing it was the latter. He did his best to find the words that seemed to satisfy the curiosity of those who asked.

"That's right," he answered. "She was on holiday to visit friends." The lie came so easily now after two years of telling it. Hell, he almost believed it himself.

The truth was much more sinister. Rula hadn't been in the Italian Alps to visit friends. She'd been there because she was leaving him.

He hadn't been able to love his wife enough to have her stay with him. And it had cost her everything.

But neither Banti, nor the rest of the world, needed to know that. So he continued to tell the lie. "She was out for a drive when she lost control of her car. There's speculation a falling boulder might have been the catalyst."

Banti blew out a low whistle. "My sympathies, man."

"Thank you," he replied.

Like countless times before when the topic came up, Dante would leave it at that. Of course, he couldn't divulge the whole story. The details that Sierra didn't even know. Details like the fact that his wife wasn't alone at the time of the accident. In fact, she'd been in the company of one of his most trusted advisers. The man had asked for an emergency leave the day before for "private reasons."

No, Dante wasn't going to share any of those details with Banti. It was a miracle that the press hadn't found out. Dante guessed it was enough of a story that the fantasy marriage of a royal couple had so tragically come to an abrupt end.

He supposed one day the truth might come out, but he'd worry about that when and if it ever happened.

"It must be difficult to carry out your royal duties without a partner."

"Thank you, Banti," he answered. Somehow the man sitting next to him now seemed more like a friend even though they'd met merely hours ago. "But I'm not quite ready to move on romantically. Not for a while."

"I understand. I'm sure your heart is still broken."

Dante ignored that. "Let's just say my wife would be a hard act to follow as the future queen of Nocera."

She must not have closed the netting over her bed all the way. Left a gap somewhere despite the miles of fabric draped over the canopy. Because there was definitely something in there with her, buzzing around and feasting on her skin. Sierra uttered a mild curse and kicked off the thin sheet covering with her feet. So much for getting some much-needed sleep.

Crawling out of bed to go look for some type of lotion, she heard the low rumblings of male voices outside. Apparently, she wasn't the only one still awake. Maybe there was someone out there who could help find some kind of balm for the itchy spots on her legs from the all the bug bites. Leaving her room, she made her way to the patio in the direction of the voices. Then nearly turned around when she noticed who it was out there and heard the last thing he'd said to his companion. Dante.

...my wife would be a hard act to follow...

Sierra started to pivot—she could deal with the itchiness until morning. Too late; he must have sensed her presence as he immediately stood. "Sierra? Is everything all right?" It took her a moment to answer, too distracted by the way his eyes roamed over her from head to toe. A silky tank and loose boy shorts that fell just below her thighs comprised her usual sleep attire. In this moment, she wished she was wearing something a tad less revealing. Why hadn't she thought to grab a robe?

"Yes," she finally answered. "I just seem to have a few bug bites. I was wondering if there might be some type of lotion available. To help with the itching."

Dante's gaze traveled over her once more. "Well, I can tell you your first problem."

"What would that be?"

He gestured toward her middle. "The color you're wearing. Tsetse flies are attracted to colorful clothing. That deep red is certainly colorful."

"I don't think what I'm wearing is much of the issue. Apparently, many beings find me fun to dine on."

A wolfish smirk appeared on his lips before he tightened them closed. Heaven help her, she'd noticed before he'd done so.

Banti broke through the tension that seemed to have thickened the air around them. "I have something you can use. I'll go get it. Though I have to warn you, it smells pretty bad."

She gave him a grateful nod. "Small price to pay. I'll come with you to get it."

No way she was going to stand out here alone with Dante a minute longer, his words from before echoing through her head. The image of the hungry expression on his face seared into her mind.

CHAPTER FIVE

SIERRA AWOKE THE next morning and scrunched her nose to the offensive stench that permeated the room. Banti hadn't been kidding about his remedy for the bites smelling bad. A complete understatement as far as she was concerned. Still, it had done the trick, allowing her to finally get some sleep. Restless as it was.

She'd been hounded by vivid dreams all night. Not quite nightmares but unsettling just the same. Images of her dancing around a large fire that grew and grew until the flames licked her legs. Her darting away from the heat only to fall into Dante's arms. He set her down immediately then reached for a golden crown that had materialized on her head before walking away, leaving her to evade the flames on her own.

Wow. A heck of a dream, one she didn't need a psychology degree to infer the symbolism behind.

Sierra shook her head briskly to push away the images. Her imagination was in full active mode, which made sense; she was a creative professional after all. But at times like this it could be quite disruptive to her peace of mind.

Right. As if any part of this trip had been at all peaceful in any way. Today would probably be no different. Given that she and Dante would be attending their first game drive together. Of course, they would be in the company of the others, with Banti as their tour guide. Still. Why did everyone around them seem to be narrowing to a distance whenever she was in his company?

...my wife would be a hard act follow...

The sentiment wasn't surprising. The truth was, Rula was in a class all by herself. She always had been. Classically beautiful, and she'd always made sure to stay fit and trim. With a charming wit to boot. Of course, Dante wasn't going to get over her anytime soon. Sierra had never bothered to compare herself to the bright star that had been her dear friend. There wouldn't have been any point.

Sierra sighed and turned on the shower. There was no point in dwelling on any of this either. Once this trip was over, she could go back to her life in New York, try to make a real name for herself on the fashion scene. Everything would go back to normal. The fact that she'd already come up with new designs as a result of being here was icing on the cake.

She'd just shut off the shower and thrown on her clothes when a knock sounded on the door. Sierra glanced at the digital clock on the wall. Unless something about the plans had changed, she wasn't running late.

The person on the other side came as a surprise. The reporter. What was her name again? Cathryn? Caitlin? Katy? Something along those lines. "Yes? Can I help you?" Sierra asked, genuinely curious as to what this unexpected visit might be about.

Cathryn/Caitlin/Katy ducked her head before answering. "Sorry to bother you, but I wanted to catch you before breakfast. Do you have a minute to chat?"

Sierra immediately began to protest. "Any official statement—"

The other woman cut her off. "This is strictly off the record."

Sierra hesitated before opening the door wider to let the other woman in, out of curiosity more than anything else. She motioned for her to sit down at the settee in the center of the room, then took a seat on the wooden chair across from her.

"I don't mean to intrude, Ms. Compari." She actually looked nervous, further piquing Sierra's curiosity.

"Call me Sierra, please."

She smiled before saying, "Thanks. Please call me Cathryn."

That was one mystery solved. Now, to discover the reason for this visit.

"What is it that I can do for you, Cathryn?"

"Well, I'm a little embarrassed to even bring this up, but girl code."

Okay. That did nothing to clear up the reason she was here. "I'm sorry, girl code?"

The color rose in her cheeks, accented by her fair skin and reddish blond hair. Sierra was right, whatever Cathryn was here for, she was more than a little embarrassed by it.

"You know, I just want to be sure that I'm not stepping on another woman's toes. Or intruding on her territory."

What in the world was this woman talking about? Toes? Territory?

Then it snapped into place in her mind. Sierra felt her jaw drop as realization dawned. Dante. This visit was about Dante. Her suspicion was confirmed a moment later by the other woman's next question. "Is there anything—" she hesitated just a moment before pressing on "—anything romantic between you and the crown prince? Again, strictly off the record."

Sierra's mouth went dry as she tried to figure out a way to answer.

"I'm asking for personal reasons." Cathryn stated the obvious.

"I see," was the best Sierra could come up with in response.

Cathryn held her hands up. "I mean, I know it can't be anything serious. He is a royal, after all. But I wanted to make sure that you wouldn't be—"

Sierra didn't need further explanation. "A fling then?"

The other woman nodded slowly. "Can you imagine? An ordinary gal like me with an actual prince? That would make for a memory of a lifetime."

"I have no doubt."

"And before you say this isn't very professional of me, I just want to clarify that once I file this piece, I'll still have a few days here. On my personal time."

A storm of conflicting emotions rushed through Sierra. The most prominent one, she didn't even want to acknowledge—a stinging bite of jealousy. Pure and strong. Which made no sense. She had no claim to Dante. No right to feel even the slightest bit possessive. He was perfectly entitled to a fling with a journalist if he so desired. Consenting adults and all. So why was she finding it so impossible to just answer the simple question? Of course, she and Dante had nothing between them. Why in the world had this woman even speculated that she had to ask?

"But I wanted to make sure to ask you about it first."

Say something! Other than what she wanted to say most, that Dante held a special place in her heart that no one else had ever been able to fill. That she'd left her home kingdom and moved a world away rather than watch him make a life with the friend she considered a sister.

No, she couldn't say any of those things. She could barely admit it all to herself.

"No. There is nothing between the prince and myself. Feel free to make your move, Cathryn."

Just when Dante had decided Sierra was going to skip breakfast, she appeared in the doorway of the dining hall. A strange rush of pleasure almost overwhelmed him. But then he took a look at her face as her gaze found his. Something flickered behind her eyes, and she visibly bristled at the sight of him.

Huh.

Sierra clearly wasn't happy. And if he had to guess, he had something to do with that unhappiness. Which made no sense. He hadn't even seen her since last night when she'd hightailed after Banti to get her insect bite medicine.

"How's the itching?" he asked, standing as she approached the table.

"It's fine," she answered, brisk and short, before pulling a chair out and sitting down. At the very opposite of the table, as far from Dante as she could get.

A server immediately appeared with a steaming pot of coffee and a fresh cup for her. The smile she flashed the man was pure sunshine and warmth. Very different from the reception he'd gotten. Somehow, Dante figured it had less to do with caffeine and more to do with him. No, it was definitely him who had caused her ill humor, not some general state of irritation.

For the life of him, he had no clue what he might have done to cause it.

"You left so soon last night I didn't get a chance to introduce you to the new friend I'd just made."

"Friend?"

"Yep," he said, lowering his hand to knee level. "About this tall. Real hairy with beady eyes. Poor hygiene. I don't think he's showered in a while."

She blinked up at him. Clearly, his attempt at humor was falling flat. "A monkey," he explained. "Banti said he was a menace, but I found the little fella somewhat charming."

Her eyebrows drew together. If she was at all curious about what he'd just said, Sierra was hiding it well. "Huh, you'll have to tell me all about him. Or her."

At another time was the silent yet implied addendum.

"Sure. Will do." Saints above. He'd had less trouble charming feuding dignitaries all those times he'd served as international mediator.

"Do you mind terribly if I have my breakfast alone?" She pulled a small booklet out of her pants pocket. "I wanted to work on some designs while I have my coffee."

Ouch. Far be it from him to stick around where he wasn't wanted. Still, he couldn't help the concern that grew in him that she would only be having coffee before the busy day they had in front of them. When was the last time he'd been concerned about whether a woman had eaten? He couldn't recall a single time, not even when he'd been a married man. Dante didn't want to examine too closely the ramifications of that.

"Sorry. I'll go and leave you to it. But I think you should eat something too. Coffee is hardly enough, given what we have ahead of us. Besides…" he added, gesturing to the extensive spread on the table—fruit, cheeses, various pastries and assorted breads.

She inhaled, her chest visibly rising and falling again dramatically. "Sure, I'll grab a bit while I draw."

Why did he get the distinct impression she was merely humoring him in her haste to have him disappear?

Without another word, Dante turned on his heel and made his way outside to the patio. Maybe his new friend the monkey would be more tolerant of his company. Even if Dante did have to bribe him with the banana he'd slipped into his back pocket at breakfast, just in case the vervet showed up again.

To think, he'd gone to the dining room early then lingered at the table, waiting for her to show up. Only to be effectively dismissed like some sort of pest. Like the tsetse flies that had been biting her all night.

That thought brought forth images of the way she'd looked last night. Her long shapely legs exposed under those, oh so short bottoms she'd had on. The way the tank had hugged her in all the right places and revealed the elegant slant of her shoulders.

Stop it.

The woman didn't even want to be in the same room with him right now, for heaven's sake. And he didn't even know why.

When he'd happened upon her drawing last night, she'd asked him to stay. So what had changed so quickly? Maybe he'd held her a bit too tight after catching her fall near the bonfire. Or he'd held on to her just a moment too long. Maybe he'd imagined that she'd been in no hurry to step out of his grasp. Or the way the glowing light of the fire had intensified the heat he could have sworn he saw in her eyes while she was in his arms.

He swore out loud. Enough already.

Well, Sierra could hardly avoid him all day. They were about to spend the next several hours together riding through the African grasslands. Maybe he'd manage to garner some clue as to exactly what he'd done to win her sharp ire. Judging by her pursed lips and rod straight spine, she wasn't going to divulge the reason herself. So different from what he was used to. When he was a married man, his missteps were pointed out to him almost immediately with great clarity by his parents or advisers as conduct unbecoming of a married prince.

Now, when it came to Sierra, he didn't have the slightest clue.

Sierra waited, watching through the doorway until Dante stood up and left the patio. Then she finally rose and walked out there herself, plopping herself down on one of the lounge chairs. The sun was a dark, burnt orange, like an orb sent down from the heavens. It turned the clouds around it into a burst of color, various shades of red.

A large splashing noise sounded from the distance, coming from the direction of the meandering river. She wondered what kind of animal had just gone in for a swim or a refreshing drink. It triggered all sorts of pulse points in her imagination.

Opening up her notebook, she began to draw the idea for the dress that was slowly forming in her mind. She hadn't been lying to Dante when she'd said she wanted time to do some sketching. But she couldn't deny how petty she was being.

It made no sense. Why was she so annoyed with him? It wasn't his fault that another unattached female on this trip with them was interested in him. Sierra wanted to tell herself that she was merely perturbed out of loyalty to his wife. But she wouldn't lie to herself that way or dishonor Rula's memory in that manner.

The truth was as plain as the rocky hill in the distance. Her already complicated feelings for Dante were being pushed to the surface. And she didn't know what to do about it.

For heaven's sake. The man was a prince. The heir to a crown. He was also a man who hadn't gotten over the loss of his wife and who had females yearning for him in the middle of southern Africa. What choice did she have but to keep her distance? For the sake of her sanity. And her heart.

Sierra sucked in a breath at the last thought. With a mild curse, she closed the book and crammed it back into her pocket. Though she had a clear idea of the dress in her mind's eye, suddenly her focus was too shot to try to draw it on paper.

A rustling in the trees in the distance had her wondering what kind of animal might be jumping through the branches. Maybe it was Dante's monkey. A chuckle spilled from her lips before she could help it. She really had wanted to hear about the encounter. But she'd been snippy to Dante instead. For something he wasn't even aware of. He had no idea one of the journalists accompanying them had her sights set on him.

How would Cathryn make her move? Sierra wondered. Would she show up at his door late at night? The woman was clearly not the shy type. Part of Sierra wished she could be the same. To just go after what she wanted, be bold enough to just announce it the way Cathryn had. The problem was, Sierra had no idea exactly what it was she wanted. Aside from her career, she had no idea what would fulfill or enrich her life.

One thing was certain—she had no social life to speak of. That would have to change. No doubt it was part of the reason her inappropriate and inconvenient attraction to Dante was making itself known. Sierra would have to find a way to fill that void. As soon as she got back to New York, she was going to take Camille up on the offer of the blind date with her cousin's friend. Or was it her friend's cousin?

It hardly mattered. Maybe Sierra would even sign up for one or more of those silly services that let you swipe left or right on your phone screen based on a simple photo and brief write-up. Sierra sighed and rubbed the tension out of her forehead. Rather than feeling any kind of excitement or anticipation at the prospect of a blind date or online dating, she felt pathetic and morose.

A shadow fell over her lap and she looked up to find Kaliha standing next to her chair. Sierra hadn't even heard her approach.

"Well, you look deeply pensive," Kaliha said. "How do they say...? A few lira for your thoughts?"

Sierra had to chuckle. "Not quite. Though I suppose it might work given inflation."

Kaliha narrowed her eyes on her in confusion.

"Never mind. I was just admiring the beauty of the skyline."

"Yes, lovely, isn't it?" Kaliha pulled the chair next to her and sat.

Sierra nodded. "Very different from the island nation I grew up on. Or the island city I call home now."

"Tell me about your birthplace. I mean your thoughts about it. Aside from what an outsider might know from simply reading an encyclopedia site." She patted Sierra's arm. "I've always wanted to visit but never got a chance."

For the first time that morning, Sierra felt a lightness in the vicinity of her heart. Thoughts of Nocera always lifted her spirits no matter her current state. "Oh, you must come see it. It's a mountainous island off the Greco-Turkish coast surrounded by the bluest, most tranquil waters that turn a shade of turquoise depending on the season. The beaches are as luxurious as any Club Med. Cruise ships from all over the world bring tourists to our pristine coast."

"And Prince Dante is the one who will inherit the throne of the monarchy," Kaliha said. "Though I hope it won't be anytime soon. Long live his father, the noble king."

A pang of anxiety tightened in Sierra's center. How could she have forgotten for a moment the reason the king and queen weren't here themselves? The sole reason she was entrusted to accompany Dante on this trip was because the king's health was a concern. How selfish of her. She should be doing all she could to ensure the trip was a successful one. Instead, she was letting her schoolgirl crush impact her actions. The king and queen deserved better from her. And so did Dante.

She turned her focus back to the conversation at hand. "That's right. The monarchy of Nocera has always been a working family. Queen Naila supports various causes and charities throughout the world, such as the reason for this trip. And the king and Dante work hard to ensure the economy is healthy and robust, with a profitable export industry, everything from olives to citrus fruits."

Her mouth began to water thinking of the fruit trees she'd climbed when growing up. "The oranges and tangerines taste like nectar, especially picked straight from the tree. Which I did my share of when I was younger."

Kaliha gave her an indulgent smile. "Quite the spokesperson. You might have a second career in the tourist industry. You sound like you miss it quite a bit, dear."

Kaliha was right. Sierra did miss Nocera and its people. More than she wanted to acknowledge.

CHAPTER SIX

BY THE TIME Sierra was dressed and had slathered herself in sunblock and bug repellent, she was running late. To her chagrin, everyone else had already gathered by the three-vehicle caravan that would take them on the day's adventure—a game drive through the nearby reserve.

Hurriedly, she made her way down the steps of the lobby toward the first open-air SUV. Dante stood leaning against it, his ankles crossed. Sierra's breath caught at the sight of him. The man looked like he could be posing for an African travel catalog. Or a cologne ad. Khaki pants belted at the waist and a fitted maroon shirt that showed off all the contours of his muscled chest. Dark aviator glasses with gold rims covered his eyes, so she couldn't quite read his expression as she approached. But the thin line of his lips told her he hadn't forgotten her coldness that morning. His words when he spoke confirmed it.

"You're set to be riding with me in the first car with Banti driving," he told her. "Unless you have an objection to that arrangement. If so, we can see about an adjustment."

She shook her head. "No objection. I'm anxious to get going. This is so very exciting"

With a small wave to the others behind them, she let

Dante help her into the back seat then scooted over so that he could sit next to her.

Banti bid her a good morning and started the vehicle.

And then they were off.

Sierra did her best to focus on the landscape rather than the man sitting next to her. Luckily, it wasn't long before Banti was slowing down to show them something. When he came to a stop, he pointed to a tall patch of grass about three meters away.

"We're in luck," Banti said in a low voice. "Take a look."

Sierra didn't see it at first, but then a gasp of surprise and thrill escaped her lips. A spotted leopard lay resting in the blades of grass, licking at her paw.

"Oh, my. She's beautiful." Images flooded her mind with gowns of flowing fabric, covered in irregular spots.

"She's not alone," Banti added.

Again, it took a moment for her to see it. Squinting her eyes against the sunlight, she noticed a movement near the animal.

"Is that—"

Dante was the one who answered. "She's got a cub."

Sierra watched in awe as the small cat strolled around its mother, nuzzling against her with its button-sized snout. When it reached her backside, it swatted at its mom's swinging tail with its paw.

She turned to see Dante's reaction to the delightful scene to find another surprise. He was holding a professional looking camera to his face and snapping a photo. Sierra had been on enough photo shoots to know the equipment in his hands wasn't designed for amateurs.

Since when had he learned his way around a camera

meant for a professional? He was handling it like he'd been doing it for years.

She gave him an inquisitive look when he lowered it. He merely shrugged. "Just something I picked up a couple of years ago."

A couple of years ago. That would mean right around the time of Rula's death. Even behind the glasses, she could see Dante was aware she'd figured out the timing of when he'd started his new hobby. A distraction from his grief then.

She didn't get a chance to ask any more about it as Dante leaned over, holding the camera out to her. "Here, look through the lens. To get a better look at the leopard and her cub. Better than the best binoculars."

He was right, Sierra realized as she did what he suggested. She felt as if she was standing less than a foot away. Instinctively, she reached her hand out, as if she could reach out and touch the leopard.

She heard Dante's low chuckle next to her. He was less than an inch away now, the camera still hung by a strap around his neck. The smell of his aftershave tickled her nose; the warmth of his skin brushing against her arms sent an electric current over her skin. For one insane moment, she imagined yanking the strap to pull Dante's face closer to hers. Then her lips would find his and she'd finally be able to taste him like she'd so often dreamed of doing. Her breath heaved in her chest at the pictures running through her mind.

Just. Stop. It.

Focus on the beautiful animal and its young one. Much safer than where her thoughts had just wandered.

She cleared her throat and handed the camera back to

him. "Thank you. It was incredible to see her up close that way."

He shrugged. "You're welcome. Feel free anytime for the rest of the trip."

"Thanks," she repeated, unsure what else to say. She had no doubt she was going to take him up on the offer to look through his camera lens repeatedly through this adventure. Which would mean he'd be moving that close to her over and over. The scent of him filling her nostrils, his warm breath against her face. The way her body responded to his nearness. She had no choice but to try to ignore it all.

As best as she could anyway.

They lingered several more minutes simply staring at the scene in silence. Not a sound could be heard from inside the vehicle. It was if even their breathing had slowed as they took in the beauty of the scene. But an orchestra of noises played around them from the grasslands, like a concert performed by the wild. Insects and birds and running water. Along with a steady drumbeat that seemed to be ringing through the air.

Or maybe that was just the pounding of her heart.

He should have gotten a longer camera strap.

Dante shifted in his seat, moving away from Sierra and the sensations that rushed through him whenever she was close. The insect repellent lotion she wore couldn't mask her distinctive feminine scent. It reminded him of vanilla with a hint of cloves. She'd always smelled that way. Even dressed in safari friendly clothing, Sierra looked chic and fashionable, like the esteemed designer she was. A tan long-sleeved jacket over brown leggings that showed off the shapeliness of her legs. A loose scarf around her neck that matched the straw-colored cowboy hat she wore. She looked like some kind of novel cross between a female rancher and a fashionista.

He found it adorable. And more than a little enticing. Dante sighed. He should be noticing the sights around him instead of the woman in the seat beside him. Easier said than done.

Banti gave them a nod over his shoulder from the front seat then shifted the vehicle and they were moving once more. About three kilometers later, they approached another breathtaking scene. Clearly, Banti knew what he was doing as their guide.

To their right a few meters away on Dante's side stood four tall giraffes browsing and picking at the leaves of even taller trees.

"Those are acacia trees," Banti explained. "Giraffes are particularly fond of that type."

Without having to turn around, Dante sensed Sierra had moved closer to him to get a better look. He had to resist the urge to shift her onto his lap so that they'd both be on the same side of the vehicle. As tempting as that idea was, it was out of the question, of course. So he did the next best thing, he moved out of the way and handed her the camera again, the strap tethering them together once more. She held it up to her face and her mouth fell open, forming a small o.

"They're majestic!" she exclaimed, breathless. "Absolutely beautiful."

The giraffes weren't the only things of beauty out here. He cursed silently at the thought, then he made a derisive sound and gave himself a mental kick. Now he was waxing poetic like some sort of besotted fool.

Sierra lowered the camera. "What?"

"Nothing. Just admiring the view." If she only knew.

She gave him a speculative look before lifting the camera back to her face. She held on to it the entire time they were there, her chest heaving with excitement at what she was witnessing. One of the giraffes chose that moment to swivel its long neck in their direction, as if watching them the same way it was being watched. Sierra's gasp was audible.

She lowered the camera, eyes wide with awe. "That felt like I was looking right into his eyes," she said, her voice shaky. Then she blinked and looked down at the camera she held as if realizing for the first time what was in her hands. "I'm so sorry. I haven't even given you a chance to see." She held the camera out to him.

Dante immediately shook his head. There was no way he was going to diminish this experience for her by even a fraction.

"You hold on to it," he told her. "I can see just fine."

It wasn't until they'd driven away from the giraffes and Sierra handed the camera back to him that it occurred to Dante that he'd neglected to take their photo.

Their next sighting didn't take much longer to get to. Banti took a few wide turns, the terrain growing rougher with each one. Finally, they pulled up beside a formation of large boulders. It was Dante's turn to be awestruck. A pride of lions, including two with thick manes, lounged upon the rocks. As the Landcruiser came to a stop, the animals eyed them lazily, appearing rather bored.

Dante couldn't tear his gaze away. As stunning as the leopard and giraffes had been, the sight of a pride of lions was a different experience altogether. An element of danger hung palpable in the air. These animals were apex predators who might attack to kill on a mere whim. Knowing that they were in the capable hands of an experienced guide like Banti tempered the risk of course. Not to mention the two burly men in the last car serving as his bodyguards. But nothing could erase that risk entirely. Sierra's thoughts must have led in the same direction. She'd gone absolutely still next to him, her pallor the shade of a bleached bedsheet.

Without thinking, Dante reached over and took her hand in his, gave it a gentle reassuring squeeze. "They're not interested in us. Don't be afraid," he told her.

She visibly swallowed, her eyes never leaving the pride. "They're not interested now. But what if they suddenly get hungry?" she whispered in a low voice, almost imperceptible. As if she were afraid to disturb the lounging predators just a few feet away.

He had to chuckle at that. "That might be a problem."

"I'll say."

"Rest assured, I'll protect you at all costs," he said, with a dramatic clap of his hand to his chest. "Even if it means throwing myself in front of you in case of an attack."

She glanced sideways at him. "I know you're merely making a joke, but I fully expect you to do so if it comes to that."

He bowed to her. "Without question, my lady. I shall not even hesitate," he said, trying his best to sound like what he imagined a knight from medieval times might sound.

He extended the camera to her, but she held a hand up and shook her head. "No, thanks. I have no desire to see these guys up close. Not their sharp teeth or razor-like claws or…" She shuddered as she trailed off.

Dante began to get ready to snap a photo, not wanting to miss his chance when it came to this pic. But Sierra still held fast to his hand.

He didn't pull his hand away. It looked like he wasn't going to get a picture of the lions either.

Joking or not, Sierra's fear about the lions would have been tenfold higher if Dante hadn't been sitting by her side back there. Her pulse still hadn't returned to normal by the time they reached the clearing where they'd been having lunch middrive.

Though the rapid pulse might have had less to do with the predators and more to do with the man himself.

She watched Dante now as he helped Banti bring the coolers out while Sierra and the others set up the folding chairs around the makeshift table—a flattened bolder near a small stream. Dante had an easy way with almost everyone she'd ever seen him with. Now, he was chatting good-naturedly with the other man while he effortlessly lifted the handle of one cooler and carried it over to where she sat with the others.

Sierra felt ravenous. All the fresh air, sunshine and excitement of a game drive could sure work up a girl's appetite. Not to mention, the prospect of being the meal herself.

As soon as the sandwiches were delivered, she waited with no small amount of impatience until everyone had settled into their seats and unwrapped their portions. Then she tore into hers.

The crisp baguette and vegetable spread tasted better than any gourmet meal she'd been treated to at any five-star restaurant in Manhattan. The frosty bottle of water tasted better than the finest champagne. Or maybe she was just really thirsty.

She looked up to find Dante's gaze on her, amusement dancing in his eyes. Tilting her head, she gave him a small shrug. "I was hungry."

"Hope you saved some room," he told her.

"Why's that?"

He bumped her shoulder. "I eyed some chocolate chip cookies in one of the coolers. I think they're meant for later as a snack, but…" He reached behind him and pulled out a white paper bag.

Sierra glanced around at the others in the circle. No one seemed to be paying any attention to them. "You snuck cookies? How naughty of you. So unbecoming of a future monarch," she teased, keeping her voice to a whisper.

He shrugged, made a motion to put the bag back where he'd retrieved it. Sierra grabbed his upper arm to stop him. "Don't you dare put that cookie back."

Dante's smile thinned as his gaze dropped to where she touched him. His eyes darkened when he looked back up at her. A rush of heat swept through her, starting from the palm of her hand where she touched him. She dropped her hand back to her lap.

Sierra forced her mind back to the cookie. "I promise to share if you hand it over." He did so with a smile. Sierra polished hers off in a couple of bites. The others slowly scattered after their meals, strolling nearby, taking in the scenery.

Sierra simply felt too full and too hot to do the same. Whether Dante felt the same or simply stayed put to keep her company, she couldn't be sure. They were the only two left sitting at the "table," though Dante's bodyguards hovered nearby, somehow close enough to keep an eye on them while still affording them the ability to carry on a private conversation. She had to wonder what they thought about the two of them. Did they have the same suspicions Cathryn had about a potential relationship between them? The thought of the other woman and her interest in Dante sent a frisson of unwarranted anger down her spine. She didn't want to think about that right now. Or ever.

Sierra picked up a stick near her seat and started scribbling in the dirt by her feet. As comfortable as she was with the silence, she was curious about Dante's new hobby.

"So, how'd you come about getting a camera?"

His gaze turned to the horizon. "I needed a lot of time alone those first few days after…" He trailed off. Sierra didn't need him to finish the sentence. He was referring to Rula's accident.

"So many people offering condolences, pity really." He sighed wearily. "I'm ashamed to say that after a while I couldn't really stomach any more, though I know everyone meant well."

Sierra felt a pang of guilt. She could have been there for him, helped him in his grief. But she'd had to get away, had to find a way to deal with her own loss.

Dante continued, "Rather than hole up in my suite, I started taking long walks. First around the castle gardens. Eventually I wandered farther and farther out around the island. The beaches, the villages, wooded areas. Each spot had its own characteristic charm, its own beauty. And I'd never even bothered really seeing it before. It took a tragedy for me to even look at all the wonder I had around me since birth."

"You wanted a way to capture it permanently," she said.

He turned back to face her. "That's right. That's it exactly." He seemed surprised that she understood.

Sierra knew what he meant. "It's how I feel when I see

something that calls forth an idea. What makes me want to sit down and sketch the images that come into my head as soon as they appear."

Something suddenly scurried by their feet, interrupting the conversation. A small animal that she wouldn't be able to name. It snatched a morsel of food someone had to have have dropped by one of the empty chairs, then ran back toward the tall grass with its haul.

"What in the world was that?" Sierra asked.

"Some type of Valhalian rodent, I would guess."

"It appeared to be the size of a small terrier."

Dante chuckled. "I guess rodents are bigger around these parts."

"Huh. I don't know. I think some of the rats in the New York subway system might be comparable. Particularly on garbage day."

Dante's eyes narrowed on her face. "What is it?" she asked. Was there a smear of chocolate on her face from the cookie or something? If so, he might have mentioned it before all this time.

"Nothing. I just always wanted to ask if you're happy there. If you like it in New York."

Wow. The question came out of nowhere, wholly unexpected. The answer was complicated.

Dante continued, "After all, you're half a world away from your home and everything that's familiar to you. Is it all you hoped it would be?"

Huh. He'd clearly given this a lot of thought. How long had he been pondering such questions? What did it mean that he was still doing so?

"Maybe I simply wanted to see if I could make it on my own," she answered, though it was only part of the story.

He simply nodded. "I get that." He hesitated, as if he might be weighing his words, before adding, "Was that the only reason?"

Sierra sucked in a breath, waited several beats trying to find the words before giving up. "I had to leave, Dante," was all she said. "I couldn't stay there any longer." As far as answers went, she knew how inadequate that was.

But it was all she could offer him.

CHAPTER SEVEN

SHE JUST HAD to get through the next several hours. The event she'd been dreading this whole trip was set to begin in about four hours. Sure, Dante would be the center of attention, but she'd be front and center, and she had to be ready to answer any question directed her way. Not to mention all the photos. She'd watched Dante and his parents enough over the years to realize what a paparazzi magnet the royals could be. It was even worse when Rula was alive. Unlike Sierra, her friend reveled in the attention of the press, found ways to draw their attention and was always prepared to give them a money shot.

The activity in the lodge had grown considerably busier over the past twenty-four hours. The peace and quiet of the place when they'd first arrived was gone. Now, there were strangers with heavy equipment and large messenger bags traipsing around whenever Sierra stepped outside. Otto and the other bodyguard stayed much closer to her and Dante than they had been upon arrival. Both men seemed much less relaxed.

The entire atmosphere had changed.

Sierra sucked in a breath. She was just going to take the day one step at a time. Starting with the team that was on its way to her cabin to help her prepare for the news conference. The palace had arranged for a hair and makeup artist as well as an attire stylist. Sierra wasn't sure how she felt about that last professional the palace had insisted on. She was a fashion designer for Pete's sake. She clothed some of the most famous people on the planet and designed for the world-renowned House of Perth. But she wasn't about to argue with protocol. Sierra knew when to pick her battles.

Except you didn't fight for what you wanted when it mattered most.

Her wayward mind began replaying the days leading up to Dante and Rula's nuptials years ago. The moments she'd debated whether to let her true feelings be known. Or confided to one or both of them that they needed to re-think their marriage of convenience. Then common sense had intervened and she'd resisted the urge. How could she risk upsetting her closest friend right before she was about to marry a prince?

But maybe Rula would still be here if she'd done just that.

Her friend had deserved so much better. Rula's parents had only seen her as a means to an end—a way to ensure their elevation in Nocera's high society. On the surface, Rula appeared to have led a charmed life. Wealthy family, a beautiful home, close ties to the royals. But Sierra knew just how little love or true affection her friend had been afforded. And how much Rula longed for only that. Then when she'd finally married her prince, a tragic accident had claimed her life. Sierra's eyes began to sting with tears, and she fought to keep them at bay.

She pushed the errant thoughts away just as a knock sounded at her door. Throwing on her dressing gown, she ran to answer it. She'd been instructed to have her face scrubbed, her hair washed and be ready to get dressed.

If only Camille was around to offer her some tips about being the one poked and prodded.

Two smiling faces greeted her when she opened the door. One carried a heavy silver case, the other was pulling a clothing rack. The woman with the case had an eyebrow piercing and a complicated bun of thin braids atop her hair. Her companion had deep ebony hair cut in a sharp-edged bob, slanted down from her ear to her chin on one side of her face, and an undershave on the other.

The woman with the pierced eyebrow introduced herself as Galen. The other woman's name was Tracey. Tracey was the stylist while Galen was there to do her hair and makeup.

"I'm a fan of your work, Sierra," Tracey said immediately upon entering the room, which made Sierra warm up to her instantly. Galen's warm, friendly smile was enough to do the same.

"Thanks." Sierra smoothed the skirt of her dressing gown. "I have to admit, I'm not used to being on the other side of this process. I'm a bit nervous."

"Nothing to be nervous about," Galen told her in a charming accent. She guided Sierra to her vanity bureau and pulled out the rolling chair in front of the mirror. Sierra sat down and studied her reflection. Dark circles framed her eyes; she hadn't gotten much sleep. Galen should probably start with covering that up first.

"Not just about all this," Sierra found herself admitting. "But about the news conference itself. I'm not used to being in the spotlight."

Tracey walked over and gave her a reassuring pat on her forearm. "I'm sure you'll do great. And with our help, you'll look absolutely stunning up there."

Her looks weren't her only concern. Not even in the top

three, in fact. She was much more worried about saying the wrong thing, making a fool of herself by appearing unknowledgeable. Demonstrating that she didn't belong up there with the likes of Crown Prince Dante Angilera.

Behind her, Galen bent down to lean over her shoulder. "You are going to have to try to relax," she said with sympathy. "I can't apply color to your lips when they're thinned out like that. And the foundation will cake on your forehead if you don't stop creasing it."

That was the second time she'd been told that in the span of a few weeks. Hadn't Camille mentioned something similar back in New York? She really had to work on it apparently.

"I'll do my best," she promised.

Tracey pulled out her cell phone. "I think we're going to need some kind of guarantee. Something to soothe your nerves." She made a call and spoke low into the phone. Within moments, a server appeared at the cabin door with a rolling cart of chilled sparkling wine and ripe fresh fruit.

"Now, just remember how knowledgeable you are and how successful you've been. You can do this," Galen reassured her, combing out her hair while Tracey poured wine into three long-stemmed glasses.

"That's right," Tracey added. "You're going to knock their socks off. I have no doubt."

By the time the two women were done with her, Sierra felt less like she'd been prepping for a major news conference and more like she'd just attended a fun girls' night out. Galen's and Tracey's cheery attitudes and encouraging words had taken some of the edge off her nerves and helped to alleviate some of the sadness the memories of Rula had brought forth earlier.

She'd barely touched her glass of sparkling wine, yet

she was much more at ease about facing all those journalists and cameras.

Not that she was looking forward to it in any way.

Dante had to remind himself to breathe when he saw Sierra approaching the makeshift stage where he, Sierra and a group of conservationists would be taking questions. Some kind of transformation had taken place since he'd seen her last. He knew the palace had arranged for some kind of stylists to help her prepare. But he didn't pay much attention to such things.

He was certainly paying attention now.

Her hair was done up in some kind of tight bun at the base of her neck. The navy dress she wore fell just below her knees and showed off her tanned lower legs. She was carrying a tablet and a stylus pen.

She looked like a cross between a serious solicitor and the sexiest, most alluring cover model. A potent combination that had his libido jumping to life.

So not the time.

They were here to face a slew of press to answer questions about the reason for this trip and about Maman's foundation. He had to focus.

By the time he assisted Sierra to the chair next to him and the questions began, his breathing had just started to return to normal. Somehow, he managed to get his brain to work enough to deliver the response for any question directed at him.

To her credit, Sierra was holding her own despite her being a novice when it came to such events. She jumped in at various moments to make relevant points and even cracked a joke at one point that had the entire group chuckling.

When it was all over, Dante finally let himself breathe a sigh of relief. The news conference could undoubtedly be called a success. A lot of that success could be attributed directly to Sierra. She'd performed like a star. He shouldn't be surprised, but the woman seemed to be able to impress him at every turn.

He had no doubt that she was completely unaware of just how impressive she was.

The next morning seemed to go past in the blink of an eye. With the news conference over and the press gaggle working on filing their interview stories, some of the pressure of royal duty had begun to taper. Nothing official was scheduled on the itinerary. Only an activity Kaliha had spontaneously arranged for them to celebrate a successful Q and A with the reporters—a river cruise. Dante spent the hours until then going over the photos he'd taken on the game drive and organizing them in a file on his tablet.

Funny enough, he had just as many pictures of Sierra on his camera's memory card as he did the sights and animals they'd seen. He hadn't even realized he'd taken so many of her. Sierra staring at an exotic bird as they drove by an acacia tree. Sierra adjusting her hat to wipe away a loose tendril of hair. Sierra smiling at the sight of a large flock of quelea birds flying overhead in the sky.

In the photos he'd taken on the game drive, she looked carefree and casual, enjoying herself. Her sun-kissed cheeks and bright smile adding to her already photogenic features. Yesterday, she'd looked regal and composed. The transformation had been rather striking. Either way, she was breathtakingly beautiful. Something he was certain she wasn't aware of. Sierra Compari could give the runway models she worked with a run for their money.

But there was more to her. So much more. The way she'd deftly answered the questions thrown at her by an overzealous gaggle had sent a surge of pride and admiration through him. Sierra had been ready with facts and data, better prepared than he could have hoped for. Maman knew what she was doing when she chose her as his companion on this trip.

Dante paused in the act of cropping a photo. He was dangerously approaching Sierra Compari fanboy status, and he had to get a grip already.

He would have to show these pics to her. But then he would have to explain why his lens had found her as the subject so often. Damned if he'd be able to come up with a plausible explanation. He should have at least included one or two of the prime minister and his wife who'd been traveling in the other car. He would have to be sure to do so today aboard the cruise.

The cruise. He glanced at his watch. It was just about to time to meet the others and ride to the Chobe River, where they would board a luxury houseboat and stay overnight drifting on the water.

Kaliha had arranged it for them after the game drive to give them a taste of the more luxurious excursions Valhali had to offer visitors and tourists. Something told Dante the woman was ready for a bit of luxury herself.

Saving the files and powering down the devices, he grabbed his overnight bag and made his way to the meeting spot in front of the lobby. Banti was already there, scrolling through his phone. He greeted Dante with his usual wide smile when he saw him approach. The prime minister arrived with his wife a few moments later.

Finally, Sierra appeared. In her typical fashion, she arrived at the agreed upon time right on the dot. Never later, not even a moment sooner. Pretty efficient, he would have to say. He was about to ask her how she managed to do so for every single meeting, but then he got a look at her as she came down the steps. Words escaped him. If he thought she looked beautiful yesterday, today she looked downright jaw-dropping.

The jade green wrap dress she wore draped her curves in all the right places and fell just above her knees to expose shapely calves. The color brought out the specks of gold in her hazel eyes. She had her hair up in a clip, showing off her neck and the delicate gold earrings dangling from her lobes. Fabric sneakers a shade lighter than her dress rounded out the ensemble.

She held a different hat from the one she'd had on the other day. This one much was more decorative, with a ribbon wrapped dangling over the brim.

Stunning was the first word that came to mind. Followed by a litany of others that he would never dare say out loud.

Banti took her bag and loaded it in the back of the SUV with the others. She flashed everyone a wide smile. "Good afternoon."

Kaliha and Nantu responded in kind. Dante still couldn't find his voice, so he simply nodded. He hadn't seen her at breakfast, figured she'd taken it in her room. It had been worth the wait.

Resisting the urge to stare during the drive, he tried to focus on the scenery instead. Lucky for him, the two women kept up a constant flow of chatter during the ride. By the time they reached the river twenty minutes later, he'd finally managed to eradicate the wholly inappropriate images flooding his mind and starring Sierra. Images of her unwrapping that dress from her body and having it fall to the floor. Then he would... A tingle ran down his arm to his fingertips.

Stop it.

There he went again.

"Something wrong?" she asked him, her eyebrows furrowed. He hadn't realized he'd actually said the words out loud. How embarrassing. He had to get a grip. The sight of a woman in a dress had turned him into a mound of putty and it was completely unacceptable.

"Just anxious to board," he said. "Looking forward to this cruise."

"To take more pictures?"

"Something like that."

She pointed at his chest. "Where's your camera?"

He motioned to the car with his thumb. "Packed away safely in one of the bags back there."

"Same as my sketchbook," she said with a smile that had his gut tightening. "I'm certain this outing is going to trigger a slew of inspiration." Excitement resonated in her voice.

"I can't wait to see what you'll come up with," he told her, absolutely meaning it. Surprising, really. He'd never been interested in women's fashion before.

When they reached the bank of the river, a tender boat about eight feet long awaited to take them to the houseboat in the middle of the river. Nantu helped his wife to board and Dante reached for Sierra's hand to do the same before Banti could reach her.

Banti noticed and gave Dante the slightest smirk but didn't say anything. Though he shot Dante more than a few knowing looks as they approached the larger vessel and boarded.

Smiling members of the crew greeted them on the deck.

One held moist towels while another handed them frosty glasses of ruby red punch.

Then they were off. Sierra walked to the railing of the boat, her smile growing wider as her gaze darted from the water to the woodlands in the distance. She appeared to be trying to decide which part of the landscape to focus on.

Whereas Dante knew exactly where he wanted to look.

She would have to thank Kaliha for setting up this trip.

As much fun as the game drive had been, this was a different experience altogether. Sierra felt like she'd just checked into the Waldorf, the houseboat was that ritzy. Only, the hotel was floating on one of the most breathtaking rivers in the world. She'd seen pictures of the Chobe on various travel sights before upon learning she'd be traveling to Valhali, but none of them had done the river justice.

The water was a shade of azure blue she'd never seen, the riverbank dotted with all sorts of fowl. Thick cotton ball clouds hung in a baby blue sky with the sun shining bright.

Her senses were in complete exhilaration mode.

Whatever lucky star had led her to be here today, she was more than grateful. Dante strode over to stand next to her. She had him to thank as well. Dante was the real reason she was here.

He pointed to the distance. "You see that?"

She followed the direction of his finger, her mouth falling open upon realizing what he was pointing to. "Is that a crocodile?"

He nodded. "It sure is," he said, then added, "Wait. Maybe it's an alligator. I never could keep track of the difference."

She laughed at his exaggerated confusion. "Either way,

it's a sight to behold. I've never seen one of those outside of a zoo."

"Don't you want to get your camera," she asked, "to take pictures of all of this?"

He shook his head slowly, turned his focus on her face. "I think I'll just enjoy the scene firsthand today rather than through a lens." His gaze never left her face as he answered her. The words were innocuous enough, but the tone in his voice and the way he was looking at her with darkened eyes sent a shiver of awareness down Sierra's spine.

She couldn't help where her mind drifted, imagining how things might have been between them if circumstances were somehow different. If fate had given Sierra a far different role in the life of Nocera's crown prince.

The idea that she might be enjoying this outing with the man she loved was almost tear inducing. If Dante were her man, he might step behind her now, wrap his arm around her waist as they took in the view together. He might nuzzle her neck then turn her face toward his, tilt her chin to drop a soft kiss on her lips. A soft kiss that might lead to longer, deeper ones.

She looked at him now. He hadn't bothered to shave, and a hint of a beard dusted his chin. The wind ruffled his hair. What would it feel like to run her hands through the waves at his crown? Or to feel the stubble on his chin against her skin. A shudder racked her body.

"Where did your thoughts just drift off to?" he asked, his voice velvet rich. Heaven help her, he sounded as if he knew the answer to that question, and that possibility had her insides shaking.

My wife would be a hard act to follow.

His words from the other night drifted through her head. How could she forget for even one moment what the true reality actually was? There was no way Dante could ever be more to her given their history. Rula's death had left a gap his life that Sierra could never fill. He would be monarch one day. The woman Dante needed by his side at that time had to be someone more befitting the role of queen. A woman who could hobnob with the upper crust. Someone who knew how to entertain heads of state or movie stars and felt at home among people like that.

Just like Rula had been.

"Sierra?" Dante asked, pulling her away from her meandering thoughts. That's right. He'd asked her a question, hadn't he? But it wasn't as if she could answer it truthfully. So she changed the subject. Leaning at the waist over the railing, she gestured downriver. "Look. Water buffalo."

A herd of the animals stood huddled together on the riverbank, muzzles in the water for a refreshing drink. Others simply lay on their stomachs, to seek relief from the heat.

"They're not as big as I would have thought," Dante said. A conflicting swirl of emotions ran rampant in the pit of her stomach. Relief that he'd allowed her to dodge his question. But a twinge of disappointment as well. She felt further conflicted when Banti walked over to stand by them, shutting the door fully on the intense moment between her and Dante. For now.

"Come to the other side," he told them. "You're in for a treat."

Sierra and Dante followed him around the cabin to the other side. Banti hadn't been kidding. A large herd of elephants splashed in the river, their trunks spouting water like fire hoses. They ranged in size from a small house to small calves. The little ones dropped and rolled, splashing each other and their parents.

"It's absolute chaos," Sierra said, delighted laughter bubbling free.

Her laughter faded as she noticed one of the older calves hovering off to the side. When it did move, it was clearly hobbling. "What's wrong with that one?" she asked Banti. "Is it hurt?"

"I see what you mean," Banti said, then stepped to the cabin and came back with a pair of binoculars. When he lowered them from his face, his eyes were dark with worry.

"It's hurt," he said. "There's a large gash on one of its hind legs."

"What might have caused it?" Dante asked.

Banti shrugged. "Several possibilities. It might have been attacked by another elephant. It does happen in certain circumstances. Gotten too close to a snare. Or a predator took a swipe before momma and the rest of the herd chased it away."

"Oh, no. Poor little guy." Sierra's eyes stung, feeling for the poor animal who had to be hurting. "What will happen to it?"

"Don't worry. I'll arrange to have a veterinary team come out first thing to search for the herd and to treat the injured calf. The team has an excellent tracker, and the lead vet listens to me."

"Are you two close friends?"

He shook his head. "There are times I want to launch him into the desert," Banti answered, with zero edge in his voice, but more of a tone laced with what might be described as affection. "But, yes, we're close. He's my younger brother."

Sierra breathed a sigh of relief. In her concern over the calf, she hadn't even noticed until now; Dante had taken her hand in his own. He gave it a comforting squeeze.

* * *

He had to admit the truth to himself. He didn't want this cruise to end. He didn't want this trip to end. Because once this was all over, he would have to go back to reality. A reality in which everyone wanted something from him. Where nothing but responsibility and duty awaited him from sunrise to sunset.

Who was he kidding? He'd never been one to shirk the demands on him. What he didn't want to end was time spent with Sierra. He'd always been fond of her. Both as a friend and...well, more. But this trip had awakened that part of him that he'd pushed aside for as long as he could remember. That part of him that had called to Sierra instead of the woman he'd been duty bound to marry.

Dante waited for the familiar flood of guilt to wash over him at such thoughts. Guilt that was always there, simmering just under the surface. To his surprise, the wave was just ever so slightly weaker than usual.

Now, as he waited above deck while Sierra freshened up for dinner, he wasn't sure how well he'd be able to continue hiding the truth. That he had feelings for her. Even though he knew how wrong it was. How disruptive to her life it would be to ask for anything from her.

Not to mention his own. As it was, Maman pestered him daily about this princess or that heiress she wanted him to meet. Each one of them bringing their own contribution to Nocera in the form of a trade agreement or much-needed import.

It was always about Nocera.

He sensed Sierra's approach before he saw her. The now familiar tightening in his gut every time she was near alerting him to her presence. His breath caught in his throat when he turned to face her.

She'd removed the clip from her hair, which now fell in soft waves around her face and down her shoulders. The fabric sneakers had been replaced by strappy leather sandals that revealed brightly colored toenails.

Saints above. He was noticing her toenails.

Clearing his throat, he held his arm out to her. "Ready to go to the upper deck?"

She nodded with enthusiasm. "More than ready. Something smells delicious."

He led her up the steps to the higher level, where several highly polished wooden tables had been set up with place settings and tall, lit candles.

Pulling out her chair at the nearest table, he sat down opposite her. They had a clear view of the river below and the setting sun in the sky above. A gentle breeze rustled the trees in the distance.

"Are we the first ones to arrive for dinner?" Sierra asked the server who appeared immediately once they'd sat down.

The young woman filled their glasses with water from a frosty pitcher. Several wedges of lemon floated on the surface above the ice. "It will be just the two of you, my lady," she answered when she was done.

Huh. That was rather unexpected.

Sierra's eyes grew wide. "Just us."

The woman nodded. "The prime minister sends his apologies. He wanted you to know that he's suffering from a touch of motion sickness, so he and his wife will be dining in their cabin."

"What about Banti?" Dante asked. He'd given his bodyguards permission to stay in their cabins if they so pleased; it wasn't as if he needed protection aboard a boat traveling down a river. Both men had apparently taken him up on the offer.

"Banti is good friends with our captain. They are eating belowdeck to catch up."

Right. The prime minister's queasiness was one thing, but why did Dante get the impression that Banti's absence was due to an ulterior motive? Recalling the knowing smirk the man had had on his face during the drive to the river, Dante had his suspicions. He wasn't sure whether he wanted to thank the other man or ask what in the world he'd been thinking.

Sierra rubbed her hand over her chin, then started fidgeting with her earring. He might say she was nervous.

"Don't worry, Sisi. I won't bite." He knew better but couldn't seem to resist teasing her.

Her eyebrows lifted clear to her hairline. "I'm not worried, Dante. Just hungry."

Right.

"And concerned about Nantu," she added a moment later.

Again, not terribly convincing.

She went on, "Plus I wanted to ask Banti whether he'd gotten word to his brother about the wounded calf."

That all was undoubtedly true, but her assurances were clearly a case of "doth protest too much."

Was she really that nervous to be alone with him? The way she ran her finger over the rim of her water glass gave him a small clue as to the answer.

Curious. What had her acting so anxious about dining alone with him? He had to admit, it was a rather romantic setting. Aboard a triple-decker boat floating gently on the Chobe River, the sun setting in the sky casting a luminous glow on the surrounding clouds, the sounds of wildlife echoing through the air. Anyone witnessing the scene might think they were a couple in love on vacation or even on their honeymoon.

"We haven't seen any hippos yet," she said, completely changing the topic at hand, snapping him out of fantasyland. In a rather clever way, actually.

"I'm sure it's just a matter of time," he said.

She nodded. "I hope so. I'll keep on the lookout while we eat."

The server appeared with salads and a steaming basket of bread rolls, followed by another server carrying a large platter of barbecued meats.

Dante watched as Sierra dug into her food, her eyes darting from her plate to the landscape then back. She wasn't making eye contact with him.

He would have to find a way to change that, put her at ease so that she could begin to enjoy the evening as much as he was.

Once again, it occurred to him just how badly he didn't want any of this to end.

The universe was toying with her. There could be no other explanation. How else would one explain the way she found herself dining alone with Dante aboard a romantic cruise in one of the most stunning settings on earth? Particularly after the way she'd reacted to him earlier that afternoon when they'd first boarded.

She absolutely could not be falling for this man. He was the last person on earth she should be lusting after.

Lust. That's all it was. It wasn't as if she was falling in love or anything. Sierra stopped short, her fork raised halfway to her mouth. Except that she was. There was no way to deny it any longer. If it were at all possible, if the circumstances were different and life was fairer, she'd give herself over to this man. Completely.

The thought could easily send her spiraling into a panic attack.

Just a few more days. Once this trip was over, she'd go back to her own life, try to forget that any of this had even happened.

Only, these weren't the kind of memories a woman might easily forget. Another thing that scared her.

The truth was, she'd be thinking of this time spent in Africa for the rest of her days. She would compare every man she met to Dante, and without a doubt they would all come up woefully short. He was charming, handsome, witty. Everything a warm-blooded woman with a pulse might want. Even without the whole prince angle.

As for him, she had to wonder what his return to Nocera would be like. Would he feel any kind of nostalgia for the time they'd spent together? She thought of the way he'd looked at her on the lower deck earlier, the huskiness in voice as he'd spoken. Would he recall any of it?

Probably not. Most likely, he'd simply return to his princely duties, resume honoring the memory of his deceased wife, and eventually find a replacement who ticked off all the appropriate boxes.

Sierra barely tasted her food before it was cleared away. A shame, really, it was so well prepared, the meat tender, the bread crusty on the outside and soft as cotton candy inside. The side vegetables were crisp and fresh. But her taste buds weren't quite registering. Her mind was too scattered, her heart too full with feelings she'd tried to keep at bay for too long.

So when dessert arrived accompanied by a tall cocktail with a sugared rim, she took the glass without hesitation.

Liquid courage and all. She downed it much faster than she should have, ignoring the dense chocolate mini cake on her dessert plate. When the server appeared with a replacement glass, she didn't refuse.

"Sierra?" Dante's rough voice reached her from across the table.

She kept her eyes leveled on the drink in front of her. "Yes?"

"Weren't you supposed to be the lookout?" he asked.

What on earth was he talking about? "What?"

He gestured toward the water. "You're missing the hippos."

She snapped her head up, then zoomed in on the riverbank. He was right. Not one but two gray leather-skinned hippos swam leisurely in the water. A small bird was catching a ride on the back of one of them.

"Wow, they're magnificent. Though I hear they can be vicious."

"They can be ferocious, as can any wild animal I suppose," Dante said. "Though hippos are known to be particularly aggressive and dangerous, not only because of their large size but also because they have very sharp teeth."

He flashed her a grin followed by a playful wink. "I can give Banti a run for his money."

Sierra returned his smile. "Hey, if the whole prince thing doesn't work out, you can start a second career as a tour guide out here."

It was a ludicrous statement. Dante Angilera was the crown prince of Nocera, a role he was literally born into, and would perform with utmost grace and success. Which reminded her of all the reasons she had to keep her feelings toward him in check.

Suddenly, the excitement at seeing the hippos and the

headiness from the liquor evaporated into thin air. Dante clearly sensed the shift in her mood. "Something the matter?" he asked, concern etching lines at the corners of his eyes.

Sierra wiped her mouth with the cloth napkin. "I'm suddenly very tired," she lied. "Probably all the food."

He tilted his head, studying her. "Or perhaps the two days of nonstop adventuring."

"That too," she said, rising out of her chair. "I think I'll retire. Now that the hippos on my check list can be crossed off."

Dante stood. "I'll walk you to your cabin."

"That's not necessary, Dante. Please stay and enjoy your evening." But her protests were futile. He'd already reached her side.

"I insist," he told her.

In silence, they made their way to the bottom deck, which housed the suite of guest rooms. Finally, they reached her door.

"I guess I'll see you in the morning," she told him, reaching for the doorknob.

But he made no move to leave. Against her better judgment, Sierra lifted her face to look at his, immediately realizing what a mistake that was. She should have twisted the doorknob and stepped into her cabin without another word or hesitation. The way Dante was looking at her had her knees weakening. A dipping sensation settled in her midsection that had nothing to do with motion sickness.

Dante's eyes landed on her lips, hooded and dark with emotion. Without knowing she intended it, she stepped closer to where he stood, their mouths now barely an inch apart. That tempting scent of his aftershave teased her, had her mouth going dry.

"Sierra." Her name on his lips sent a shudder through her core.

"Yes?"

He blinked, swallowed. "Good night. Sweet dreams." Then he leaned toward her. The next instant somehow his lips were on hers. Time stopped. As did her heart beating in her chest.

Sierra couldn't help the moan that escaped her as Dante's mouth fitted over hers. He cupped her chin with one hand, the other resting at the small of her back. Every point of contact sent a burning warmth over her skin. She ran her palms up his arms and over his shoulders, relishing in the feel of him against her. Nothing could have prepared her for the longing and desire coursing through her body. Finally, Dante was in her arms, kissing her with abandon, and she was certain she'd never be able to get enough of it. Enough of him.

He tasted like citrus and mint and some exotic spice she wouldn't be able to name.

He tasted as good as she'd always known he would.

A peck on the cheek. That was all he'd intended. But something had gone awry. One of them had turned the wrong way, at the exact instant they shouldn't have. He couldn't even be sure which of them it had been. But the next moment, his mouth was on Sierra's. Her soft delicate lips like rose petals against his own. She tasted that way too. As sweet as the smell of fresh roses in the spring. Or the finest honey or nectar.

He meant to pull away, he really did. But then the soft sound of her moaning under his lips sent a surge of burning desire over every cell in his body. And he was lost.

Fate played a hand when the boat hit some kind of wave

and jostled her further against him. Or maybe he'd pulled her closer himself without even thinking. The sail had been smooth up until now, after all. She was pressed against his length, running her hands up to his shoulders.

Heaven help him, he wanted to ask her to invite him into her room.

But that would have to be her offer to make. So he stopped himself from asking her outright. For now he would enjoy the moment, enjoy the feel of her, the taste of her.

It would be over all too soon.

He couldn't get the kiss out of his mind. Dante tossed and turned in the darkness of his cabin, sleep eluding him now for hours.

Nor could he erase the image of Sierra's face when they'd finally broken apart. Stunned, wide-eyed. Like a startled doe. Then she'd turned and darted into her room without a word. He'd shocked her. Well, he'd shocked himself. And maybe it was merely his masculine pride, but he'd felt her pleasure as clearly as he'd experienced his own. For one thing, she hadn't pulled away immediately. Her mouth had lingered on his. Exploring, prolonging the moment. He wanted to kick himself for not prolonging it any further while he had the chance. Because he wouldn't get another one in this lifetime.

He'd have to come up with something to say to her; they couldn't exactly ignore that the kiss had happened. The only question was, what exactly was he supposed to say? That he was sorry? That would be a lie. He hadn't intended to kiss her. But he didn't regret that it had happened.

He wanted to do it again.

Which was sadly out of the question, of course. He

could explain away one time. As a momentary loss of judgment. A friendly peck that had somehow turned into something else, which was true enough.

The pretending that he didn't want to do it again would be a lie. But only out of necessity, because he had no choice. He couldn't very well have a fling with his dead wife's best friend. The thought of the kind of worldwide gossip that would create had him cringing where he lay. Dante could just imagine the juicy headlines plastered all over the websites or magazines. There were journalists back at the lodge they'd be returning to, for Pete's sake.

Not that any other kind of romantic relationship with Sierra was an option either. She had a life back in New York, had made no secret of the fact that she didn't consider Nocera her home any longer. It would be the only home Dante would ever know given his birthright.

No, any kind of real relationship with Sierra was impossible. As was any kind of fling.

Which left him in quite a predicament, didn't it? Because the taste of her still stubbornly clung to his lips. And he wanted more of that taste than he had a right to.

CHAPTER EIGHT

UNLIKE THEIR DINNER last night, Sierra hadn't found herself alone with Dante since they'd left the houseboat and returned to the lodge.

A heavy awkwardness hung between them now, their conversations stilted and stony. She knew the others had noticed, if the speculative glances cast between Kaliha and her husband were any indication.

They couldn't spend the rest of the trip that way.

Determined to prove to him that their kiss on the cruise was nothing to be skittish about, Sierra made her way to his room. They could be adults about this. The kiss had happened. It wouldn't happen again. That was that. Yet she had no idea how she was going to go about saying any of that. She'd figure it out once she got there.

She was only a few feet away when Dante's door opened. But he wasn't the one who stepped out over the threshold. Sierra's steps faltered, and she nearly tripped over her own feet.

Cathryn.

Ha! So much for the reporter's declaration that she would wait until she filed her story before she made her move. Apparently the temptation had been too much.

It looked like Sierra didn't need to see him about their

misbegotten kiss at all. He'd clearly already forgotten about it, while she'd been reliving the kiss in her head ever since she'd felt his lips on hers.

Sierra pivoted on her heel to head back to her own room before the other woman could lay sight on her. She had no interest in discussing the way Cathryn and Dante had spent the afternoon together. She could just imagine how that might have been.

Not that it was any of her business. Cathryn had been blunt about what she was after when it came to Dante. And Dante was a grown adult who'd been single for quite some time. If he wanted a meaningless fling while on a safari, it was his prerogative and his own business.

It had nothing to do with her.

So why were Sierra's fists clenched so tight that her fingernails were digging into her palm? Taking a deep breath, she loosened her fingers, sprinted to the door to her cabin, opened it then shut it firmly behind her. Then she started pacing the wooden floor.

Sierra let out a bitter laugh. She was such a fool. Served her right for making more out of a silly kiss than it had obviously been. Dante had simply been lost in the moment. A romantic dinner on a luxurious cruise must have that effect sometimes. He'd probably gone back to his room last night and slept soundly, without giving Sierra or their solitary dinner another thought.

A cry of horror escaped her lips as a realization occurred to her. That could have been so much worse. What if she'd made it to Dante's door and knocked on it only to find Cathryn in there with him? He would have seen the shock of humiliation on her face right away. He knew her well enough.

See, she should consider herself lucky. Someone up there was looking out for her. Saving her from herself. So why did she feel like smashing something against the wall?

Or collapsing in a crying heap?

Sierra spent the evening in her cabin, asking for a tray of sandwiches and fruit to be delivered to her instead. The right call. The solitude had done her a world of good. She'd even managed to get some sleep.

Maybe it was cowardly of her, but the risk of running into Dante, or worse, into Cathryn with Dante, wasn't one she'd been ready to take last night.

But she couldn't stay holed up in here another minute longer. For one thing, she wanted to find Banti and ask if his brother had been able to check on the wounded elephant calf yet. On top of everything else, she hadn't been able to stop thinking about the poor little guy and wonder how he was faring. Silly, really. There had to be hundreds of wounded or hunted animals out there right at that very moment. But she hadn't seen any of those others firsthand. Hadn't watched one of them hobble in pain as it had tried to keep up with the others only to fall over.

The calf had tugged at her heartstrings, and she hurried her shower then toweled off in record time to go see where Banti might be. There was nothing on the itinerary today as Nantu had a daylong conference call about another problematic poaching incident outside the village. Banti's brother must have his work cut out for him. Being a vet out here had to be demanding and draining.

Sierra wandered the grounds until she found Banti behind the workers' quarters hosing off the Landcruiser. He put down the hose when he saw her.

"Good morning, Sierra. I missed you last night at dinner."

She wondered if Dante had been at dinner. And if he'd been alone. Sierra had to stop herself from asking the question out loud. "Thanks, Banti. I just needed some downtime."

He cast a smile at her. "Fair enough. Are you feeling rested then?"

"Sure am. I wanted to ask you about the calf. From yesterday. The little one who was hurt."

Banti's eyes softened. "You have a good heart, don't you?"

Sierra wasn't sure how to answer that, felt mildly embarrassed at the question. Did she? Sometimes she felt selfish and self-absorbed. How many decisions had she made in life out of a desire to protect herself from any hurt?

"Did your brother and his team get a chance to check on him?" she asked, refocusing on the matter at hand.

He glanced at the large watch on his wrist. "They should be doing so right about now. Or at least trying to. Mama elephants can be very protective. I was going head out that way. See how it went and say hello to my brother."

"Is there any chance I can tag along? If it's not a nuisance, that is. I'd love to be able to witness how they take care of a wounded calf."

"No nuisance at all. Though we'll have to keep our distance. Can't get in the way of the veterinary team."

Sierra tapped two fingertips to her forehead. "Got it."

"Give me a chance to dry off the car and we can be on our way." He grabbed the thick towel thrown over his shoulder.

Sierra noticed another one folded on a stool nearby and took it in hand. "Only if I can help."

Within moments, the thirsty towels had the Landcruiser clean and dry. Sierra climbed into the front seat next to Banti and they drove around the quarters toward the lodge.

They didn't get past the patio. Dante jumped the three steps and reached the vehicle in a flash of movement that could only be described as agile and athletic.

The smile he flashed her sent a shiver down her spine. Stupid. Stupid. Stupid. The man had probably spent the night in the arms of Cathryn the reporter.

"And where are you two sneaking off to?"

Banti put the vehicle in park. "No sneaking. I was going to go see my brother and his team take care of the wounded elephant calf. Sierra wanted to come along."

Dante turned his gaze on her. She resisted the urge to look away and meet his eyes straight on instead. "You've been worried about the little thing, haven't you?" he asked her. Rhetorically apparently as he didn't wait for an answer. "I'm not surprised, knowing you."

What was she supposed to say to that? Thank you?

He didn't give her a chance to decide, turned his attention back to Banti. "Mind if I come along too?"

Sierra sucked in a breath. No. No. No.

That was the last thing Sierra wanted or needed. Aside from her concern about the baby elephant, she was hoping for a few hours without the risk of running into Dante. But she could hardly be the one to answer. Her heart sank as she knew what the man's answer would be. There was no reason to turn Dante away. Not for Banti anyhow. Sierra herself had all sorts of reasons.

"What about your bodyguards?" she asked.

Dante shrugged. "They're not with me twenty-four

seven," he answered. "I'll be back before they'll notice I'm gone."

"Then, sure," Banti said, restarting the ignition. "Hop on."

Bingo. She'd been right. Great. Just great. Rather than avoiding him, now they'd be spending the next few hours together. So much for that great entity above who she'd thought was looking out for her yesterday. Apparently, she had decided to take the day off. Dante jumped into the back seat before the last word was out of Banti's mouth.

"You don't mind if I'm along for the adventure, do you, Sierra?"

Another rhetorical question clearly. And a belated one. What could she possibly do about it now, after all? Ask Banti to stop the car and send him back to the lodge? How in the world might she explain why?

"It's not for me to say how you spend your time, Dante," she answered over the roar of the engine.

How true a statement it was.

If the cold shoulder Sierra was giving him from the front seat was any frostier, it might send the searing heat lower several degrees. What was it about the woman? She seemed to run hot and cold without any kind of warning. Today it was the latter.

The kiss. That had to be why her hackles were up. Was he to apologize for it then? The notion didn't sit well with him. Still, it was clear they needed to talk about it at some point.

One more thing was clear—Sierra didn't want him along on this little jaunt. Well, too late now. He was already here, and he wasn't about to turn back. They drove most of the way in silence, save for Banti occasionally pointing out an exotic bird in a branch above or spots that might have been dens for wild dogs. At one point he stopped the car so that they could listen to the call of a roaring lion. Soon they rounded a bend and another SUV came into view. A van was parked beside it.

Several meters from the vehicles stood the herd of elephants. Four men were nearby. One of them appeared to be trying to lure a small calf toward him with what looked to be a large watermelon, while keeping an eye out for the calf's mother. Another man in green fatigues stood nearby with a lasso. Dante figured they were trying to isolate the injured calf.

Banti parked the vehicle a prudent distance from the veterinary team. "This is probably as close as we should get," he said over his shoulder.

They sat in silence for several moments. The rushing sound of the river providing a soothing backdrop to the scene unfolding before them, a crystal blue sky overhead. Dante reclined in his seat, admiring the men trying to help the wounded animal.

The peaceful atmosphere didn't last long. In the next moment, all hell seemed to break loose. It happened so quickly, Dante thought he might have been imagining it. A large elephant seemed to explode out of the nearby river. Before any of the men could do anything, the elephant charged at the man who'd been approaching the calf. Presumably, that man being Banti's brother.

He'd guessed right. Banti shot out of the vehicle and ran toward the chaotic scene. "Stay here you two," he yelled behind him.

Sierra jumped out of her seat, her hand to her heart. She'd gone pale, her eyes wide with disbelief.

Dante reached her side, took her tightly in his arms. She was shaking. "Hey, it's all right. The elephant seems to have stopped its attack."

Which appeared to be the truth. The animal was standing in one spot, pounding its foot into the ground with menace. But it wasn't charging. It was over before it really began. But the damage was done. The vet sat squirming on the ground in pain. Banti and the other men lifted him gently and carried him back to the van.

Banti ran back a few moments later. "I need to get you to back to the lodge."

Dante held a hand up to stop him. "How is your brother?"

Banti sucked in a breath, his hands trembling at his sides. "We don't know for sure yet. The good news is the mother elephant clearly only meant to scare him. She was protecting her calf."

"Good, that's good," Sierra said in a breathless whisper. She didn't sound terribly convinced anything was good at all.

Banti continued, "But Tiejo needs to be checked out. We need to make sure there's no serious damage." He jumped into the front seat and started the Landcruiser. "I'll get you two back to the lodge then I'm going to head to the clinic to check on him."

Dante gripped the man by the shoulder. "Banti, go. Run back there before the second car leaves. I'll contact someone at the lodge to bring us back. I'm sure they'll be here in no time. Go be with your brother."

Banti hesitated, his eyes darting from Dante to where Sierra stood, clearly torn. "I don't know…"

Sierra stepped over to where he stood, touched his forearm. "We'll be fine. Go, Banti."

Banti hesitated just another moment before bolting back toward the other men, yelling at them to wait. They heard him just in time.

Dante waited several beats until his breathing returned to normal. He'd felt so helpless just now, unsure of what to do. But the best course of action seemed to be to get out of the way.

Sierra had been mesmerized by the chaotic incident, shocked, but some of the color was beginning to return to her cheeks. He reached into the back trunk to the cooler where he knew Banti kept the water bottles and handed her one.

"Thanks," she said, opening the lid and taking a long drink. Her shaking had slowed considerably as well.

"You're welcome," he answered, then held out his hand. "Mind if I use your cell phone?"

She blinked at him. "Cell phone?"

"Yeah, you know. So we can call someone at the lodge and tell them to come get us."

Sierra blinked some more, and he had a sinking feeling in the pit of his stomach. Then she said the words he was dreading. "I didn't bring my cell phone."

Not good. Because his was sitting back in his room at the lodge.

"Don't tell me," Sierra said, her voice shaking. "You don't have yours either."

"How do I answer if you don't want me to tell you?"

She swore, using such an unexpected, uncharacteristic term that Dante couldn't help but laugh, despite their dire circumstances.

"What part of this is funny at all?" she demanded to know.

"Relax. I'm sure there's some kind of communication device in these vehicles." But when he reached for what looked like a receiver and pressed the various buttons, all he got in response was a bunch of loud static.

Sierra leaned over his shoulder. "Do you mean to tell me we're stranded out here? With no way to contact the lodge?"

Dante shook his head at her. Did she really have such little faith in him? "Relax, Sierra. The SUV is equipped with GPS. I'll just use it to figure out how to get back."

Her shoulders sagged with relief, and she blew out a deep breath. "All right, please try not to get us lost."

"Oh, ye of little faith," he said, putting the vehicle in gear and turning it around in the direction in which they'd come. The GPS monitor was different from anything he'd seen before, but he was betting he could figure it out through trial and error as they drove.

And that's when it started to pour.

Yep, her so-called protective spirit was definitely MIA. Either that or a vengeful deity was toying with her, one who'd just opened the skies to pour buckets of hard, punishing rain over her and Dante. Only one of them deserved it, she thought with no small amount of pettiness. For the record, that would be him.

For his part, Dante looked absolutely miserable. The expression of shock and dismay he currently wore would be funny if their current situation wasn't all so…well, un-funny.

Within seconds, she was soaked. Her clothing plastered to her skin. Her hair a soppy mess atop her head. Water was starting to pool in the floor of the vehicle.

"Now what?" she asked over the noise.

"Hang on," Dante answered, navigating the dirt road that was quickly turning to mud. "I have an idea." Then he mumbled a few words under his breath that sounded something like "if I can figure out how to get there."

The "there" turned out to be a large sprawling tree. At first, Sierra figured Dante meant to park underneath the branches as cover from the rain. But when she realized where they were, she had to begrudgingly admit that his idea was even better than that. Looking up, Sierra saw there was a good-sized tree house nestled among the branches. Shelter!

As angry as she was with him, at the moment, she wanted to fling her arms around his neck and smack a big, wet kiss against his mouth.

Steady.

"I noticed it when Banti was driving us down," he told her, shouting over the sound of the rain. "Let's get up there."

Sierra ran to the base of the tree, where a spiral series of steps began about a foot off the ground. She was about a third of the way up when her soggy shoe slipped and she dropped three steps. The good news was a set of strong hands stopped her fall before she dropped any farther. The bad news was that she'd practically landed on Dante behind her, and he was now cupping her rear end to keep her steady.

"Whoa, are you okay?" he asked, his mouth against her cheek, his breath hot on her skin.

As fine as she could hope to be with his large palms wrapped around her backside.

"Just great," she answered, then resumed her climb. Moments later, they were both stepping through the doorway into the tree house. The rain pounded heavy on the roof, but it seemed to be holding strong.

"What is this place for?" she asked, stepping all the way inside. The house was the size of her closet back home. Tight quarters, but at least it was a dry roof over their heads.

"I'm guessing it's some sort of lookout for hunters," he answered, wiping the moisture from his face. He'd let his facial hair grow even longer. His wet hair curled around his tanned face. He looked like some kind of rugged rancher or misplaced cowboy. And wasn't this a swell time to be noticing such a thing? But even now, in his soaked clothing and with his dark hair plastered against his forehead, Sierra couldn't deny the man was simply drop dead handsome. She could hardly blame Cathryn for making a move on him. Heaven knew, if their circumstances weren't what they were, she would have done the same. Sierra might have been the one leaving his room yesterday having spent a pleasurable afternoon in his arms, in his bed.

A shudder racked her body.

Dante breached the short distance between them. "You're cold."

He began rubbing her upper arms in an effort to warm her up. Little did he know, the effect of his hands on her only served to amplify the cause of her shudder. She stepped out his grasp with no small amount of reluctance.

What she wanted to do was step deeper into his embrace. Wrap her arms around his neck and lose herself until she could forget where they were and how they'd gotten into such a precarious predicament.

"Thanks. I think I'm good now," she said instead.

"You sure? You're still kind of shaking like you're cold."

She would go ahead and let him believe that mistaken assumption. Better than having him guess what had really caused her body's reaction at being so close to him.

"Wait here," he told her. "I'll be right back." He stepped back out through the door.

Wait? He'd really told her to wait? As if there were any choice in the matter. What else would she do? Where did he think she might possibly go?

When he reappeared moments later, he was carrying a large duffel bag. One she'd seen in the back of the Land-cruiser when she'd been helping Banti towel it off earlier.

"There might be something useful in here," he told her, dropping the bag by her feet. "I also threw in some snacks out of the cooler. In case we're here longer than we want to be."

That was already the case as far as she was concerned. She was tired, cold and wet. So very wet.

Just for something to do, she unzipped the bag and opened it. "For a pampered prince, you're pretty resource-ful in an emergency."

He had to know she was teasing him. Dante had com-pleted Nocera's required military service and had been de-ployed in some of the most dangerous places in the world on humanitarian missions. He was far from pampered.

"Thanks? I think," he said, crouching next to her to look through the bag.

To Sierra's relief, the bag appeared to contain emergency supplies for just such an occasion, including a towel. Thin and small, but a towel none the same. There was also a fleece blanket in there, along with a flashlight, some wipes and a long canvas tunic of some sort. Like the towel, it was rather thin. But it was dry.

"Thank God. This stuff will come in handy." She yanked out the towel first.

"Great," he agreed. "That's good. Now all we have to do is wait out the storm."

"Right. We can try to dry off in the meantime."

How long could it rain, anyway?

Dante couldn't recall a single time he'd been in a tree house before. He didn't exactly come from the type of family that went camping or built forts in trees. However, there was a first for everything.

"What's that?" Sierra asked behind him.

He hadn't realized he'd spoken the last few words out loud.

"Nothing," he told her, then glanced out the square opening in the wall. "Just wondering if the rain is tapering down at all."

"I don't think it is. Unfortunately."

Sierra stood toweling herself off with the square of a towel they'd found in the duffel. She might as well have been raking the ocean. Water dripped from her hair, her clothing, even her nose.

He thought she looked adorable. But she was clearly uncomfortable. Dante reached inside the bag for the tunic he'd seen in there then held it out to her. "Why don't you put this on? You'll feel better once you're wearing dry clothes."

She eyed it with speculation. "What about you? You're wet too."

He shrugged. Being soaked didn't really bother him. Despite Sierra's shivers, he didn't find it cold at all. Especially now that they'd found shelter from the wind. "It's not really my color." Not to mention, the thing wouldn't even reach his knees.

She took the tunic out of his hands, did a twirl motion with her finger. Dante turned his back to her.

"I hope Banti's brother is all right," she said behind him.

He hoped so too, but it was hard to concentrate at the moment. All he could think about was the fact that Sierra was undressing merely a foot or so away. He heard the sound of a heavy thud as she dropped her wet clothing to the floor. Which meant…well, it was obvious what it meant.

Focus on something else. Anything else.

It wasn't easy, but Dante forced his attention on his surroundings instead. The rain pounded heavily on the wooden roof, but the underside stayed dry. All in all, the place was pretty well constructed, not so much as an uneven floorboard.

A red-breasted bird with black wings and head landed on the sill of the window. Dante began to turn around to ask if Sierra was seeing it. He caught himself just in time. He didn't really need to defend himself against any Peeping Tom suspicions right now.

After what seemed like an eternity, Sierra finally finished changing. "I'm done," she said. "You can turn around."

Dante wasn't sure what he'd been expecting. But the sight of her had him struggling to keep from reaching for her and pulling her into his arms. Somehow, she made the simple tunic look incredibly sexy. It draped over her curves like the finest designer dress, reaching just below her knees. Not exactly see-through but thin enough that his mouth had gone dry, and he had to avoid looking in the vicinity of her chest.

Yeah, he had it bad.

She spread her arms wide and did a slow 360-degree turn. "You know, it's pretty plain and a little drab. But with the right accessories, I think I can make it work."

She had no idea just how well the tunic was working for her already. "If anyone can pull it off, it's you."

She glanced around the small room. "You'd think these hunters might have furnished this place. You know, in case a couple of clueless stranded tourists needed to wait out a storm in here or something."

"Yeah, well, wild game hunters aren't exactly known for their consideration or hospitality."

He didn't want to tell her about his real suspicion about this place. His best guess was that it was used by poachers to track their game.

Sierra crossed her arms in front of her chest. "So, now I guess we just wait."

"Not much else to do until the rain clears up."

"I guess not."

"May as well make ourselves comfortable," Dante said, grabbing the blanket and scrunching it up on the ground by the wall. "Your seat, my lady."

Sierra sighed, lowered herself to the floor and sat on one end of the spread blanket. Dante hadn't forgotten the feel of that luscious bottom in his hands when she'd lost her footing climbing the tree earlier. And he wouldn't forget it anytime soon.

Sierra tucked her legs under her and patted the stretch of blanket next to her. "There's room for both of us," she said, then added, almost under her breath, "Though it will be tight." She didn't sound thrilled about the prospect.

Dante sat down, making sure to avoid any contact. He was still dripping wet whereas Sierra at least had managed to get dry.

"I can't believe neither of us have our cell phones," Sierra said with a shake of her head. "I didn't think to grab it because I thought I was just going to ask Banti about the elephant calf then head right back to my room."

Dante nodded once. "Makes sense."

"What's your excuse?" Sierra asked.

He shrugged. "I didn't think I'd be leaving the lodge either. And my phone needed to be charged. I was on it most of last night speaking with my father."

"Long conversation?"

"He was catching me up on all the developments back home, so that I can hit the ground running as soon as I return."

"How is he?" Sierra asked. "Your father?"

Dante leaned his head against the wall. So many ways to answer that question. "Still being monitored by his team of doctors. No real change." But there was no denying that Papa was getting older. Each year, his energy level dipped a little lower, his health giving them another small scare. Dante would have to pick up more and more of the king's responsibilities and eventually take over altogether.

He had to be ready.

Dante rubbed a hand over his face. Plus at some point, probably fairly soon, he would be expected to remarry. Nocera's people would be waiting on Dante to provide heirs of his own. They needed reassurance, stability in their leadership.

So much to think about before it all came looking for him.

Was it so wrong to try to forget about it all while he was a world away with Sierra by his side? Reality would intrude soon enough. Despite the disaster this day had turned into, Dante knew the demands on him wouldn't make life any easier when he did get back home.

Judging by the pounding rain on the roof and the messy view out the window, the storm wasn't abating even a little. Sierra adjusted the neckline of the tunic and shifted in her "seat." Dante immediately moved over to give her more room. As if another inch was going to make a difference. As it was, the close quarters were wreaking havoc on her senses.

"Bet you're sorry now that you asked to come along with Banti and me this afternoon."

He nudged her shoulder with his. "And miss all this alone time with you?"

"The last time we were alone, we were on the houseboat." Why in the world had she brought that up? For all she knew, Dante might have forgotten all about that night. Forgotten about the way he'd kissed her outside her door. He certainly wasn't acting like he remembered any of it, not their isolated dinner. And certainly not what had happened afterward. He'd even had a liaison with Cathryn since then.

His tongue darted out to lick his bottom lip. "Yes. I recall."

He could have fooled her. "Huh. Surprised to hear that. I was beginning to doubt that it happened at all." She hadn't meant to say that, almost an admission, like she was some sort of jilted lovesick teen with a crush who'd ignored her in the high school hallway. How pathetic of her.

Dante sighed deep, his chest falling. "Look, Sierra," he began. "I know it was inappropriate of me, what happened on the houseboat."

Really? That's where he thought she was going with this?

He continued, "I lost myself for a moment."

"I see," was all she could come up with to say.

"It won't happen again."

Ouch. Sierra felt a tightening in her midsection, not quite sure what to attribute it to. He was right, of course. But as the cliché went, it took two to tango. They were equally to blame. She shouldn't have kissed him back. She should have stepped away instead, bid him a polite goodbye and locked herself behind her door. But sharing the blame didn't take the sting out of hearing Dante say he regretted it had happened, that he wanted to take it back.

At least she had some answers now.

"You sound awfully close to apologizing, Dante," she said, faking a lightness in her voice that she didn't feel. "There's hardly any need for that. I got carried away too. It was just a meaningless kiss. Let's just agree to leave it alone."

He nodded slowly, his eyes roaming over her face. "Sure thing. If that's what you want."

"It is," she lied.

That settled it then, didn't it? Their little interlude on the river last night was all sorted. Dante had simply been carried away with the romantic setting. He hadn't meant to kiss her. She didn't need to give it another think. Good thing. Because she suddenly felt so very tired and weary. In both body and mind. Leaning her head back against the hard wooden wall, she slowly let her eyes close, then focused on the darkness behind her lids. The pattering of the rain outside served as a meditative background soundtrack, almost. She just needed a moment to breathe, a moment of silence.

When she opened her eyes again, the world around her had changed. It took a few seconds for Sierra to get her bearings, but two things registered immediately. For one, the rain appeared to have stopped; the humming background noise of the storm was gone. All she heard now were the myriad of jungle noises that had become so familiar these past few days. For another, she could see through the square opening in the wall that served as a window that the sun was shining once more.

Okay. Clearly, she'd had her eyes closed for longer than she'd thought. In fact, she must have fallen asleep.

There was more.

Something else was different about her surroundings. Something much more alarming. Sierra was no longer on a flimsy blanket on the hard floor. Apparently she'd shifted in her sleep to find a more comfortable accommodation. On Dante's lap!

His arms were wrapped around her, cradling her against his chest. Her head was tucked under his chin. The scent of him filled her senses. For a moment, she was too stunned to move. Finally, she made herself blink away the remaining grogginess of sleep and try to pull herself together. She had to remove herself from Dante's grip before he awoke.

Too late. Before she could so much as move, he blinked his eyes open. Heat immediately darkened their depths. His arms around her tightened ever so slightly. Sierra's heart pounded in her chest as she tried to come up with something to say, words that might cut the tension or somehow lighten the mood. But her mind had gone blank. Dante blew out a deep breath. His hand reached up from her waist to cup her face. Sierra forgot how to breathe. Several moments passed in loaded silence. Both seemed to have forgotten how to speak.

Finally, Dante's lips parted. "Hey, Sisi." He spoke the nickname softly, his breath hot on her lips. "I gotta be honest about something."

"Yes?"

"I don't think I'm going to be able to keep my earlier promise."

Her mouth went dry, her tongue felt heavy. "You're not?"

He shook his head, oh, so slowly. "No. I'm afraid I'm going to kiss you again, after all."

Heat rushed through Sierra as she braced herself. She wasn't going to stop what was about to happen, though she knew well that she should be doing exactly that. But she didn't want to.

Dante tilted his head closer, lifted her chin with one finger.

Sierra's body seemed to move of its own accord. Her hips rotated just enough that she was squarely on Dante's lap. The intimate contact had her breath hitching in her throat. Still, she couldn't seem to make herself move away

so much as an inch. Dante's clothes were still damp, seep-
ing moisture through the thin fabric of her dress straight
through to her skin. The heat darkening his eyes told her he
felt every sensation she was feeling. Sierra leaned closer,
inching her face toward his.

The loud noise of static sounded from below. Another
noisy burst followed a second later.

Dante blinked twice. Then he gave a brisk shake of
his head.

"What is that?" Sierra asked.

"It's coming from the Landcruiser outside," Dante answered, his voice rough, and heavy with desire. "I think
it's the radio."

It took several moments for Sierra to process the words.
Her body was throbbing at every point it connected with
Dante's. Her mind a scrambled mess of desire and confusion. Then she finally managed to come to her senses, and
she suppressed a horrified sob. She was ready to give herself completely to this man, atop a tree house of all places.
Scrambling off his lap, she leaped to her feet.

Dante rose slowly, his gaze never leaving her face.
"Guess we better go answer that," he said.

She couldn't find her voice to respond, so she merely
nodded then followed him down the tree's steps to the car.

CHAPTER NINE

HEAVEN HELP HIM, he'd almost done it again. What in the world was wrong with him? Dante returned the receiver to the dashboard after listening to Banti's instructions about how to work the GPS and get them back to the lodge. It was a wonder he even processed the man's instructions. His insides were still a churning mess. Waking up with a beautiful woman on your lap, one you'd been attracted to since as long as you could remember, would do that to a man.

Dante righted the wheel of the vehicle after hitting a rather large dip in the muddy terrain. He had to slow down. They'd turned down Banti's offer to come get them as the tree house was halfway to the lodge as it was. But he was already anxious to get back there to rip off these wet clothes then take a long hot shower. He glanced over at Sierra in the passenger seat. She still wore the tunic but had also wrapped the blanket around herself. No doubt she was looking forward to showering as well.

Too bad they couldn't do it together.

When they arrived back at the lodge a few minutes later, Banti awaited them by the patio. He gave them a once-over and lifted an eyebrow in question. "Are you two all right?"

Dante nodded, stretching his legs. They still felt tight and stiff from the hour or so spent sitting on a hard floor with Sierra on his lap. Not that he was complaining about that last part. It wasn't likely that would happen again anytime soon. "Just need to get cleaned up. And then maybe some food. Speaking of which, you're going to need to restock the supplies in your emergency kit."

"Sorry about leaving you. That freak storm wasn't on any radar. If I'd known, I would have never—"

Sierra cut him off, wrapping the blanket tighter around herself. "Banti, don't apologize. We're fine. How is your brother?" she asked.

Banti clasped his hands together. "He's going to be okay. Just a few scrapes and bruises. Like we thought, the calf's mother was only trying to protect her baby. Tiejo treats the ailments and vaccinates the herds that regularly stop at that point in the river. She must have recognized him on some level so as not to cause any real damage."

Sierra's shoulders dropped a couple inches in relief. "Thank goodness."

Banti continued, "And the team went back to treat the calf. He was isolated from his mother and given the necessary vaccines to aid his recovery."

"Good news on all fronts, then," Sierra said. "Now, if you'll excuse me. I could really use a shower and need to find some real clothes."

Too bad, Dante thought, watching her walk up the steps then head toward her room. She did look rather fetching in her current state. He'd been telling the truth earlier; Sierra really did pull off the disheveled look rather well. Then again, she was the kind of woman who would look good wearing a potato sack.

"You sure you're all right?" Banti asked again. "You look a little dazed."

He *felt* a lot dazed. Desire still coursed through his body, the need to chase after Sierra and pull her back into his arms almost overwhelming. "I'm fine," Dante answered, clapping the other man's shoulder in reassurance. Except for the bruising his ego had taken earlier, that was.

Sierra's words sounded in his head again. *It was just a meaningless kiss. I got carried away too.*

"If you say so," Banti said, looking unconvinced. "You just seem kind of out of it."

A rather apt description. His mind was still trying to process what had happened.

She'd told him just minutes before that their kiss on the houseboat hadn't meant anything to her. Had he been imagining it then? Her reaction? She'd appeared angry with him for the past couple of days. The kiss had to be why. He couldn't think of any other reason for it. So he'd felt the need to explain himself and his behavior the previous night.

"Dante?" Banti's question pulled him out of his thoughts. Oh, yeah, he'd asked Dante a question.

"All good, my friend. I just didn't get much sleep last night on top of all the chaos of the afternoon." That was all true enough. He was spent, between the hours-long phone call with the king and being stranded in a storm, it was no wonder he'd almost made the mistake of kissing Sierra again back at the tree house.

He really had to get a better hold of himself.

"I'll go have the kitchen prepare you two some sandwiches then."

"Thanks, Banti. And I'm glad to hear your brother is okay." He was no wildlife expert. But it wasn't hard to imagine the damage a large elephant could do to a man if it wanted to.

"Thanks. Those sandwiches will be ready in no time. Should I have them sent to your rooms?"

Dante shook his head. "I can't speak for Sierra. But I think I'd prefer to eat out here on the patio once I get changed, to enjoy the poststorm fresh air." First, he would have to get the lecture from Otto over with. The bodyguard was not going to be happy with him. Dante had left the lodge for hours without even a cell phone or so much as a heads-up to the other man.

"You got it," Banti answered, and turned to head toward the kitchen. "I don't blame you. There's nothing like the aftermath of an African rainstorm."

Dante wasn't going to admit the truth out loud. The fresh air excuse was just that, an excuse. He wanted to come back out here in the hopes that Sierra would make her way back outside too.

It made no sense really. Despite being up close and personal in tight quarters just now, damned if he couldn't wait to see her again.

Sierra took so long under the steaming spray of water, her fingers and toes were pruned by the time she turned the shower off.

A message pinged on her cell phone. She reached for it where it rested on the end table, vowing to never leave the room without it again.

Heat rose to her cheeks when she thought about the way she'd moved onto Dante's lap in her sleep. Not to mention her reaction to him upon awakening.

If it wasn't for Banti's call on the vehicle's radio, she shuddered to think of what she might have done in her groggy, disoriented state. She had to thank her lucky stars that static from the radio had sounded when it had.

Take that, vengeful deity! Banti had been her guardian angel in this case, coming to her rescue in the nick of time before she made a fool of herself again. She must have still been waking up and had been dreaming the part where Dante said he wanted to kiss her again. No way that had really happened. After all, he'd practically apologized for doing so the first time.

What was it about the man that had her forgetting herself so easily?

The message on her phone had been sent by the man in question. Dante wanted her to know that a tardy lunch had been prepared just for the two of them and awaited her on the patio.

Clipping her wet hair in a topknot, Sierra threw on a pair of jeans, a long-sleeved cotton flare blouse and slipped on a pair of hiking boots. Her stomach rumbled in anticipation. The granola bars from the duffel bag weren't much in the way of sustenance.

When she stepped outside, the effects of the unexpected storm still lingered in the air. Tendrils of steam still rose off the wet ground in ghostlike curls. The heels of her boots sunk into gooey mud as she made her way to the patio.

Dante sat in one of the lounge chairs, and a silver tray sat before him on the wicker center table. Next to it was a steaming teapot. Her stomach rumbled again, and the thought of a soothing cup of tea almost had grateful tears swimming in her eyes.

Dante stood when he saw her. He hadn't touched any of the food yet. Sierra couldn't help but feel touched that he'd waited for her.

"You clean up pretty well," he told her with a small smile. "Not that you didn't look great in a tunic with a blanket cape."

He really had to stop saying such things to her. Sierra

knew it was all in jest, some lighthearted banter. But the words made her feel a certain way nonetheless. A way she had no business feeling. As it was, look at what her imagination was doing already when it came to Dante.

"You didn't have to wait." She lowered herself into the seat opposite him. "I'm sure you're as hungry as I am."

He'd changed into a pair of khaki pants and a teal-colored V-neck shirt that emphasized the tanned color of his skin. Both to her delight and her dismay, she noticed he still hadn't shaved the stubble from his face.

"What kind of gentleman would I be if I ate before the lady was present?" he asked with a playful wink. There he went again.

She ignored his question, took one of the cucumber sandwiches off the tray. Dante poured her a cup of tea without bothering to ask. Not that he needed to. "Any sign of the others? Aside from Banti?" she asked.

Dante shook his head. "Not that I've seen. Nantu and Kaliha are probably out exploring. And I'm guessing the reporters are working on their pieces."

That's right. Cathryn had said she'd be filing hers later today. Which meant she'd be on her personal time afterward and free to pursue Dante. She scoffed mentally. As if the woman had waited like she said she would. Despite how hungry Sierra had been just a moment ago, the sandwich she'd just taken a bite out of suddenly tasted like sand in her mouth. It went down that way when she swallowed.

Dante took a sip of tea, holding the cup in his hand without setting it down. "Cathryn's the only one who asked me for a quote," he told her before taking another, longer sip.

"A quote?"

"That's right. For her article. She wanted an official palace statement. She came by to see me."

A puzzle piece fell into place in her mind. It appeared very likely that Sierra had come to the wrong conclusion when she'd seen Cathryn leaving Dante's room. So the woman had kept to her stated commitment to professionalism, after all. Sierra's felt a rush of shame for being so quick to judge the other woman. She'd been true to her word. And along with the shame came no small amount of relief that she'd been wrong about her and Dante getting together. Yet.

"Wait, is that why she was in your room yesterday?" Sierra asked before she could stop herself.

Dante's left eyebrow rose about an inch higher. This time, he did set his cup down, so fast and hard some of the tea splashed over the rim and onto the table.

Damn it. She'd given herself away.

"You knew about that?" he asked. "How?"

How in the world could Sierra possibly answer his question without admitting that she'd been upset to see it?

She couldn't think of a single way.

She'd been jealous. Dante had no doubt about it. Suddenly it made sense—why she'd been acting so angry with him. Not because he'd kissed her that night. But because she thought he might have kissed someone else the very next day.

He wanted to reach for her, to take her hand in his and tell her she was a beautiful little fool. To think for even a moment that he would look at another woman after she'd just left his side.

Truth be told, he'd definitely picked up on some flirtatious vibes from the reporter yesterday. But there was no way he'd even consider reciprocating in any way. Not with Sierra so near. Or even on the same planet.

Wow. That had come out of nowhere. He couldn't examine that sentiment too closely.

It would lead to all sorts of roadways and paths better left unexplored.

Sierra still hadn't answered his question. Dante considered pushing for one before deciding against it. He didn't need an answer to know the truth. So Sierra wasn't as unaffected as she'd claimed to be back in the tree house earlier. Not that it changed anything. After this trip, what would it matter? Neither one of them could do anything about the pull between them. Sierra was wise enough to know it. It wasn't as if he could drop everything once or twice a month and go see her in New York. And she'd already made it perfectly clear that her life was there now. Maybe he could persuade her to come visit Nocera more often than she had since the loss of her best friend.

But then what? What happened when he ultimately had to find a fiancée? Heaven knew he couldn't put it off much longer. What would he do then? Tell Sierra to stop coming around? Not even a possibility.

She deserved better.

As elated as Dante was that Sierra felt enough for him to be jealous of another woman, the simple reality was that there was nothing to be done about it.

So he would be letting it go.

"There's Nantu and Kaliha now," Sierra suddenly announced, standing and waving in the direction of the porch. She looked so relieved at the sight of the other couple, Dante thought she might have somehow summoned them through sheer will. Her smile of greeting when they approached was luminous.

"So glad you're both back safely," Kaliha said as soon as

they reached the patio. Her husband nodded in agreement behind her. Soon they'd all taken seats around the table.

"We were very worried when the storm started and you two were nowhere to be found," Nantu said, helping himself to some tea.

"Thank you for your concern," Sierra told them.

"Apologies for having caused you any alarm," Dante said at the same time. "It was harrowing for a while there, but we managed to find shelter until it passed, in a tree house believe it or not. Then Banti made sure we got back here safely."

Sierra's cheeks turned a bright shade of pink when he'd mentioned the tree house. Was she recalling all that had happened in that shelter, perhaps?

"Well, thank goodness," Kaliha said. "I know the four of us have only just met, but we feel a closeness with you two, I must admit."

Dante couldn't help but feel touched by the woman's words. As crown prince, he had no shortage of people around him every day offering fake platitudes. That Kaliha's words were genuine was clear as the raindrops on the grass nearby.

"We feel that way too," Sierra said, glancing at him for confirmation to speak on his behalf. He gave her a small nod.

Nantu took his wife's hand in his. "It occurred to us that we wanted to ask you something," he said.

"That's right," Kaliha agreed.

"What's that?" Sierra said, just as Dante spoke.

Why were they speaking over each other so often, all of a sudden?

"Our youngest daughter is getting married next month,"

Kaliha began. "We would very much like you to attend the ceremony. As personal guests of the bride's parents."

An invitation to a wedding was definitely not on his radar. A look at Sierra's open mouth told him she was just as surprised.

"We would hate to impose that way," Sierra immediately began to protest.

"It's not an imposition in at all," Nantu assured her. "You'd be our guests," he repeated.

"But I'm sure your daughter already has her guest list," Sierra said.

Nantu nodded. "Yes, and it continues to grow. Good thing the venue is so large," he added, shaking his head.

"Your daughter and her fiancé are fine with two strangers attending her wedding?" Dante asked. The older couple's ask was unexpected, but hardly unusual. As a member of the royal family, Dante got invited to all sorts of ceremonies—everything from weddings to christenings to bar mitzvahs. Often, he didn't even know the parties personally.

Kaliha chuckled at his question. "Rest assured she's more than fine with it. We've already asked her, of course. And her response about those strangers ran along the lines of just how much she'd be thrilled to have the Nocera crown prince and the most anticipated designer in the world of fashion there to share in her special day."

Sierra cleared her throat, leaned forward. "I'm so honored, Nantu," she said, and turned her gaze to the other woman. "Kaliha. But I'm not sure how I would manage to come back here in a month. My schedule is stretched enough as it is."

"That's the best part, dear," Kaliha said, clasping her hands in front of her. "It just so happens that her husband to be is a Wall Street banker. She'll be getting married in Manhattan. You won't even have to travel anywhere, Sierra."

Sierra glanced at Dante, her eyes wide as if seeking his help. Darned if he could come up with a way to do so. The wedding would be taking place in Sierra's figurative back yard. How could she possibly say no?

Her tight smile told him she couldn't come up with an answer either. "Then it would be a privilege," she finally said. "Thank you for the honor of inviting us."

A server appeared to ask them if they needed anything.

"In fact we would," Nantu answered. "Something chilled and sparkling, please. To celebrate that the four of us will be seeing one another again in a few weeks for a most festive occasion."

That settled it then. If Sierra would be attending, then so would he. Suddenly, it appeared he had something to look forward to.

There was no way she was going to get any sleep tonight. It didn't help that she'd retired to her room ridiculously early to avoid running into Dante.

Her mind kept replaying the day's events. The scare with Banti's brother, the storm that came out of nowhere. Being stranded several feet above ground with Dante. Falling asleep only to awaken in his lap and what had almost happened afterward.

And the coup de grâce with the way it all ended. With the knowledge that she'd be seeing him again in New York at a lavish wedding of all places.

Sierra wasn't sure how her heart was supposed to handle that. Once she left Africa, she figured it would take all her effort to try to forget him and the time they'd shared together down here. So much for that plan. Her heart would hardly get a chance to recover before she would have to see him again.

With a frustrated sigh, she pulled apart the canopy above her bed and crawled off the mattress. She needed some air. Grabbing the bug lotion from the bathroom vanity, she lathered a thick layer on her skin then threw on a pair of leggings and a long-sleeved top.

Going out this late was probably asking for trouble in the form of a thousand bug bites, even with the smelly repellant on. But she was going stir-crazy in her room with her mind racing like a Thoroughbred at a derby.

Stepping out onto the porch, Sierra sucked in a deep breath of air. Apparently she wasn't the only one roaming about. A faint light glowed from inside the dining room. Curious, she made her way toward the entrance and through the lobby.

She was right. There was someone else awake. Cathryn sat at one of the long tables, an open bag of chips, a frosty bottle of beer and an open paperback in front of her.

Sierra debated turning around and leaving her to it when Cathryn suddenly looked up. A smile appeared on her face, inviting Sierra to walk farther into the room.

"You couldn't sleep either?" she asked rhetorically.

Cathryn shook her head. "I'm always too ramped up after filing a piece. This is how I wind down and celebrate meeting my deadline." She gestured to the items sitting in front of her. "Join me."

"I don't want to intrude on your celebration."

Cathryn waved a hand in dismissal of her comment. "Nonsense, I'd love the company." She reached for a second frosty bottle in a small cooler by her leg, twisted the cap then pushed it across the table to Sierra.

Sierra pulled out the chair opposite and sat. There was no good way to bring up the question at the forefront of her mind. So she decided to just blurt it out. "So, now that you've finished writing the article, do you plan on talking to Dante?"

Cathryn took a swig of her beer. "Yeah, I've changed my mind about that, actually."

Something loosened in the pit of Sierra's stomach. She released the breath she'd been holding. "Oh?"

"Yeah. I went to see him about a quote for the article and decided pretty much right away that it wasn't a good idea to start anything."

Huh. "Why's that?"

Cathryn shrugged, brought the bottle back to her lips, speaking before taking another swig. "The vibes were off. We weren't really meshing. I can tell right away when a man isn't interested, you know what I mean?"

Sierra couldn't help but be impressed with the reporter. Cathryn wasn't afraid to go after what she wanted but knew when to say when. Exactly the type of woman Sierra would want as a friend.

"I think any man would be lucky to have you come on to him. Dante's loss," she said, surprising herself.

Cathryn tipped the bottle head in her direction. "Hey, thanks for saying so."

"You're welcome."

A sly smile spread over Cathryn's mouth. "You know, your name came up a lot during my conversation with Dante."

Her ears began to hum at Cathryn's announcement. "It did?"

"Sure did. It was one of the reasons I knew to back off.

And also the reason I asked you first about him before I did anything."

Sierra rubbed her forehead. The woman was too observant by half. She supposed that's what made for a good journalist. "Things are complicated," she answered. "Between Dante and me. And after this trip ends in two days, we'll be on our separate ways and off to separate lives." Until she would have to see him again at the wedding in New York.

Cathryn's eyes narrowed. "That may be so, but it doesn't look all that complicated from where I'm sitting."

"He used to be married to my dearest friend in the world."

Cathryn whistled out a breath. "That's right. Now that you mention it, I remember from my research that the person accompanying the prince on this trip was someone with whom he had some sort of connection. His sister-in-law, or something."

The description was close enough. She and Rula had been like sisters, after all.

"It must have slipped my mind," Cathryn added.

That said quite a bit about Sierra's relative importance as a member of this mission. One of the journalists here to cover it had barely made note of her until just now. It just reaffirmed what Sierra already knew, that she had no real business in Dante's world in any kind of permanent way. If Rula were here, she'd be sure to be noticed. She would behave the way a future queen would behave. Rula wasn't the type of person who ever slipped someone's mind.

"You're right," Cathryn said after a pause. "I stand corrected. That is complicated." She polished off the rest of the beer and set the bottle down. "But maybe it doesn't have to be?"

* * *

Sierra made her way back to her cabin, her thoughts a jumble of confusion. Cathryn had no idea. Things between her and Dante couldn't get much more complicated. They had a history as childhood friends. He'd been married to her closest friend, whom they'd both lost. There'd always been an undercurrent of tension between them. Tension that had come perilously close to the surface during this trip. Soon, he would be on the search for a suitable wife in order to be better positioned to take his place on the throne when the time came.

It didn't get much more complicated than that.

Speak of the devil, she found him outside the door to her room as she approached from the other side of the shared porch. He lifted his hand to knock then dropped it when he saw her approaching. His smile widened into a grin. "There you are."

"Hey, Dante. Something I can do for you?"

The grin faltered ever so slightly at her lack of enthusiasm at finding him there. What exactly was he expecting?

He lifted the object he was holding. A sweaty bottle. "Thought you might be up for a nightcap."

Sierra stepped past him to her door. Of course she would be up for a nightcap, given who was asking. But it was late, her emotions were in turmoil. And Dante looked so devastatingly handsome in a deep blue button-down shirt that brought out the steel gray of his eyes, and khaki pants that fit his long legs like they were tailored for him. Which of course they were. Her willpower could only be able to withstand so much.

"I just had a nightcap," she told him, knowing full well how rude and dismissive she sounded. "With Cathryn."

He eyebrows drew close together. "The reporter?"

She nodded. "That's right."

"Oh." Disappointment washed over his features. "Maybe we can just talk then."

Sierra wanted to turn him down. She really did. It would be the smartest and most prudent course. But she couldn't do it. She wanted to talk to him, wanted to have one more night in his company.

That made her all sorts of a fool.

She stepped inside her room and motioned for him to follow. The grin reappeared above his chin, and she couldn't help the smile that lifted her own lips.

He reached for her hand then, and Sierra made herself not react to the jolt of electricity that shot through her arm and into her lower belly at the contact. Why did she react in this manner whenever this man touched her? Even in the most innocent way?

"To what do I owe this visit?" she asked, pulling her hand away and dropping onto the mattress of her bed. She curled one leg under the other.

Dante set the unopened bottle on the coffee table and pulled over the chair from the sitting area so that he was about a foot away from Sierra. Thank heavens he hadn't attempted to sit down next to her. Her mind filled with images of where that scenario might have led, and she had to force herself to focus on Dante's face.

"I wanted to run something by you," he told her.

Something about his tone and his demeanor sent alarm bells ringing in her head. She got the distinct impression she wasn't going to like whatever was about to come out of Dante's mouth.

"What's that?"

"I was thinking, Nocera, and particularly the Angilera

palace grounds, just haven't been the same since you left the kingdom."

The alarm bells grew louder. "Um…thanks?"

"More selfishly, I have to confess to the fact that I miss having you around."

Huh.

Dante continued, "You've always been such a big part of my life. It's felt so much emptier after your move."

Sierra's breath hitched in her throat, and a nervous knot tightened in her center. Where exactly was Dante going with this?

He leaned over, braced his elbows on his knees. "Lots of fashion designers have more than one city where they're located. Many of them have fashion houses all over the world."

What in heaven's name was he possibly getting at? "Those would be actual fashion houses, Dante. Run by titans of the industry. I'm merely an assistant designer working my way up. Big difference."

He winked at her conspiratorially. "But you don't have to be."

Sierra crossed her arms in front of her chest, some foolish part of her heart deflating with disappointment. "Maybe you should just come right out and say what it is you're getting at."

"What if you could be the lead designer working out of your own empire. I would back you. Nocera could become another power player in the fashion industry. And you would be in charge of the launch."

There it was. Sierra could hardly believe what she was hearing. For an insane moment, she'd thought maybe he was about to admit to something deeper. How downright foolish of her.

"So you're offering me a job. Is that it?"

He leaned back against the chair. "I suppose I am. What do you say?"

She might have laughed if it wasn't so darn heartbreaking. Dante wanted her back in Nocera with him. But he couldn't just say so. He couldn't admit that he felt anything for her. She could only think of one reason.

He still hadn't gotten over Rula's loss.

So he was offering her a job working for the kingdom in order to have her near. Sierra would be a crutch until he could find the proper replacement for his perished wife, which Sierra clearly wasn't.

And what would become of such an arrangement when he eventually remarried? Was she to turn into a fixture in the background then? A fragment of his former life?

Without giving herself a chance to think, she blurted out the question that had been plaguing her subconscious. "Why do you never talk about her?"

"Talk about who?" He had to know the answer to that. Sierra got the impression he was just buying time.

"Rula. You never so much as mention her name. That afternoon with Banti, you said your wife would be a hard act to follow."

He blinked at her in confusion. "What I'm offering you now has nothing to do with Rula."

"I think it does."

His gaze narrowed on her face. "I could ask you the same question."

Touché, dear prince. Her answer might have surprised him. That her hesitation to speak of Rula had a lot to the with the guilt she carried regarding her friend's loss. Guilt that Sierra might not have been there when Rula had needed her, pursuing a dream in New York rather than being available to her friend. All because she'd had to get away rather than watch Dante and Rula begin their married lives together.

Dante rubbed his forehead then began to speak, apparently giving up on waiting for Sierra to answer. "Things between Rula and me, they were complicated, Sierra."

There was that word again. So many complications between them. How would they ever get past it all?

She couldn't see a way. Slowly, she rose off the mattress. "Thank you for the job offer, but I'm not interested."

Dante rose, his lips tight, his eyes pleading. "Sierra…"

She didn't wait for him to continue, went to the door instead and opened it. "I think I'd like to retire for the evening."

Dante washed his hand across his face then strode to the open doorway. He turned back.

"Sierra," he repeated.

But she was done listening. "Good night, Dante."

And goodbye, she added silently.

CHAPTER TEN

Four weeks later

DANTE SLAMMED THE drawer of his desk hard enough that several items fell off the top and a priceless painting on the wall behind him dropped to a slant. Biting out a curse, he looked up to find his mother entering his office.

"Is everything all right, dear?" she asked.

No. The answer to her question was a big, fat resounding no. Nothing was all right. Everything was irritating him. Even a simple email about a slight delay in shipping due to a canal backup had him irritated and ready to snap.

Of course, he wasn't going to tell Maman any of that.

"Why do you ask?" he asked instead.

His mother tilted her head, her lips drawing tight. "Please don't be a smart a—" She caught herself before finishing. "Don't be a smart aleck," she amended. "Let's not pretend you haven't been in an absolute terror of a mood since returning from the safari."

Dante pinched the bridge of his nose. "I apologize, Maman. I've just had a lot on my mind."

That was a lie. He'd only had one thing on his mind. Sierra. In fact, he couldn't stop thinking about her.

"Well, I can only hope this trip to New York will perhaps lighten your mood. Am I to understand Sierra will be there?"

"That's correct." There was no way to explain to his mother that Sierra was the source of his torment.

"That's good then," his mother said with a smile. "She's always had a way of brightening your disposition. It's a shame she lives so far away. Perhaps you can convince her to come back to Nocera somehow."

Dante studied his mother's face, the understanding in her eyes. *She knew.* And perhaps she'd always known. He should know better than to underestimate the woman. But the reality was what it was. Sierra had gone back to her life in New York without so much as a second glance at him when they'd landed back on American soil. What choice had he had but to jet back to Nocera alone?

"Why would I do that, Maman?"

His mother reached across the desk, patted his forearm. "Oh, son, I think you know why."

Dante leaned back in his chair. No use pretending he didn't know what she meant. "I'm afraid there's no use. I have responsibilities. I need to put Nocera first. And Sierra's decided that her new life is in New York. She's moved on. The same way I need to."

His mother squinted her eyes at him. If he didn't know better, he might say she was disappointed in his words. Or maybe she was just disappointed in *him*.

"Have you asked her that, son? Or are you just assuming? If it's the latter, then I'd have to say that's rather arrogant of you."

Arrogant? Of course that wasn't it. Was it? "There's nothing for her here. She's made that quite clear."

"Are you sure there's nothing? Nothing she might consider a life change for? Or no one who might possibly make her change her mind?"

Dante's aggravation skyrocketed once more. As much as he loved and respected her, his mother didn't know what she was talking about. "Sierra had every opportunity to tell me so if she felt that way." In fact, he'd given her an ideal opportunity to return to the kingdom that was her home, and she'd turned him down flat.

Maman nodded slowly. "You're right. She did. And you had every opportunity to tell her how you felt. Instead, you made her some kind of job offer."

Well, when she put it that way...

Dante cursed under his breath. His mother was right, as much as he wanted to deny it. What Maman just described was the very definition of arrogance.

"Maybe it's time to forgive yourself, son."

Dante jolted upright at his mother's words. So unexpected, so jarring. "What's that supposed to mean?"

Maman gave him a smile full of affection. And sympathy. She reached over and patted his cheek. "I think you know the answer to that question."

Yet Dante was still pondering his mother's words long after she'd left the room. Self-forgiveness hardly came easy. Certainly not in his case. Where would he even begin? Out of duty, he'd married the woman he'd been expected to wed. It had resulted in tragedy. Rula had eventually and gradually decided she wanted more than a loveless marriage. She'd made it known to him in many subtle and not so subtle ways.

Dante had never been able to bring himself to even try. Maybe if he had, she wouldn't have felt the need to flee. He'd driven her away. For that, he had no one else to blame but himself.

Dante swore out loud and leaned his head back to stare at the ceiling. Maman knew all this.

Still, she'd said what she had. Her words echoed once again in his head.

Maybe it's time to forgive yourself...

"I can't believe you've scored an invite to the most talked about wedding in Manhattan this year."

Camille was much more excited than Sierra herself was about her plans for the evening. Sierra adjusted the hem of her silk dress and slipped into the matching navy stilettos. "Neither can I." And she couldn't wait for it to be over.

The butterflies in her stomach multiplied with each turn of the second hand on the vintage watch that she'd scored from the pop-up market in SoHo. Each revolution on the clockface meant that Sierra was that much closer to seeing Dante again. She had no idea what she would say when she did. The safari seemed like years ago, another lifetime perhaps.

Did he think about her as often as she thought about him? Highly unlikely. And no use dwelling on.

"Thanks for coming by to let me borrow these," she said now to Camille, toying with the diamond drop earrings the young model's latest boyfriend had gifted her. They were something Sierra would never be able to afford.

"Sure thing. It gave me a chance to watch you get ready." She eyed her up and down. "You look amazing. The prince is going to go gaga at the sight of you."

Sierra had to laugh at that. Camille had such a way with words. Part of her wanted desperately for the other woman's prediction about Dante to be true. Another part was scared to death at the prospect.

Would they be seated together? It made sense. They'd been invited by the bride's parents. Sierra assumed there would be specific tables for such guests.

A thought suddenly occurred to her that had a wave of horror crashing through her core. What if Dante wouldn't be coming alone? What if he was bringing a date? One of the many possible women who would make a great candidate to be the next queen. Nausea rolled around her stomach at the thought. How in the world would Sierra sit there and watch him accompany another woman into the hall? Watch him dance with her, hold her in his arms, the way he'd held her the night of the bonfire.

"What's the matter?" Camille asked, concern etched in her eyes. "You've just gone pale as a ghost."

"Nothing," she lied. "I guess I just haven't eaten enough today." That last part was true enough. She'd been too nervous to eat. Or to do much of anything, for that matter.

Her fingers still stung from all the times she'd pricked herself with a needle today during fittings due to her distraction.

"Saving room for the wedding dinner, huh?" Camille said. "I heard it's being catered by none other than Simone Billieu of the Parisian."

If Camille thought that name was supposed mean something to Sierra, she was sadly mistaken. Her lack of appetite these past few days had nothing to do with the menu of a distinguished chef and everything to do with seeing Dante again.

She really needed this wedding to be over so that she could get back to her life.

A life where she could finally put thoughts of Dante Angilera out of her mind once and for all.

* * *

She sensed him before she saw him. The air in the banquet hall seemed to stir. The rumble of voices grew a fraction quieter. Heads began to turn in the direction of the entry-way. Leave it to Dante to make an entrance. Sierra braced herself to turn and look his way. Her breath caught in her throat when she did. Out of respect for his hosts and following tradition, he was wearing his official uniform—a military jacket in a deep rich burgundy with all his honors and medals pinned to one side of his chest and the crest of the house of Angilera on the other. Black pants with precise, razor-sharp pleats, and polished black shoes completed a look that only a prince like Dante could wear. Sierra hadn't seen him at all at the ceremony earlier. He must have made a relatively quick entrance then sat in the back of the room in order to avoid drawing any attention to himself.

Now, he looked like something out of a painting that might be hanging in one of the finest museums in Europe. He looked like the king he was destined to become.

"Yowza!" came an impressed cry from a female voice somewhere in her vicinity. As good a reaction as any. Heaven knew she herself had been rendered speechless at the sight of him.

"Oh, my God," a different voice nearby said. "He's coming this way."

That he was. Sierra's heart pounded in her chest as he made his way across the hall. When he looked up and his gaze zeroed in on her, she thought her heart would stop altogether. The man she'd been on safari with had been casual and relaxed. Here, he was the epitome of regal. This was the side of Dante that had always intimidated her, made her feel like an alien in the world he inhabited. It was a stark reminder of what she could never be and where she would never fit in.

He was at the table in a few long strides, most of the eyes in the room following his path. He smiled when he saw her and Sierra was grateful she was sitting down; her knees had gone weak. Actually, every joint in her body felt as if it might have turned to Jell-O.

"Good evening, Sierra," he said, as if they'd just left each other's company the other day as opposed to several weeks ago. Pulling out the empty chair next to her, he sat down.

Sierra cleared her throat and forced her mouth to work. "Dante, how lovely to see you again."

So formal, but it was all she could come up with. If he had brought somebody with him, they were nowhere to be seen at the moment. Maybe he had and the woman was merely in the ladies' room powdering her nose, or preparing to make her own entrance. But that made no sense. Any woman in her right mind would want to step into any room on Dante's arm. Still, Sierra had to know for sure before she could resume any kind of normal breath. "Are you here alone?" she asked, before she could lose her nerve and find out the answer the hard way.

He lifted an eyebrow, clearly surprised by the question. "Yes," he answered, then after a pause added, "And you?"

"Yes."

Was it her imagination, or had he just clenched his fists until hearing her answer?

The bride and groom walked in at that moment to thunderous applause. The bridal party followed, including Nantu and Kaliha. They all took their seats at the head table.

Several waiters appeared from various corners wheeling carts full of food.

"Nantu and Kaliha look like the quintessential example of proud parents," Dante remarked. "They're both beaming."

"They are," she agreed. "And how are your parents?" she asked. "The king and queen."

"They're doing well. They send their regards."

"I'm glad to hear it. You must give them my best when you return." God, she hated this small talk. They were speaking to each other like strangers. While a few weeks ago, she'd been on this man's lap while clad in nothing but a thin tunic.

Don't go there.

She had to force that image out of her mind before her cheeks turned the color of the tomato in the salad that had just been placed before her.

Sierra could barely pick at the food on her plate, despite having not eaten all day. Her stomach was simply in too many knots.

If Dante noticed she wasn't eating, he didn't comment on it.

By the time their plates were cleared away and the bride and groom moved to the dance floor for their first dance, Sierra's pulse still had yet to slow.

It didn't help that Dante leaned over to whisper in her ear. "You look amazing."

She had to swallow the lump that formed in her throat at his compliment.

He continued before she'd even begun to recover. "Like I told you once already, you clean up really well."

"Thank you," Sierra managed to say, trying hard not to

follow the path his words were leading her down, back to Valhali and the afternoon of the storm. "You don't look so bad yourself."

He stood suddenly, extended his hand to her. "In that case, perhaps you'll grant me the honor of this dance."

Oh, no. In alarm, Sierra glanced at the dance floor to discover that other couples had joined the bride and groom there, moving along to a slow ballad.

The prospect of being in Dante's arms again, moving with him, feeling his warmth against her skin—she wasn't sure she could handle it. But what choice did she have? She couldn't exactly say no while he stood with his hand out to her. She'd already hesitated a second too long; the others at the table had begun to stare.

Bracing herself with a steadying breath, she stood and placed her hand in his, then followed him to the dance floor.

Maybe he shouldn't have put her on the spot that way when he'd asked her to dance. But Dante couldn't take another minute of sitting so close to her, inhaling that vanilla and rose perfume of hers. The need to touch her and to hold her pulsed like shots of electricity through his system.

The way she'd hesitated had sent a figurative dagger through his heart. Now that she was in his arms again, he wasn't sure he'd ever be able to let her go again.

He could feel the heat of her skin through her silk dress. The familiar scent of her shampoo had him longing to nuzzle his face into her hair and inhale deeply. Was he imagining her slight tremble? Did he dare hope she was as affected as he was right this moment? If so, he would guess she was doing her best to try to hide it.

Well, there was no hiding his own reaction at having her in his arms again. He'd missed her. More than he would have ever anticipated. He thanked his lucky stars that Nantu and Kaliha had made this meeting between them possible. He wasn't going to let the opportunity go to waste. When the song ended, Sierra immediately stepped out of his arms, and it felt like a bucket of ice water splashed over him.

"I could use a drink, if you don't mind," she said, not quite meeting his eyes. If he didn't know better, he might think she was being shy with him. That wouldn't do. Not at all. Not given what he had to say to her as soon as he got her alone.

"Sure, I'll get it for you."

When he returned to the table with two glasses of champagne and handed one to her, Sierra appeared still unwilling to make eye contact. A rush of exasperation flushed through his system.

Enough.

He waited silently until she finished her drink, his patience hanging by a thread. When she was done, he pushed his chair back and stood, holding his hand out to her once more.

Sierra looked up at him finally but immediately shook her head. "I don't think I'm up for another dance just yet."

"No. I don't mean another dance. Can we go somewhere to talk? Alone?"

She blinked in surprise. Once and then again. Still, she didn't stand. For one excruciating moment, Dante thought she might turn him down. Finally, after several awkward beats, she pushed her chair back, rose to her feet and took his hand.

He led her toward the exit. Otto immediately started following them. Dante gestured to him, a movement of his hand so small it was almost imperceptible. But the body-guard got the message and immediately stopped, though he didn't look terribly happy about it.

Soon, the two of them were out the main doors, down the hallway and to a doorway with a bright red exit sign above it. They found themselves at the foot of a stairway that went up several flights.

Sierra smoothed down the skirt of her dress, as if the fabric was the most interesting thing on the planet and required all her attention. "Well, this certainly is private, Dante."

He took a steadying breath before speaking. "Sierra, look at me."

It took her a few beats, but she eventually did as he asked. Finally. When her eyes met his, Dante hated that he couldn't read what he saw in their depths. However, there was no turning back now. In for a penny and all that.

"I have a confession to make," he began.

Her tongue darted out to swipe at her bottom lip, and Dante lost his focus for a moment. He wrangled himself back to the matter at hand with no small amount of effort.

"Yes?"

"I missed you. I need you to know that. There hasn't been a day since we parted that I haven't missed you. The way I went about asking you to come back to Nocera in Valhali went all wrong. I should have thought out better what I was going to say and how I wanted to say it."

She sucked in a breath. "Which was what, exactly?"

Couldn't she see it in his eyes? Didn't she understand how hard it was to speak the words? "That I wanted you to come back with me to Nocera. That I needed you by my side." The rest of it was on the tip of his tongue—that he loved her and always had. But the dark torment behind her eyes kept him from saying the words out loud.

She squeezed her eyes shut, and Dante felt the need to hold his breath until she responded. Which took an agonizingly long time.

"Oh, Dante," was all she said.

"Sierra, say something." As much as he loved the sound of his name on her lips, he needed more from her right now. Much more.

"What would you have me say?" she asked, her voice a low whisper that sent shards of glass through his heart. The heart he'd just laid at her feet.

"You don't know?" he asked. "Nothing comes to mind?"

Like maybe that you missed me too? Or how about that you've been thinking about me? Or maybe you could throw me a paltry bone along the lines of "I'll call you sometime."

At this point, he would take it. He would take anything.

But Sierra didn't seem inclined to offer him anything.

When she opened her eyes again, Dante felt a small sprig of hope when he saw the wetness in them. If she was on the verge of crying, surely that had to mean she felt something for him. Sierra crushed that hope with her next words.

"I'm sorry, but I can't say the words you seem to want to hear."

The air left his lungs like a pricked balloon. What a fool he was. Standing here declaring his love for her only to be rebuffed.

She went on, rubbing her forehead. "If you'll excuse me, I'm feeling rather light-headed."

He couldn't help the concern that washed over him, despite what was happening between them at the moment. "Are you all right?"

She moved out of his reach and another stabbing sensation pierced his gut.

"I'm fine," she said. "I just haven't eaten much today, and I shouldn't have drunk the champagne so quickly. I think I'll pay my respects to our hosts and make it an earlier night than expected."

All right. If that's what she wanted. "I'll come with you, see you home."

She held a hand up. "No, that won't be necessary. Please, you've come all this way to attend this wedding. I'd hate for you to leave on my account."

Right. As if he could spend one more minute here at this party given that she was about to leave.

"Sierra, just let me see you home. I just want to make sure you get there safely."

She squared her shoulders, lifted her chin in a stubborn movement that left no room for question. "Dante, please don't follow me. There's no need. I know my way around this city. I'll be fine by myself. I live here. Permanently."

Her double meaning couldn't have been more clear than if she'd etched it on his chest with a knife.

Without another word, she turned on her heel and stepped out the door.

Leaving him standing there, with no other choice but to watch her go.

Sierra was on the second box of tissues an hour after she'd left the banquet hall. Not too many sheets left in this one. Still, the tears would not stop falling. Her heart was shattered, irreparably damaged. Dante would never forgive her, would never understand that she'd merely done what she had to do in that stairwell. She couldn't be what he needed; it wasn't in her makeup to be any kind of queen. The very idea was petrifying. He would have realized it soon enough, the first time she fell flat on her face at a royal event. Or when she made a fool of herself because she didn't know what fork to use at a state dinner.

By then it would be too late.

Dante knew it too. That's why he couldn't say the three words to her that might have had her giving in to her feelings for him. He hadn't been able to say them back in Valhali, and he hadn't been able to say them tonight.

I love you.

No. They both knew Sierra could never be Dante's queen. And what was the other option? A meaningless fling? Some type of shallow relationship that would need to end when he did move on to someone more suitable?

Sierra couldn't survive that. She couldn't watch him walk down the aisle with another woman, stand idly by and nurse her wounds when he eventually had children with someone else.

The mere thought had her gasping for air.

Finally all cried out, she fell asleep where she sat on the couch, sheer heartbreak and exhaustion eventually gaining the upper hand.

It was Rula who woke her up. Somehow back from the dead.

Her dear friend's voice rang clear in her head. Though the word she kept repeating made no sense: *journey.*

Sierra jolted up in her seat, waking with a start. The neon lights outside her window had dimmed, the street was quiet. A glance at her watch told her she'd been asleep for three hours.

That was the most realistic dream she'd ever had. As if Rula had been right there in the room with her. A stab of longing pierced her chest. If only Rula was really still here. Sierra would give anything to seek her advice, ask her what she might do to ease the anguish. Although that notion was downright nonsensical given the reason Sierra would need to ask in the first place.

Rula's familiar voice echoed through her head again. *Journey.*

Why was she hearing what she was? Her mind had to be playing tricks on her. Of course Rula wasn't trying to tell her anything from beyond. And even if that were somehow miraculously possible, why would her friend be referring to a journey?

Sierra gave her head a shake. Her mind was simply trying to call up the memories of the journey she'd been on with Dante. That had to be what the silly dream was about.

But the voice persisted.

Journal.

Not journey.

Sierra sucked in a breath. She could no longer deny that something was trying to give her some sort of message. Even if it was in her own mind.

Journal.

The word triggered an idea in the back of her head. Sierra had been given a box of Rula's things upon her passing. Her parents weren't exactly the sentimental kind or much of the grieving type. They'd offered the personal belongings to Rula's best friend, uninterested in the sentimentality of knickknacks.

Sierra hadn't had it in her to go through the box two years ago in the depths of grief. Was there a chance Rula had kept a journal? Sierra had never considered herself a very spiritual person. But she couldn't shake the sense that something, or someone, wanted her to go find out the answer. Without giving herself a chance to overthink, Sierra stood and walked to her closet. Using a stool, she reached to the back of the top shelf until she felt the velvet cover of the box that held her friend's things.

As soon as she removed the ribbon and lifted the lid, her eyes began to flood again. Photos of the two of them as children, riding horses, eating ice cream, splashing in the crystal blue water in the ocean at one of Nocera's more popular beaches. Another picture of Rula in her wedding dress. Yet another one where she was having a tiara placed on her head by the king.

Surprisingly, there were none of her and Dante together. Or any of Dante at all, for that matter. Maybe the royal couple wanted to keep those at the palace. It made sense; it was the only logical explanation.

Sierra looked through the other items, removing them carefully and setting them aside—everything from theater tickets to newspaper clippings, to press announcements. Nothing really of value but obviously full of sentiment. Finally, at the very bottom, Sierra found a thick notebook bound in a buttery soft leather cover. Her hands shook as she lifted it. Judging by the outside, it definitely appeared to be some type of journal or diary.

Sierra almost dropped it right back in the box to seal everything up again. A journal was meant to be confidential, wasn't it? A way to vent and purge some of a person's most private thoughts. She couldn't bring herself to read

Rula's most intimate writings, couldn't intrude on her late friend's privacy that way.

Before she put it away, Sierra granted herself a small allowance and thumbed the edge of the pages like a deck of cards, just to have a look at the handwriting. Rula had had the most beautiful penmanship, each letter almost a work of art.

Then she saw it, blinked to make sure she wasn't imagining things. But it was unmistakable. Sierra's name was written at the top line of every page.

Her friend may have been writing in a journal, but she'd been writing to Sierra.

CHAPTER ELEVEN

DANTE STUDIED THE glass of amber liquid he'd poured about two hours ago but had barely sipped. As much as he wanted to obliterate the pain of the past few hours by drowning himself in drink, he knew in the end that was only prolonging his suffering.

The sooner he got it over with, the better. Then he could move on and do what he should have done in the first place—go forward with his life and do his best to forget Sierra Compari ever existed.

And somewhere along the way, he would have to forget what a fool of himself he'd made over her.

Ha! Easier said than done.

Suddenly the frustration and disappointment of the past few hours became too much. All the weeks of missing her, wanting to somehow deny that he was. Followed by days where he'd thought maybe if he professed his feelings, she would confess to hers. Only to have it blow up in his face. Rather than take another sip, he instead flung the drink against the hanging mirror with such force that both the mirror and the glass shattered.

He felt only marginally better.

And now he had a mess to clean up on top of every-thing else. First thing first. He wasn't going to waste another minute pining for a woman who either didn't want him or didn't want to acknowledge that she did.

Either way, he was ready to move on. Making his way to the desk in the corner, he fired up his laptop and began composing an email to his personal secretary.

Time to get the ball moving on his future.

Sierra hadn't left the floor of her closet since walking in there an hour ago. A cursory glance through Rula's notebook confirmed her suspicions. Her friend had been journaling in the form of letters to Sierra.

They hadn't been particularly close as adults, something Sierra would always regret now. But Sierra had always been the one Rula had confided in with her deepest secrets. And this notebook had a fair share of those.

Rubbing her eyes, Sierra read the first page once more, somehow keeping the tears at bay this time.

Dearest Sierra,

One of these days I'm going to rip all these pages out and send them to you. Or maybe I'll just send you the entire book all at once. But right now I just need to get everything down and out of my system.

You see, my dear sweet friend, I've made such a mess of things. I've realized too late that the life I pursued for so long wasn't the life I wanted after all. I married for status, for prestige, for a title. I married for all the wrong reasons and not the only right one...the only reason that matters.

My husband is a good man. I do love him. But I didn't really know what passionate love was until I met *him*. The man I should have waited for and married instead.

Sierra sniffled onto the sleeve of her sweater before she could continue. The rest of the pages were variations of the same theme. Rula had fallen for one of Dante's closest advisers. Dante had to have known. But he'd never said anything to her. Had kept his wife's confidence even after her death. Not just from her, but from the entire world.

Sierra's heart twisted as she remembered the fight back in Valhali. She'd been so unfair to Dante, the things she'd said. The accusation she'd hurled at him. Still, he'd kept silent about Rula's betrayal. He hadn't so much as defended himself.

Despite all that, he'd shown up tonight and swallowed his pride for her. And what had she done in response? Dismissed him like he was an errant admirer she didn't have time for. It was almost too much to bear to think about. Yet another sob escaped her throat as she recalled his stricken expression when she'd simply turned away and left him in that stairwell, admonishing him for daring to ask about taking her home. How would she ever explain that she'd only done all of it to protect her own heart? Dante had every right not to give her the time of day after tonight.

She'd been such a fool.

Sierra turned her focus back to the journal in her lap. The last page was of the most consequence. Sierra's heart broke for the woman she'd once viewed as close as a sister while she reread it.

Dearest Sierra,
We've decided it's time. Ronaldo and I are leaving
for the Italian Alps first thing tomorrow. We're going
to take a few days to decide our next course of ac-
tion and just spend time together.
I'm so excited to leave. I know this is the right

decision for everyone. I'm certain Dante knows. He has to. He's a smart man who'll put two and two together. I think he will recover quickly.

You see, I don't think he's fallen in love with me any more than I had with him. He's handsome, of course. With everything going for him. He's a prince! But ours was a match made out of convenience. I think it's best for both Dante and I that it be dissolved.

I'll be mailing you these pages as soon as I return. To give you a chance to learn it all before we can finally meet face-to-face once more, and you can celebrate my new life with me and you finally meet the man who's stolen my heart.

That was the last entry. Sierra closed the book gently and held it tight to her chest. Rula would never return from the Alps, would never get a chance to mail these pages to her.

But Sierra had managed to get them all the same. If Sierra knew her friend at all, Rula had somehow made sure of it.

Sierra continued to sit in her closet with her back against the wall until the bright rays of the sun shone through the large pane window. The irony of it all wasn't lost on her.

Rula had prepared her whole life to marry the crown prince so that she could become queen. Ultimately, it hadn't made her happy. Judging by her own words, she hadn't found such happiness until she'd found the man she really loved. It had ended in tragedy instead. Her dear friend had discovered too late that titles and crowns weren't important. In the end, love was the only thing that mattered.

A hiccup escaped Sierra's throat, and she finally stood on wobbly, shaky legs. She felt raw and spent. But there wasn't any time to lose. It may be too late for Rula, but Sierra still had a chance. Rula wouldn't want her to waste that chance. Rula would want her to be happy. His former wife would want Dante to be happy too.

She just hoped Dante still believed that Sierra might be the path to that happiness for him. After the way she'd reacted to him at the wedding, she wouldn't be surprised if he'd hopped on his jet and returned to Nocera already. Dante wasn't the type of man who swallowed his pride at all let alone twice. Was it at all possible he might do so for her?

Only one way to find out.

The words echoed through her head. She couldn't even be sure if it was her own voice she heard. Or if it was Rula's.

His secretary phoned him bright and early the next morning. Dante wasn't surprised. He'd been expecting the man's reaction to the email he'd sent last night.

"Am I to understand, Your Highness, that you would like this visit scheduled as early as next week?"

"That's correct. If the sultan and his daughter are available, please clear my schedule so that I may fly out as soon as they're ready to receive me." Dante had no doubt they would indeed be available. The sultan had been trying to get his daughter to meet him for the better part of a year now. Dante figured they were a good start on his fiancée-finding mission. A logical and thought-out approach to what needed to be done. He should have done it months ago, had just been putting off the inevitable.

"That would mean you're canceling some very important meetings, Your Highness. Are you sure?"

Dante pinched the bridge of his nose. He really needed his agenda to move forward before he had a chance to change his mind. "Yes, I'm certain, Duvall. This takes precedence over everything else."

"Consider it done."

Good. That was one check mark off the to-do list. Dante thanked the man then ended the call. Now he had to get ready for a long day of travel. It had been nice seeing Nantu and Kaliha and meeting their daughter and her husband last night. But in all other respects, this trip had been a waste of his precious time.

Not to mention the blow he'd taken to his pride. And his heart.

Served him right for going against everything he believed in and taking a chance.

Dante had just stepped out of the shower and toweled off when the knock sounded on his hotel room door. Throwing on a pair of sports shorts, he ran to answer. Room service was early by an entire hour.

But it wasn't a hotel employee across the threshold when he flung the door open.

"Sierra?"

She smiled at him shyly. "Good morning, Dante. Hope I'm not intruding."

What in the world was she doing here? After what she'd said last night and the way she'd hightailed it away from him, she was the last person he'd been expecting to see.

Just when he'd thought he had his future figured out, when he'd finally made the decision to get past this stage in his life and had finally acted on it, here she was at his door. Would he ever understand women? This one in particular vexed him like no other.

"How did you know which hotel I'd be at?"

She ducked her head. "I called your mother."

He almost laughed at how childlike that sounded. But the situation was too serious for laughter. Even now, he couldn't help but notice how beautiful she looked. Her hair was wet, her cheeks glowing from the exertion of rushing uptown. Her lips were swollen and red, as if she'd been chewing on them in concentration. He knew from their days on safari that she only did that when she was sketching. It took every ounce of will he had not to reach for her and take those plump lips with his own, taste her the way he'd imagined doing for these past few weeks.

Then he took a closer look at her face. Her eyes were red, framed in dark shadow. It looked as if she might have been crying.

The thought that he might have caused those tears sent self-reproach shooting through him like lightning. For that alone, he supposed he would hear her out.

But it had to end there. His heart couldn't take much more.

Sierra half expected to have the door shut in her face when Dante opened it. For a horrifying moment, he looked as if he wanted to do just that. Right before he gave her a resigned sigh and crossed his arms over his bare chest.

Why did it have to be bare? Getting through what she planned was going to be difficult enough without the distraction of Dante's naked upper body in her line of sight. His hair still glistened wet. She must have rushed him from the shower. He hadn't toweled off completely, and moisture still clung to the muscled skin of his arms and torso. For a second she lost her train of thought. She also forgot the start of the speech she'd rehearsed all the way over here. Maybe she could ask him to go put a shirt on so that her brain could start functioning again.

"You called my mother to find out where I was?"

She could only nod.

"Why? What exactly are you doing here, Sierra?" he asked, not even bothering to invite her in. Sierra swallowed past her trepidation and forced herself to continue. She had to go through with this or she'd wonder for the rest of her life exactly what she'd thrown away so carelessly.

She held up the sketchbook she'd carried all the way up here from her apartment. "I wanted to get your opinion on something. If you have a minute."

Dante hesitated, his eyes skeptical as they glanced at the book in her hand then back to her face. He repeated the cycle twice more before he spoke. "I suppose I have a few minutes. Come in." He might have uttered the invitation, but Dante made no effort to move to let her inside.

Sierra stepped past him and into the room, brushing against his naked skin. Electricity shot through her core at the contact.

So not the time.

The man was not going to make things easy for her. Not that she could really blame him.

The room was dark, the blinds and curtains still drawn. His laptop screen lit up a small square in the corner. Paperwork was strewn about the floor. She knew Dante to be much tidier than the appearance of this room indicated. But what really alarmed her was the smattering of broken glass and mirror in front of the fireplace mantel.

"Did you have some kind of accident?"

"Something like that," Dante answered. "I tried to clean

it up…" He trailed off. It was then that Sierra noticed the bandage on his hand.

He didn't give her a chance to ask about it. "Let's get this started then, shall we. I have a jet to catch."

Right. He was a busy man. And she was about to turn his life upside down. Hopefully.

"Sure thing." She walked over to the mahogany table in the center of the room and laid her sketchbook flat. A professional one this time, large with high quality drafting paper. Much different from the mini pocket-size ones she'd been sketching on back in Africa. This particular drawing deserved no less. She opened it up to the middle page.

Dante moved next to her to take a look. He stared at it blankly.

"What do you think?" she asked after several moments of silence.

Pinching the bridge of his nose, he released a long sigh. Sierra knew she was testing his patience. But this was the only way she could think of to say what she had to say without chickening out.

"I think it's a wedding dress," Dante finally answered after several more awkward beats. "For a bride."

She nodded. "That's right, it is."

"And?"

"Do you like it?"

He shrugged noncommittally. "It looks like a dress. With a long skirt. And a veil. Definitely a wedding dress."

She had to chuckle at that. "We've established that."

He turned away from the table to face her. "Why are you showing it to me? I'm not exactly an expert on women's fashion. Let alone wedding dresses. Or any dresses for that matter."

She swallowed. This was so much harder than she'd

even imagined it would be. "Well, the truth is, neither am I."

He gave a brisk shake of his head. "I'm sorry. I don't understand. You design clothes for a living."

"Yes, but wedding attire is an entirely different industry. I design for the runway, or for magazine shoots."

"Yet you drew this." He pointed to the open book.

"I did, yes."

He gave an exasperated shrug. "Do you want me to say I'm impressed. Yes, you're very talented. You didn't have to come all the way up here to hear me say that. I've said it several times over before now."

Sierra pulled out the nearest chair and sat down before her knees gave out.

"The thing is, I was hoping to wear something like this myself. But only if you like it. I think it might look pretty flattering. It's exactly the kind of dress I'd hope to wear on my wedding day."

His brow furrowed and he stared at her for so long that Sierra figured he really wasn't getting what she was trying to say. Then she watched as a glimmer of understanding flashed over his face.

His jaw dropped and he rubbed an open palm down his face.

"Sierra, just to be clear, are you saying what I think you're saying?"

She nodded, determined to take the chance she'd come here to take, no matter the consequences. "I'm saying that I love you. That I've loved you for as long as I can remember knowing you. And I wish I'd admitted it sooner." To herself and to him.

Dante squeezed his eyes shut, remained silent for so

long that Sierra felt a trickle of apprehension run along her spine. Had she made a colossal mistake?

No. No mistake. Whatever Dante's reaction to her declaration, she'd had to get out in the open her true feelings for this man. It was beyond time.

Finally, when he opened his eyes to look at her again, she knew she'd had nothing to be apprehensive about. A wealth of emotion darkened their depths, his features awash with tenderness. No man had ever looked at her that way. No one had. What a fool she'd been not to have seen it earlier—this man loved her! She should have seen it in his eyes, in the way he'd held her, in every word he'd spoken to her throughout the years. He proclaimed it out loud with his next words. "You have to know that I love you too. I always have, Sisi."

A torrent of affection flooded her system at his words. She'd only just sat down, but her jubilation had her jumping right back up again. "I guess women don't typically drop to one knee, but I will if you want." To his clear astonishment, she began to lower herself before Dante grabbed her by the wrist to lift her back up.

"Sierra, what are you doing?"

She grinned at him. "Isn't it obvious? I'm proposing."

Her breath caught in her throat at the expression that fell over his face at her words.

"Dante Angilera, please do me the honor of making me your wife. I'm going to need some help with the whole future queen thing, but I'm willing to do whatever it takes—"

Her words were interrupted when Dante cut her off by taking her upper arms and yanking her to him. Then his lips were on hers in a deep, crushing kiss. Sierra's arms flew around his neck, his damp skin wetting the front of her shirt. He cupped her behind, lifted her up onto the table in front of them and continued to kiss her some more.

When he finally let her go, Sierra didn't think she'd ever be able to catch her breath. It caught once more at the look on Dante's face. An ocean of emotion swam behind his eyes. "The wife part was all I needed to hear. And you would look amazing in any dress. Even a knee-length canvas tunic." Pulling her against him again, he delved into her mouth once more for a deep, mind-blowing kiss that melted her heart and her soul. When they finally parted, Sierra wasn't entirely sure she was back on earth and not on some heavenly plane where all her fantasies had just come true.

It took several long moments before she could speak again. "I take it that's a yes."

Dante didn't need any words when he answered her.

EPILOGUE

GALEN ADDED ANOTHER layer of color to Sierra's lower lip, then pulled back. The smile she flashed in the mirror above her head was one of sheer joy. Sierra felt pretty joyful herself. She was living a true fairy tale. About to marry a crown prince. *Her* prince. More importantly, she was about to marry the man she'd always been in love with.

Next to them, Tracey clasped her hands against her chest, a lace veil draped over her forearm. The moment brought forth a wave of déjà vu. The last time Sierra was in this chair with these two women seemed a lifetime ago.

And now her new life was about to start.

She would do her best to not take a single moment of it for granted. Closing her eyes, she gave a silent nod to Rula. Her deceased friend had played a major role in the path that had led Sierra to this joyous moment. Not only through her journal of letters but also during her years of friendship.

"You look beautiful, Sierra," Galen said, giving her shoulder a squeeze and pulling her out of her contemplations.

"Absolutely lovely," Tracey agreed.

"I think it's obligatory to say that to the bride," Sierra said. "Plus a lot of it is your handiwork."

Galen waved her hand dismissively. "Nonsense. We're

saying it because it's true. But I will take the compliment about my skills."

"As well you should," Sierra told her, gently standing up to avoid wrinkling the body of her bridal gown.

"Now, let's get this skirt and the veil on you," Tracey said, stepping forward with the items in question. "It's almost time."

Sierra didn't need the reminder; the butterflies in her stomach were doing that well enough. She was only slightly more nervous than the last time she'd been prepped by these ladies. She would never have guessed that morning of the news conference that the trip to Valhali would lead her here, about to finally tie herself to the only man she'd ever loved.

She couldn't wait to spend the rest of her life with him.

Tracey helped her slip the skirt and train of the gown on her then gently placed the tiara and veil combination atop her head. Galen made a few adjustments to her hair.

"You're ready," both women declared in unison.

Sierra took a fortifying breath then followed them to the door, around the porch to the back of the Melekhanna lodge where her father waited to walk her down the aisle. Her mother was in the front row of the audience chairs in front of the dais, probably on her third package of tissues. Both her parents had been beyond surprised at the announcement that she'd be marrying Dante. As was most of the world.

"The Ever Grieving Prince finally discovers new love!" read one headline.

The others were rather similar.

Little did anyone know their love wasn't new by any means. They'd just needed to find what was right there under their noses.

Sierra's father beamed at her when she made it to his side. He gave her a small peck on the cheek then led her down the steps, and onto the wooden pathway leading to the dais. Audible gasps sounded from the guests in attendance, which included a large number of fellow Nocerians, including Dante's mother and his father, who'd finally been given the medical clearance to resume travel, as well as so many dear friends she and Dante had made here in Valhali—Banti and his family, Nantu and Kaliha...even Tiejo had taken leave from his veterinary duties to be here. And no small amount of international press and photographers were hovering on the outer perimeter.

But Sierra hardly registered any of it. Her gaze was focused on the man standing waiting for her on the dais. Dante looked so handsome she thought she might forget to breathe. In his ceremonial royal dress, he looked every inch a regal leader who would be crowned king one day. More importantly, as far as Sierra was concerned, he would soon be her husband.

Dante couldn't believe his good fortune as he watched Sierra walking toward him. His soon to be wife. He'd be hard-pressed to find the words to describe her. A vision. It was the only description that came to mind. So much time wasted. He should have admitted years ago that she was always the only woman for him.

But the only thing he wanted to focus on right now was the joy of this day. Even nature seemed to be helping them to celebrate. The setting sun cast a burst of color in the sky above them. The hum of the cicadas seemed to rise and fall in tempo, almost as if performing a tune in their honor. Or maybe he was simply being fanciful because he was simply so happy.

There was no other location better for their wedding day. Valhali was where they'd both found the courage to finally acknowledge their true feelings and stop resisting the mutual pull of their love.

As a bonus, the publicity would serve as a further boost for NEWEF. Maman was very pleased about that. Not to mention the romantic setting with such stunning views as a backdrop.

Once they'd said their vows and bowed to the applause from the audience, Dante led her to the head table to await the festivities.

The dancers from their first night here appeared and began a ceremonial matrimony dance in their honor. Dante took advantage of the diverted attention to focus on his beautiful bride. Splaying his hand on her lower back, he turned her toward him and pulled her closer. Her response was immediate. She lifted her chin and met his lips for a soul-shattering kiss that had his insides turning to lava. When he finally managed to begrudgingly pull away, he didn't think he could bear the loss.

Sierra gave him a knowing look, the desire in her eyes matching his own.

Pretty soon, several of their guests had joined the dancers on the floor. Just as he and Sierra had on that night many months ago.

"I'm so grateful that so many friends and loved ones are able to be here to celebrate with us," Sierra said.

Dante nodded. "Me too. Father seems to be back to his old energetic ways. One of his doctors speculated that our wedding gave him a positive boost toward recovery."

"Thank heavens."

"Though I think there might be at least one uninvited guest," Dante declared with mock seriousness.

Sierra pulled back with an alarmed expression. "Oh? Who?"

He pointed to the tree line in the distance. "I'm pretty sure my friend the vervet monkey is in that tree just waiting to make his move and steal a banana from the buffet."

Sierra chuckled and snuggled in tighter against his shoulder.

"Would you like to dance?" he asked his bride after a few moments of simply enjoying her closeness and warmth. "The way we did all those months ago?"

"In a few moments," she answered. "Right now I just want to sit here next to you."

That was fine with him. "As you wish, Princess Sisi," he told her, playfully tapping her nose.

Dante draped his arm around her shoulders and they watched the dancers.

"When we do dance, please remind me to take the skirt and train off," Sierra said, settling tighter against him. Dante had to resist the urge to pull her onto his lap and kiss her until neither one of them could breathe. Patience. He would have to wait until they were alone together that night unfortunately. Sierra was worth the wait.

"We don't need a replay of my clumsiness that night," she added.

He chuckled at that. "I wouldn't complain. I rather enjoy catching the woman I love in my arms."

He would be prepared to catch her for the rest of their lives together.

* * * * *

COMING SOON!

We really hope you enjoyed reading this book. If you're looking for more romance be sure to head to the shops when new books are available on

Thursday 12th October

MILLS & BOON

MILLS & BOON®

Coming next month

THE CHRISTMAS THAT CHANGED EVERYTHING
Faye Acheampong

"Will, put your arm around Naomi."

Naomi chanced a look at Will, only to find he was already assessing her coolly. After what felt like an eternity, he repositioned an arm so that his hand was hovering hesitantly by her waist. Naomi wasn't sure if it was his body heat that was permeating through the material of her costume or her own temperature elevating at rocket speed.

"May I?" Will requested, in a strained and lowered tone.

"Uh-huh," Naomi murmured, liking the way his palm fitted snugly over the curve of her hip.

She supposed Will had first-hand experience of marriage and husband-wife unions, seeing as he'd worn a plain gold band on his wedding ring finger up until his November meeting with Harpreet—not that Naomi had been keeping track or anything!

An unsatisfied Kwame was speaking. "Naomi, you're out of the frame. I'm going to need you to get closer to Will."

Naomi awkwardly shuffled towards Will. In return, he enacted a slow sidestep that brought him even closer. One after the other they moved with calculation to close the obvious gap between their bodies.

Will's eyes narrowed, as if he was sensing her cautiousness. "Are you sure you're okay with this?"

"I said it was fine."

"Well, you don't exactly sound "fine"."

"You're not really qualified to speak on whether I seem out of character..."

Irritation blazed in Will's pupils, but she was relieved when he opted for silence instead of creating a retort of his own.

Their actions were like a peculiar dance that resembled chess pieces navigating a board during a high-stakes match. At its culmination, Naomi felt as though she was losing the ability to think logically. The game had suddenly changed into a puzzle. Her and Will's frames seemingly fitted together with ease—her shoulder slotted into his armpit, and the arm he'd stiffly slung around her waist continued to provide a snug accommodation. The scent of his aftershave settled over her like an appealing blanket of cleanliness, amber and rich musk that somehow reminded her of how much she enjoyed the art of being cuddled.

Continue reading
THE CHRISTMAS THAT CHANGED EVERYTHING
Faye Acheampong

Available next month
www.millsandboon.co.uk

LET'S TALK

Romance

For exclusive extracts, competitions and special offers, find us online:

- **f** MillsandBoon
- **🐦** @MillsandBoon
- **📷** @MillsandBoonUK
- **♪** @MillsandBoonUK

Get in touch on 01413 063 232